WINTER WHEAT

Mildred Walker

WINTER WHEAT

HARCOURT, BRACE AND COMPANY

NEW YORK

"*There is but one victory that I know is sure, and that is the victory that is lodged in the energy of the seed.*"

—ANTOINE DE SAINT-EXUPÉRY,
Flight to Arras

To

MARGARET WALKER ABEL

*Who quickens her teaching with understanding
and her living with faith and humor.*

PART ONE

*"I shall not fret about the loam if some-
where in it a seed lies buried."*

—ANTOINE DE SAINT-EXUPÉRY,
Flight to Arras

I

SEPTEMBER is like a quiet day after a whole week of wind. I mean real wind that blows dirt into your eyes and hair and between your teeth and roars in your ears after you've gone inside. The harvesting is done and the wheat stored away and you're through worrying about hail or drought or grasshoppers. The fields have a tired peaceful look, the way I imagine a mother feels when she's had her baby and is just lying there thinking about it and feeling pleased.

It was hot, though, like a flash-back to July. I was glad we weren't cooking for harvest hands. There wasn't any fire in the stove and everything was spick-and-span because I had just washed the dinner dishes. Mom was out having another look for the turkeys that were always wandering off. Dad was lying on the couch in the other room waiting for the noon broadcast of wheat prices to come on. We had to sell our wheat this month and not hold it over; that is, we did if I was going to the university that fall. It might go higher along toward Christmas, but we couldn't wait for that.

The house was so quiet I could hear Mom calling the turkeys down by the barn. Dad told Mom not to bother, they'd come back by themselves, but Mom worried if anything was lost or left unlocked.

"When I've got something, I take care of it," she always said.

I washed some cucumbers while I was waiting. They were bright-green and shiny in the water. I used to play they were alligators when I was a child. Then I fenced them in with my hand and poured off the water into the kettle on the stove. When you have to carry every drop of water you use half a mile, you don't throw away any.

And then it began. I knew before Dad turned it up. The voice of the man who announces the wheat prices is as familiar to me as Dad's. It's different from anybody's voice around Gotham—more like one of those city voices that broadcasts the war news. That voice touches us here, and all the ranches spread out over the prairies between the Rockies and the Mississippi. It touches all the people in Clark City, thirty miles from here, who live on the ranchers, even though they try to forget it.

"Here is your Grain Market Broadcast for today: Spring and Winter . . . up two."

I could add two to yesterday's price, so I didn't have to hear any more, but I listened out of habit and because I love to hear it.

"One heavy dark Northern Spring . . . fifty-two." The words came so fast they seemed to roll downhill. Nobody ever calls it all that; it's just spring wheat, but I like the words. They heap up and make a picture of a spring that's slow to come, when the ground stays frozen late into March and the air is raw, and the skies are sulky and dark. The "Northern" makes me feel how close we are to the Rockies and how high up on the map, almost to Canada.

"One dark hard Winter . . . fifty-three."

It's just winter wheat to the people who raise it, only to me it means more than that. It means all the winter and all the cold and the tight feeling of the house in winter, but the rich secret feeling I have, too, of treasure in the ground, growing there for us, waiting for the cold to be over to push up strong and green. They sound like grim words without any comfort to them, but they have a kind of strength all their own.

"Durum, Flax, and Rye . . . up one." The broadcast ran on. Mom came in while I was standing there listening.

"Wheat's up," I told her.

Mom nodded. She stood there untying her bandanna and I watched her as though I didn't know her face better than my own. Mom's is a quiet face with a broader forehead than mine and dark brows and eyes and a wide mouth. She doesn't show in her face what she thinks or feels—that's why people in Gotham think she's hard to know—but when she laughs, the laughter goes deeper down in her eyes than anybody's I know.

I look more like Dad. He is tall and thin and has light hair and blue eyes and his face shows what he thinks or feels. Mom is square and stocky with broad shoulders and hips. It's just as well that I am more like Dad in my body. I like being slender and straight. I am strong like Mom, though, and I like working in the fields better than in the house.

Dad clicked off the radio and came out to the kitchen. "Well, we'll go over and tell Bailey we're going to sell. Fifty-three is good enough. Come on, Ellen, you can drive me over."

I took off my apron and was running across to the barn for the pickup before Dad had taken his hat from behind the door. I felt so excited I couldn't walk soberly.

Glory, it was hot! I had the doors of the truck tied open with a piece of rope so the air could rush through, but it felt hot enough to scorch my bare ankles, and the heat of the engine came up through the rubber soles of my sneakers.

You can't see the elevator till you get past our place. There's only one in Gotham, but it stands up from the crossroads like a monument. That and the railroad station are the only things to let people know Gotham's a town.

"I feel I'm going for sure, Dad," I told him.

"You bet you're going," Dad answered. "The war spoiled college for me, all but one year. Nothing's going to spoil it for you. Might's well drive way in. It'll keep the car from burning up."

So I drove the truck up the ramp inside the high shelter of the elevator. That's fun. Dad says that's the way covered bridges feel back East where he comes from.

"Hi!" I called out to Bailey. He's the one who runs the elevator. Mr. Mathews was with him. Mathews is the inspector from the Excelsior Milling Company. Dad leaned against the wall of the office, talking to Mathews and Bailey about the heat. It seemed a long time to me before he said:

"Well, I thought I might as well sell. It isn't going much higher."

"Nope, it ain't," Bailey said. "Mathews and I were just sayin'."

"I doubt it," Mr. Mathews said kind of carefully.

"This girl's going to college on that wheat money, so I guess I'll take it now," Dad said. "It's up to you, Bailey, to keep the price of wheat up so's she can stay there."

I sat down on the running board of the truck while the men were talking, because it was cooler. All of a sudden, a swallow flew out of the shadowy corners way up in the roof. It made a quick shadow on my face as it swooped past. A swallow flying always makes me feel cool. Then I felt Mr. Mathews looking at me and that made me hot again. I had on my oldest pair of jeans rolled up almost to my knees and a white polo shirt that was maybe a little tight. I snapped my fingers at Bailey's big tiger cat so he'd look at her instead of me. The cat's too lazy to move usually, but this time she yawned and stretched and came over to me. Dad was talking. He loves to talk, and I suppose it's hard on him that Mom says so little. Dad isn't a rancher naturally. He'd be happier, I think, if he had done something else.

"No, sir, most folks are changing over to winter wheat, but I'm going to stick to raising both. I had a hundred acres in spring and it gave twenty-five bushels, but of course you take more of a risk. Year before last, I only got ten bushels to the acre. Winter wheat you plant in the fall and you don't have to worry so much about moisture, but my wife's the one that holds out for planting some spring too."

I stood up, spilling the cat off my lap. I'd heard all that so many times before. But I liked hearing him say "my wife" that way, as though he was proud of Mom's judgment. The people in Gotham, Dad too sometimes, act as though Mom weren't quite . . . quite equal to Dad. It hurts me. I stood leaning against the wall idly reading the calendars and notices posted there: "No Smoking." "This Elevator Does Not Sell Clean Seed"—that means the seed you buy there for planting may have weeds in it and you can't come back and blame them for it. There was an advertisement of Karmont wheat that Dad says was developed especially for me because it has Russian and American parents, too—from Kharkov and Montana. He calls me Karmont, sometimes, to tease me. A big fly-specked placard read "Heavy Northern Spring . . . Dark Hard Winter"—the words are like something you know by heart, something you know without learning. They have a deep solemn sound . . . I couldn't explain it to anybody. Suddenly, it seemed to me as though those words I had always known—"Heavy Dark Northern Spring . . . Dark Hard Winter"—held in them all my living here.

"Ellen, you go ahead. I'm going to stay and have a game," Dad said. He and Bailey and Mr. Mathews went inside the little office.

"Okay. I'll leave the pickup for you. I'll walk back," I told him.

6

I stepped out of the shadow of the elevator and the sun seemed to wrap around me and press down on my bare head. Mom says that's the way you get sunstrokes, but I like it on my head. I like my hair brushing hot against my neck, too.

In two weeks, I thought, I'll be far away from here—and I'd never been more than three hundred miles before. I looked at the corrugated tin sheds below the elevator where they store salt and oil and feed and thought how I used to slide down them. I'd just as soon right now, only the tin would be so hot it would blister my seat. I looked at the store. It didn't do much of a business, because most people sent away for big mail orders. There was the cellar hole they dug one time for a community church, but folks didn't agree and they didn't have a crop that year, so they never finished it. I felt as separated from Gotham as though I didn't even know it. I was so excited I could have run in spite of the hot day. Then I discovered something funny: my hands were ice-cold. I pushed them down into the tight pockets of my jeans. I had known I was going and yet, with deciding to sell the wheat today, I could feel it more.

2

UNLESS there is company, and there seldom is, Dad and Mom
and I sit in the kitchen in the evening. In the summertime, if one
of the boys from Gotham comes to see me we sit out in the pickup.

That night Dad was reading the morning paper that gets to
Gotham in the evening. Mom was ironing. I sat at the table with
the plate and knife and fork pushed back so I had room for my
tablet. I was figuring up my expenses again.

It was bright in the kitchen. Mom had a hundred-watt bulb on
the one cord that hung down from the ceiling. It was so bright
you couldn't look at it, but Mom liked lots of light. We hadn't
had electricity at the ranch so very long. Mom said all her life in
Russia she had cooked and ironed and mended by the light of a
wick in a bottle of kerosene, and she liked the feeling of being
able to turn on the light the minute it got dark and have it shine
on everything. She didn't like the shades pulled, either. Our house
was like a lighthouse for people coming up past the coulee.

"If I get the job in the cafeteria," I figured out loud, "that'll
leave only my room and books and railroad fare, besides my
tuition."

"And if you don't like working in the cafeteria, you needn't,"
Dad said, almost angrily, putting down his paper.

"That wouldn't be much to do," Mom said. They're often like
that. And then I try to turn them both the same way.

"Oh, no, I won't mind that," I said. "That'll be fun."

I drew a line under the figures. At the top stood "railroad fare"
and just seeing it there made it hard to keep my mind on anything but going. Tomorrow . . . tomorrow night at this time I'd
be on the train.

"You go ahead and do what you want, Ellen, and if you want

8

to join a sorority you do it. Have yourself a good time. If we should have a bad year and not be able to send you the whole four years, you'll have had your year, anyway. I remember how I felt when I was in college."

He meant to make me feel good and free; he couldn't see that he put fear in my mind at the same time. If they did have a bad year! It was like a drop of temperature in the middle of a summer's day; you begin to worry about hail striking. I looked over at Mom. She was folding a shirt on the ironing board, buttoning the little buttons down the front. But I could see by her lips she didn't like Dad to talk that way.

"You'd always rather eat to bursting one meal than spread it out over two," she told Dad. "If she take care, her money'll go longer."

I made little marks on the page. I felt pulled two ways again. I have since I was a child. I love Dad's way of talking that makes him seem different from other ranchers. He's lived here twenty-three years, but he still says "back East where I come from." He's the one who gets excited when I do about spring coming or a serial running in the magazine we're both reading, but it's what Mom says that I depend on. When Mom used to say "Don't worry" about my pet chicken or dog or new calf, it always got well. Dad is always talking of going some place, not now, but next year, maybe. Mom seems to think of nothing farther away than today or perhaps yesterday or tomorrow morning.

Mom folded the ironing board and put it inside their bedroom that was just off the kitchen. She carried in the freshly ironed clothes. Dad went back to his paper. When Mom came back she took beans from the cupboard to soak for tomorrow. Dad always said Mom could make all the dishes he'd had back in Vermont as well as though she were a New Englander herself, instead of a Russian. All of a sudden, I realized that tomorrow when those beans would be ready to eat I'd be going away. It gave me a funny feeling.

"I'll be taking the train tomorrow night," I said aloud, more to hear it myself.

"We can drive you into town in the afternoon," Dad said, dropping his paper on the floor.

"There's no need to go to town; she can catch the train at

Gotham just as well. We haven't nothing to take us into town for," Mom said.

"Well, we don't have to decide tonight," Dad said, but I knew he wanted to go into Clark City. It wouldn't be so flat as just seeing me go off on the train from Gotham. My going away was hard on both of them; they were so different—and I was part of them both. It made me uncomfortable to think of leaving them.

While I was getting ready for bed in my room that's off the front room, I saw how it would be if I left from town. We'd go in right after dinner and go around to the stores, Dad going one way and Mom and I another. Dad would probably have his hair cut at the barbershop and stop in the bank and meet someone he knew to talk to. Then we'd meet at the big store on the corner and go to the cafeteria for supper. The train stops ten minutes or so at the station in town and there are other people and excitement and you have time to wave from the platform and then again from your window by your seat. We went to the station in Clark City to see the Goodals off when they went back to Iowa.

If I left from Gotham, we'd just drive down in the truck and wait till the train came. It only stops long enough for you to get on and you hardly have time to taste the flavor of going away.

I sat on the bed in my pyjamas with my arms around my knees. I couldn't keep from thinking of that time Dad went back East. I tried to, and then I just sat still and looked straight at it. Sometimes that's better than working so hard to keep from looking at what's in your mind.

Dad went all the way back to Vermont when his mother died. It was in November and it was already dark when the train came through Gotham. Even now, I could feel how cold and dark it was. I held Mom's hand. Dad was so dressed-up he seemed strange. He had gone to town and bought a new dark suit and a hat and gloves, not work gloves or warm gloves, but soft gray ones that made you feel gentle to touch them. Mom didn't like it. We stood there without saying anything until Dad told Mom to remember to call Mr. Bardich, our neighbor, if the cow didn't calve tomorrow.

"I'll manage," Mom snapped back.

"I wish you could go, Anna," Dad said to Mom, "and we could take Ellen."

"I don't want to go," Mom said, and the tone of her voice hurt to hear. I could feel more than the night coldness around us; I could feel Mom and Dad drawing away from each other. I wanted to say something to bring them together. Dad mustn't go this way, but I couldn't say anything.

Then I heard the train and the big round beam of light cut through the darkness like a harrow turning the dark earth. It shone hard on our faces, making them look queer and unreal.

Dad was going.

"Dad!" I screamed, jumping up and down. Dad lifted me off the ground to kiss me and held me so tight I could feel how he loved me. Suddenly, all of me rushed out to him and I loved him so much I forgot all about Mom and the sharp, hard sound of their voices a few minutes ago. I felt then, at eight, how much Dad and I are alike.

The train was rushing toward us. Over Dad's shoulder I watched it come. It was going to take him away.

"Dad, please take me with you," I sobbed in his ear.

I felt his soft gloved hand on my cheek.

"I won't go away without you next time," he whispered, and set me down. He picked up his bag. I wanted him to kiss Mom; I had never seen him kiss her. But he didn't.

"Good-by, Anna Petrovna," he said, looking at Mom. I had never heard him call her by two names before.

"Good-by," Mom said, standing still, without smiling.

Then he was gone and the crossroads were darker than ever. The train light shone on the high window in the top of the grain elevator for a moment and then that too was dark. We got into our old Ford and Mom drove back to the house. My throat ached all the way. The name Dad had called Mom kept saying itself in my ears: "Anna Petrovna, Anna Petrovna." I wanted to ask Mom about it, but it was tied up somehow with that bitter cold sound of their voices.

Our house seemed lonely when we came back to it. It seemed to be hiding under the coulee. I went with Mom to put the truck in the barn that was bigger than the house. I think Mom was prouder of our barn than the house, anyway. We walked back to look at the cow that was going to calve. She was just a big light blob in the dark, waiting. I had thought she was exciting this morning, but now she seemed sad, too.

The wind blew when we walked across the open space to the

house and I couldn't help shivering with the cold. Inside the house it was warm, but empty.

"Bring your nightgown in here and I heat you some milk," Mom said.

I drank the milk sitting on a stool in front of the stove. It tasted good, but the lonely ache in my throat was still there. I picked up my clothes and hung them neatly behind the stove and put my cup on the sink board. Mom was fixing oatmeal for tomorrow morning.

"Good night, Mom," I said almost timidly, standing beside her. She seemed wrapped around in a kind of strangeness. Then she turned around and drew me to her. The front of her dress was warm from the stove. I felt the comfortable heat through my gown. She laid her hand against my face and it felt rough and hard but firm. I dared ask her something I wanted to know.

"Mom, was that really your name—what Dad called you?"

Her voice sounded surprised. "Why, Yeléna, you know that; Anna Petrovna. You know I am born in Russia, in Seletskoe."

"Yes, but I didn't know your other name," I said.

"Anna Petrovna Webb." She pronounced it slowly. "Once I think what a funny name Ben Webb is!" She laughed. Her laugh was warm and low like our kitchen, and comfortable. The house seemed natural and right again.

"Mom, can I sleep in your bed with you while Dad's gone?"

"Yes, Yólochka moya." Mom called me her pet name for me, and I was comforted. It meant small pine tree. "Pine trees are strong trees, Yeléna. You should see the great black forests in Russia," she used to say.

But now that I am grown I feel the wall of strangeness between them, more than when I was a child. I wondered how they would get along without me.

Dad went past my window and I could smell his pipe. Mom was in the kitchen still.

"Anna, come outside and get a breath of air," Dad called to her. I heard the screen door close sharply.

"The windbreak's stirring like it rain tomorrow." Mom's accent makes what she says sound final.

I slipped my feet into my sheepskin slippers and went out as I was, in my pyjamas, my hair loose around my face.

"What are you doing out here?" Dad asked gruffly but as though he was glad I had come.

"It's hot inside," I told him. It was good to be outside. The heat seemed to bring the sky down close. It was not dark even at ten o'clock. The stars were faint. Over against the house the shoulder of the coulee was darker than the sky, cutting the air from the earth. I followed the sharp line a long distance. That was the way tomorrow would cut my living here from the rest of my life, I thought unhappily, but with a kind of prickling of excitement in me. I lifted my eyes to the sky, where the lighter darkness was all of one piece. The sky drew me as it always had, making me feel light and airy. I left Mom and Dad there and ran in my slippers up the side of the coulee.

The top of the tree that makes shade by our kitchen door comes even with the ridge of the coulee. In the daytime I can see far off to the mountains. I have the whole sky to myself. I did what I used to do. I lay down flat on the ground where I could smell the sagebrush close to my face and see every star in the sky. The earth was warm and hard under me. I rolled over on my side and looked down at our house. Mom and Dad were sitting there on the bench. Somehow, I felt sad looking at them down there. I almost didn't want to go away and leave them. I ran back down the hill to them, like a child.

"Well," Dad said, "young lady, if you're going to leave us tomorrow . . ."

"Yeléna, go get to bed," Mom said shortly; she pronounced the "Ellen" differently, the Russian way, Yeléna.

3

I SHALL never get over the pleasure of waking on a train, even if I should travel all my life. But that first morning, somewhere in North Dakota, I felt unreal. I had an upper berth and couldn't see out, but there was plenty to see in the berth itself. I lay still and looked at the cunning little lights at either end and the hammock where I'd laid my clothes the night before, the bell with the sign under it, "Please call porter for ladder before attempting to climb down." I smiled at that, after all the scrambling and jumping I had done all my life. The jump from our roof to the ground that I made often was higher than the distance from the berth to the aisle. I could land like a cat, anyway.

I liked the berth being open over my head, and wondered if I wouldn't feel a little as though I were in a polished coffin in the lower berth with the shiny wood closed over my head. The smooth motion of the train was exciting. I lay still to feel it more. I was on my way. It had begun. I knew I had been waiting for this since the night when I was eight and Dad had gone away on a train. He had left the cold and the darkness and the cow waiting to calve and the house lonely and huddled under the coulee and I had felt deserted. This time I was going off myself and leaving all that behind.

Then I could lie still no longer, and I sat up so fast and so straight it's a good thing I was in an upper berth. I dressed as swiftly as at home. Every single thing I put on was, for the first time in my life, completely new. A little of the "new-dry-goods" smell of J. C. Penney's store clung to my rayon lingerie. My new rabbit's-wool and rayon dress prickled as I drew it down over my shoulders. I am too warm-blooded to wear wool in September, but the saleslady told us that was the best thing to go away to college in. It was I who told her I was going to college. I wanted to tell everyone. Mom stood by with that silent and secretive look on her face that she always has with strangers.

The dining car was more glittering and wonderful than I had imagined. The tablecloths were so long they came to within a foot of the floor. The flowers I had seen through the windows of diners were there, and they were real.

The waiter pushed my chair in for me at a table with three empty chairs. I picked up the menu and ordered the same things the folks would have had hours earlier: prunes and oatmeal and toast and coffee. Then I realized I could have had anything from strawberries or melon to sausages or ham. But I wouldn't change my mind with the waiter standing beside me. I looked out the window as though I wasn't interested in food.

We were going through North Dakota. The mountains had disappeared. A field of wheat stubble came almost to the rails. I wondered if they'd had a good crop. North Dakota didn't do as well as Montana this year. That was what had helped to raise the price for us. It was queer to look at fields and know nothing about them. There was a poor-looking ranch house, and I could tell by the iron bed moved out against the back wall that it was so hot inside they couldn't stand it to sleep there hot nights. There wasn't even a windbreak planted around the shack. Then the shack was out of sight just as I'd begun to know it. Why should I try to know it? But it was queer to look at ranch land and not care about it. We ran through a station without stopping. Next to the station was a grain elevator that looked like ours at Gotham.

The waiter was seating a young man across from me. He looked like the men who came out from the Flour Company offices to the grain elevator. I realize now that I thought that of any man who wasn't a rancher or a cowboy.

"Good morning." He smiled at me. "On your way back to school?"

"Yes," I told him.

"What year?"

"I'm just beginning." I hated to admit it, so I asked him a question. "Are you in the university?"

"Used to be. I'm going back to Minnesota to join the Army. That's where my home is."

"Why did you go West?" I'm getting over that habit of just asking people the questions that pop into my head.

"To see my girl. She lives in Idaho. Where do you live?"

"Gotham, Montana."

"Oh"—he nodded knowingly—"I imagine that's quite a place."

"Seventy-five people, counting all the ranchers. It's on the Great Northern road. The train came through there at eight-ten last night. Didn't you look out?"

"I'm afraid I didn't. Did I miss much?"

"Well, no," I had to admit, and I could see he thought I was funny.

The head waiter brought two girls about my age to our table.

"I'll just put all you college people together," he said. A warm glow spread through me. It happened so fast I don't really know who introduced us, but in a few minutes we all knew each other's names; maybe it was Bill. Bill Rand his name was. The girls were seniors. The one named Kay laid a cigarette case with her name in raised gold letters by her napkin. She opened it and her fingers were long and tapering with polish all the way down, like an advertisement. She passed it around the table. When I didn't take one, she said, "Don't you smoke?"

I told her I'd emptied out too many ash trays for Dad. They laughed as though they thought that was a funny reason, but they didn't know that the days the ash stand by Dad's couch filled way up were the days when he was so gloomy and silent and the shrapnel hurt so that Mom would have to put hot packs on the places. Sometimes when the wind blew all day he would lie and smoke one cigarette after another and not say much of anything.

The other girl was Marge. She wore a thin black dress that made my wool one feel more thick and hot. Her lips were the same shade as her fingernails and they weren't any of the shades at the Rexall Drugstore where I bought mine. It was so much fun listening to them I didn't look out the window once. It was as though the train were the whole world.

But when we finished breakfast, the girl with the handsome cigarette case said, "Let's go into the club car."

I didn't say anything at first; I thought of Dad not wanting me to go tourist and Mom saying, "That extra money would be nice to have in your pocket when you get there." I spoke right out. "I'm on the tourist sleeper. I don't believe I can use the club car."

"Sure you can with us," Marge said. "When you're on your way to college, the train's your apple. You can do everything but sit in the engineer's lap and they won't say a word." That's the way I felt, too, free and lucky. I wondered if the middle-aged people on the train didn't envy us.

The club car was a wonderful place of tan and red-purple curtains and chairs and carpet. There were mirrors at unexpected places and lamps and a writing desk and a radio. The air was clammy-cold like the root cellar in the side of the hill at home or the movie in Clark City.

"It smells and feels like the inside of a movie theater," I said, and wished I hadn't because the others laughed and I didn't feel with them for a minute.

"You're an original," Bill said. I didn't like that.

Later in the day, we played bridge. They asked me if I played. I said that I'd played cribbage and pinochle mostly, but Dad and I had played contract a few times with Bill Bailey and his wife at the elevator.

"The elevator?" Kay asked.

"The grain elevator. The Excelsior Milling Company runs it," I explained.

"Wait till you see the huge elevators in the Twin Cities. When you see them, you're practically having your first quiz," Marge said.

"Baby, can they look gray of an early morning after Christmas vacation!" Kay groaned. I wouldn't be going home for Christmas vacation, but I didn't mention that.

"I'll never forget the time . . ." Marge began. I loved hearing them talk. It was a different kind of talk. I felt part of it because I was going to college too.

We were in the very tip end of the train where it's all glass and separated by a glass wall from the other passengers, who were reading the magazines and newspapers. I looked in at them and thought how sober they looked. I couldn't help thinking, either, how Dad would have loved to be sitting there talking about the country with some other man.

"Did you know Tim Murphy?" Marge asked Bill, and then they were off, talking about people I had never heard of before.

But I didn't mind. I had always liked listening to Dad tell of the people he grew up with in his town in Vermont. I felt I knew them. When he'd start, Mom would never listen. If it was in the evening when Mom was knitting, her needles would go faster and faster and then she'd go out to tend to something outdoors, as though she didn't want to hear. Mom hardly ever told about people in her town.

In the shining lavatory I was a little shocked at the way the girls spread all over the place, as though there were nobody else on the train. They scattered powder and used so many of the cunningly folded towels I had been so careful of. I tried to act more as they did, as though we owned the train.

"Is your hair natural or do you use a bleach?" Marge asked when I was combing my hair. I had to laugh.

"It's natural. Dad says it's the color of a scoured pine board."

"Are you a Swede? Your name doesn't sound it."

"My mother's Russian, but my father's from New England," I said. "He has light hair." I had that feeling I have had so often at school that it was sort of queer to say my mother was Russian, but that saying my father was from New England made up for that. I had got that feeling from Dad. I think he felt that way. He seemed not to like to mention Mother's being Russian. I used to wonder how they had ever come to marry. He must have loved her very much I thought then.

"How exciting!" Marge was saying. "Where on earth did your father ever meet her?"

"In Russia. My father was with the Polar Bear expedition during the war." I finished my hair and brushed off my dress. It took too long to explain.

"How perfectly thrilling!" Kay echoed in the same tone. Both girls talked so much alike I wondered if I would talk like them by next year at this time.

"Well, if the war keeps on, I'm certainly going to get in it somehow. I'd love to have a war romance," Marge said.

"And marry some English commando," Kay suggested.

We went along the narrow polished little aisle to join Bill for lunch. I had never thought of Mom and Dad as being part of a war romance.

The day on the train was the shortest day of my life, and the most idle. We had dinner together again. I spent more for it than I meant to, because Bill was writing down our orders and he came to me last. The other girls were ordering fried chicken, so I did too. I wondered what the diner has to pay a pound for them. We sold some of ours last week at 37 cents.

Afterward we went back to our end of the club car. The light was fading out of the sky. The rails stretching on forever beyond our train were the only point of brightness against the pale blur of the rolling fields. The porter came through and turned on the little lights and they made it seem more luxurious than ever. I was glad we wouldn't get off till ten-thirty. We'd sort of run out of talk and just sat there, listening to the radio. I began to watch the country. It was different. The ranches—farms they were here —came closer together, the houses were larger, even the barns were all painted. Trees, not just windbreaks, grew easily in the dooryards. Smaller fields were neatly fenced, as though wood was easy to get. Sometimes a river flowed across a field. There were no irrigation ditches and no dark strips laid to fallow.

"We've been in Minnesota for ages, you dope! We'll be in the Twin Cities in three more hours," Kay was saying.

Brilliant flame sprang out of the dark. Against a sagging wire fence three figures raked up the weeds and brush and tossed them on a bonfire. The figures were dull and lumpy: a man and a woman and a child. Only the tin clasps on the man's suspenders gleamed bright. The woman's arm was outlined in red. The firelight touched the towhead thatch of the child. Somehow, it made me catch my breath. It was so familiar. It was beautiful, too—red fire against the wide soft dusk and the figures touched with red. I had never stood outside and seen it before.

Perhaps Dad and Mom would be burning the weeds at home tonight. I had been the towheaded child when they used to do it, holding my hands out to the fire and then running away from the heat, screaming when the flames went very high. The tight windows shut out the sharp smell of smoke and the burning grass, and the ice cakes underneath the car somewhere shut out the fierce heat, but I couldn't help breathing more deeply to try to catch it.

Sometimes we had guarded a bonfire like that in the evenings when the Great Northern train passed through, all lighted up and unreal as a picture on a railroad calendar. I had seen the rich inside of the train and the little lights and the people facing each other in the club car or eating in the diner or the drawn curtains where Dad said the beds were. I hadn't known then how much more brilliant our bonfire must have looked to the people in the train. Something sharp rose in my throat, and a hurting loneliness.

"Someday, you'll be riding in there," Dad had told me, "eating a steak in the diner and never looking out to see the little dark town you go through." I think he always wanted to be on every train he saw. He never quite liked belonging in a little dark town like Gotham, and he was always reminding me of my separateness from it, almost from Mom, too. All day I had forgotten them; I had had such a good time with Kay and Marge and Bill. I came back to them now.

There wouldn't be much to do today. Dad would care for the stock and go over to talk to Bailey at the elevator after a while. Mom would wash the curtains and blankets in my room, probably, and make it clean to close up until I came back to it again. When she was through in the house she'd go out and work around the chicken house. She kept it as slick as some people in Gotham keep their own places—or she'd work in the garden. She always kept busy. But they'd miss me. Supper would seem lonesome. I could feel their missing as though I were right there with them missing someone else. I wonder if a child can feel like a parent to her own parents. I do sometimes.

I tried to think of last night. It was just last night. Dad had called to Mom to come out. I thought of them sitting there on the bench together. They were happy in their way; they were just so different, I told myself.

Bill went inside to talk to the soldier he had met after lunch. Marge left to write a letter.

"It's a lot easier to write home from the train than when you first get there," she said.

I thought of writing. I would write often so Dad would have letters to take home to read to Mom. But I couldn't write tonight.

"I'm going to do my nails. I have a date meeting me at the station," Kay said.

I sat alone in the end of the train, watching the shapes of trees and barns and riverbanks hurry away into the dark. I would have given anything to be back home. I felt the train taking me away, faster and farther every minute, from Dad and Mom and all I had ever known. Or was it the train?

4

I THINK I liked everything about the university.

There was a girl named Vera across the hall in the house where I had a room who was so homesick she used to cry herself to sleep. I heard her one night and took her into my room to cheer her up.

"If you lived in one of the women's dormitories or a sorority house, it'd be different, but in a hole like this you might as well be dead and buried," Vera said in the midst of her crying.

I looked around my room. It wasn't handsome. The brown-and-green-leaf wallpaper showed tack holes and a long water stain. The couch that was my bed was lumpy. The desk was too small to rest my whole arm on when I wrote. The easy chair Vera was sitting in was a rocker set up on a kind of platform. It squeaked more than the springs in the truck. The rug had two spots on it. I guess I hadn't looked at the room very hard before. It rented for $15 a month. But I wasn't in it except at night, like the house at home during seeding or harvest.

"The room doesn't matter. You don't have to be here much of the time," I told Vera.

"I am. I come back from classes and I get so blue I can't even study."

"Tomorrow you go with me. We've got the lib. and the woman's lounge at the Union to study in. The whole range is ours."

And the next day I met Vera after class and walked the length of the mall with her. But she walked along discontentedly looking at the fur jackets on the girls we met. In the woman's lounge —that name makes me think of Bailey's cat stretched out on the ramp at the elevator—she sank down in one of the low squashy chairs and I sat down in another. The light is soft in there because the blinds and the colors of the curtains and rug and chairs are the very colors you see on the flats at sundown. And it was bigger than the dance hall at Sun River.

"Why don't you camp out here? I do when I have time."

"I might," she said. "Do you know that some of the sorority houses are furnished better than this even?"

I nodded. She made me think of Dad a little, the way she kept thinking of other places all the time. I had been invited to a sorority. Kay and Marge looked me up and took me to theirs. I could see they'd told the others I was something pretty funny, the way they looked at me and laughed at anything I said. I'd have liked to live there, but I couldn't afford it even if they wanted me. It didn't worry me any.

"Well, I've got to go. I'll meet you at the lib. and we'll walk home together," I told her. "If you eat at the cafeteria I'll see you." I thought she looked more cheerful.

The job at the cafeteria was fun. I liked it best in the morning before many people were there, and the metal counters shone like new milk cans. There was the smell of fresh coffee from the big urn, and fresh broiled bacon, or sausage. The fried eggs, laid out on a warming table, looked like daisy heads with their yellow centers and white petals. It was fun to slide one off on a plate without breaking it. But the rush hours were exciting; you had to keep on your toes. The girls who'd worked there longest said, "Wait till it gets hot and you serve fish a whole noon!" I kept thinking how easy it would be to feed a harvest crew in a cafeteria—but try to find a crew that would wait on themselves! The same people came every day and I got to know a lot of them. Some of them kidded, like the red-haired boy that always called me "Swedie." I wouldn't get fat working in the cafeteria; there was so much food around I never felt hungry.

At four-thirty, just as I started back toward the library from "Teaching Methods," I remembered I had a conference with Professor Echols on my first composition. I couldn't meet Vera then and there was no time to stop in and tell her. I hurried back to Mr. Echols' office.

Mr. Echols had a way of saying things that stayed in your mind. In our first class he told us we were the voice of a new America learning and growing and becoming articulate in the sheltered places of the earth, while out beyond, a death struggle was going on for us and for learning. It made me think of our house in the shelter of the coulee. It can be as still and quiet as a church outside the kitchen door and above the coulee the wind will be roaring and driving the tumbleweed in front of it at fifty miles an hour.

I wondered anxiously what Mr. Echols would say to my theme. "For the first theme I want you to choose your own topic," he had said. "Write about something you know or something you think or believe, but for heaven's sake don't let it be anybody else's idea and don't write me how it feels to be in a Nazi concentration camp or in a submarine, because I'll make a pretty good guess you haven't been there." He was always saying funny things like that.

I wrote about Wheat. I'd had a letter that day from Dad saying John Bardich, whose land touches ours on the east, was selling his wheat now for 70 cents a bushel. "It's a pity we didn't hold some of it back. But that's the way with the wheat business," Dad ended.

That started me off. I wrote: "The pioneers who came West in the seventies in search of gold were no greater gamblers than the prosaic-looking ranchers planting wheat on the dry-land farms. They gamble with the weather that it will be neither too dry, nor too hot, nor too wet, nor too cold; that the wheat will not be destroyed by hail or grasshoppers; and when at last they have the ripe wheat cut and stored they gamble with the market that wheat will be selling for enough money to pay for all the summer's work."

I stopped writing and thought about Bill Bailey, who runs the Excelsior Grain elevator and knows a great deal about wheat. He can tell whether it has smut or rust or garlic in it, or why the top of the sheaf is empty or what is the best seed to plant. Bill Bailey likes to talk, and he says, "If you know a man's wheat over a few years you've got a pretty good line-up on the man himself." In harvesttime he sits at the center of things, in his little office in the elevator, and sees the ranchers driving in with their loads of wheat. Sometimes they stand parked in line till midnight. Bill Bailey can see them coming all day. There is nothing to hinder his view from his little window. I wondered if the ranchers far back on the prairie roads don't make him think of ants.

I went on writing: "I love the wheat and I hate it. I love the green blades of winter wheat in the spring. They show through the snow on the ground and make the only bright color in that winter world of grays and blacks and whites. I love the spring wheat that always seems trying to catch up with the winter wheat. It is like a person without much education or background trying to measure up with a person who's had years of both. The beardless wheat always seems to me like a young boy, and the shaggy bearded wheat like an old man.

"When the wheat is an even ripeness, the color of the crust of the fresh-baked bread it will go to make, and the wind sings across it, I love it so I could sing too, just to look at it. My mother says the wind in the wheat makes her think of the wind in the forests of northern Russia, only this is a sharper, thinner sound. When I was a little girl, I used to lie on my back in the field of wheat where my mother and father were working and play I was in a forest. The trees of wheat reached high above me and the wind sang in their tops; only my forest was golden instead of black like Mother's forest. Perhaps mine was the forest of the sun and hers was the forest of the night."

I could have gone on and on. I wanted to tell about harvesting and riding the combine when you feel as proud as a king on a chariot at the start of the day, but you can't feel and are like a piece of the machinery itself by the end of the day. But I liked the sound of the words I had just written: "forest of the sun" and "forest of the night." So I stopped there. It's funny that you can put down some words on a tablet and have them leap up from the page and carry you with them. I felt like the woman in the fairy story who baked the gingerbread boy that came to life.

I knocked on Mr. Echols' door and opened it. He was sitting behind a littered desk. His eyes looked so sleepy when he glanced up I thought maybe he couldn't remember my name.

"I'm Ellen Webb," I told him.

"Yes, I know. Won't you sit down, Miss Webb?" He was hunting in the pile on his desk for my theme. I saw it before he did, telling it by the way I'd turned the corners down to fasten it together. He picked it up and looked at it as though it were something strange he had never seen before. I wondered if he had even read it. The sun came in palely across his desk. The sun is always pale here, never out-and-out bright as it is at home. I could smell the heat in the radiators and outside I heard someone calling.

Mr. Echols was turning over the pages the way you do a newspaper you're not going to read through. He came to the last one.

" 'The trees of wheat reached high above me and the wind sang in their tops; only my forest was golden instead of black like Mother's forest. Perhaps mine was the forest of the sun and hers was the forest of the night.' "

It sounded terrible when he read it aloud. I felt my face going red. He took off his glasses.

"Very interesting, the way you see the land. Do you . . . Are you fond of Montana? I take it you come from there."

"Yes," I said. "I've always lived there."

"You don't have cattle?"

"No, we have a dry-land wheat ranch."

"Do you want to go back and live there?"

"I love it there, but I can't live there, because I want to be a . . . a linguist." Our Spanish teacher in high school called it that.

Mr. Echols took up his pipe. He looked at me while he lighted it. I could feel how hard he was trying to look into my world, into Gotham, Montana. He couldn't know how different it was. I felt so safe from being looked into. I wondered if that was the way Mom felt sometime when people looked at her and wondered what she was really like.

"That's very interesting," Mr. Echols said. "Do you speak any other language now?"

"Not really, but I can understand some Russian and some Yugoslav and I can speak some Spanish and French." I hated to admit how little I knew. "Languages are easy for me, though," I added.

"Have your family always been ranchers?"

"Oh, my father isn't naturally a rancher; he just took the ranch after he was married."

"He comes from some other part of the country—or was he born in Montana?"

I couldn't help smiling a little. "Almost everybody around Gotham came from some other part of the country."

"That's odd, isn't it? Where do they all come from?"

Looking out of the window of Mr. Echols' study I could see Gotham spread out: There were the Yonkos and the Bardiches, they were both Yugoslav and the best wheat farmers around. Next to us were the Halvorsens; they were Norwegians and the

Hakkulas were Finns. Mr. Peterson, who ran the store, was a Swede, and there was one family of Germans and Bill Bailey was from Iowa and the Whalens from Missouri.

When I'd told him, Mr. Echols said, "Is there any real unity of feeling with such a mixture?"

I had to laugh. He should see them. "No," I said, "not very much. We live mostly to ourselves."

"But don't you have a church and a grange?"

"They never got the church finished. The store is pretty small. I guess the grain elevator is the center of things. But we're only thirty miles from Clark City; that's our big town, with over thirty thousand people. That's where I went to high school. I went in on the bus every day."

I guess he couldn't picture it very well. He sat there trying to think how it would be. Then he said, looking at me as though he was trying to make me out:

"What nationality is your father? I take it that your mother is from Russia."

"Yes," I said. "But my father came from Vermont."

"Very interesting." I could see that he was wondering how they ever got together. Then he looked at his watch and leaned across the desk to hand me my theme. "Go on writing about what you know, your own part of the country—what you think, what you feel."

He had put an "A" on my theme, and underneath in a little scrimped handwriting I was to come to know very well, "Freshness of viewpoint," which seemed kind of meaningless.

I ran all the way to the library to see if Vera was still there. She wasn't at the lib., so I walked on back to the rooming house. It was like Indian summer and there were a few leaves on the pavement that crackled like a piece of paper when you stepped on them. At home the cottonwood tree by the coulee would be all yellow and the aspens in the windbreak turning copper. The sage would be tall and whitish and tough-rooted if you tried to pull it up. Mom's asters would be purple and pink and red and white all along the front of the house and down the path to the fence. My eyes were glued so tight to home I almost didn't see the maple tree in a yard I was passing. It had leaves as red as apples. There was a kind of windbreak around the yard, only cut very low, that was new to me. Most of its leaves were gone, but it had

26

red berries. I found out later that it wasn't a windbreak at all but a barberry hedge.

I love the fall. I loved it even here, where there was no clear distant view, and no mountains and so much rain. I ran into the house and up the stairs feeling as though I had something rich and lovely and both pockets full of it.

We were both on the third floor, Vera near the bathroom and I halfway up the hall. I knocked on her door but there was no answer. But just as I started to go on I heard her crying. The door wasn't locked, so I walked right in and said "Hello."

Vera was lying on the bed. She had come home and put her hair up in pin curls, and if there is anything a girl can do to make herself look more pinched and homely I don't know what it is. She wiped her eyes with a wad of tissue before she answered.

"I'm sorry. I couldn't stay over there. I didn't go to chemistry lab, either. I just came on back here."

I sat down on the arm of the chair and looked at her, trying to understand how she could crumple up like that. She was for all the world like a bum lamb that's going to die; there wasn't anything to work on. Her face didn't look unlike a sheep's face as it was now. She must have felt this way all week, the room was in such a mess. I picked up the clothes thrown on the chair where I was sitting and hung them in the corner behind the cretonne curtain. I guess it was my silence that made her turn over to look at me.

"You aren't mad at me, Ellen, are you?"

"Of course not. Look, I don't work at the cafeteria tonight. How about getting dressed and we'll go some place to eat." I didn't want to much, but I couldn't leave her like that.

She started to cry again and dab at her face with tissue. "You don't really want to. You're just being . . . kind."

And then I had to tell her in five different ways that I was crazy to. She got up finally and began combing her hair while I sat watching her. Suddenly she laid down her comb and said, "You're pretty, Ellen."

I stared at myself in her mirror harder than I ever had before. I saw that my hair had a soft shine to it, but that was because I had just washed it, and I had good color because of my fast walk home. For the rest, my gray eyes and too-high cheekbones and wide mouth were so familiar I couldn't tell.

27

"See, you even think you are! I'm not. Nobody would turn and look at me twice."

Then I got sick of such talk. "Don't be a goose, Vera. How can you worry about whether you're pretty or homely when people are worrying about whether they'll be living tomorrow!" I sounded to myself exactly like Mom. There was the time Mrs. Yonko's daughter sat in our kitchen talking about how poor they were and Mom turned on her.

"You don't know nothing about poor!" she had said in a cold hard kind of a way. "Wait till you live on black bread and cabbage three year and be glad to get it! During war we don't have that some time." Mom's eyes had seemed to see way beyond us.

"Tell us about that time, Mom," I had begged. I was about twelve then. Mom closed up tight and the fierceness went out of her; but it comes to my mind when I read about poverty. Mom never wasted anything, and she'd urge Dad or me to eat the last piece of anything left on the platter till Dad used to get angry. Dad never liked having pigs, but Mom had to have them. "They eat cheap," Mom used to say, "and they sell good."

Vera was pretty when she was all ready and we had left that terrible sloppy room behind. She had on a red corduroy dress and some red shoes to match and a white lambskin jacket. Her lips matched her dress and the beanie she wore on the back of her head. She didn't have any stockings without runs, so I loaned her a pair of my white knit socks with the red and black border.

"Gee, they look hand-knit," she said.

"They are. Mom made 'em."

"Pretty hot! They're like the real peasant stuff over at the ski shop."

"They are peasant stuff," I said. I thought of Mom coming in from the barn in her big galoshes and her hair tied in a bandanna. I suppose she must have been a peasant girl when Dad met her. I knew Mom hadn't had much regular education. She could read a little and write a little, but Dad wrote me mostly. Sometimes Mom tucked in a little note. I think she didn't want him to read them. But always they told more in a sentence than Dad's long ones.

"Gus Johnson was over help your father with post holes. He is real hay-maker." Which was Mom's way of saying he was a hard worker . . . or she would write "Your Dad don't talk much.

28

Wind is bad." And I could see the whole long day with Dad sitting miserable and silent by the stove.

We went to the Beanpot because that's the most popular place near the campus. It has a big fat beanpot out over the door and they serve a full dinner for 65 cents, which is 20 cents more than you'd have to pay at the cafeteria. It was nice to sit down at a table and order, but to save my life I couldn't help noticing each plate that went by to see the size of the helpings. That's what working at the cafeteria does for you. The food did taste different. The steam table does things to food in spite of how clean and shiny the metal dishes are. We ended with a serving of chocolate pie topped with whipped cream and Vera smoked afterward while I had a third cup of hot black coffee.

Then I remembered Mr. Echols this afternoon.

"Vera, what do you want to do after college?"

"Get rich," Vera answered, so fast it took my breath away. "I'd like to be a dress-designer in Hollywood and make pots of money." Her face didn't look so thin. "I'd have a penthouse apartment that was really beautiful with a bedroom in gray and dusty pink and a bathroom opening out of it in Dubonnet with a square gray bathtub."

I thought of the messy bedroom she had at 1112 and the bathroom down the hall that was always draped with washing and the washbasin littered with bobby pins and broken pieces of soap.

"What do you want to do?" Vera asked.

"I want to be able to talk different languages and go and live in foreign countries for a while. Last year when I took Spanish I knew I wanted to do something with languages." I couldn't explain to Vera that I'd always wanted to talk Mom's language. There are English words that don't quite fit the Russian ones. Mom says something in English and doesn't look satisfied sometimes, as though the English words didn't really say it, like my name that she calls Yeléna. The Bardich girls won't let their mother and father talk Yugoslav together; they want them to be American, but I don't feel that way. Mom's Russian is something precious of her own that she brought from Russia when she came, like her icon.

"How would you make a living doing that?"

"Oh, I'd translate and interpret for people or be a correspondent." But I wasn't very sure about it.

"You don't want to go back to Montana, do you? I'm never going back to Iowa if I can help it."

"I wouldn't mind going back for a while. I may teach a year or so after college. I'm taking enough education this year so I'll have my certificate."

"For heaven's sake! My folks want me to teach school back home, but I'd starve to death rather than go back to that dump and teach kids."

We walked up Third. Two boys on the porch of a fraternity house whistled at us.

"Do you know any boys in school?" Vera asked.

"Nope, not one," I said, though the boy in history class had asked me to go to a movie Friday night.

"All the nice ones go for girls in sororities."

"You can get in next year, maybe," I said, thinking if we had a bumper crop maybe I could, too.

"If I'm asked, you mean," Vera said.

And then we cut across the campus and there was room to smell the rotting leaves and the night air. I forgot Vera. My spirits rose like a partridge startled out of the brush. I had never been inside so much in all my life as this last month and a half. I hadn't known how cooped-up I had been.

When we came to the door of the rooming house and climbed the three flights of stairs, the narrow hall crowded in on me. I thought of the feeling of space on top of the rimrock back of our house at home and the wind in the aspens in the creek bed. I undressed in the dark and lay in bed with my face turned toward the open window, but the lighted windows of the house next door blocked my view, and there was no wind stirring.

5

I HAVE reason to remember the library. Now of all the buildings on campus it is the clearest in my mind. I remember the shallow feeling under my feet of the steps leading up to it, and the weight of the front door, and the worn marble stairs inside. I know each room with its subdued shuffle of papers and feet, the smell of books that is different from the smell of periodicals and papers, and the sound of the light switching off in the stacks and the tinny tread of feet on the steel stairs of the stacks. I remember the sun across the study tables, the sun of that spring shining through green and the paler sun of that winter whitened by snow. I remember the feeling of excitement at ten o'clock when half the lights in the reading room were turned off as a warning of closing time, and I would go down and meet Gil.

I always studied in the library, never in my room at 1112. There was a table in the corner between two long windows where I usually worked, but if I sat with my face toward the window I kept looking out, studying the weather the way we do at home. If I turned toward the door, I watched people coming in and out. But I learned to look at the window and think about what I had been reading, too.

It was in October that I met Gil. I saw him sitting at a table halfway across the room. I watched him when he went over to the encyclopedias against the wall. I met his eyes and looked away. Finally, I turned my chair toward the window. It was better to be distracted by the weather than to keep glancing up at some boy. But after that I always looked to see if he was there when I went in.

One day I went over to the lib. after Mr. Echols' class to work on the next assignment. Mr. Echols wanted us to write autobiographies. "Begin with your family. Make me see them with your eyes, then make me see you growing up, your town, your house, your religion, your school." It must be interesting, I thought, for him to know all about each one of us sitting there in his classroom.

I thought it would be easy. Things I wanted to say sprang into my mind all the way over to the lib.: I would tell how the warm, melting breath of a chinook felt after days of dry cold; how it felt to pull the harrow or drive the combine; how it felt when a cloudburst struck after weeks of hard bright heat and I stood out in the open and let it drench me; how hail felt, too, when I ran out in it to get the chickens all in. I wanted to bring my whole world and set it down on paper.

But now, sitting in front of a pad of empty paper, it wasn't easy. "Begin with your family," Mr. Echols had said.

I started in: "My father and mother are very different. My father came from a small town in Vermont." I knew that town almost as well as Gotham. I could describe some of the people and the house where Dad was born, he had told me so much about it. The house was three stories tall and had a long two-tiered porch. I knew just how the parlor looked with its horsehair and walnut furniture and I knew Dad's room when he was a boy. His windows looked out into green maple leaves that sometimes woke him in the night with the noise they made, louder and more scary than the sound of the aspen leaves by the creek, Dad said. There was a big picture of the Day of Judgment that scared Dad, too. He told me that when I said I wished we had more pictures in our house and he said it was better to have none than the kind that scared you.

Dad's father was the principal of the high school and I think Dad stood in awe of him as a boy. He died while Dad was in the Army. When Dad went back with Mom only his mother and sister were there. I felt I knew a lot about Vermont, too. Dad so often talked about it—how different it was from Montana. Trees grew easily there, the way they do here in Minnesota, and there were picket fences and neat garden plots and all the houses were painted and every village had a church with a white spire on it.

Dad used to tell me about skating parties and corn roasts and the fun they had in the high school where his father was principal. Once he was telling about home and Mom looked up from the knitting she was doing and said:

"And the womans in that town would see a murder done better than have dust in their parlor. They are afraid of what their neighbors don't do, too."

Dad stopped talking about Vermont and went outside.

"Go get to bed," Mom said sharply to me. That came back now more clearly than the stories Dad had told me.

I didn't know much of anything about Mom's town. I hardly knew what she looked like as a girl, except that Dad had a candy box of old snapshots: of the boat he went to England on, and the one he sailed to Archangel in, and pictures of other soldiers and the snow in Russia, of towns that looked half-buried in snow and groups of Russians with funny hats. One of them showed Mom in a dark dress with a bandanna over her head. There was a big black coffeepot in front of her as though she had just put it down, and she had a snowball in her hand and she was laughing. Mom was seventeen then, she told me. "The soldiers always laugh and joke and make fun," Mom said. "Your father always had some-thing fun to say. The day they bring him to Seletskoe all shot up and bleeding he can make jokes."

Some of the fun had gone out of him in Montana, it seemed to me, the way so many dry years have taken the moisture out of the soil.

I knew Mom's family were very poor and she was the only girl in a family of five brothers. "I have five uncles, Mom. Will I ever see them?" I asked one time.

"Four was killed in last war," Mom said, "and one go to be a priest."

"Are my grandparents living, Mom?" It seemed as though a little part of me must be in them. I wanted to know about them in order to know more about myself, the way you do when you look at your baby pictures and listen to things you did before you can remember.

"They was both killed," Mom said. I couldn't have been more than eight when Mom told me about them. We were thinning beets in the garden; Mom was always more talkative outdoors.

"Killed, Mom?" I couldn't believe it. Children in Gotham had their grandparents living with them. How could mine have been killed?

"My father try to keep his pigs from robber soldier. The man shoot him and burn our house. My mother burn to death."

I stared at Mom. Even to a child my mother didn't hide things or make them seem better than they were. I saw in her face that she could see it all just as it was.

"Did you see it happen?" The question almost stuck in my throat and yet I had to ask it.

"I see my father shot, then I run for help. When I come back the house is burned, and my mother dead. It was in winter."

I remember how still it was out there in the garden, and since that day I have always known how red are the veins of the beet leaves and how like soft green leather the leaves themselves.

"What did you do, Mom?"

"My brother and I live in old shack for while. Then he go to be priest. I help nurse wounded soldiers. Move your hands faster. See, like this!" Mom was through talking, but all afternoon as we worked down the hot rows I thought about my grandmother and grandfather, part of me, killed. I remember wishing they could know that I was here.

I wished even now that they could know I was here in college, sitting in this big room at a polished table writing about them. But the paper in front of me was still empty except for two sentences: "My father and mother are very different. My father came from a small town in Vermont." I began now purposefully. I would start with their meeting.

"My father was sent to Archangel in the last war. In a way, I think it must have been the most important happening in his life. Before the war he had had one year of college and expected to go right on and finish. That spring he enlisted and that summer he sailed for England. While his transport was in the harbor in England, the order came that sent him to Russia."

Dad has a picture taken in the harbor and one of himself leaning over the railing and waving. He says he'd never had an ache or pain then. He'd even won his letter for track freshman year. I had studied that snapshot a long time. It seemed so good to see Dad well. I've never known him when rain or cold didn't set his shrapnel wounds to hurting and make him cough.

"The American troops were sent to Archangel to keep the Germans from gaining control of the railroad and the new Russian government from seizing the Allied ammunitions."

I knew all about that; I had heard Dad talking to Bailey over at the elevator. "Damn-fool expedition!" Dad had called it. "The Armistice was signed less than three months after we got there, but the port of Archangel was frozen up tight as a prison. You ought to see it! We don't know what cold is here. Cold fog everywhere. They told us what to do to keep from frostbite. One of the boys, a little fellow from St. Louis, insurance salesman he was, was so afraid he'd freeze his face he kept making faces every few minutes and it nearly drove us crazy. We'd bellow at him, 'Stop doing that!'" Then Dad and Bailey had laughed and Dad had lost his tired look. I've heard Dad tell how the very morning the Armistice was signed, while some of the men were still at breakfast, the Bolshies came out of the woods in a regular attack formation. "Armistice or no armistice, that's when I got filled with shrapnel!" Dad had said.

Bailey shook his head. "Don't they know what's going on in the rest of the world?"

"Russia's a world by itself. They were mad at each other and they didn't want us up there, so they kept on fighting."

I loved hearing about their escape over a trail through the woods. Some of Dad's stories Mom didn't like, but she liked the part about the soldiers being brought into the little village where she lived. That was where she took care of Dad.

I tried to put it down in the biography, but I couldn't get in so many things. When we had Mom's hot red borsch Dad would say sometimes, "This is the stuff your mother filled me with to make me well."

"That was poor stuff, not like this," Mom would answer. "You'd had so many of those cold apple pies and salt-pork meals you don't know good soup from bad." Sometimes I felt Mom wasn't joking when she said things like that. She didn't like anything about Dad's home.

"Did you fall in love with each other right away?" I asked just last summer when Mary Bardich got married.

Mom went on knitting without looking up. Her face went blank the way it can do when it shuts down over something. I looked at Dad. Dad was busy getting his pipe to draw.

"I mean," I said in the funny little silence that had spread until it was big, "wasn't it hard with Mom speaking Russian and you English?"

"We didn't find it difficult," Dad said kind of formally.

"He can say '*bol*,' pain, and 'hurt,' and 'water' in Russian," Mom said, "and 'What is your name?'" She looked at him and laughed a little.

"*Kak vashe emya*," Dad said like a child saying his lesson.

"You could say 'rest now' and 'eat it up' and 'you will feel better,'" Dad said, as though he had forgotten me and was talking to Mom. And I could see suddenly how it must have been through those few words. I think I began wanting to know different languages then.

"And '*mne holodno*,' remember?" Mom asked, hugging herself as though she was shivering cold.

"I remember the day you said 'cold' in English," Dad said.

"And how you try to teach me English," Mom said.

"You learned very fast," Dad admitted.

"That was easy!" Mom said, as she says about planting a whole field or cooking for harvest hands or even digging stones out of the field.

I sat there in the library, chewing the end of my fountain pen while I tried to sort out what was important in the story of Dad and Mom. I remembered one time I had heard her admit that a thing was hard. Judy Bailey was getting married and going to Illinois to live. I was helping Mom with the washing and I said I bet it would be hard meeting her husband's family the first time.

Mom lifted the dripping clothes out of the hot suds with a stick. "It is hard," she said. "Everything is different when I go to your father's town, everything!" She made a gesture with the stick and dripping clothes that showed how wide the difference was. "They don't eat same as I do—house, clothes, church, everything different. They don't even think same. That was hard."

"You weren't there long, though, were you?" I asked.

"Long enough!" Mom said, and her face was dark and heavy. "They was glad to see me go. We come out here."

I asked Dad once, when he was talking about Vermont, how they happened to come off out here, and Dad's face looked almost as though he didn't know either, but he said:

"I wanted to go to the other end of the earth just then and your mother wanted to live on a farm. So we homesteaded. Sort of last-call pioneers."

I heard Dad talking to Bailey one afternoon in winter when it started to grow dark at three o'clock and it was so cold in the elevator Bailey kept the door into the office closed. They both sat there with their feet on the airtight stove. I think they'd forgotten me.

"If anyone was to tell me when I was seventeen that at forty I'd be ranching it out here in Montana I'd have told him he was crazy," Dad said. "At seventeen I was hesitating between being a lawyer and teaching. My father wanted me to be a college professor. He taught in Andover for a year before he became principal of the high school at home. And I was leaning that way. I'd have liked to teach history."

"And then the war threw the monkey wrench into all your plans, eh?" Bailey said. "You could have gone on and taught anyway, couldn't you? It would be a long sight easier than raisin' wheat in this infernal country."

"No, I couldn't," Dad said shortly. "I was married and had a child on the way. My father was dead by that time. Not a chance!" He got into his heavy sheepskin and the cap Mom had knit him that came way down over his ears, and the mittens. "Good night, Bailey. Come on, Ellen."

There was one day when Dad was sick and had to lie on the couch all day. Mom and I were cleaning the barn, and some of my thinking and wondering came out in a question.

"Mom, couldn't Dad have gone back to school? Wouldn't his mother and sister help him and you could have found some position?"

"What you talking about?" Mom was scattering fresh straw in the stall and a wisp of straw was caught in her hair. I looked up at her and thought how pretty she was.

"About Dad. I think it would have been so much better for him if he'd been a teacher. That's what he always meant to do, he told Bailey one time," I said brashly.

"Did he say that? How long time?" I was too young and stupid to get the change in Mom's face right away. I saw it afterward, though.

"Oh, last month sometime. I don't see why he didn't go back to school."

"His mother and sister was afraid to death they don't have enough to go on live just as easy as always. They love that house like first son. No, they don't want to help."

37

"But why didn't they want to, Mom? They must have been hateful."

"No," Mom said slowly. "They don't like him to bring back poor Russian girl who don't talk much and don't dress right. I see now; I don't then. I hate them. I don't know then what Ben want to do. I can't stand it there. He want to go far away. I want to have just a little land. He hear you can take homestead, so we come out here." Mom shrugged. "He like it here."

"Oh, I know he does," I said quickly, wanting now to comfort Mom. I had seen the change. "It's only sometimes in the winter when he doesn't feel good that he talks that way. In the spring he loves it."

Mom nodded. That was one of the times when I felt like a parent to her. And I have not asked questions so brashly since.

But you couldn't write all this into a biographical sketch. My knowledge of Mom and Dad was made up of such little things, things felt more than known. I came back to the few sentences I had actually written and went on boldly:

"My mother and father fell in love, although my mother could speak only a few words of English. They were married by the Captain of my father's company and when the ice loosened its grip on the harbor at Archangel my mother sailed with my father to America." I set a period with a flourish. "Loosened its grip" had a proper, bookish sound. I skipped over the return to his home in Vermont in a sentence and wrote of their taking a homestead in Montana, "where I was born three years later."

I had told their story in eight sentences, but it had taken me all afternoon. I had to run to be at the cafeteria on time.

By seven-thirty I was back at the same table. I had thought it would be easy to write now, but it wasn't. I kept remembering certain happenings in my childhood, down to the silliest detail; but they weren't the kind of incidents you tell. I could only seem to compose terrible trite sentences like "My early childhood on the ranch was the usual happy life lived by children in the country, although it may seem bare in the telling."

But how could I tell about those days when I'd run up to the top of the rimrock because I had to be closer to the sky? Ever since I was seven or eight I have done that, or run out across the flats. I couldn't stand still or walk soberly, because I felt something exciting was going to happen. Sometimes the wind gave me that feeling, sometimes the first bleak day of fall, always spring and the first green pricks of wheat, and always threshing time.

I have looked at Mom often and felt that she didn't expect anything exciting to happen. I think Dad used to, we are so much alike, but he has given up expecting it now, so I try not to show how I feel.

All I wrote was: "I did not really know the difference between work and play. Work on a ranch is interesting to a child: driving the horses and later the truck or tractor, making butter or filling sausage cases. It doesn't matter much what you are doing, except the things you really hate, like washing dishes and cleaning house.

"I had toys. Dad bought most of them. He hardly ever came back from town, when I hadn't gone along, without a stuffed animal or a monkey I could wind up or a new book of paper dolls. But I was fondest of a painted wooden picture, less than a foot high, that Mom put in my room on a high corner shelf. Set back from the frame was a solemn face with round cheeks and deep-set eyes. I liked best its hands that met finger tip for finger tip with each one distinct and perfect, even to the fingernail. The paint had mostly worn off; only a faint tinge of blue still remained. The wood was so smooth it felt almost soft when I stood up on a chair to touch it. It wasn't a toy at all, but an icon that had hung in Mom's house in Russia. She found it near the ashes after her home was burned. I had it near my bed and used to talk to it without making the words, just looking over at it now and then."

I did not write of the uncomfortable feeling I had about the icon. When I had diphtheria at six, Mom hung the shelf in my room and put the icon on it and a saucer beneath with a lighted wick floating in oil. I lay in bed watching the little flame. When it grew dark outside, the flame on the wick made a secret glow in the room. As soon as Dad came home from town I called him to come and see it, but instead of liking it he was angry.

"Don't bring my child up with such idols, Anna!" he called out to Mom, and he blew the flame out.

"Don't take it away; I love it." I started to cry. Then I remember Mom coming in and lighting the wick again, her eyes thin and her mouth tight.

"What have you got in your church a child can see?" Mom

39

asked in a voice that was so cold and scornful it was like ice cracking in the water bucket.

"Please don't take the picture away," I begged, and Dad didn't say anything more. Mom took the saucer away next day and never lighted a flame again, but the icon has always been in my room ever since.

I began writing again. "All the animals on the ranch were mine, or I felt them so. The cows, the team of horses that I rode bareback whenever I wanted, all of the series of dogs; only the sow I never laid any claim to nor the tom turkeys that always looked too bloody to me with their bright-red wattles. I think I have never been lonesome.

"We went to town often, but seldom on Saturday, when most of the ranchers went. I had a feeling that Father didn't like it when the streets were filled with ranchers in clean work shirts, the little tags of their tobacco bags dangling out of one pocket, the color of their faces and necks giving away their occupation. Yet people must have told easily that we were ranchers. Dad always wore his best suit and a city hat, never the broad-brimmed Western hat. He carried cigarettes in a case that I was never tired of watching spring open at the pressure of a thumb. He wore oxfords instead of high shoes. Perhaps they couldn't tell Dad was a rancher unless they looked at his hands, but he had Mom and me along.

"Mom wore a plain cotton print in summer, a dark wool dress in winter. She bought it in "The Big Store." She never liked a hat on her head and never looked quite right in one. She never wore gloves in summer, and her hands were the color of the red-maple furniture you see in furniture-store windows; only her hands had fine lines of black that no amount of washing with the vegetable brush at the sink could quite take away, and her nails were always worn down at the finger tips. She was big-boned and solid, with broader shoulders than Father's. Her lips of themselves were—Why do I put it in the past tense?—her lips are now red and full, and there is color on her high cheekbones. Her face is so calm and still it stands out from the animated or worried or cross faces of the town women, hurrying by on their eternal shopping. I guess I was thinking, too, of the contrast with women I had seen on the streets downtown in Minneapolis.

"For years I was a slim child with pale-yellow pigtails to the waist of my clean starched dress. I never wore a hat unless it was winter, and I wore socks and oxfords that Dad took pride in buying.

"Every time we went to Clark City Dad and I stopped to have our shoes polished at the Greek shoeshine place. I think it was one of the high spots of the trip for Dad. He would sit there, reading the paper he had bought, and feel like a city man."

I held my pen still, remembering all those trips: the trip to the grocery store and to the hardware store or to the McCormick-Deering store for a piece of machinery, the briefer trips to "The Big Store" for some needles or thread or cloth. Usually we separated and Dad dropped into the lobby of the hotel to talk to someone. Mom and I went together, Mom walking along the aisles of the store, scarcely looking at the things that didn't interest her, I hanging back as we went past the perfume counter, the fine soaps, then the pocketbooks and gloves and stockings. And yet, I really only wanted to look at them; I didn't covet them; they would only have been a clutter around home.

I remembered the time when we did go to town on Saturday, the Saturday before Easter. All the women in Gotham had gone to town and bought new clothes to wear to church Easter Sunday. In the beginning, Dad had not intended to go. But Saturday came off so warm the winter wheat showed bright apple-green. We had left the breakfast dishes and gone outdoors to work. Dad set off with the drill to do some seeding. I was feeding the chickens and Mom was somewhere below the barn when all of a sudden Dad came back.

"Anna!" he called at the top of his voice.

I heard Mom answer and then I saw her running.

"Anna, tomorrow's Easter!"

"I know."

"Let's go to town today."

And instead of saying no when there was so much to do and everything, Mom laughed. "You want a Easter hat?"

"Well, you can't work all the time." Dad often said that to Mom. He tired before Mom did.

We drove into town that morning and had lunch at a restaurant. When we came out we stood together on the sidewalk the way ranchers do in town. Dad took out a five-dollar bill and gave it to me.

"Here, Ellen, go buy yourself a new Easter dress."

When Dad had gone on down the street I handed the money to Mom to put in her big pocketbook for me. She pushed it off. "Keep it yourself, your father want you to buy with it."

Without a sound my day broke into pieces, pieces with sharp cutting edges. I didn't want any new dress. I only wanted to be in my jeans and old shirt at home. Mom was hurt because Dad hadn't given her the money.

"I've got to go in hardware store and buy new ax handle," Mom said. "Your Dad'll never think. Go on, get your dress."

Wretchedly I walked into the store where dresses were sold. Nothing drew me as it usually did, not even the long sheer silk stocking on a shapely glass leg. I watched some women coming in and hated them for the way they wore their clothes, and their trim ankles and shoes and the faint sweet smell as they passed me. I had been standing aimlessly against a counter by the front door. Suddenly I knew what I wanted. I went over to the stocking counter and said in a firm voice:

"I want a pair of silk stockings like those on that glass leg." When the clerk asked what size I said, "A big size, about as large as you sell," thinking of Mom's legs as I often saw them in the row ahead of me when we worked in the garden.

"Those are three dollars," the clerk told me, and I could see she doubted whether I could pay for them.

"I'll take them," I told her. Then I gave her the five-dollar bill and had two silver dollars back.

"Are they for a gift? I could wrap them with tissue paper for you."

I didn't want them to seem anything special. I said, "No, just everyday."

I walked straight from the stocking counter to the perfume counter, where I had never had time to linger before. It was hard to know what to ask for. The salesgirl was unlike anyone I had ever seen outside a magazine.

"What scent do you have that smells Russian?" I asked.

"Russian? Let's see—we have Cuir de Russe. That's Russian leather."

"I'd like to smell it." The whiff seemed to penetrate back of my eyeballs. My eyes watered. "I'll take two dollars' worth," I said.

The lady at the counter gave me a bottle so tiny it didn't look as though it could cost more than a quarter, but I paid her. Mom still has the bottle on her dresser, along with a picture of Dad in his uniform and a hand-painted pin tray with "New York City" written on it. The perfume bottle is still half-full.

"You get your dress?" Mom asked when I found her. She had the ax handle in her hand.

"No, I bought these for you." I thrust the paper sack and the little package at her and took the ax handle. I busied myself with an assortment of screws. Mom was so quiet I had to look at her. Her face was different. It wasn't as firm as usual.

"Yeléna, your Dad won't like it."

"He gave it to me. It's mine." But I wasn't anxious to see him and have him ask me about the dress. He did ask me, and I said I couldn't find one I liked so I bought something else I wanted. He whistled and smiled. Dad never was stern or angry with me— only at life and the weather and his own illness.

"What did you buy?"

"Some perfume and stockings," I mumbled. Mom was in the back seat arranging parcels.

"So you had a hankering for perfume and silk stockings. You're growing up. Nobody would think it to see you in your jeans. What do you think of that, Anna?"

Mom didn't answer and Dad let the matter drop. He had another idea. Easter had gone to his head.

"Why don't we stay overnight and go to church on Easter like civilized people?"

I held my breath.

"We've got the stock to take care of," Mom said doggedly.

"They can wait. We'd be back by two o'clock. It would do us good. We haven't been to church since . . ."

"Since we went with your mother," Mom said. That was before I was born, I was busy figuring to myself. Church wasn't part of our living. But I wished Mom hadn't said that. It was suddenly too close to breathe easily, even though we sat in the truck on the main street. Dad started to drop the idea and close up and then he didn't.

"As I remember, you were a good Greek Catholic once. We don't want Ellen not to know what the inside of a church looks like."

43

The air cleared. That was the most exciting trip we had ever made to town. Mom and I bought nightgowns in Montgomery Ward's and we packed them in a little straw suitcase Mom carried her parcels in. We stayed at the hotel where Dad often sat and talked in the lobby, a big glittering place that awed Mom and me. We had a room I can see now. The carpet went from wall to wall. The furniture was big and shining, with a full-length mirror in the door. There was a bathroom between the rooms, with the first big white bathtub I had ever used.

I couldn't remember a time when Dad had been so gay. He called up and ordered ice water sent up to the room and tipped the boy who brought it, as though he were a king.

"Remember the hotel we stayed in the night after we got into New York?" he said to Mom. "I told you we were having our honeymoon and you thought 'honey' was the word for 'hotel,' Anna!" I walked into the bathroom and drew water out of the shiny faucet, feeling good because they were laughing.

It was a wonderful night. We didn't eat dinner in the beautiful dining room; that cost too much. We went out to a cafeteria, and I thought of that cafeteria some days when I was serving in the one here.

I lay awake that night looking at my room until I knew every object in it. Light from the alley came in the window and shone in the mirror like the moon does at home. It was better at night, because you couldn't see the dust along the edge of the carpet or that the rose-silk lampshade was punched through. I liked listening to footsteps in the hall and cars out in the street, and my body felt delicious after its hot all-over bath.

When I woke in the morning I had a funny feeling. I was afraid something would go wrong. Dad came into my room all dressed in a new white shirt he had bought himself. He'd had a shave downstairs in the hotel barbershop and he looked as though he didn't know wheat from barley.

"Well, Ellen, how do you like it?"

"All right," I told him. Something in me wouldn't let me sound any more pleased for fear . . . fear. Maybe it's because I was born on a dry-land wheat farm and I know you've got to be afraid every spring even though the wheat stands brave and green, afraid until the wheat's cut and stored, afraid of drought and hail and grasshoppers. Dad is, always. Mom used to say to him, "If

44

you're going to be afraid of drought all the time, you might as well be afraid of planting in the first place." Yet Mom is the one that feels it worst when the drought comes.

When Mom came into my room to braid my hair she had on her new silk stockings I'd given her and the scent of the perfume was on her. The stockings fitted her ankles and legs better than skin. They were too fine for the black laced low shoes she wore, but they were beautiful. Such a pride came up in me it almost drove out the little fear. I think that's why folks dress up in their best clothes when they do something special—to keep them from being afraid anything will spoil it. I had another bath that morning and I felt as light as tumbleweed, but a lot cleaner.

We had breakfast at the cafeteria down the street. Dad had a paper to read while he ate and he gave Mom the woman's part and me the funnies.

"It's been nearly twelve years, Anna, since I've had a morning paper to read at breakfast. By heaven, this is living like a white man!"

And suddenly, I was proud that Dad knew how to live, that he was used to places like hotels. Mom loved it, too. Her eyes were bright and dark. I leaned toward her a little and there was the delicious smell of "Russian leather" again, nicer than fresh hay or sweet clover or buffalo willows in the spring and as penetrating as the smell of sage. I looked at the three of us in the mirror. We might have been travelers just passing through town for the day.

"I don't like letting the cows and pigs and chickens an' all wait for their food," Mom said, but Dad didn't hear her.

"Well"—he folded the paper on the table—"it's close to ten. Where do you want to go?"

Mom looked surprised. "To church, Ben."

I remember driving along the streets, quiet on that Easter Sunday morning. Bells on one church began ringing. I had never heard church bells before.

"Let's go where the bells are, Dad," I begged.

We could pick out the churches easily from the steeples that reached up above the roofs of the bungalows. I leaned way out of the car to try to see the bells swinging in the tower, the way they do on Christmas cards. I noticed how the sun glinted hard

45

on the cross that topped the spire, like the sun on the lightning rod on the Hendersons' barn.

"Sit back, Ellen," Dad said. He stopped the car and Mom got out.

"I think I'll take Ellen over to the Congregational Church, Anna."

Mom leaned against the car door. All her face waited. I knew with dreadful certainty that the thing had come, the thing I had feared when I woke up this morning, the thing that would spoil our day. I couldn't say anything. I looked at the people going into church, whole families together. Some of them wore flowers. The bell was still ringing. The double door opened and I caught a glimpse of brightness, of candles far down in front, and the stained-glass windows.

Dad was making the engine sound louder with his foot. "We'll come back for you at twelve or as soon as our service is over, Anna. Wait right out in front."

I wanted with all my heart to go with Mom. It was no good this way. I held my hands tight together. Why didn't Mom say something? Her face was firm like it is when she goes to kill a turkey.

"Now I don't want any church," she said.

"Oh, Mom, come with us," I said as she opened the door of the car. Mom shook her head. Her lips came out farther than usual. "I go to his church once. Everyone is too busy look at me to say prayers." The hard cold feeling was there. Nothing could help now. It was no use.

Dad pushed his foot down hard on the accelerator. The engine roared so loud people on their way to church looked at us. Dad drove back down from the quiet shady streets where people lived, out the road toward home. I watched the road straight ahead without looking at Mom or Dad. They didn't speak. After a while I looked down at Dad's shoes with the city shine on them, at Mom's silk stockings so thin and smooth they showed a blue vein through.

We were more than fifteen miles toward home when Dad said, not to Mom or me, just aloud, "I guess we've lost our religion out here along with some other things." He didn't sound mad, only discouraged. We never drove into town to go to church again.

"Tell about your religion," Mr. Echols had said. "How much it has meant to your family, to you." The sheet in front of me was blank. I hadn't written a word for an hour.

It was just there that I looked up and saw Gilbert watching me. I always remembered that meeting him was mixed in with my writing my biography, as though I must have known how deeply he was to be part of my life. He met my eyes and smiled. I smiled a little in return. He picked up his book and came over to my table and I saw again how slender and tall he was. He took the chair next to me.

"I've seen you here for two months. It's time we knew each other. How about calling it a day and going over to Pop's Place for a coke?"

I hesitated, then I put my pencil down. "Okay," I said. We went down the marble stairs together.

"My name's Gilbert Borden—Gil. I've been trying to find out what yours is."

"Ellen," I told him. "Ellen Webb."

"I like that. It fits you. Where do you come from, Ellen Webb? You must be a freshman, because I'd have seen you if you'd been around here."

"I came this fall from Montana."

"It would be some place far away and unusual."

I remember laughing at that. I remember how we laughed at all kinds of things. Everything we told each other seemed exciting. He was a senior in the school of architecture.

"Any other year I'd have been working for the Paris fellowship. If I got it this year, I'd have to take it in Cincinnati or Cleveland or some place. Anyway, I'll probably go into the Army in June."

That, too, gave a deeper color to everything he said. We had a booth in Pop's, the last one. Gil kept punching out "Tomorrow Is a Lovely Day" on the jukebox. He played it over again three times. I felt as though I'd known him for years.

We walked back across campus and sat on the steps of the auditorium. The lights along the mall seemed to lie at our feet. We sat against one of the pillars, so we weren't cold.

"No kidding, I've watched you in the library ever since the first week in October. You came in and sat down there at the

47

end of that same table and the sun on your hair made it shine like silver."

"I've seen you, too," I said.

"You didn't take much time from your work to look my way!"

"I can't. I have a job at the cafeteria and it takes quite a lot of time. Don't you ever go there?"

"I will now. But that's no job for you."

"I hope to get a job in the library next year if I can."

"Maybe Dad can help you. He teaches history."

"You live here, then?"

"Oh, I live at the fraternity during school."

He walked back with me to the rooming house. I ran up the stairs that night not feeling that they were narrow or that the upper floor was stifling. I looked at the biography, but all that had happened to me before seemed unimportant beside the future. I wrote that at the end and copied the whole thing neatly before I went to bed. Mom and Dad's story seemed less important than my own.

6

WHEN I got that biography back, Mr. Echols had written across the top "C. Disappointing, stereotyped. You write with more feeling about objects than about people. Characterization poor."

I would have minded more if it hadn't been for Gilbert. But by now my days were measured off by seeing him. I was in love. Once in a while the marvel of it struck me, when I'd stop in to see Vera down the hall, or when I would see some of the very stunning girls on the campus, but most of the time it only seemed natural. Gil said that was the way it was with him, too.

We were different, but we were excited about the same things. Nothing was dull when we did it together, even studying in the library. I hadn't meant to fall in love so soon, but there's nothing you can do about it. It's like planning to seed in April and then having it come off so warm in March that the earth is ready. The spring doesn't wait.

Gil came to the cafeteria for lunch when he could have eaten at his fraternity house. He looked so funny carrying his tray I loved him all the more. He chose the craziest, most unbalanced food and there were so many things he didn't like to eat I told him he'd be hard to cook for. Sometimes he'd come by and say: "Only twenty-nine minutes more. I'll meet you by the corner." He never would believe that I didn't mind serving in the cafeteria. He acted as though I were delicate and kind of frail, and I'm not. I'm as strong as Mom.

"You're like silver," he used to say.

I laughed at him and told him he should see me after I'd been working in the field, haying or threshing. I get so burned my eyes look light and my hair looks almost white against my skin. He never seemed to get any picture of the way I was, really. And

I never stopped to think how different Gil was from anyone at home. I used to think Dad must have been a little like him when he was well and young and in school. Gil liked to talk a lot, the way Dad does.

One night in Pop's Place he got to talking about how the war would change his life. "I don't mind doing my bit; but for an architect, every year after college counts." He looked moody and discouraged the way Dad does. "This 1940 is a cockeyed year for me. I'm starting my aviation training in June—and then I meet you."

I'm a little like Mom, I guess; my mind gets so full of one thing it moves slowly to the next. Gil's mind jumps so fast it keeps me breathless. I was thinking about his work and he was already back to us.

"But we did find each other," I said. "Think if we hadn't."

"What if I get across and am shot up and come back minus a limb? There's that, too."

I thought of Dad and the days when the shrapnel hurts and he's moody and quiet. I tried to think of Gil that way, but it would be different. I would have known him this way, the way he really was. I could always remember that. If he were changed it would be the war that had done it.

"That wouldn't make any difference," I said slowly, thinking about it hard.

"You think so now."

"Why, Gil, if I loved a person I wouldn't change." I don't know how I could be so sure so soon, but I'm made that way. "Would you, Gil?" I knew he wouldn't, I just wanted to hear him say it.

Gil wasn't listening to me. "Ellen, you're beautiful," he said. But there are times when you don't want to be told something like that.

"Would you, Gil?"

"What?"

"Change if you loved a person?"

"Never, Ellen." We looked at each other across the table in the end booth that we called ours. I didn't even know what the jukebox was playing. I felt as though I were in a little room alone with Gil and I wasn't afraid of what the war or illness or Time— any of the big and terrible things—could do to us. It was the kind of feeling you have when you read the words "They plighted them their troth."

The month after I met Gil I had a note from his mother inviting me to dinner before a concert.

"Aren't you kind of scared, Ellen?" Vera asked me.

"Why, no, I want to meet Gil's family." I wasn't. I hadn't thought of it that way.

"I would be. Anyway, you'll knock them over by the way you look," Vera said. She made me wear a black dress of hers with nothing on it except a pin that was Dad's mother's, and black velvet ribbons in my hair. I thought I looked like a war orphan. I was going to curl my hair but Vera wouldn't let me.

"You don't want to look like any girl with a date!" she said scornfully. "You know you could get a job as a model; you're tall enough and you sure have the figure."

"No, thanks," I said. "I don't like to stand still that well."

I was ready the minute Gil came, because he always acted as though he didn't like the parlor. I hadn't thought anything about it until I saw it through Gil's eyes. I was never in it, anyway. It was just a kind of dark little room with lace curtains and green drapes and a lot of furniture. I used to glance in on my way upstairs.

"What a parlor!" Gil said the first time I left him there. "I couldn't hear myself think, it screamed so."

Gil's family lived in a gray stone house set way back in some trees. The way the roof came down in front, low over the door, made me think of a sheep shed, but I couldn't tell that to Gil, because he'd never seen one. It would be so much more fun when he'd been out to Montana and knew what I was talking about.

Mrs. Borden was sweet. She was so little I felt huge beside her.

"This is Ellen, Mother," Gil said.

"My dear, Gilbert has told me so much about you. Come in." She wore a long dress and her hair was brushed up high on her head. I liked to watch her when she talked. Dr. Borden was just coming across the hall. Gilbert looked like him. He was very tall and gray-haired, with long white hands like Gil's. He didn't often put his eyes on me as though he were really seeing me, but when he did it was worth waiting for, his eyes were so kind. He was almost too gentle for a man.

51

Sitting in their parlor—I mean living room—I understood why Gil shuddered so at the parlor in the rooming house. I looked around trying to fix in my mind the differences. The colors in the room were as soft as the summer colors of the prairie. There was an open fire burning white birch logs; it seemed a pity to burn a white birch tree.

"You come from Montana," Dr. Borden said at dinner. He made it sound as though it were Australia. "Were your people pioneers?"

"No," I told him, "my father came from Vermont and homesteaded after the war." And at my saying Vermont Mrs. Borden told of several summers they had spent in Vermont. They even knew the town my father came from.

"Some of the houses are beautiful; they are so dignified and simple and old, particularly the ones around the common."

"Oh, my father's house faced the common," I told her excitedly, and I was describing it as though I had lived there. All of a sudden, I began to wonder if Dad's family hadn't been the same kind of people that Gil's family were, and I felt warm and at home.

Mrs. Borden took me upstairs before we left, into the daintiest bedroom I had ever seen. It was as big as our front room, with a four-poster bed and wallpaper. I never can get used to wallpaper; we have only calcimine at home. While I was powdering my nose Mrs. Borden said:

"My dear, you are as lovely to look at as Gilbert said you were. He cares a great deal about you."

I saw myself going furiously red. "I care a great deal for him," I said.

I felt so happy all the way over to the concert. We separated at the auditorium and Gil and I found our seats.

"Like the family?" Gil asked when we were seated.

"I loved them," I said. "You are like your father, Gil."

"Not so bookish. Dad doesn't live outside his books. Mother's always plotting on how to get him out of them. They liked you. Dad said you made him think of the women of ancient Greece. That's tops for Dad."

I had all this to think of as we listened to the music. Gil held my hand. At first, it seemed odd to sit still and just listen. Most of the music I've heard has been over the radio and I've been doing dishes or studying or cooking. I could feel Gil beside me really loving it. He played the piano himself, but I hadn't heard him. I stole a glance at his face in the half-dark. His face is finely cut; his features are smaller than mine. My eyes touched his hair waving back from his forehead. His mouth is shaped almost like a woman's and yet it isn't feminine. I wasn't hearing the music at all. Guiltily, I brought my eyes away from his face to his hand lying across his knee. You could never tell a man you loved his hands, and yet I did. I turned mine quietly in my lap, the one Gil didn't hold. It was as large as Gil's. It didn't look like a hand to be held.

The music didn't seem to touch me, but I liked sitting there beside Gil in the half-dark. I had plenty of time to think. I tried to make the music sound to me as the program said it did, "gaiety finally giving way to despair," but it didn't, so I just sank back into the joy I'd felt when Mrs. Borden told me Gil cared a great deal for me.

Gil lifted his hand and laid it on his knee. His face looked far away and secret as Mom's does sometimes, so I went on with my own thoughts.

I was always trying to explain myself to Gil. I suppose all people in love do that. I wanted to know all the things he had felt and wondered about and hated or been afraid of. I wanted him to know the excitement I felt when the wind blows above the coulee or when we're threshing and working so fast that I forget that I'm a separate person. Maybe he would learn that feeling in the Army.

I wanted him to know the terrible feeling of sadness that creeps into my mind sometimes, like rust on the wheat. I wanted to know if he felt that way. Maybe I never would again, now that I had him. I stole another look at Gil and felt suddenly how little I knew him, even yet. I wished he would take my hand again, so I'd feel nearer.

Then something happened to the music. It was different. It had a swing and pulse to it. I could feel it now. I glanced at Gil, wanting to tell him I knew how he felt. The music was as familiar as though I had heard it before. I looked at the program, but I wouldn't know it by the name. It took me back suddenly to a concert in Clark City one early spring. I must have been about nine. Mom saw the concert advertised and wanted to go. I remember, because it wasn't like Mom. I remember Dad saying, "Well, if you're set on it, but it seems a lot of money for a little fiddling." I remember the program had a lot of Polish and Russian names on it.

We had good seats in the balcony that time. I sat watching the curtains, waiting for them to open. When they did, there was only an empty stage and a shiny black piano. Then a man in evening dress came out and people started clapping. Another man came after him and sat at the piano. When everything was still, the man lifted his violin under his chin and began. I was disappointed. I had expected something more. Once I looked at Mom and her eyes were like the big water barrel when you look into it at night. You can see the stars in it, sometimes. There were notes way up high that were so sweet you could almost taste them and some lower notes that made you feel warm and comfortable and there were times when the music was wild and made you want to dance. I glanced at Dad and he winked at me, the way he did when he was in high spirits. I looked at Mom wanting the three of us to be together. She was leaning forward. The light from the stage fell on her face so it seemed lit up too. Her hands were held tight together. I reached out to touch her hand, but she didn't seem to feel it. She had forgotten about Dad and me.

"Well, did you get your money's worth, Anna?" Dad asked in the car. Mom caught her breath and her teeth were shining in the dark.

"So much worth, Ben!" Dad bought us hamburgers to eat and made it a real party.

When we got home Mom went around to cover her tomatoes against the frost. I heard her humming, not soft and low as she did sometimes around her work, but deep down and full. Then the humming stemmed out into words that I knew were Russian, but they didn't sound hard and strange; the night or the music in them gave them a meaning that was deeper than word meaning. Suddenly, I knew what Mom had felt when she sat there, separated from Dad and me. The music swept over me as though it had hung in the air all this time, as though I had heard it before. I ran across the garden.

"Mom!" I cried out breathlessly, catching hold of her coat. "Mom, the music is Russia. That's how it is!"

Mom put her hand on my head and I smelled the cold dirt and the sharp scent of tomato plants on her fingers.

"*Solnieshko moyo*, that's how it is. Run now, you'll have cold."

But I sat a minute on the gate feeling the power of understanding was in me. It was like a miracle. "*Solnieshko moyo*—I knew that much; that meant "my sunshine"—but I knew so much more. I wanted to tell Gil this. I wanted him to know what I felt. When you love someone you're no judge at all of what's important and vital. A little thing seems important to share. But I went on sitting quietly beside Gil.

We went out during the intermission. Everyone loitered in the lobby, but I wanted to go way out. "Let's walk around the block, Gil."

"We better stay right by the door. I don't want to miss any of it," Gil said. "There's nobody like Kreisler, really."

We were quiet at first, then I tried to tell Gil: "I was sitting there thinking about both of us, Gil, and the music was just a kind of windbreak to sit against and think, and then he played something that seemed familiar. It was the 'Hungarian Rhapsody.' It made me remember the only other time I ever went to a concert. Mom made Dad go . . ." I had the feeling that Gil wasn't listening. I didn't go on.

Gil threw away his cigarette. "Let's go back in, Ellen."

All through the second half I sat listening to the music with Gil's hand on mine, but the music didn't carry me up to the gate again. Maybe what I was trying to tell him wasn't anything anyway, I thought.

I spent Christmas Day at the Bordens'.

I gave Gil's mother two towels that Mom had embroidered with a wide border. She was pleased.

"Why, Ellen, what beautiful work!"

"Mom did them," I told her. "She used to do that work when she was a girl in Russia."

"Did she live in Russia?" Mrs. Borden asked.

"Oh, yes, she was born there. My father met her during the war."

"How interesting! John, did you know that Ellen's mother was Russian?"

"Yes, my dear, Ellen told us that before," Dr. Borden said in his mild humorous way.

"That's what gives Ellen those high cheekbones and that light hair," Gil said, looking up from his drawing. He was doing a head of me, but he wouldn't let me see it until it was finished.

"I think of Russian people as being dark. They're a picturesque people," Mrs. Borden said.

"And a people of tremendous courage and endurance," Dr. Borden added.

I gave Gil a picture of myself, the one I had had taken for high-school commencement, but he said it was terrible. He gave me his, all wrapped up, under the Christmas tree. It looks as though he were just sitting talking to me. He has a cigarette in one hand and the little thread of smoke shows in the picture. His white shirt is open at the neck and his head is thrown back the way he does when he likes something. I wish, though, that he were smiling in it. His eyes and mouth have a sober look and he isn't looking right at me.

Before Dr. and Mrs. Borden left us that night we drank a toast to Christmas and to Peace on Earth in wine that Dr. Borden poured into tiny glasses, and then Mrs. Borden lifted hers again and said, smiling at both of us:

"To your happiness!"

I couldn't get my breath for an instant. I felt that Mrs. Borden was waiting for us to say something, but I could only look into the fire. Then Gil laughed and said:

"Well, thanks, Mother!" He said it so offhandedly it hurt me.

After they had gone we sat down on the rug in front of the hearth. There was an uncomfortable feeling in the room. I was waiting for Gil.

"You're so quiet, Ellen," he said at last.

I smiled at him. That wasn't saying anything, really. He leaned over and kissed me.

"Do you love me, Ellen?" he whispered.

"You know I do, Gil," I whispered back, but I wondered how he could ask.

"I love you, too." The room was comfortable again. "Will you marry me, Ellen?"

I said, "Yes, Gil," out loud.

"Of course, with my going into the Army there's no use trying to make definite plans, but it will be wonderful to know you're waiting for me," he said, playing with my hair. The words seemed too much like someone else's, but I guess I was just crazy. People have to use the same words, but sometimes the words seem to belong to a person and sometimes not. I would have married him the next day if he had wanted me to.

"Only knowing each other a couple of months is a pretty short time, I suppose," Gil said.

I hadn't thought of Time at all. It didn't seem to have anything to do with it.

"I mean, most people know each other longer than that. Do you think we know each other well enough, Ellen?" Of course he was asking it in fun, but his voice sounded worried.

"Well enough to know we love each other," I said. I felt so sure. I couldn't pretend about a thing like that.

"You're wonderful, Ellen." Gil kissed me.

"I'm going to tell the family tomorrow." Gil sounded suddenly sure and so much happier, but I was startled.

"About us, Gil? I thought they knew. I thought that was what your mother meant."

"I guess she hoped that. No, I told them I was crazy about you. I didn't tell them we were engaged. We are now, did you know?"

"Yes, I know," I repeated stupidly. "Maybe they aren't asleep. Why don't you go up and tell them?"

"Oh, no, I'll wait till morning," Gil said. "We want to keep it to ourselves that long."

It was after two when Gil brought me back home, but I wasn't tired. I started to write Dad and Mom, then I realized I'd already told them about Gil and me; I had told them two weeks ago.

It was funny to have spring come and not be running the tractor. I gave up the job in the cafeteria in the spring term and went to the job in the library. It worked out better with my studies and I knew Gil liked it better. He waited for me every evening, downstairs by the steps. Sometimes when I came out all I could see would be the burning tip of his cigarette, and a rush of joy would come up in me. I'd try to come up without his seeing me and then when I was right beside him, I'd say in a low voice as though I were surprised to find him there:

"Hello, Gil."

"Hi, Ellen. Last one out, as usual!" I never could make him sound surprised.

We did so many things that spring. I went canoeing for the first time in my life. There can't be anything more smooth and gentle than slipping through the water like that. It seemed as though it made up for all the dry summers at home. I didn't know I loved water so much. I went to sleep some nights thinking of a lake with willows hanging over the edge, a lake right where we planted the crested wheat grass last spring. The ground slopes up from there like a shallow bowl. It could make a beautiful lake; only there isn't a drop of water anywhere around!

We danced that spring, at the dances at Gil's fraternity house, at the big Senior Ball, but I liked best going into the city for dinner alone with Gil and dancing afterward. Gil knew people; we were always running into them and they stopped to talk to us, but all the same we were alone. I had always loved to dance, but the dances around home always got rough after a while.

"We were meant to dance together," Gil murmured when we were doing a fancy step without even touching our hands, his eyes on mine. I nodded, not wanting to talk, we danced so smoothly.

We were dancing on the roof of the hotel. Between dances we went out to see the night and lean against the high stone wall. It was close and hot down in the street. I knew how it would be in the rooming house, but up here a breeze blew my hair back from my face. It smelled fresh. I took a long breath. Last week, Dad wrote that they were going to plow if the ground ever softened up; that they'd miss me. Standing there with my thin skirt rippling against me and the big linen hat Vera made me buy, I wanted to be in jeans, sitting up on the seat of the tractor. We always work late at home spring evenings, it stays light so long. I don't know what made me think of it, but I said to Gil:

"Mom says that in Russia the girls and boys dance out in the fields summer nights. After haying all day they go down to the river and bathe and then put on clean clothes they have brought with them and the girls braid poppies and daisies together and put them in their hair. Sometimes they dance all night. And they build big bonfires and dance around the fire and sing."

That picture was something rare and bright I had to give to Gil. Mom is so stocky now, I had never been able to think of her as slim, and I had never seen her dance, but tonight I could think of her as dancing, feeling her body thin and good, following the music and her partner. I could see her with poppies around her neck and her dark hair brushed back and fastened with ribbons. She never wore it up on her head, she said, until she was married.

"How would they dance on rough ground like that?" Gil asked.

"Oh, they dance differently. Somebody'd play an accordion. There's something about an accordion that won't let you sit still."

Gil laughed at that and said: "You're part Russian after all. Here, let me tie a bandanna over your head and see how you'd look." He took his big white handkerchief and folded it three-corner-wise and tied it under my chin. Then he tipped my chin up with one finger and kissed me.

The music began and we danced, still with Gil's handkerchief tied over my head.

"I can't wait to have you at home, Gil. June is wonderful in Montana; you must bring your drawing things." I thought how green the prairie still was, and there'd be wild flowers, even the cactus blooms in June, and there's a clear trickle of water in the creek bed. The seeding's done and the hardest work hasn't begun. It was a wonderful time for Gil to come home.

"What if your mother and father don't like me?" Gil teased.

"They will. They couldn't help it. They're different from your family, you know, Gil. Dad isn't so different, but Mom speaks with an accent and she's very quiet and a little shy until she knows you."

"Is she beautiful like you, Ellen?"

"She isn't beautiful, but she's . . . oh, you'll have to see her, Gil." And then I began to plan the things we'd do. "We'll take the truck and drive up one of the canyons of the Rockies one day."

"How far is that?" Gil asked.

"Not far—eighty miles, about."

"I call that far."

"Not in Montana. Distances are all great out there."

59

And always we'd talk about the fall. "How about October, Ellen? I'll have my commission then."

"I'll be back in school then."

"But you could take a week off to come and see me, couldn't you?" Gil teased.

"Oh, Gil . . ." He held me so tight and kissed me. We stood shoulder to shoulder, lip to lip. He looked taller because his hair waved back from his forehead. Mine was smooth and tight to my head.

"Gil, do you wish I were little?"

He laughed. "You're wonderful as you are, Ellen."

I loved him so much I couldn't say anything at all, but I kept wanting him to talk. Afterward, I would remember every word and go back over it when I lay in bed and couldn't get to sleep.

When I came back to my room there was a letter from Dad. The people and things he wrote about seemed far away. Mom had bought a hundred baby chicks in town. I could imagine how they cheeped all the way home in the truck, and without half trying I could see Mom fussing over the brooder out in the chicken house. The Hendersons were building a new granary. "The snowfall has been way under average; it had better be a wet June or there won't be any crop," Dad ended.

7

I WAS home two weeks before Gil came. It seemed longer than that, though I was busy every minute. I had to tell Mom and Dad about him. I wanted them to know him so they wouldn't be like strangers. I had his picture to show them. Dad liked him right away.

"He's a handsome-looking chap," Dad said. "So his mother and father knew Plainville, did they?" He was pleased by that.

Mom took the picture on the kitchen table and studied it so long that I said:

"Do you like him, Mom?"

"I have to see him first."

"You'll love him when you see him," I told her, but I was disappointed with her and took the picture back into my room.

Everything looked beautiful to me. I went out to see if the wild flowers on the prairie were still in bloom. The grass wasn't very green, but there were bright blue and yellow and pink patches. I went up on the rimrock and felt the sun and looked way off to the mountains. It was almost as though I told all the places I loved that I'd be back and bring Gil.

It had been a late spring. I helped plant the low field to wheat that week and I ran the harrow. It was so good to be out of a town and to wear only a shirt and a pair of jeans and sneakers.

"Better not let your young man see you like that," Mom said.

"Why not?"

Mom shrugged. "He look to me like he want a girl dressed-up."

"He's not that way at all! He'll have to see me in them."

Monday afternoon I washed the windows. I wished we had curtains, but Mom didn't like them. Her geraniums were in bloom

61

by the sink and in the front room the windows were small and you didn't seem to miss curtains so much. Dad let me take the truck to town and I bought stuff to cover his big chair that was through on the arms. I tried to find a soft green the color of the sage, but I could only get a deep blue-green that was the color of the wheat before it turns. Mom helped me make the slip cover and we got it done, but I'd rather run the tractor any day than sit at that old machine and treadle it. I waxed the linoleum rug and polished the brass strip that is nailed down around the edge. I brought a pale-green paper shade home from the ten-cent store and put it on the electric bulb in the center of the ceiling. I wished there were floor plugs so we could have a lamp.

Mom stood in the doorway and smiled. "You think he look at the house or you?"

It did seem silly. "I guess I just like to be doing things for him," I said. Mom didn't answer, so I looked over at her.

"You have love for him all right," she said.

I brought back some white piqué from town and Mom made it into a dress for me. I didn't want her to, I meant to make it myself; Mom is always out in the garden this time of year. She does all the work in it herself, but she is quicker than I am. The pattern had a red cross-stitch design to stamp around the skirt, but I wouldn't bother with that till later.

"You don't do the embroidery?" Mom asked.

"Not now. Maybe I will sometime," I said. I was impatient for each day to be gone. I was at the post office before the mail was there each day. Bailey keeps the post office in the little building on the side of the elevator. The first day I was home I had the first letter from Gil. He wrote it on paper that had his family's house number in little raised black letters like the pattern the printer sent for our high-school graduation announcements, the one we didn't get because it was too expensive. Gil wrote:

"Dear Ellen,

"Believe it or not, I have been to see about a job! A friend of Father's who is an architect in Chicago has promised me an opening as soon as I am out of the Army, so you are apt to live in Chicago when we are married, Mrs. Borden! How will you like that? But I'll be seeing you a week from Monday and we can talk about all this. I'll buy my ticket, as you said, to Clark City."

My eyes skimmed over the words, just barely taking in the sense, hunting for other words. Then I found them and it was like coming to a water hole on the prairie.

"I have thought of you steadily since you left. Without you this place is as empty as the stadium. I had to go to the library to return the books I had out and I looked in our room over at your table by the window. I resented seeing someone else there, someone fat!

"Commencement was terrible, like hundreds of others. Mother lapped it up, of course, and I had to trail around all morning in a cap and gown. I spent the evening at the fraternity house and got a little plastered, so I stayed overnight. This morning the place was a mess with everyone packing and leaving. The others at least had to see about trains and going home. I had only to walk eight blocks and be there . . . very flat.

"I put the finishing touches to the sketch of you, but I am disappointed in it as I always am with anything I do. I shall try again when I am out there. I can see you as you were at the station. You were beautiful even in that terrible brown hat. You must not wear brown.

"I love you, Ellen,

"Gil."

I sat out on the ramp at the elevator and read and reread it. Bailey's tiger cat come over and brushed against me as I sat there. Some of the words seemed as clear and shining as a pool of water. Then I wished I hadn't thought they were like a pool. Out here the shallow pools that in June have ducks on them are dried up by August and look like nothing but the bottom of a burned saucepan. I liked best his saying the place was empty without me, and his looking for me in the library, and his last sentence. I put the letter in the pocket of my jeans and started back home. Mathews from the office in town drove up to the elevator.

"Hi!" I called out.

"Well, hello," he said. "How's college?"

"Swell," I told him, but I kept right on going. I didn't want to stop to talk to anyone.

Walking up toward our house from the elevator you can only see the top of the chimney above the coulee and the tops of the trees that grow in the coulee. I've always loved the way it was tucked down in. That was Dad's idea. He wanted to get out of the wind and he liked the way there was some green shade in there. But as I came up today I almost wished it stood out bigger. I wished it were painted. The barn is painted, but the house is just the color of the earth that wind and rain and sun make everything if you give them a chance. If Gil didn't like my brown hat, maybe he wouldn't like the gray-brown house. Then I put the idea away hurriedly.

"When we are married . . ." Gil said. I went into the house with the paper for Dad, feeling somehow unreal.

"Did you hear from Gil?" Dad asked.

"Yes," I said. "He's coming next Monday." I loved just saying it.

I was up at six Monday morning. There was so much to do. Gil would have my room, and I had cleaned it till it shone. Mom had painted the floor while I was away. She had painted it a bright blue and calcimined the walls a peach color, so it was pretty bright, but the quilt Dad's mother sent me once was a nice faded color. Mom says lots of things made in New England can't stand Montana sun. I cleaned off the dresser and laid a clean towel on it and put clean towels on the closet door. Then I picked a bowl of wild flowers for the dresser, and because I had talked so much about the sage out here I picked some sage and put it in an old olive bottle on the window sill. The little icon still stood on its shelf on the wall.

I was going to sleep on the glider out on the porch. I loved sleeping out there anyway and Gil's window would be just around the corner.

To think he'd be here tonight was such a joy I could hardly keep from singing. I stood in the doorway looking at the dining room. Dad had bought a fresh carton of cigarettes home for him and left it on the table. I took a couple of packages out and laid them on the two tables. I saw the tied-and-dyed plush scarf on the table as though I were seeing it for the first time. Somehow the long silky fringes seemed too gaudy to me today. I wondered if Mom would care if we had the table bare.

"Mom, where did we get this cover?" I asked.

Mom came to the door. She was fixing chickens so I could take a picnic lunch to eat halfway home.

"First fair we go to, I hit down a wooden Indian with a ball and get it for prize."

I left it there. What if it was awfully bright? Gil wouldn't notice it any more than I had until today.

While Gil was here we would eat in the front room. Mom wanted to have it all set, but I said I'd do it when I came. I had a big bowl of blue lupin in the center and the shades drawn halfway to keep the room cool. It was hot for June. Everybody wanted rain, except me. I wanted it to stay bright and clear for Gil.

While I was in school Dad had traded the pickup for a ton truck. Mom was proud of the truck. It would be fine for driving alongside the combine to load the wheat in and carry it to the elevator.

"Will you mind driving in for Gil in the truck?" Dad asked almost anxiously. I wondered why.

"Why, no," I said.

"Do you suppose he's driven in a truck before?" Dad said.

"I don't know. He'll like it anyway."

I drove off at ten o'clock so I'd surely be there. Dad and Mom came out to watch me off. I could feel their love over me like warm sun.

"You look like a girl in love all right, doesn't she, Anna?" Dad said, and Mom laughed.

I wore the gray linen dress Vera had picked out for me at school and I had my big hat in a bag in the truck to put on when I got out at the station, but I'd feel silly driving the truck with it on. The lunch and a thermos bottle of hot coffee and two bottles of coke were on the seat beside me. I knew just where we'd stop to eat by a creek where it was shady. I sang all the way to town. Nobody could hear me above the noise of the truck. Once in a while I'd tip the mirror so I could see how I looked.

And suddenly the train was there and Gil was coming down the train steps. In two weeks' time I had forgotten how he looked.

"Oh, Gil!" I was so glad to see him I think I kissed him first.

"Ellen, it's good to see you. Wait, I want to see to my bag."

It was a beautiful bag, as soft and smooth-looking as a new saddle.

"Over here, Gil, in the truck."

"Well, there's certainly room!" Gil put it in back. I could see that he was worried for fear it would get scratched.

65

"I wish I'd brought a blanket to wrap it in," I said. It hadn't a scratch on it. Even as I looked at it, I was loving the initials G.H.B.—Gilbert Hinsley Borden.

"It looks as though it might get bracked in there. Maybe I better take it in front with me."

I remember now how hot the seat was when we got back in. The lunch and the thermos bottle were on the seat between us.

"Can you drive this thing? It looks pretty big to me."

I laughed. "It's fun to drive a truck. Oh, Gil, I'm glad to see you."

"I'm glad to see you. Minneapolis was dead as a doornail. By the way, Mother and Father sent their love to you."

"Thank you. Give mine to them."

"So this is Montana!" Gil said as we waited at the intersection of the main street for the bell to ring and the arm that said "go" to bob up.

"Wait till you get beyond the town, that's more . . . that's my part."

"We bumped over the approach to the bridge and my hat that I had put behind me came down. I had forgotten to wear it. Gil rescued it for me.

"Oh, Gil, I meant to wear it to meet you in. Did you notice I didn't have a hat on?"

"You looked beautiful to me," Gil said, and I loved the way his eyes looked at me. "You handle this truck with a professional hand."

"I've been driving trucks since I was twelve, not on the highway, of course, but over the fields."

"Did you get my letter?" Gil asked, though he knew I had because he had mine in answer.

"Yes. I loved it. I liked your looking in the library for me. Did you get mine?" I asked idiotically.

"Yes. Thanks for the piece of sage. I had never smelled any. It's a little like catnip, isn't it?"

"I don't know catnip. When do you start training?"

"I passed the aviation exam all right, and they tell me to expect orders to report within two weeks, but don't let's talk about the Army. If we don't get into the war, I'll be discharged in twelve months and we can be married next June!"

We were driving over the uninteresting part just out of town, where the mountains are far away and the rimrock looks dry and baked in the sun, but today I blessed it with my eyes. "We'll be married next June" sang in my head as I kept my eyes on the highway.

"That would be wonderful," I said. "It seems a long time away now."

We drove into the place I knew where willows and alders and aspens made a green shade along a brook. I wished again I'd brought a blanket. Gil's suit was awfully light, but the earth was hard and gravelly there, not dirty.

"I'm not hungry. It's only twelve-thirty—I could wait just as well," Gil said.

"I know we could, but I thought it would be more fun. We've never had a picnic."

"That's so," Gil said, but he didn't sound enthusiastic. I was busy laying out the fried chicken on a linen napkin. I had thought he would love a picnic.

"This is in memory of Pop's Place," I said, handing him a bottle of coke that was a little warmish. He laughed at that and we had some of the feeling of Pop's.

"I'd like to do a water color of you with that yellow-green shade on your face."

"Those are aspens. I'll sit under one at home for you."

"I couldn't get it. Just that light would take a Renoir or a Van Gogh. I just daub."

"Why, that's not so, Gil! You haven't worked at it very long. Maybe you'll be just as good some day."

He shook his head. "Could be you're in love!" And then he changed the subject as though it annoyed him. "Were you glad to get home?"

"Oh, yes, but it was so different, Gil, because I kept thinking of you all the time. I had no idea how it would change things— loving you, I mean."

"It does that," Gil said. "For me, too. I like it that way."

I started to tell him how it changed things for me. That it made waking up in the morning and going to bed at night and the sun itself different, but Gil went on:

"You see, I've never . . . been swept along by any one drive . . ." Gil was trying so hard to make me understand I sat still with my eyes on the shallow creek water. "Most fellows

67

are; it used to bother me. I used to think I'd never really fall in love, and then I saw you that day in the library. I had to know who you were. I had to know you. I watched you all those days almost afraid you'd spoil yourself, someway—oh, you know, powder your nose or have runs in your stockings or . . ." He laughed and I saw he had colored like a girl. "You probably think I'm crazy, but you were so lovely I wanted you that way. Every day, you were just the same. On a bright day, all the sun would seem to center on your head and on a dull day your hair would give it brightness and you'd look cool and gentle and quiet and yet so alive, Ellen."

"Why, Gil!" His words sounded like poetry. He had never opened so much of his mind to me before.

"And then after I knew you, I found I was in love, really and deeply. Mother noticed the difference right away. Do you see, Ellen?"

I watched his long, straight fingers breaking a stick into little bits and laying them in a tiny heap. I was so happy I didn't want to speak. Gil's fingers left the little pile of sticks. I lifted my eyes and met his that are brown and sometimes sad. He drew me into his arms. The little shallow trickle of water under the thin shade of the willows seemed almost to stand still. I could see the sky mirrored in it. I looked at these things thinking I could come and look at them any time and hear Gil's words.

"I don't know why it's so easy to talk to you, Ellen—things I couldn't say to anyone else." He laughed.

"That's being in love," I said.

"You know, do you?" Gil teased.

"Yes, I know," I told him soberly, for it was the truth.

After a while I folded up the picnic things and we walked over to the truck. "I'm glad we stopped there," Gil said, "so we could be alone for a little."

"Yes" was all I said, but of course that was why I'd brought the lunch.

"Don't you want me to drive?" Gil asked.

"Okay. It's fun. You have more power under you than you have with a regular car."

Gil drove so easily in the city. I had always liked to watch him and I'd admired the way he slides a car into a narrow parking place, but he wasn't used to the truck and he looked so funny sitting up straight on the seat and frowning. We drove off with such a jerk that I laughed at him.

"Stop that!" he shouted at me over the roaring he made with the starter. "There! After all, I had to get the feel of it."

"After all!" I mimicked him, but I loved seeing his hands on the steering wheel. I reached over and laid my hand on his knee and we drove that way into Gotham.

"That's the elevator where the post office is," I told him. "Where your letters come."

I waved to Mr. Peterson on the store steps and I saw him call something in to his wife. Everybody in Gotham would know by tonight that I was seen in the truck with a stranger driving me. I wondered how soon the Bardich girls would make some excuse to come over.

"How far are you from Gotham?" Gil asked.

"Only a mile by the road. We're just in the next coulee."

"Coulee?" Gil didn't know even the names of things out here.

"Kind of a gully, a cut in the land. In spring a little creek runs along the floor of the coulee, that's why there are trees there. When Dad came out from Vermont he hated the wind, so he built his house in the coulee. There, Gil! There's where we turn." I've always loved having the road to our ranch turn toward the mountains.

Across the bright green of a field of winter wheat you could just see the chimney and a piece of gray roof that was our house.

"Where? What are you looking at?"

"Our house—turn right by this post. The road dips, you better shift." Gil shifted with such a grating I knew the folks would hear it. I felt the dip in the road happily all through me, as you do a place you know. "Drive on to the barn; we'll put the truck in later."

Dad came out to meet us. He was dressed in his town suit for Gil. I introduced them and we walked back to the house.

"Where's Mom?" I had expected her to come to the door.

"She's right there," Dad said. He was busy talking to Gil. "Well, if this is your first trip West you'll find you have to revise a good many of your preconceived ideas. I know when I came out here . . ." Did Dad always use such big words?

I went in the house ahead of them. Mom was in a clean print dress. "Come and meet him, Mom," I said.

Dad had taken Gil around to the front door that opened right into the front room. We never used it. The stoop was sort of high and the walk led up to the kitchen door.

There seemed to be wide spaces between us: Dad and Gil coming in the front door, Mom not quite in the doorway from the kitchen, I between. "Mom, this is Gil."

Gil came over to her and bowed in that easy graceful way he has. Mom shook hands with him, not smiling, her eyes looking so steadily at him.

"Pleased to meet you," she said heavily. I wished she would smile.

"We had a delicious luncheon," Gil said. "And Ellen let me drive the truck home. You know, I have always wanted to drive a truck since I was a little boy."

"Trucks they make now is easy to drive," Mom said.

"Sit down over here," Dad urged. "Have a cigarette?" I wanted to run and get an ash tray or matches, but I knew they were already there on the plush scarf. Gil looked hesitatingly at Mom still standing in the doorway, then he sat down in the chair with the new slip cover.

"Yeléna, you sit down and visit," Mom said.

"You come too, Mom. It isn't time to get dinner." I looked at my watch. It was only four. Mom sat on the straight chair by the door to the kitchen, I sat on the couch with Dad.

"The best time of year here is really fall," Dad was saying.

"Oh, I love spring, too. I'm glad you came in June, Gil. Next time you'll come in October. Look at these. I picked them this morning." I brought him the bowl of shooting stars and harebells and crocuses.

"Do they grow in your garden?" Gil asked.

Even Mom smiled, and I laughed at him. "Oh, no, they grow wild right out on the prairie. I should have shown you some on the way out. We were so busy talking I forgot. Look, Gil, the crocuses make me think of your mother the first time I met her, all in kind of lavender-gray."

"I see what you mean," Gil said. But I wished I hadn't said that. Mrs. Borden was different from Mom.

"I hear the people in your part of the country are talking war harder than we are here," Dad was saying as though he were talking to Bailey at the elevator.

"Well," Gil answered, "I suppose that's natural. The farther east you go, the closer people feel to Europe."

"I was younger than you, I guess, almost twenty, when I threw everything over and enlisted. Three months in Camp Devens . . ."

I was too excited to listen. I leaned over and smelled the sage I had put in a pitcher on the table at the end of the couch. Before dinner I wanted to take Gil out around the barn and up on the rimrock.

". . . In the end I sailed with a Michigan regiment. Well, sir, we weren't in the harbor at Liverpool more than twenty-four hours when we got orders to sail for Russia. Some folks think of hell as a fiery furnace, but I'll tell you my idea of hell is a frozen God-forsaken village in Russia."

I glanced over at Mom. She hadn't said a word. Her face was still; all the expression was hidden. Her eyes were on Gil. I wished she would laugh, so Gil could hear her.

"You wouldn't dare call the village where Mom lived that, would you, Dad?" I said, looking at Mom.

"That was the one I meant," Dad said. "Even your mother thinks that, don't you, Anna?"

"Winter is cold most places," Mom said, without laughing.

Dad shook his head. "Not like that."

I was afraid Dad was going to tell Gil all about Russia, then.

"I want to show Gil around a little," I said. I tried not to see Dad's disappointed expression. "I'll be back in time to set the table, Mom."

As we went through the kitchen the smell of the kettle of borsch was fragrant and warm. "That's Mom's famous Russian soup, Gil. Have you ever had borsch?" I had asked Mom to make it.

"No, I can't say that I have. I've been to a smörgasbord," he said.

"It's very special. Dad doesn't admit that he likes it, because they don't make it in Vermont, but he does."

We went out around the house. I wished the asters were in bloom against the gray clapboards.

"You don't have much view with the hill so close, do you?" Gil said.

"No, not from the house, but I always run up here. See, I have a regular path up the side. Dad calls it my game trail.

How's that, Gil?" We stood on the top. "There's no end to the sky up here, and see the mountains; that faint blue line over there, that's the Main Range of the Rockies."

Gil shaded his eyes. " 'Sister Anne, Sister Anne, what do you see?' "

I had to laugh. " 'Nothing but the dust blowing and the green grass growing,' " I quoted back from Bluebeard.

"Mother wouldn't read me the story of Bluebeard because she thought it was so hideous, so when I found it myself I went all out for it." Gil laughed.

"It was in a fairy book my aunt sent me from Vermont," I said. "See, there are crocuses, Gil." They were growing in the grass not more than a foot from us. "There should be cactus plants in bloom." Then I found one. It was a pale amber and looked as though it were made of plastic. The blossom was as soft and smooth as the leaves of the cactus are prickly. "You have to get down close to see it."

"I never saw a cactus growing before, either," Gil said, but I felt he was being polite and wasn't really interested.

I looked around the soft grass-covered hill at the yucca plants and the patch of shooting stars with a queer lost feeling, like you have in an exam when you can't think of the answers. What was it I had meant to show Gil? I couldn't think now. An empty silence spread between us.

Gil said: "How did your father happen to marry your mother—I mean, when she spoke Russian and he spoke English I should think it would have been so difficult." But I saw that wasn't what he meant. He meant how had Dad ever happened to marry Mom. I was suddenly hurt and a little angry.

"Why, he fell in love with her, I suppose," I said, "and Mom learned English very fast."

"Your father, though, must have had such a different kind of background."

"Mother is always quiet with strangers. You have to know her awhile. She seems sober, but you should hear her laugh. And she loves fun and music. . . . She loves music the way you do, Gil." All the time inside I was crying, "Please like her, Gil. Please see her as she really is."

We sat there looking down on the roof of the house, not off toward the mountains at all. The screen door banged and Mom came out. We saw her walk across to the barn with a pail. She

72

looked big and heavy except for her head and shoulders and the easy way she walked. I couldn't say anything at all. I had meant to tell Gil how I always ran up here whenever anything exciting or sad happened, but I didn't. I was afraid it might sound childish.

"Well, we better go back down," I said finally. I ran down the path and it gave me the feeling it always does of plunging head-first. "I dare you to run," I said, trying to feel natural.

"Not I, Mrs. Bluebeard. I value my life."

Dad and Gil sat out on the glider on the porch while we got dinner. I set the table in the front room. The cloth was shining white but it wasn't very thick. I took a sheet from the bureau drawer in Mom's room and laid it underneath for a pad. For the first time in my life I noticed how thick the plates and cups were; that they didn't match. Only the dozen spoons that Dad's mother had willed me were sterling. Then I was ashamed of thinking of things like that when Gil was here. The food would be so good, I told myself, no one would think of the table.

We sat at the table. Dad and Gil were talking about New England. Mom was silent. Was she always as quiet as this? The soup was hot and red.

"This is delicious, Mrs. Webb," Gil said. I wondered if he would ever call Mom Mother easily.

I took out the soup dishes and brought hot plates to put in front of Dad. We had steak from our own beef. Mr. Hakkula came over to butcher for us, but Mom did as much as any man.

"I'll tell you one thing, if the United States sends our boys over to Europe again, when they come back they're going to want a changed world and they're going to insist on getting it. We came back from the last war and accepted things as they were. That's why we're having another war."

Dad looked younger when he was talking, even though his voice sounded a little oracular. I saw how Mom was watching him. Did Gil notice how big and dark her eyes were? I couldn't keep my mind on what Dad was saying. I was aware of our hands on the white cloth—of Mom's that were large and red and checked with black. I saw the broken nail on Mom's finger as she cut her steak. Mom's hands looked kind, but perhaps that was because I knew them putting on compresses for Dad, doing things for me. Dad's were brown against the white cloth; they looked tired. I never noticed before that hands could look tired. I knew Gil's hands better than any of our hands. I loved again their shapeliness, the wrists that were as slender as mine. I looked at my own hands. They were large like Mom's and already roughened from the little work I had done outdoors, but I always forget to wear gloves and I don't like the feeling of them anyway. Our hands, all moving, seemed to say things to each other. Gil's hands didn't seem to belong with ours. I put that thought away quickly as I got up to take off the dishes.

Once Mom held up her hand to make Dad and Gil stop talking. "There comes the rain; that's good."

"For the wheat," I explained to Gil.

"You go on, now. I do the dishes," Mom said when we were through. I hesitated. Dad and Gil could talk in the front room while I helped Mom, but I felt I'd been separated from him all during the meal. I wanted to be alone with him.

"Thank you, Mom," I said. "We'll take a little walk."

We couldn't walk far. It didn't take much rain to stir the gumbo to a slick, slippery paste. I said as I would to any boy from school:

"Let's sit in the truck awhile."

Gil laughed. "That's an idea!"

It was snug in there with the rain on the cab roof; the seat was as comfortable as any in the house. "This is like Pop's Place," I said.

"Quite. Do you want to drive into town?"

"Oh, no, Gil, not tonight; you just got here."

"Okay."

But Gil was quiet so long that I said, "What are you thinking, Gil?"

"Nothing, really. What were you thinking?"

"Nothing much, I guess. I . . . Gil, I love your being here."

"It's nice. It's different from the way I imagined a ranch would be."

"You've seen too many ranches in movies. This is a dry-land wheat ranch."

"I should think people would go stark, raving crazy out here in winter," Gil said.

"Why?"

"Well, there's nothing to do, except the work, I suppose. You're so far away and dependent on each other. Take your mother and father; I would think they'd have been talked out years ago."

"They're pretty busy, of course," l said.

"But in winter."

I had never thought about it before. "There's work to do in winter, too."

"It makes you think of some novel or play you've read, something Russian, Gorky for instance." Then he stopped and I knew he had just remembered that Mom was Russian.

Dad came to the kitchen door and switched on the yard light. It was a big light mounted on a tall pole so it flooded the house and the barn. Mom loved it. She felt it made the place so safe. From the highway you could see an aura of light spreading up above the shoulder of the coulee. People said, "That's Webb's ranch."

Gil and I sat in the truck and looked at the house and the shed and the barn. It looked bare in the electric light. Maybe it was bare; I had never thought of it before. But I tried to be funny.

"And there's the stage set for Act I of a Russian play," I said.

Gil was looking at it. "How do people stay in love with each other after years alone in these places? I should think they'd end by hating each other."

"Why should they, Gil?"

"They shouldn't, but . . ."

"Well, look at Mom and Dad," I said.

"That's right," Gil said. He leaned over and kissed me, but there was something kind of sad about it, as though he were sorry he had said anything.

I loved the rain when I lay on the glider on the porch. The porch was so narrow I only had to reach my fingers out a little way to feel the drops. I lay still so the glider wouldn't bump against the house and disturb Gil. I had turned down the bed for him the way I had seen the beds turned down at his mother's house. I wished the electric-light bulb didn't shine so hard on the bright peach walls and blue floor.

I was so wide-awake I couldn't go to sleep. Gil must be too. Somehow, I wasn't satisfied with the day.

"Gil!" I called softly. Then I whistled. He whistled back. "How're you doing?" I called.

"Just fine. Good night."

"Good night." I shucked deeper under my blanket, ashamed that I wished he had come out to sit with me on the swing.

8

THE next afternoon, on our way back from seeing the grain elevator and Bailey, Gil told me he could only stay three days; that he had to leave Wednesday. I stopped in the muddy road and stared at him.

"But, Gil, I thought you were staying a week, anyway."

"I know, Ellen. I didn't tell you at first because I didn't want to spoil everything, but I have to be in Florida by the first and I promised to spend a week at home before I left."

He went on talking, explaining, but I didn't hear him clearly. He had his drawing things he hadn't even unpacked. We hadn't done any of the things we had talked of doing. I searched his face, trying to understand. His eyes looked unhappy. His mouth had that moody line.

"What's wrong, Gil?" I asked. Nothing mattered if he would just tell me, but he said, "Nothing's wrong," almost as though he didn't like my asking. "I hate to leave you, that's all." This was the way he must speak to his mother when she wanted him to wear a raincoat, I told myself to take the sting out of it. I waited for him to speak next. We walked in silence up back of the store and along the highway. Gil had on some galoshes of Dad's because of the mud. We turned off the highway on our road that runs down into the coulee. Mom and Dad built that road themselves, I almost told him, and then I didn't.

"It must be lonely for you here sometimes," Gil said, as though he were being kind.

"No, I've never been lonely here," I answered. I wanted to go on talking, about anything, but I couldn't.

The kitchen was warm and cheerful after our walk in the rain. Mom and Dad were both working outdoors or down at the barn. They hadn't expected us back so soon. I hung my jacket back of the kitchen door and took Gil's from him. I loved the room because we were alone in it together. I shoved the teakettle over and put a fresh shovel of coal in the stove.

"We'll have tea in a minute, Gil." I set out the cups and saucers on the kitchen table and sliced bread. "You make the toast." I gave him the toaster and the bread. He was so quiet. Why didn't he say something?

When we sat down I noticed the rain had stopped. A yellow-gray light came over the field and the yard through the uncurtained windows. I hoped Mom and Dad wouldn't come in for a while.

"The tea tastes good," Gil said.

I wanted to ask him again why he was going so soon—what the matter was—but I knew with a kind of sixth sense that Gil didn't like to be asked uncomfortable things.

And then Mom came in. I heard her kicking off her galoshes on the back step. She had her bandanna tied over her head and a chicken she had killed herself in one hand. When she opened the door she smiled at us.

"Hi, Mom, come have some tea," I said. Gil stood up.

Mom waved the chicken at him. "Sit down. I just wash my hands."

But of course we weren't alone any more. When Mom was there Gil seemed embarrassed; Mom didn't. I thought Gil's nostrils twitched with distaste. I put the chicken in a bowl and covered it while Mom was taking off her bandanna. Then we sat down again. Mom loves tea any time and likes it strong. She looked like a painting sitting there. I wondered if Gil didn't think so, too.

"You're not gone long," Mom said.

"No. Gil had never seen the inside of a grain elevator. I showed him that and all of Gotham. The road's pretty muddy."

"But we need the rain." Mom's eyes shone. "It look like rain again some more."

While I was starting dinner Gil sat in the front room, reading a magazine. We had no bookcase. Dad kept the magazines in a neat pile on the floor under the window. I set the table in there, looking over often at Gil.

"This is like playing housekeeping, Gil," I said.

"You are the happiest person, Ellen." Gil sounded irritated.

"Why shouldn't I be, Gil? Aren't you?" Yet I felt he wasn't.

"Of course." Then he said, "Tell me about that little carved figure in your room."

I told him that it was an icon Mom had saved from her home. "I've always had it there. I used to talk to it when I was a child."

"I wondered about it," Gil said.

We had the chicken for dinner and biscuits and mashed potatoes—the kind of a meal Dad loves. I wasn't hungry. I saw that Gil wasn't either. Dad was in high spirits. He came in from working on the tractor and bathed and dressed for dinner; we could hear the water splashing in the bedroom.

"I don't mind being a rancher if I can forget it at dinnertime," he said. But the meal was the same as all the others. Mom was silent. Dad and Gil talked. I saw our hands moving again over our plates.

Gil wiped the dishes for me after dinner. Mom sprinkled clothes that she had washed before the rest of us were up. Dad sat smoking his pipe.

"I'm sorry that I'm going to have to leave tomorrow," Gil said.

I saw Mom's hands still on the clothes.

"Tomorrow! You better stay longer than that," Dad said. I poked the corner of the dishcloth down through the spout of the teapot.

"I only wish I could. The Army doesn't wait for you, I guess. I have to give the folks a few days before I leave for camp."

"Well, I thought you were going to make us a real visit," Dad said.

I couldn't say anything. I emptied the dishpan outside where Mom had planted nasturtiums and asters. A little more water wouldn't hurt them any. The air was cool and damp on my hot face. I saw Dad follow Mom into the bedroom. I knew what they had said when Dad came in. Gil must know, too.

"We didn't know this was to be your last night, Gil. We promised Bailey we'd come down and have a hand of bridge with him," Dad said.

Mom never went anywhere in the evening. They thought we wanted to be alone.

When they had gone I got some dance music on the radio. We danced around the table and out in the kitchen.

"I bet you never danced in a kitchen before," I said, laughing.

"This is all right," Gil answered.

When the announcer broke in on the music I was standing close to Gil. "Oh, Gil, don't go!" I whispered.

"I really have to, Ellen," Gil said.

We sat on the couch and talked. I don't know what we talked about—things we did last year in Minneapolis, people we both knew. We seemed closer together talking about things there than here. But I had thought it was important to show him the places I knew, that they would make him know me better. I tried to say that to him.

"Isn't it funny, Gil, we've been such different places together there and here? We could be anywhere if we were together and it wouldn't matter."

"That's right," Gil said. "You'd like to live here, wouldn't you?" I thought he asked it almost eagerly.

"Oh, no, I don't care where we live, Gil, but I was born here. I suppose that's why I love it."

"I wonder if you could ever be happy in the city."

"I could be happy where you were, Gil, I know."

Mom and Dad came home but they didn't stay with us long. Mom made hot coffee and told us to have some when we wanted it. There was fresh cake to eat with it. She called me into the bedroom and showed me the white dress. She had finished the red cross-stitch border around the full skirt.

"I finish it down at Baileys'. Mrs. Bailey like it good. I'll hang it up here."

We didn't stay up very late. And neither of us wanted any coffee or cake. There was too short a time to talk of some things. Others didn't seem important. Just as we were saying good night Gil stood in the kitchen door.

"Isn't it too cold and damp for you on the porch? Let me change places with you. I didn't realize last night that I was putting you out of your room."

"Oh, no, it's just a June rain. Come out and breathe it; it's sweet, Gil."

He kissed me there on the porch in the dark and for a minute I was happy.

"Gil, you don't have to leave so soon." I almost said I wanted to go with him if he were leaving.

"Yes, I do, Ellen." His voice was muffled against my hair. We were both as sad as death, and why should we be? We belonged to each other. He was going only for a short time—the time between two seedings. That wasn't so long.

"You can drive me into town early, can't you, Ellen? We can have the day together. The train doesn't leave till ten-thirty," Gil said the next morning. "Or will that make you too late getting home?"

"No, that won't matter. We'll leave right after lunch." All I wanted was to be off alone with Gil.

Dad and Mom didn't do any work except the chores. There was a feeling of waiting. When I tidied Gil's room I saw the two suits in his suitcase he hadn't worn. He had meant to stay longer. I couldn't get that out of my head. Something must have happened here to change his plans, and yet nothing had.

I was glad it had cleared off; the sky was a bright clear blue above the coulee. The blossoms of the prickly pear cactus shone in the sun like yellow and red glass. I started to tell Gil to come and look, and then I didn't. I felt with a sick sense of disappointment that he was going before he had seen anything, before he had any feeling for the country. But why did that matter? Wasn't I separate from the country?

I was in the truck first. I wore my new white dress because Mom expected me to. She had cleaned my shoes for me, too. It didn't occur to her that I might look a little silly sitting up high in the truck all dressed in white. As I went out the door Mom said:

"The geranium match the cross-stitch, Yeléna. Wear it in your hair." Mom loves bright flowers. I broke off the blossom and fastened my hair back with it instead of with a bow. I looked at myself in the mirror over the sink. I looked very gay and happy.

Mom gave me twenty dollars to stop at the McCormick-Deering and get the new part for the combine. I watched Gil standing at the door with his beautiful leather bag. He thanked Mom so politely. Mom shook hands with him. They were still like strangers. Dad laid his hand on Gil's shoulder and walked with him to the truck. I couldn't hear what Dad said, but I could see how he liked Gil, how he had adopted him already.

"Can I drive? I don't get a chance like this very often," Gil said.

"The road sticks!" Mom called as we drove off.

I nodded. "I won't stop for the mail today," I said to Gil. "I won't stop till day after tomorrow. Have a letter for me then, Gil."

Gil was shifting gears. I was glad when we had passed Gotham. Somehow I felt Gotham seemed horrible to Gil. The road ran between the fields; the strips of faint green were spring wheat; the strips of olive-green were winter wheat. They were beautiful under the sun. I could never drive through the country without noticing the wheat. I felt happier.

"Don't you like the wideness, Gil?"

"It's so wide it's depressing," Gil answered. "Look at that shack without a shrub or a tree around it!"

I looked. It belonged to the Peter La Rouches. Guy La Rouche was in my class at high school. We used to drive in to Clark City on the school bus together every day. He had ten brothers and sisters in that house. They made a living and kept off relief, but they didn't have any time left over for gardening. I didn't tell Gil I had gone to a dance once with Guy La Rouche. But the sun drove out all my worries of last night. It was enough to be riding along in the truck with Gil beside me driving.

On a stretch of gumbo about eight miles from Gotham we slued violently to the side. Gil put his foot on the brake too hard and we swung way around.

"Scare you?" Gil asked, looking pretty scared himself.

I laughed. "It takes more than that to scare me. You better go slow, though. This road's all gumbo to the main highway. Want me to drive?"

"I can do it." Gil sounded irritated. The truck had to follow the deep ruts gouged out in the mud. He was driving too fast.

"There's an awfully bad place about a mile ahead," I said.

Gil liked the novelty of the truck. "Wonder what a fellow that drives one of those big oil trucks thinks about, thundering along like this?" he said. Of course, our truck weighs only about a ton; that's some different from an oil truck, but I let him pretend.

"His girl," I said.

"Poor devil, probably worries for fear she's two-timing him."
He looked at me, smiling.

"I bet she isn't. She's probably waiting for him at the end of
his run."

"You think love's pretty important, don't you?"

"Don't you?"

"Yes, but I think a lot of other things are important, too."

Suddenly, I knew as clearly as though he had told me what was
wrong. Gil was going away because he was afraid to marry me;
he didn't mean to come back, ever. I was thinking so hard that
I didn't warn him about the place in the road. It was so chopped
up by other cars there were no clear ruts. I felt the truck settle
down in the gumbo. I came out of my thoughts in a hurry. The
truck stopped. The racing motor gave back a hopeless sound. I
was sorry for Gil's sake.

"Try backing, Gil," I said.

Gil tried. The wheels churned up the mud and settled down
deeper.

"Well, I'll be . . ." Gil muttered, pushing his hat back on his
head. I liked him that way.

"Somebody'll come along, maybe," I said, but there wasn't much
traffic. People out our way were busy this time of day. The place
seemed loudly quiet after the noise of the motor. "Let me get in
there a minute, Gil. You slide over so you won't have to get out
in the mud." That was the wrong thing to say. I thought maybe
I could get it out, because gumbo was such an old story to me. I
tried, but the road had no bottom.

"Satisfied?" Gil asked, grinning at me. I think he was glad I
couldn't get it out either.

"We should have brought chains," I said. "This road's awful
in the rain." Then I laughed; it was pretty funny. "Oh, Gil, look
at us, you all dressed for the train and I in white!" I couldn't
stop laughing. It was a relief after the way I'd been feeling.

Gil laughed a little, too. "Woman, you're stark, raving mad,"
he said, and he sounded like himself. "I suppose there's nothing to
do but sit here till somebody comes by."

"Oh, no, we can do something," I said.

"What would you suggest?"

"Well," I said slowly, "if we could find some branches to put
under the wheels . . ."

Gil looked around. There were no trees, only some low bushes along an irrigation ditch.

"What a country!" Gil said.

I stepped gingerly out on the mud, but I went down to my ankles.

"Where you going?" Gil said.

"To make mud pies!" I don't know what made me flippant. I was sorry the next moment. "Gil, you're all ready for the train, there's no use in your getting muddy too." I squshed through the mud to the side of the road. I had to lift my full skirt carefully over the wire fence. I jerked at the little low bushes. They were hard to pull out. I looked back at Gil, expecting him to come after me anyway. He was trying the motor again. The roar didn't seem powerful out here, just useless. I called to him to stop, but he couldn't hear me. I pulled so hard at the bush it came over with me. At the fence I got one of the rotten fence posts loose. I came back to the truck and spread the bushes and the log in front of the back wheels. Then I pulled the blanket from around Gil's bag and laid that in the mud. I was dirty and my hands were scratched, but I didn't care. I came around to the door.

"Now back slowly," I ordered. "Slowly!" I yelled again as Gil started up too fast. The big wheels threw up the mud like water. A soft, wet chunk hit my hair. Then one wheel was on the rotten fence post. I tried to hold the blanket out straight. The geranium fell out of my hair in the mud.

Gil let the motor stall. He hadn't given it enough gas at the right time. It made me mad.

"Let me get it out, Gil." Gil moved over. I slid in and backed the truck hard until I felt the wheels take hold and the rear end rise a little. Then I shifted like lightning and drove full-power ahead. I let out a yell. If we slued off the edge we were done for, but we couldn't ever get out if we didn't give her everything she had. The truck plunged ahead like a sheep coming out of the sheep dip. I didn't dare slow down. I kept her going. I felt triumphant. In the car mirror I could see the blanket lying in the mud, chewed to ribbons. I didn't care; let it stay there. I bet Gil's suitcase was thrown around, too.

When we were out on the dry road, Gil said:

"Good for you!"

I was so hot I pushed my hair back from my face, muddy hand or not. I looked down at my feet.

"I'm a mess!"

"If you'd been driving in the first place, you wouldn't have been stuck," Gil said. I had wanted him to tell me I wasn't a mess or that he loved me anyway.

"Oh, I might have. That's a regular sumphole." Gil was angry because he'd got stuck. We drove a long way in silence. "When we get to town, I'll buy some new shoes and stockings and a new dress," I said.

"I'll pay for them," Gil said. Tears filled my eyes so I could hardly see where I was driving, but I kept my voice cool.

"Oh, I'd be getting them anyway," I said, but I wanted to stop the truck and put my face against Gil and cry. I wanted to say: "Gil, what's happened? Where are you? Gil, I'm sorry I got the car out of the mud. Oh, Gil, I love you, don't you see?"

We came into town and it was only a little after three. I tipped the mirror down so I could see myself. I looked awful. Six hours was all I'd have of Gil. He'd go away then and never come back. He wanted to go now, and he was uncomfortable because he was trying to explain to me. But he wouldn't have to explain. I'd act as though everything were all right between us.

"Gil, I'm such a mess, I'll go in and buy a dress and stockings and shoes. It won't take me long. Then I'll go to . . ." I was going to say "to the station rest room to change," but Gil would squirm at that, so I said "the hotel."

When we were in front of the store Gil said: "I wish you'd let me buy these things for you. After all, it was my fault, I meant . . ." I was glad he fumbled a little for his words.

"No, thanks," I said again.

It was lucky I had the money for the piece of machinery. I don't believe anyone ever bought a dress and shoes and stockings faster. I didn't waste any time explaining to the salesgirl why my dress was muddy, either. I bought a dress that made me think of the city, all black, and black sandals with soles so thin they couldn't stand anything like mud. On the way down through the store I bought a black turban to wind around my head, a big flat black purse, and gloves. When I came out of the door of the store Gil was sitting in the truck just as I had left him.

"Did you see the mud on the wheels?" Gil said when I got in. "The stuff's like clay."

"Gumbo's bad, all right," I said.

"I'll get you a room," Gil said when we walked into the hotel. He went up to the desk and I could see he was uncomfortable, but I didn't care.

"I'd like a room for this young lady to change in. We ran into some mud coming in." He laughed a little while he talked to the hotel clerk.

"I'll say she did," the clerk said. "You came through pretty good yourself." That made Gil angry. I could see him flush. He wrote my name on the ledger while I stood there like a child. I couldn't help thinking how it would be if he had written Mr. and Mrs. G. H. Borden.

I went upstairs in the elevator and followed the boy down the corridor without a word. I thought of that other time when Dad and Mom and I stopped here. The rooms had been done over since then; they were very modern now, but I hardly looked at the room. No one ever took a bath and dressed faster.

Gil was sitting in the lobby in front of the elevator when I came down.

"I feel better," I said and started to pull on the gloves as though I hadn't seen the quick change of pleasure in Gil's face as he stood up. Then I saw the price mark was still on the gloves and started picking it off with my nail.

"Ellen, you look like the first time you came to dinner at our house."

I sat down on the arm of the chair and looked across the room in the wall mirror. I didn't look as though two hours ago I'd been dragging a fence post along the road.

"Then it's a good thing I got muddy," I said.

"I should have been the one," Gil said. It still bothered him that I had got the truck out.

"Don't be silly. My dress will wash."

"Do you know, Ellen, you are the most unbelievable person. You change with whatever you put on."

"No, I don't, really," I said. "I'm just the same whether I have on jeans and an old shirt hanging out or this outfit." We went over to a corner of the lobby and looked out the big front window of the hotel onto the main street. We were by ourselves over

85

there. A big fern and an aquarium shut us off from the rest of the hotel.

"Ellen, there are so many things we haven't talked about yet," Gil began. I could see how hard it was for him.

"Yes," I said.

"I realize how much I'm asking you to change your whole way of life when you marry me. I didn't know before."

I waited. What was a "way of life" but being with a person you loved?

"I mean, seeing how you love the ranch, and how differently you've been brought up from the way I have, makes me wonder."

He had almost said it. I waited so hard I could feel my heart pounding. I looked over at him and loved him so much I was afraid he could feel it. Something had made him afraid to love me, I knew. I believe he really wanted everything to be the way it had been before.

"Wonder what, Gil?" I said gently.

"Whether you'd be happy, living with me."

But he couldn't doubt that. He was afraid about himself— whether he'd be happy with me. I could see how wretched it made him, how ashamed, but I wouldn't say anything to help him.

"Ellen! Why don't you say something?"

There were so many things to say, but I mustn't say the wrong thing. When you love someone you ought to be able to talk to him without testing your words.

"Ellen?" Gil didn't like silences. The silence became strange, like another person standing beside us.

"You know I would be, Gil. I'm not like that."

"I know you aren't, Ellen," Gil said. He reached out and held my hand tight. He couldn't tell me. I was unhappy for both of us.

"Let's go, Gil. Let's have some fun before you go. It's almost six o'clock."

"Why don't you come back and stay overnight at the hotel, here, after the train goes?" Gil suggested. "Your mother wouldn't worry, would she?"

"Oh, yes, she'd worry," I said. "But if I were there in the morning early, it would be all right. Perhaps I will."

I thought of that hotel room, the beds without any footboard and a silly print on the wall of some flowers that never grew in the earth. I couldn't think of anything worse or lonelier than coming back here after Gil had gone. If Gil had loved me here, it might be different, but Gil was afraid to love me. I wondered as we walked across to the dining room whether if Gil had wanted to stay here with me tonight, I would have stayed with him.

It was a little early for dinner, but the doors were open. The waitresses stood in starched patience waiting by the empty tables. We had a table for two under a shaded light. I studied the big menu, but I didn't take any of it in. If Gil had said even one little word, if he had shown he wanted me, I knew I would have loved him with all my body and my heart.

"Sherry to begin with?" Gil asked.

"Yes," I said. "That will seem like being at your house with your mother and father."

Gil smiled. When it came, I held the thin-stemmed glass in my fingers. I thought how big my hand looked.

"To us!" Gil said. We had said that with cokes in Pop's Place. Then it had always seemed exciting and gay. I tried to make it seem that way again, but I felt as though this was the end of the world.

I was quiet at dinner. Gil was talkative. He was relieved that he was going so soon. I watched his hands, long and carefully cared for and shapely. Maybe I loved them because they were so different from any hands I had known. Mine were like farm horses, strong and well fed, but Gil's were like fine saddle horses —the kind they showed at the County Fair now that people in Clark City were taking up riding.

It was quarter of nine when we finished dinner.

"Let's go some place to dance," Gil said as we came out.

We went to the Bijou, a funny little place in the basement of the biggest movie house, but it had a four-piece orchestra. There was only one couple there, it was so early. The orchestra played everything we ever liked. They played "Tomorrow Is a Lovely Day" over twice. I was happy while we danced. I didn't look at the time. And then it was twenty after ten. We took a taxi to the station. Gil hardly had time to kiss me good-by. It was easy, after all. He stood on the platform, bareheaded, waving his hat as the train pulled out.

"It's been wonderful, Ellen," he called.

"Yes," I called back. I watched until I couldn't see him any longer.

The taxi-driver who brought us down wanted to take me back. He said the gentleman had paid for the trip back to the hotel. I said no, I wanted to walk back. I took off the turban on my head and carried it in my hand. The truck parked out in front of the place where we went to dance looked big and friendly. I climbed up in the seat and slipped off the black high-heeled sandals and put on the muddy white ones. It was good to hear the engine. The big wheel was something to take hold of. I left her in second gear all the way out of town so she'd make more noise. I don't know why. When I came beyond the town where the road stretched out into distance, I shifted into third. She ran as quietly as a kitten purring.

There was nothing on the road. I could let her out. I went the first ten miles like a streak, then the dark sky with the stars scattered as carelessly as sagebrush across it calmed me and I slowed down. The air was cool for June. All month, June had meant Gil coming. Now Gil was gone. He had come loving me and something had happened to change him. What was it? I didn't know. I tried to think about it driving along in the empty night.

I passed the place where the alders and willows shielded the creek bed. That was where Gil had said, "I was afraid you'd spoil yourself someway." But how had I?

I came to the place where we'd been stuck on the way out and I blamed that mud for my losing Gil. I put my foot on the accelerator and rode through recklessly. The ruts grabbed at the wheels like one of those crazy cars at the fair, but the truck came through. It just took a little more drive than Gil gave it.

I thought of Gil standing on the train platform. He had kissed me as though he loved me, hadn't he? Everything was all right. There'd be a letter for me day after tomorrow—but underneath, I knew.

I came to Gotham. The truck lights lit up the grain elevator and the gasoline station and caught the tracks of the railroad. Above the dark shoulder of the coulee shone an aura of light. I swerved off the main road a little faster than I usually took it. The unpainted box of a house and a barn and a shed stood out ugly and bare in the glare of light. There were lights, too, in the uncurtained windows. The folks were still up.

9

I HATED to go into the house. I meant to tell them right off that we weren't engaged any more, that I had lost Gil. It seemed a worse failure than if I had failed at college. Dad would be eager to talk. He had enjoyed having Gil here. When I opened the screen door, I noticed how it sagged on its hinges and how narrow the doorway was. The bright light was hideous.

"Well, did he get off all right?" Dad asked.

"Yes," I said. I knew how Mom felt when she doesn't want to be talked to.

"I liked him, my dear," Dad said. "Whenever you young people are ready, you can have my consent." His tone of voice started goose flesh along my arms. "He shows considerable background," Dad went on. His tone of voice gagged me.

Mom was making cottage cheese. I saw her coldly, with Gil's eyes. She wore a bright-blue print dress she had never bothered to have fitted. It bloused around the belt, making her look bigger than she was. It was warm and her hair was pulled back into a tight knot. She must have been outdoors, because there was mud on her shoes and her legs were bare. Once, I thought she looked at me almost fearfully. It would be a queer thing if Mom should see what had happened, and not Dad.

I looked at the gaudy calendar on the wall in the kitchen, at the sepia copy of "The Sower" that Dad had bought one time in one of his moods of liking the ranch, at the plush tied-and-dyed scarf on the table and the imitation-leather davenport. Tonight the bright light slid across the shiny linoleum, making more vivid the blue leaves of the printed design. For the first time in my life the frank ugliness of the house struck me full in the face. It made me almost sick. I wanted to run away and hide.

89

"Where you get that dress?" Mom asked. It was so long ago since this afternoon I had forgotten I had a new dress. I had forgotten for a moment that I'd spent all the money for the combine part on it. I might better have worn my muddy dress and said good-by to Gil when we got to town.

"Oh, we got stuck in that sumphole a mile beyond Heath's turnoff. I got myself covered, so I bought a new dress in Clark City, because we were going to the hotel for dinner."

"You buy new shoes, too?" Mom asked, looking down at my mud-caked white ones.

"Good for you," Dad approved. "Didn't Gilbert think that was a pretty fair hotel for a town that size?"

Mom's hands were still. I could feel her eyes looking at me under her heavy black brows. "Can't he get the truck out himself?" she asked.

"Oh, I didn't have much trouble, and he was all clean for the train," I said lamely. "I've got to go out and bring in my things."

I was glad to get out of the searching glare of that room and Mom's eyes. I took the box with my muddy dress and the fragile-looking black sandals and went back into the house. Mom had said something to Dad. He looked up at me anxiously.

"Gil won't be coming back," I said, and my lips drew down so I could hardly get the words out.

Dad straightened up in his chair. "Why, the . . ." he began.

"He say so, Yeléna?" Mom asked.

"No," I said, "but I know. We're too different from each other. . . ."

"Oh, young people have fallings-out . . ." Dad began.

I couldn't stand to listen. "No, that isn't it. We . . . he isn't in love with me."

"Come here, Ellen," Dad said gently, holding out his arm. I felt his tenderness. I knew he wanted to comfort me and I didn't want to hurt him, but I couldn't go to him. I didn't dare speak. I didn't want them to feel badly about me or to blame Gil. I shook my head. I felt my eyes sting. I was afraid they would see them. There was no hiding anything in that terrible light.

"You're all in. Go get to bed," Mom said. She knew I wanted to be alone. I felt grateful to her.

I went in and closed the door of my room and undressed in the dark. But the room was too small. It had held Gil just a little while ago. I took out the collapsible screen and climbed out the window as I had done dozens of times before. I ran up the side of the coulee in my pyjamas. The clumps of sage were still wet from the cloudburst, but the ground was already dry. I sat up on my ridge.

I couldn't think clearly. I could only go back over things: the way Gil had sat silent up here and then had said, "How did your father happen to marry your mother?" and then as though he felt that was too abrupt, "I mean, when she spoke Russian and he spoke English I should think it would have been so difficult."

I thought of his hands at the table and the fine slender look of his wrist. I loved his hands and I loved him. I hadn't thought how our ranch might strike him, the bareness and ugliness of it. It ought not to have mattered, something in me said, but I crowded it down underneath. It didn't help any to blame him. I should have talked to him about it—made him see that I was separate from the ranch. I had been away to college. I was more like Dad, I could write and tell him.

Maybe I was all wrong; maybe he had meant what he said on the platform at the station. He had kissed me. He was looking forward to next year. . . . All these things I told myself, but I didn't believe them. It's hard to lie to yourself when you're alone at night under the sky.

Ever since spring I had counted on Gil's coming, his being here with me. I had never thought how it might turn out. All the plans we had talked, all the times he had told me he loved me, crumbled into so much dust. The wind could blow it away like topsoil. Then, as though to save even the dust, my mind went back to things we had done together in school: walking down the mall together, dancing, Gil telling me I was beautiful. I didn't believe it, but I loved his telling me.

"Gil, do you wish I were little?" I had asked.

"You're wonderful as you are, Ellen," he had said.

I had had some idea of running off up here to cry by myself, but I didn't, any more than I did on the way home. I looked up to see the Northern Lights in the sky, as though that were what I had come up here for. They were like ropes, pulling the whole pale tent of sky toward the center. They moved as I watched. One rope came free of the canvas. It was green, and there was a yellow rope. Then the white tent billowed over them again. Any

91

other time I would have called out to the folks to come and look.

I went back down the hill by my game trail that ran past Mom and Dad's room.

"Yeléna don't try hard enough to keep him," Mom was saying.

I stood still listening, then I knelt down, leaning against the slope of the side of the coulee that was covered with wet grass. The room was lighted. I looked in and saw Mom lifting the blue print dress over her head. I couldn't keep from looking at her wide shoulders and big bosom. She looked younger in her cotton slip. She sat down on the side of the bed and started taking out her hairpins. Dad stood leaning against the closed bedroom door, smoking.

"I see him look at Yeléna like he think pretty much of her." Mom gave a quick backward shake and her heavy hair came down in dark braids on her shoulder. She looked pretty, or maybe what she had said about Gil warmed me. "She could keep him if she try," Mom muttered.

Dad finished his cigarette. I watched him walk over to the dresser to rub the end into the ash tray.

"Not Ellen," Dad said. His voice had a tight sound to it. Mom turned around so fast on the edge of the bed her hair swung back from her shoulder. I could just see her face as she turned toward Dad, and it was white and her eyes blazed.

"I know what you think. You say to yourself Yeléna don't think to trick him into staying like I trick you! It's long time to think that, Ben Webb!"

Dad said nothing. He wasn't even looking at Mom and she went on in a fast, angry voice.

"I know, she won't never pretend to her young man she was going to have baby like I do. No, you want her like your sister to sit in parlor and drink tea and never let him touch her hand!" Why didn't Dad say something? I ached with waiting for him to speak.

"You liked your Russian girl to love you; you liked to lie with her an' put your head on her shoulder. Then when you get order to go home you say good-by. You say you come back when you get job an' can take care of me. . . ."

I could hardly believe it was Mom talking so fast, with Dad standing there with his eyes on the cigarette stub in the ash tray.

"Nice girl wait to see how much money you get; if you

can build big house. Nice girl wait till you come back." Mom's voice had a taunt in it. "I never care what money you get; I can work myself. I know sure you forget when you go back and don't come for me. I love you so much I can't stand to see you go. I tell you lie . . . one little lie in all these years, Ben Webb."

"Anna, for God's sake don't go back over that. I don't hold it against you." His voice sounded as though it hurt him to speak, as though he wished she would stop. "I was to blame. You were right in a way; I probably never would have gone back, but that's all over long ago. I brought you back home and when you weren't happy there, didn't I come out here because you wanted to?"

"You want to get your Russian girl out of your old town; that wasn't for any love." Mom's voice was quieter, but it was cold.

I couldn't look into that little square room at them. I was ashamed to have my own eyes see them or to listen any longer. I crept back to my room and climbed in noiselessly. My own breathing sounded loud to me in the stillness. I lay down on my bed, but Dad's words followed me and I raised up on my elbow to hear them.

"Well, Anna, if that boy's made Ellen unhappy, we've got paid back for our sins," Dad said, and his voice was older and sadder than I had ever heard it.

I stared into the darkness of my room and thought over what I had heard.

After a while, I heard Dad's steps going barefoot across the kitchen floor, past my door into the front room. I heard the old couch creak. Dad was going to spend the night there. It seemed to me that hate and hopelessness filled our house to suffocation. Maybe Gilbert had felt that hate between Mom and Dad. Maybe that was what drove him away from me, because I had seemed part of it. All these years Dad and Mom had lived together, pretending to be fond of each other, even having me, when all the time they had hated each other.

I wanted Gil more than ever. I wanted him to take me away from here, back where we had been so happy.

Then I came back to what I had just heard. Little bits fitted in together: the way Mom was angry that time when Dad went back to his home; the way she had taken the doll Dad's sister sent me and put it away. She had said it was too fancy to play with on a ranch. Dad's calling Mom Anna Petrovna, sometimes in fun, but sometimes when he was angry with her. What I had overheard was the reason for the bitterness that I had so often felt between them.

Maybe Mom had loved Dad as I loved Gil. If I could have held Gil some way—but Dad was right; I knew I could never have lifted a finger or spoken a word to keep him. A feeling of shame, deep in myself, crept out for Mom. If she had really loved him, she couldn't have done that.

Suddenly, she wasn't Mom; she was Anna Petrovna, someone strange whom I hardly knew. And he wasn't Dad, tired and tormented by shrapnel; he was Ben Webb, a strong, healthy young soldier.

How could they ever have stood it out here all these years where they were shut in together?

"I should think people would go stark, raving crazy out here," Gil had said. "I should think they'd end by hating each other."

And I had said: "Why should they, Gil? Look at Mom and Dad!" I turned wretchedly in the bed and I saw how the shade hung crookedly. Gil had seen that while I had lain on the porch and been happy.

I heard Mom moving around in the next room. She opened the door of her room and crossed the kitchen.

"Ben, don't sleep there. You'll be all lamed up in the morning."

I lay still, hardly breathing, straining my ears to hear what she said.

Dad gave a kind of groan that hurt me. "It's a funny thing, Anna, how a little circle hangs on a big one. If there hadn't been a war, we wouldn't be here. I wouldn't be a physical wreck. Ellen wouldn't be eating out her heart, maybe."

Dad's voice wasn't angry. He was standing outside the row, now, looking at the whole field.

"Yeléna'll get over it," Mom said in a voice so low I had to lean out of bed to hear her.

I wanted to go in there and tell her I wouldn't get over it, that I hated all of this that Gil had despised. I hated her being a Russian peasant and Dad being sick so much. I hated even myself for being so big and tall and strong and simple.

I heard the couch creak. Dad was going back to bed. I listened to each sound. Mom was turning out the light. They must be lying there, side by side, now. How could they?

Slowly the thing I didn't want to know bore in on me like the awful rising heat at harvesttime. People made messes of their lives and then they had to live with them. Life didn't turn out right because you expected it to. There had never been any real love between Mom and Dad. For a little bit, I forgot Gil, thinking of them.

10

AFTER that night, I began to watch Mom and Dad, wondering what they were thinking. We all watched each other, sitting across the oilcloth-covered table from each other. I could feel Dad's eyes on me. I could feel him wondering how badly I felt. When Mom and I were quiet too long, he talked. He invented errands for me to do in Clark City, but I made excuses. I'd rather stay home, I said. Why didn't he and Mom go?

Maybe there was one good thing about it; I thought about Anna Petrovna and Ben Webb as much as I thought about Ellen Webb and Gil Borden. I could feel the weight of their lives weighing on my own. Sometimes, up on the rimrock, I would look far off and try to separate their lives from mine. They had nothing to do with me, I told myself.

I was free in myself, in my own body and mind. I would look at Mom and think how my hair was as light a yellow as the wheat and my eyes were gray and my body was slim. I would notice coldly how red Mom's neck was below the strong, black hair. I would hear Dad's cough and look at the tired lines in his face and think how unwearied I was after a whole day's work outdoors. But it didn't do any good; we were all bound together.

There were two letters a couple of days after Gil left, one addressed to Mom. She opened it and made out most of the words. It was very polite, thanking her for her gracious hospitality, saying what a new experience it had been for him, saying how he would always remember her hot borsch. Every word hurt me. It seemed insincere, because he hadn't appreciated Mom.

There was a letter for me. I couldn't make myself read it for a long time. I looked at the ending first.

"Always, Gil."

I took it with me down to the barn and climbed up in the seat of the duckfoot to read it.

"Dear Ellen,

"First, thank you for all you did to make my visit such a pleasure. It was all so new to me and made me realize how limited my life has been.

"I want to be very frank and honest, because you are yourself. I have thought a great deal about us. I am afraid that we are too separated in background and interests and ways of looking at things to be happy together. You are a little like your country and I feel a sense of strangeness with you as I did in that wide desolate country. I didn't want to say this while I was there, to spoil our time together. I felt the best way was just to leave as I did. I shall always remember how lovely you were standing there in the station as the train pulled out,

"Always, Gil."

I crumpled the letter into a hard ball, then I opened it up again and tore it into pieces so no one could ever read it. I didn't let myself think; it would hurt too much. I went up to the house and saw that Mom had left her letter on the table, but she had gone out to the chicken house. I put it in the stove. I couldn't stand looking at myself or the house. The smell of a soup bone simmering on the stove nauseated me. Outside I could see Dad running the harrow over the fallow strips. I walked down there and told him I'd do it.

Dad looked at me and his face was full of questions, but he didn't ask any of them. I saw that he was a little afraid of me, and that made me feel more separate from him than ever.

"All right, I'll go to Bailey's and get the gas for the truck."

I felt it a relief to have Dad gone. I watched him going slowly back to the house; then I had the sky and the hard clumpy earth to myself. I started to put on Dad's gloves he had handed me, but I stuffed them in the pocket of my jeans instead. Why should I care how my hands looked? I didn't care if I got burned with the sun or if I drove back and forth all day in a deadly monotony of rows, with the harrow dragging after me across the field like my own unhappiness.

I didn't go up to the house for lunch and Mom brought a pail of lunch and some milk down to the fence. I wished she hadn't. I wished she would let me alone.

"Your Dad an' me eat up at the house," Mom said.

I ate it and I noticed how thick the crusts were and I thought with anger how I had cut the bread so thin for Gil.

We had more rain that June, but not enough. Mom watched the sky anxiously. Dad complained about it and discussed it with anyone who stopped at Bailey's. All he thought of was the land and crops and weather, I thought critically. No wonder that Gil was bored when he was here.

Chuck Henderson was home helping his father. I used to go places with Chuck. He was going to the University of Montana. He came over one night and asked me to drive to town to a movie. I could feel Mom and Dad behind me, wanting me to go.

"Why don't you go ahead, Ellen?" Dad urged. A hard anger burned inside me. I had trouble keeping my voice pleasant.

"Okay," I said. "I'll just get my coat."

"Wear that black dress you get," Mom said.

"I'm all right as I am," I said, and put my coat over my cotton dress. I ran my comb through my hair in front of the kitchen mirror and put on some lipstick. I didn't bother to look very closely, but even in that quick glance I could see my face looked dull.

Chuck was nice enough, but I wasn't interested in him. He was taking agriculture and coming back to help his dad on the ranch. He talked about school and the football games and the girls down there. I didn't listen very hard. I was feeling the road going by, the same road Gil and I had driven over. It seemed to belong to us. I saw the light in the La Rouche shack and felt the mud suck at the wheels in the place where we were stuck. Why hadn't I sat still in the truck and wrung my hands and acted scared? But I knew it wasn't my getting the truck out that mattered. It was something bigger than that and harder to understand.

"When does school open down there?" Chuck asked.

"The seventeenth," I said.

"Why don't you switch to Missoula? That's where you ought to go," Chuck said.

"Oh, I'll finish where I started. They have a good language department there; that's what I'm majoring in," I said, but it seemed a long time ago that I had been interested in studying.

"Language! You mean French and Spanish . . . not me!"
And then Chuck came back to the weather and ranching. I thought
of Gil talking to a girl about crops.

". . . We may get a good summer after all. Dad says there's
nothing to keep us from having rain for a week steady. I'm going
to own a place of my own someday and believe me, it's going to
be partly irrigated. The day of the farmer praying to God for
rain while his crops fry up is over. . . ."

I couldn't keep my mind on what he was saying. All I could
think of was driving to town with Gil. I looked at Chuck's hands
on the wheel and thought of Gil's.

We went to a movie and sat and watched a play about two
sisters. One stole the man the other sister loved. That was different: to have someone else take your man. That was different from
having him change and cool and no longer love you because of
something in yourself.

Chuck put his arm inside of mine and measured our finger tips
together in my lap. I let him. Why not? We went out of the movie
and had hamburgers and I remembered the night after the concert when Dad bought them. I wished I were eight years old
again. It isn't good to wish you were a child; it's like hiding your
face in your warm collar out of the wind. When you lift it again,
the wind seems twice as cruel.

"Want to stop in at the Bijou?" Chuck asked. "I'd like to dance
with you again."

"I'd just as soon," I said. I had a sudden fierce desire to hurt
myself. I even picked out the place where we had sat, Gil and I.
I told Chuck to ask the orchestra to play "Tomorrow Is a Lovely
Day."

We had cokes and danced. "You dance just as well as you used
to," Chuck said, "but you seem quieter. You didn't use to be so
quiet."

"I'm sorry," I said, but I couldn't think of anything to say to
him. I dreaded the ride home. I meant to let him put his arm
around me going back, but when he tried to, I couldn't stand it.

"Don't, Chuck!" I said, so sharply he was cross.

At our gate Chuck said, "How about going to the dance at Sun
River Saturday night?"

"I'm sorry, Chuck, I can't go."

"Well, if that's the way you feel about it . . ."

Then he drove off and I had to go into the house again and face Mom and Dad. I dreaded that. I felt them both sitting there watching me, looking to see if I had had a good time.

"Hello," I said. "You're getting so you sit up late."

"Why didn't you ask young Henderson in? He's developed considerably," Dad said, trying to be offhanded about it.

"I didn't want to," I said and went into my room, and I could feel their silence through the thin wall.

Until there was hay to be cut, I worked in the garden. Once a week I drove the truck down to fill the big barrel with water from the creek. It was almost a joy to attach the hose and spray the hard-packed gumbo. The water spread out over the hardpan surface like a map, peninsulas and islands of moisture creeping out farther. When the dirt was wet black I felt easier in myself; some tightness that had held me loosened.

I used to like to run in wet black mud when I was a child. In summer the ground was always so hard; the roads that had been puddings of mud turned to dust that stuck in your throat and tickled your nose, and made your hair lie flat and lusterless on your head. Dust was what bodies of people and animals alike turned into; it was part of death. But mud was elastic and springy; there was life in it.

I remembered, one time in the spring, coming home from school with Judy Bailey and seeing Mom down by the fence. We ran across the field instead of going to the house first. When we came up to her I saw that Mom was barefoot. She had left her shoes way round by the gate. I didn't mind until I felt Judy looking at Mom's feet. I could feel her thinking right through her silly fat little head.

Judy and I were walking on the stubble to keep our school shoes out of the mud. Mom was walking in the plowed fallow that was so soft that the mud squshed up between her toes.

"Don't your feet get hurt going barefoot, Mrs. Webb?" Judy asked.

"Not where it's soft," Mom said. I was thinking how Judy would tell about it in a hateful, sly whisper to the girls at school. Then Mom laughed. "You girls, take off your shoes and stockings; run up to the house that way. It feel good!"

"No, thank you," Judy tittered. "I'll have to hurry over home."

When she was gone, I went barefoot with Mom, not because I wanted to, but out of a kind of loyalty. We looked at the footprints we made in the mud. We set them together over by the firm edge, mine shorter than Mom's then and not so broad.

"You feel like it was spring through the bottom of your feet!" Mom said. "Feel?"

Then I did feel it. Mom laughed at me. "We hurry up to the house an' wash our feet before your dad come. He don't like me barefoot."

On the porch steps Mom brought out a basin of warm water. "Wash your feet, Yólochka; they feel like new," Mom said. She washed her own and put on the heavy men's shoes she wore around the ranch. My own inside their heavy laced boots still kept that cool springy feeling.

"They feel dancy," I said. Mom laughed again.

"That's right, they do, Yólochka moya."

But today when I thought of that, I could feel Gil wincing at the sight of Mom and me going barefoot in the mud. I hurried with the watering, only to be through with it.

I did nothing to keep my skin from sunburn or my hands from calluses, or my hair from going coarse and flat in the hot sun, and I felt how slovenly I looked. I kept on wearing shirts that were faded and ragged and the jeans that had patches over the knees, yet I despised myself in them. I couldn't be content the way I used to be, liking whatever I was doing.

All the time I kept listening, spying on Mom and Dad, picking over anything they said to find a hidden meaning in it. I had no feeling of sadness for them, only distaste and aloofness. How could they help but see how I felt? I was glad when there was more work to do. I would be glad when it was time for threshing.

I dreaded meals more and more. I listened to what we said and thought how stupid it sounded.

One day, I came in with Dad and Mom had the table all set in the front room with the cloth we had used when Gil was here. I knew she did it to please me, but instead of thanking her, I was cross.

"Well, Anna, that looks nice," Dad said.

"You make yourself a lot of extra work, Mom," I said.

We had a steak broiled rare, the way Dad loves it, and onions fried in deep fat and a salad of pears in gelatin that I had learned to make in school. Mom even made a strawberry shortcake. I was hungry, and all these things I ate knowing Mom had made them especially for me, but I felt her pitying me and the pity made a sour sauce. I felt anger just behind my eyes, stinging them without tears. I saw their kindness clear on Mom and Dad's faces, and my own stiffened. Why should they love me so much when they must have conceived and borne me in hate?

We were eating dessert when Mom said, "Gilbert was poor eater."

Having his name spoken out loud was like being flicked with a whip. Dad looked at me quickly as though he realized how I might take it. I just sat there eating the tasteless berries without saying anything. When we've lost a field of wheat with grasshoppers or hail or drought, it's always Mom who can talk about it first. And then, since Mom had said Gil's name out loud, I wanted to hear her say it again.

"This was all awfully strange to him. He had never seen anything like this country and our ranch," I said.

Mom's face looked stolid and secretive the way it goes when she meets a stranger. But Dad nodded.

"Well, it's different from the East. I remember when I first came out here, I thought it was pretty strange, too."

"Dad, did you hate it?"

"No," Dad said, "I didn't hate it. It was too big and strange and new. I liked being on my own out here. When I first got back to Plainville, after the war, I felt cramped. There was plenty of room out here." Dad's face wrinkled the way it does when he's talking with Bailey. "I didn't know enough about ranching to fill a tin cup. If it hadn't been for your mother we'd have been back in Plainville before the next spring."

"We never go back to Plainville," Mom said.

"Oh, you'd have come to like it back there. You didn't give it a chance."

Mom shook her head. "Not me. We stay too long then."

"Did you have any fun when you first came?" I asked shrewdly. I knew they were making things sound good for me.

"We worked too hard to think about it, and I was sick that fall. All we asked was to get a crop the next spring."

"We get thirty bushels a acre," Mom put in as though that made up for everything.

"And I was born the third winter," I said, wanting them to go on.

Mom's eyes gleamed with fun. "I can't have you in summer, I was too busy. February was good time." Mom piled her dishes on top of each other and took them out to the kitchen. Dad went over to his chair with the *Post*. I finished clearing the table and wiped while Mom washed.

"Were you glad I was coming, Mom?" I asked, ashamed of my own slyness.

"I want you long before you come," Mom said.

"Mom, were you glad to get out of Russia?" I asked after a while.

Mom shrugged. "Things was bad in Russia, but I was used to hard times. My people was gone, all but Peter; he go to be priest."

I dried all the plates before I asked another question.

"You must have been very much in love to come way off here. You hadn't known Dad very long."

Even in the bright glare of the electric light, Mom's face told nothing. "From November all winter. We leave next spring when ice is out of the harbor. Almost so long as you know Gil."

I wondered if Dad were listening. I crossed the kitchen to put the cups on the shelf. He wasn't reading, anyway.

"We had good time on boat. There was only fifteen womans, only eight Russian woman." Mom wasn't often so communicative. "I dance on boat for the soldiers, gapak an' mazurka an' valcs, all Russian dances. Ben dance valcs with me, Russian way, not hugged up tight together. Your Dad can dance fine."

"Oh, Dad, Mom says you were a good dancer!" I leaned against the doorjamb. I made my voice like a child's. I felt deceitful and underhanded.

"You should have seen your mother dance. Anna, whirl for her," Dad said.

Mom shook her head at first. I could see her color come up under the sunburn. Mom lifted her skirt, her apron flew out. She whirled as lightly as a young girl, her face all lit with laughter.

"Mom, you're good," I said genuinely.

"When we dance at Plainville your Aunt Eunice say I dance with too much 'abandon.'" Mom gave the word a funny pronunciation, as though she had carefully remembered it. A kind of reserve seemed to shut down on Dad's face.

"Didn't you dance any out here, when you came?"

Mom shook her head. "Too much to do." She was big and heavy-looking again. It took a lot of imagining to think of her as young.

I sat out on the steps after the dishes were done. It seemed to me that I could see clearly how it had been with Anna Petrovna and Ben Webb. They must have been happy enough together until they reached Plainville. Even there, Ben Webb must have defended her against any criticism from his mother and sister and taken care of her, thinking of the baby coming. But the summer must have come and gone and there would be no sign of her body growing bigger. Dad must have asked. I wondered how Mom could have found the words to tell him the truth. Dad had a temper that had lost him one hired man and spoiled a good sale once. I knew how he must have lashed out at her in his anger. But she had had a child, after all, three years later, carrying it with Dad's hate against her, I thought. It was awful to remember that I was that child. I felt like weevily wheat, the sound grains of beauty or pride or joy spilled out on the ground, leaving the sheaf empty.

The nights were warm and I slept out on the glider. In my own room Dad and Mom seemed too close to me. I couldn't go to sleep for thinking of them.

Mom liked to leave the light on the post by the barn burning all night, but I got up and went across the yard to switch it off. It was a relief to have the dark hide our house and the three of us.

II

THEN began the days of heat; the wheat grew before our eyes.
I wished Gil could see the moving forest that hid the bareness of
the earth now. There was a sense of order that I liked about the
wide strips of green beside the wide strips of fallow ground. It
made me feel as though my life this last year had been without
any pattern.

It was hard to get help on the ranch. Dad and Mom and I did
the haying. We worked from sunup till eight or nine at night, as
long as the sky stayed light. We cooked dinner after that and
didn't get through till nearly eleven. There was no time to think,
hardly to talk. We fell into bed and were asleep.

One night, with only two days' haying left, I woke, aware of a
soft shuffling noise. I raised on one elbow. The sound came through
the screen door. Then I lay back. I had heard that sound since I
was a child. Dad was walking up and down because of the pain
in his leg.

There was nothing I could do to help, so I lay still with a hopeless feeling. I knew Mom was awake, too. I stared across the sweet
warm dark to the shoulder of the rimrock. I had learned as a child
that if you stared at something long enough, it made something
you didn't want to be seem not to be.

Dad groaned softly as though he were trying to stifle it, and
the selfish hypnotism I had been practicing broke completely. Dad
was out on the couch now.

I heard Mom in the kitchen. The light glared across the porch.
Then it was not so bright. Mom had pinned a newspaper around
the bulb like a shade. I knew without seeing her how Mom would
look with her hair in a braid down her back and her crinkle-crepe
nightgown hanging shapeless and clean. She struck a match and I

knew she was lighting the two-burner oil stove we used in summer. Then all my senses seemed to wait for the pungent smell of the flaxseed mash she was boiling up for a poultice. I knew that scent so well. Sometimes the hot mash we made for the baby chicks smelled a little like it.

I heard Mom going into the other room. The light burst from the front window and laid a path across the dry mud of the road.

"Turn off the light, Anna. There's enough light from the kitchen." Dad's voice was irritable and tired.

"Too hot, Ben?" Mom's voice was low and without any tiredness, but it didn't sound sympathetic. Dad just murmured, then he let out his breath in a little sigh. It was so hot I pushed my cover back. How could Dad stand a hot pack against his skin on a night like this?

I thought of the fields where we had worked all day, stretching out under the gentle covering dark, and tried to think of this spot of pain here. I must have fallen asleep. I heard Dad say:

"That's enough, Anna." There was a long silence. Mom was already back in the kitchen when Dad said: "Thank you. You'll be tired tomorrow." I thought it sounded grudging.

"Come to bed now," Mom said.

"It's cooler here. Maybe I'll read awhile."

But Dad didn't read. The house was dark and still. I could feel all our breathing and our wakefulness, and the fields that began so close to the house, breathing, growing, awake, too. There was too much life. It was like a pain to think of it; life in the wheat that could be dried out and pinched off by drought, or beaten out suddenly by hail; life in us that could suffer and ache and want. I tried to think of something still and not living. I felt better when I thought of the rimrock that was gray and too hard and unchanging for life, then I must have fallen asleep again.

Mom woke me at five. She was already dressed in overalls and an old shirt of Dad's.

"We let your father sleep," she whispered. "He was awake most the night. I been over by Bardiches and get Tony to help today. It'll make your father rest up."

I got into my jeans and shirt and shoes and washed outside the kitchen. Mom made tea for herself, but I had milk and fruit and bread. We didn't talk lest we wake Dad, but I felt good. I could just dimly remember last night when I had tried to think of something without life. This morning seemed separated from last night by the width of a whole valley.

Once, Mom knocked a spoon off the table and I pointed my finger at her and we both laughed noiselessly like children at school. Mom tied a clean towel over her head and motioned me to come outside. There was still a pink freshness over everything.

"I go get Tony started. You stay up. I don't like your father to wake up alone. If shrapnel hurt bad you put poultice on. This afternoon we need you, too."

I wanted to work in the field. I wanted to be rid of the house, but I nodded. I tiptoed in and pulled the seldom-used shades in the front room. I felt shy looking at Dad. Mom had thrown a sheet over him and the white sheet made his face and neck look sallow and tired. But he was good-looking in spite of the beard on his face. How awful that he had ever had to grow old—well, forty anyway. Since I had known how he and Mom had come to marry I hadn't quite looked at him. Now I stood there, feeling half-guilty, thinking how he must have been as a young soldier; he and Mom in love once. It's queer that being young yourself and in love doesn't make it easy to see how it was for your own mother and father; but in this they seemed stranger to me than people I hardly knew. I was afraid my thoughts and my looking at him would waken Dad, so I went back to the kitchen.

When he woke he asked right away where Mom was. I told him she had Tony Bardich working and that seemed to make him feel better. He limped outside and washed and I could see how it hurt him to move. I fixed him his breakfast and asked him if I could put the compress on again.

"Oh, not for a while, but the old Adam surely did try to get out last night!" It was what he used to tell me when I was little, about the tiny sharp pieces of shrapnel that worked their way up to the skin from time to time, festering and hurting until they finally came out. He was too sick in Russia for the doctors to try to get them all out and all these years he had carried them.

"I wanted to finish that southwest piece today. With two of them working they won't," Dad said.

"After I get your lunch made I'm going down and help," I said.

Dad nodded and lay back against the pillow with pain. I washed the dishes and cut vegetables into the soup kettle and swept out the kitchen. Then I went in to tell him I would go and help with the haying now. I leaned over the back of the chair.

"Feeling any better, Dad?"

He was looking over yesterday's paper again.

"Yes, thank you, Ellen." He said it differently from the half-grunt he had managed in the night. "Just reading about the war. We'll be in it by next spring, all right. We're working up to it just like last time."

I was glad Dad felt enough better to talk, but I wasn't much interested at first. Then I remembered how he had said to Mom that night: "If there hadn't been a war, we wouldn't be here. I wouldn't be a physical wreck." My mind felt stealthy and sharp.

"I wouldn't think you could forgive the last war for . . . for this, Dad?"

"Why not? You have to take a chance. Other men had lots worse things than this." Dad's voice was mild and unresentful.

"Do you wish you had never been a soldier, Dad? You would be back in Vermont, wouldn't you?"

Dad lit a cigarette. "Yes, I presume I'd be still in the East; probably be teaching somewheres. There are things I wouldn't have missed, though."

I felt a little ashamed, but I asked anyway. "What things, Dad?"

"Oh, a lot of things, Ellen. It was a pretty big thrill sailing for Europe when I was nineteen, feeling the world was counting on me. I felt sorry for the boys back in Plainville whose parents wouldn't let them go. You had to have your parents' consent if you were that young.

"Oh, it wasn't all patriotism, I don't suppose. My family was very strict. When I was home I couldn't miss church or stay out with a girl after eleven o'clock or drink or smoke. I liked being free and on my own. Some people wouldn't think of the Army as letting you be very free, but I did.

"And I had a good time with the other men in my company, fellows I would never have known in Plainville. There was a fellow named Josef Podoroski, a Polack from Hamtramck, Michigan. He'd worked since he was fourteen in a factory. I wouldn't ever have met him if it hadn't been for the Army. I never liked any man so well."

"Where is he now, Dad?"

"He was killed in that fracas Armistice Day when I got this bird shot in me."

"Oh," I said softly. I wanted him to go on. Then, because I wanted to get back to Mom, I said, "Did Mom know him too?"

"No. They took him on a sled to Seletskoe. It was forty degrees below zero, and he died on the way. On our way out to Montana your mother and I stopped in Detroit and hunted up his family. They were poor Polish people, living in a tenement. Anna could talk some Polish, but I couldn't understand much of what they said. Anna told them he was my best friend. They wanted to give me everything they had."

"Do you wish you were living back in your old home, Dad?"

"Oh, sometimes, when I don't feel good, I'd like to be back in my own room. It was always cool there in summer because of the maple trees."

I felt sorry for Dad because the sun was burning down full-force now on the low roof of the house. In spite of the shades being drawn the front room was hot. There wouldn't be any coolness till late tonight. Suddenly, I wished we weren't out here on a dry-land wheat ranch under the burning sun. I wished we were in Vermont and that Dad was a teacher and that I had never worn jeans in my life. When Gil came to see me Mom would have served tea out on a green lawn. I went over to the couch and sat down beside Dad. I couldn't think of anything to say. I looked down at the white, thin places in the knees of my jeans.

"Well, it was a great experience, even if I paid for it. A third of the men in our company lost their lives. I think I would have, too, except for your mother."

"You didn't know Mom very long before you were married, did you, Dad?" I asked him as I had asked Mom.

"No," Dad said, "I didn't. Things are different in wartime, though, especially over in Europe."

"I don't think it matters how long if you love a person, do you?" I couldn't look at Dad, but I had to say it. Maybe it was the heat and Dad being sick and the way I felt about Gil . . . everything pressed on me. I wanted to force Dad into a corner and say: "I know you didn't love Mom; Gil felt you didn't love each other. That's why I lost him; because of that and this naked little ranch and the way we live. You could have been like Gil's father, but you came out here and tried to be like a peasant, too. You never read anything but the newspaper and a magazine or two; you can only talk about the last war or the weather or the wheat!" The words crowded at my mind to be said. "I don't blame Mom as much as I blame you," I would like to have told him.

Dad put his arm around me and I writhed inside, wanting to get away.

"Ellen, stop thinking about Gil. He isn't worth worrying over. You don't want to let him ruin your life."

I moved away from the couch. "He isn't ruining my life," I said, and my voice broke shamefully. If I had known how to get out of that room I would have run. I couldn't stand to have *him* pitying me. He had no right! The room was so tight and still. I had to say something.

"It's just one of those little things," I said, and I tried to make my voice flippant. "I think I'll go back to school a little early this fall, Dad. I'm going to take more hours the first semester."

I went inside the door to my bedroom and took quite a while to fix my hair. I made a pompadour in front and pinned a bow on top. It looked pretty crazy with my stretched-out polo shirt and jeans.

When I came back Dad didn't look at me and he didn't say anything for a long time. It seemed as though the room were filled with heat and pain and sadness: sadness of Dad wanting to be back in his cool bedroom at home, of his not loving Mom and living off here with her all these years, of Gil's not loving me.

"If you'll heat up that flaxseed, I think I'll try another poultice on here," Dad said.

When I brought it to him hot, he wouldn't let me put it on. "Thank you, Ellen. Now if you can take your mother's place out there, you might ask her to come back up here."

They were haying in the field farthest over. I was glad of the walk down, though it was so hot I knew the butter on the bread I took would be all soaked in. I had the big thermos jug of hot soup, and oranges bulged the pockets of my jeans. I didn't want to eat with Tony, but I thought Mom would like to eat up at the house with Dad.

I could see Mom a long way off, standing on the stacker. She was making Tony Bardich hump himself to keep up with her.

The sky, all one deep-blue, came around her head and shoulders and made her look bigger than she was.

"Hi, Mom!" I called up. Somehow, it was a relief to see her. She didn't look as though she wanted to be any place else. "Let me get up there. Dad wants you."

Mom stopped. "Is pain bad?"

"I don't know. He said it was better awhile ago, but just now he asked for a poultice again. Do you want me to take you back up in the truck? I can go while Tony's eating."

"No. Put the lunch over there. We finish this first," Mom said.

"Say, I might fall down in a faint if I don't eat pretty soon," Tony Bardich said, grinning at me. He's an easy-going kind with nice teeth, like all the Bardiches, and black hair. He plays the accordion at country dances, but he gets drunk too easy. I thought Mom was going to slap back at him, but she said:

"All right, eat, but we don't waste no time. We got to get the haying done today."

We ate sitting on the running board of the truck. There was enough for the three of us, anyway. Tony and I talked a little, but Mom was quiet. She kept looking away beyond the growing haystack over the fields as though she was thinking about what still had to be done. And she was through first. She sucked her orange and wiped her hands off on a handful of hay. Then she wiped her mouth on her arm.

"Come on, Yeléna . . ."

"What about Dad's lunch, Mom?"

"It's all there, isn't it? He can help himself if he's hungry. I go up soon. The work go faster with three of us."

When I came up alongside Tony in the truck, he shook his head. "The old woman sure can work!"

"Mom's good, all right," I said.

I think we all tried to outdo each other. When you think there's a chance of finishing a long job that day, it goes easier. Even I could tell that the hay wasn't as heavy as it was last year. The dry weather had dried it, too, so the bottom of the stem was brittle, not sweet when you sucked it between your teeth.

Working hard made me feel better. I began to think that maybe I would drive over to the reservoir a mile to the east of us and take a swim tonight. Maybe Mom would go, too. She could swim twice as well as I could. I could feel the delicious coolness of the water on me even while my shirt stuck to me with sweat and the hay that had crept up the leg of my jeans prickled.

Then I saw Dad. He was limping and coming painfully slow. He looked paper-thin against the sky. He hadn't worn a hat, and I knew he shouldn't have come. Mom was turned the other way, so she didn't see him. The truck was making too much noise over there for her to hear unless I shouted, and suddenly I didn't want Tony Bardich to turn and stare at him.

When Dad was close enough I waved. I was sure he saw me, but he didn't wave back. Tony saw Dad as he turned in from the road and came limping across the hay stubble toward us.

"Say, I thought you was s'posed to be sick in bed! That's what your missus said when she came crying for me to help," Tony yelled out in his big hearty voice. Dad never had liked the Bardiches. He always called them "ignorant foreigners."

Mom turned around and saw Dad.

"Ben Webb, you ought not come here. You get your sore infected like you did other time before!" Mom was hot and tired and her voice was loud. Then she softened it as though she were talking to a child. "We get done today, you don't need worry."

Dad kind of jerked.

"Oh, I know you can run the whole ranch by yourself—run it better alone." He sounded so hurt and he looked so thin I wanted to say: "No, we can't. We can't do it without you at all."

Mom didn't say anything at first. Her eyes were glued on Dad, but she didn't look big and strong, just hot and tired.

"*Proclyatye!* That is not so," she said in a low voice, as though she didn't want Tony to hear her. I looked back; Tony was standing in the truck, grinning a little. Dad saw him and turned toward him suddenly.

"I can do as much as you're doing standing there, even if I am sick," he said. "You can have your time."

My throat ached, I was trying so hard not to cry out. I knew the way he felt. I knew so well that I hated Tony patronizing him with his health. I even knew how he hated Mom's strength. I hated it, too, just then, and my own.

"You are a fool, Ben! We have the hay done by night if we don't talk all day. Tony, come on now. He don't mean nothing."

Tony chewed on a blade of grass. He laughed an easy-going

silly laugh, like boys laugh when they take you out the first time
—boys around Gotham, I mean. He turned to me.

"Which pays the wages here? That's all I want to know. Your
old lady hired me, but your old man looks pretty mad."

Dad didn't usually carry much money in his pocket. I don't
know how he happened to have it, but he took a ten-dollar bill
out of his pocket.

"I'm paying you today. Get along." He limped over and
dropped the bill on the hay by Tony's foot. Tony picked it up.

"It's okay by me. I get off a couple hours sooner and get paid
for them just the same. Well, s'long."

It was four miles over to the Bardiches. We would have taken
him home after work, but we stood still as though we were frozen.
And the feeling was worse because of the sun blazing down and
making us hot on the outside. I was ashamed to look at Tony,
going off across the field. I knew that he would tell his family
and the story would go all around Gotham. I couldn't look at
Dad or Mom. Something in me cried out:

"Don't! I can't stand living this way!" But no sound came out
of my lips.

Mom started to work again. From the ground I could just see
the back of her head and shoulders. She knew how to build a
haystack as well as any man. She kept working with the pitchfork,
like a toy figure when the spring is wound up. Dad still stood
there by the fence.

By now he was sorry. Help was so hard to get and we would
never be able to get any of the Bardiches again. But he couldn't
bring himself to say anything. Couldn't Mom see? I felt Mom's
hardness. I didn't look at Dad, but I felt him standing there,
sorry and hurt and wanting Mom to stop so he could take Tony's
place and not wanting to call out and have her tell him his leg
was too bad.

Oh, why didn't we give up the hay? What good was it to cut
it and feed the cows just so they'd give food for us, if all we
ate was soaked in bitterness and hate? Then I saw Mom standing
still, looking at Dad.

"You go rest while the leg is bad, Ben, an' keep soaks on
it so you don't be sick when threshing time come. We do this
easy; we can't do threshing without you."

Mom saw how he felt. It was as though she was walking a

little way across the field to meet him. If he would only come as far.

"I guess you can manage the threshing as well as the haying," Dad said stubbornly. He got out a cigarette.

"Oh, Dad, you know it takes three. Please go back. We want you to be feeling good." I couldn't wait for them to come together. It was too far and too hard for them.

"Well," Dad said, "it's kind of tough to feel you're so much dead wood."

I don't think he expected to be answered. Even the way he said it was like the exit line in a play that lets you go off the stage without feeling silly. He started limping away.

Mom and I worked like—well, like haymakers. It was an awful handicap not having Tony, but we didn't say anything about it. When I got thirsty I kept right on, because Mom didn't stop. When I was little, I used to play that a spot out on the fields was an island and I was marooned there, between the sky and the sea. I wasn't a child any more, but I felt that way today. We worked until it was too dark to see the hay at the end of a pitchfork.

"We got to stop," Mom said, and a little wave of relief washed up over the island. We were too tired to be hungry. I drove the truck home and Mom sat beside me.

"We let the other field go. The hay isn't much good anyway," Mom said out of her tired silence. I think she wanted to be through with haying. A half a mile away we could see the lights of our place, the big yard light showing everything up clearly, like a prison that is floodlighted so the prisoners can't get away.

Mom was lame when she got out of the truck. The hay smelled sweet in the cooling night air, but I closed my senses to it. No use to wish on the load of hay, tonight. What could I wish now? For Dad to be well? For Dad and Mom to be different? But there was no getting those wishes. For Gil to be here?

If Gil were here, how would he like me? I asked myself, walking across the yard in my dirty jeans and sweaty shirt. I wiped my face and my hand smelled of rusty iron and grease from fixing the truck hitch. I knew how my feet looked in their boy's work shoes, though they were hidden in the dark. I felt them plodding ahead of me, big and heavy. What was the use of wishing, anyway? I went on into the house.

Dad had made supper for us. There was a clean cloth spread

on the kitchen table and three places set. Usually, summer nights we just sat down at the oilcloth-covered table. Dad stood at the stove making scrambled eggs and bacon.

"Why, Dad, how nice," I said, trying to make my voice sound excited and pleased, but I was too tired. Mom had gone on into the bedroom.

"There's plenty of hot water to wash with," was all Dad said.

I felt better when I was cleaned up, and I was hungry after all. But we couldn't seem to talk much or make what we said sound natural.

"This tastes so good, Dad," I said, but my voice stayed up in the air.

"You shouldn't walk on your leg," Mom said.

"If you're going to do the work in the fields, the least I can do is to keep house," Dad grumbled. The hot uneasy silence settled over us again. Dad had opened a can of pears for dessert. They were still a little cool from the root cellar and I let each piece lie on my tongue for a second.

"Did you get through?" Dad asked.

"Near enough," Mom said. "We let the rest go. It's no good anyway."

Dad didn't make any comment.

"I see the wheat's got a little color already," Mom said. The haying and Dad's firing Tony and our not getting through was in the past now. Mom could as well have said, "Forget it, there's the wheat to think of."

When I was in bed on the swing I could see Mom fixing Dad's bandage. I looked at them through the open window as though I were watching a play. A day like this when Dad felt guilty he must hate to have Mom take care of him. Maybe Mom hated it, too, but she didn't show it. They both bent over the sore on Dad's leg.

"There!" I heard Mom say. "It's big piece."

I knew just what it would look like, a hard, irregular piece of shrapnel, no bigger than the tip of a knife blade, shot so long ago, taking all this time to work up through.

"Maybe that's the last of it," Mom said. She always said that, and it never was.

I thought of our modern-history class at the university. Everyone talked about the last war as though it were as long ago as the Napoleonic Wars. They didn't feel it still, as I did.

But if the last fragment of shrapnel were out, there would still be the hate and resentment between Mom and Dad. Those were bits of shrapnel, too, sown by the war.

12

LAST fall, going away to school, and last winter had been full of excitement. Last spring I had known so much joy it had made me almost breathless, but since June there had been nothing to look forward to. One day was like another, hot and bright and full of work. I was glad when it stormed.

The sudden darkening of the sky and the wind springing up out of no place to blow the dirt across the barnyard and lash the sunflower plants like giant pendulums back and forth gave me a kind of excitement. The sudden dropping of the temperature was a relief after the long continuous pressure of the heat. The chickens scuttled together against the wall of the chicken house, the hogs planted their great fatness together like a fortress and let out frightened squeals. Mom and Dad and I all came in from the fields. Dad stood on the porch looking anxious.

"Worst country for extremes," he muttered.

But I like the swift cruel changes. They make me feel that this country isn't just flat placid farm country, that it's as violent as the dark Doone country or any wild Cornish coast you read about in English novels.

We could watch the storm come, steellike against the yellow-gray sky. We could see the first drops hit. They whacked like the scattering of broken beads and looked on the ground like rock salt. We had a little hail insurance, but never enough to amount to anything. We sat dumbly on the porch, waiting. The hailstones were bigger now. Tomorrow at the store and the elevator they'd swap stories of how big they were. We watched them smashing the nasturtiums I had kept watered with dishwater all summer. There wasn't much left of them.

Then I realized, sitting there on the steps where the hailstones just hit my shoes and bounced back down the steps, that I didn't care what they ruined. Always there is a chance that the next ranch will be hailed out instead of ours. Ever since I was a child I have had a tight feeling in my throat when it hailed, but now I just sat waiting for it to stop. It isn't so hard on you when you don't care, but it's an empty feeling. I looked quickly at Mom and Dad, hoping the way I felt didn't show through on my face. Mom's lips were moving tight together as though she were biting something tiny like a grape seed between her teeth. I'd seen her do it before when she was worried. I think she really bit at the skin of her lips. But otherwise her face was still. Dad smoked a little faster than usual, letting the ash grow out on his cigarette until the wind blew it off.

"Get your jacket, Yeléna, and bring out your father's hat," Mom said. She wore her old brown sweater that had the front ends stretched way down from wrapping them around her arms.

Inside the house the hail beat on the roof as loud as a drum. It was too warm and shut-in. I picked up my denim jacket and Dad's hat and started back outside, but Mom and Dad were coming in.

"It gets too cold," Mom said.

"No man ought to try to raise a crop in a place where it can hail in August," Dad grumbled.

But I went outside and sat astride the porch railing. The air was as cold as though it came down off the mountains. The sudden change made me think of the sun drawing farther and farther away and the earth growing colder. When that happened it would come like this, I told myself. But the cold was a relief after the heat.

When the hail was over the sun came out, like a child that was over its tantrum. We drove around in the truck to see what damage it had done. It had riddled the cabbages in the garden that were just beginning to head up, and the hay we hadn't had time to cut lay draped every which way like a tumbled bolt of cloth. We crossed the highway in one place to get to the extra land Dad had bought and we saw a whole mile-long strip of the Bardiches' hailed out. I looked at it without caring, but I heard Mom catch her breath.

"*Gospode Boge!*" she said very low. I think it meant "Lord God."

Then we came to our own. Three strips were hailed out; the stalks looked as though they'd been chewed to shreds and then spit out, as ugly a sight as you could ever see. The hailstones lay all over the fallow ground, peppered through the stubble. The three of us on the seat of the truck, just sat there a minute.

"It looks pretty sick," Dad said. He pushed his hat back on his head and his voice sounded tired.

"I look at this piece yesterday and I think we get maybe twenty bushel a acre." Mom shrugged with a kind of down-settling of her shoulders.

I couldn't say anything. Maybe I couldn't go back to school. I'd have to stay here. I felt penned in between Dad and Mom in the cab of the truck. Dad started the motor again. I looked hard at the fields as we passed. When we came to ours again Dad stopped and Mom got out. She broke off a head of the starting wheat and rubbed it to see the seeds. She made a kind of grunt.

"Look at that. Half-empty."

"What makes it, Mom?" I asked.

Mom shrugged. "Wind, maybe." When she shook it, dust sifted out.

"It's better farther in," Dad said, "but it's been too dry."

I had heard talk like this always, every summer. Every spring when we saw the first pricks of green through the thin scattering of snow we felt good and full of energy and we planted the spring wheat full of hope. Then slowly through the summer our hopes grew less.

"We won't get five bushels a acre," Mom said in a kind of final tone. "More like we get four."

Enough to live on till next year and buy some new seed and oil and gas and tires, but not enough to go away to school on. Dad talked about how independent the rancher was, but he talked to make himself believe it.

As we drove we could see how the grain that was untouched by the hail was coloring up fast. The kernels shelled out of the sheaf when you rubbed them. They tasted sweet and hard between your teeth, the way your life should taste to you in the morning when you wake up and at noon when you're hungry and again at night when you're through for the day—only mine didn't, I thought, and spit the grain out of my mouth.

"We ought to get started combining about Monday," Dad

said. "The hail wouldn't have had to hold off much longer to make us a crop."

We listened to the Grain Market Broadcast each noon now as we had listened last August.

"This is your Grain Market Broadcast for today: Spring and Winter up four . . . Repeating . . ." The news of the hail and the heat and the lack of rain in the Northwest had reached all the way back to the grain markets of the cities. Wheat was up. The price was good this year. They needed wheat in Europe. War needs wheat always. But we would have so much less to sell this year.

"One dark Northern Spring . . . eighty-two."

But it hadn't been like that. Mine had been one tender, happy spring, too beautiful to last.

"One dark hard Winter . . . eighty-three." The words sounded like a melancholy prophecy of what was ahead.

"Durum, Flax, and Rye . . . no change."

"Minneapolis futures for September . . ."

There wasn't any Minneapolis future for me, I thought. Maybe I could borrow the money for school, but what if we had a crop failure the next year? Dad and Mom said nothing about my going away next month. Were they worrying about it, too?

But in the morning the worry slipped from me. I went out after breakfast and looked across the country. Gil should see it now, I thought, and a kind of hard anger came with my thinking of him. Anyone who loves beauty, I told myself, would be blind if he couldn't see it here now. The wideness that Gil had thought was depressing was here, but it was beauty, too. The deep-yellow grain, laid against the fallow strips, was beautiful beyond anything you could think of. The damage of the hail didn't show from here. There isn't anything prouder than a field of ripe grain. It makes you stand a little taller so you can see farther across it.

Mom and I were putting up chickens. It was blazing hot in the kitchen with the fire roaring in the range, and the dishpan in the sink was piled with dishes. We'd been working outside so much the house was just a place in which to sleep and cook. Dust would be thick on everything in the front room, but we didn't have time to go in there anyway. Mom's face glistened with sweat, but it didn't look heavy or dull. She likes this time of year for all the work is hardest.

Dad came by and called to me to come and ride over to the elevator with him.

"Go ahead," Mom said, and I went like a child.

We drove out of our way to look at the Yonkos' wheat. It was no heavier than ours. Afterward, when the wheat is all cut and sold, the difference between what you get and what you expected strikes in on you, but while it is standing in the fields you don't think of that.

Even Bill Bailey at the elevator had a new briskness. His busy time was just starting. Ranchers came to the elevator like cattle to a water hole. Nobody had time to lean against the wall and talk or play pinochle in the office. They had to get right back. Gotham showed its reason for being: carloads of grain were going out of Gotham every day now, bound for all parts of the world. We had a reason for being, too. Maybe that's what everybody is after. Mine had been Gil this spring. Now it was getting in the wheat. After the wheat . . . I didn't know.

"Hurry up, Ellen. We want to get right back," Dad called. There was a kind of importance in the sound of his voice. I wished it could be that way all the time.

We must have gone a mile before Dad reached into his pocket and brought out a letter for me in Gil's handwriting. He gave it to me without taking his eyes off the road.

"I didn't know whether to give it to you or not," he said.

I didn't want to read it there with Dad sitting beside me, watching, but I couldn't not read it, either. It was postmarked "Tampa." I tore off the end of the envelope and the "Dear Ellen" in his handwriting made me weak and shivery as though I'd had a sunstroke.

"*Dear Ellen,*

"*I can't go on without writing you. I have not heard from you since June. That must mean that you are angry or hurt. I wrote as I did because I feared we didn't have enough in common to build a happy life together. Won't you write me and tell me that you understood?*

"*Always,*

"*Gil.*"

121

I stuffed the letter in my pocket. I felt he didn't want anything changed, but he wanted to be sure I wasn't angry so he could feel right with himself. "Won't you write me?" What would I say if I wrote him? "I loved you but you didn't love me enough."

Suddenly, Dad reached his arm around me.

"Oh, Dad," I whispered.

"I know, Karmont," he said gently.

Dad didn't say anything against Gil—that wouldn't have helped any. But I could feel how much he loved me. I handed him the letter and took hold of the wheel so he could read it. He folded it and handed it back to me.

"He can't get you out of his mind."

"Like a duty," I said. "Something you feel you should have done and didn't." Then I thought of Dad and Mom. Dad must have felt Anna Petrovna was a duty. He could have gone off and left her; instead he had taken her back to his home. He had come to depend on her, but I didn't believe he had ever loved her.

"Could a man come to love a girl if in the beginning he felt it his duty to?" I was ashamed after I had asked it.

Dad was slow in answering. "Don't let any man think of you as a duty, Ellen," he said very soberly. "You don't want Gil back because he feels obligated."

It seemed to me that he had as good as said that he hadn't loved Mom. I felt the kind of coldness I used to feel as a child, even in the truck with the engine throwing up heat in our faces and the sun beating down on us. I tore Gil's letter into pieces and dropped them over the car door.

We took the combine out of the shed that afternoon. That starts the threshing the way setting up a Christmas tree begins Christmas. I get as excited over one as the other. Dad went right to work on it, oiling and cleaning out straw and seeds and dust. I put on old jeans and covered my head with a cap and got underneath to put grease in all the little grease nipples. It looks so complicated from underneath it makes your head ache to try to understand it. As I crawled out I saw the shadow of the combine laid out on the hard gumbo of the yard as clear-cut as a photograph.

We were one of the first ranches around Gotham to get a

combine, the first of the small ranches, that is. Mom kept coming out to watch us and look at it. Every rancher's wife is proud of the combine; it does the work of so many men that there aren't any big threshing crews to feed any more. Mom's so proud of it that when anything happens to it she acts as though it were a hurt child. Mom and Dad and I can thresh the wheat in ten or fifteen days by ourselves if the weather's any good. We used to be cooking and setting tables and washing dishes at harvesttime. Now we can be in the field all day.

Dad had the combine ready Saturday night. He could have begun Sunday. Way over to the west we could see by the cloud of dust rising from their combine that the Yonkos had started. But Mom said it was bad luck to start on Sunday. Dad laughed at her for that, but it was hard to go against Mom when she said something so firmly with her lips set.

Mom made bread and pie and cake; we wouldn't have much time to cook next week. There was such a festive air in the house that I said to Dad, "You'd think Mom was getting ready for company."

And Mom said: "I am. I got The Harvest here." Mom says quaint things like that with a different twist to them that gives them a foreign sound, but it's as much the thought behind it as the words themselves that make it sound foreign. She doesn't think like anyone else.

Monday I was up at five. I knew Mom had been up long before that. By six we were down at the field. The combine was all ready to go, but there was too much damp yet on the wheat. It has to be bone-dry if the wheat is going to come out clean. It was hard to wait. We were kind of quiet and excited. Mom went back up to the house to do something. Dad fussed with the combine and the tractor. I sat against the fence and chewed a stalk of wheat and watched the morning grow wider. It was cool now, and in less than half an hour it would be like a furnace.

The Bardiches came by on their way into town to the fair. Jake Bardich yelled at Dad:

"Aren't you going to the fair?"

Dad shook his head. "Comes at the wrong time for me this year."

Tony Bardich was in back, but he didn't say anything. A year ago I'd have wanted to go to the fair, but this year I didn't care. I guess that's a sign of growing up.

"Want to go some day this week, Ellen?" Dad asked.

"Nope," I said. "They're all alike." I thought of Gil writing that about commencement. Gil had known commencements all his life; I had known State Fairs. Then I stood up and kicked at the dirt with my foot. I wasn't going to think of Gil any more, but I thought of what Dad had said. "He can't get you out of his mind." I was glad of it.

It was good to get started. We took our places like old troupers, Mom in the tractor and I running the combine. Later we'd change off. Dad stood on the combine to see that it was running smoothly. He'd come alongside with the truck as soon as there was enough grain cut. He'd get a load and then take it back to shovel into the storage shed. The shoveling was the hardest work. Mom and I took a hand at it sometimes, but Dad didn't like us to.

Now the sickle was flashing back and forth, shearing off the grain that bent beneath the reel. The noise of the machinery, the look of the tractor, the sight of the stream of wheat falling out of the elevator spout into the grain bin, were all so familar it might have been last August or the August before that. I wondered how many Augusts would find me here threshing the wheat. I didn't care much; I just wondered.

We were out in the field, almost dead-center. The big combine seemed like a ship out on a sea, just as it had when I was fourteen and Dad bought our first combine. I lowered the reel to get a clump of wheat that grew shorter than the rest. There was a small patch of poor soil in the field. I knew it well enough, like a mole on my own face.

An airplane flew over our heads, one of the Army planes from the new air base in Clark City. The pilot waved and I waved back. When he was right over us I couldn't hear his motor because our own was so loud. But when he got off away I could hear him. His plane disappeared and made me feel as though we were standing still in the field.

I tried to keep my mind on the chains and rollers, to look at the wheat falling out of the spout and think how lucky we were not to have to bind and shock the wheat before we threshed. I could remember taking a nap against a shock of wheat when I was a little kid and Mom and Dad were both working in the field.

I wondered about Mom driving the tractor. She had a blue cotton handkerchief tied over her head today—that was all I could see, and the square look of her shoulders. I pulled the cord that ran from the combine to the tractor and had a sheep bell on it. I couldn't hear the bell back here, but Mom could hear it right back of her. She slowed down and looked around to see what I wanted. I shook my head and smiled at her and waved to go on. Mom got it. She knew I just wanted to see her turn around. Her face lighted up. She liked all this: that it was the first day of threshing and that we had good weather and that we were all three here working. I liked it, too. I pointed over to Dad. He was coming behind with the truck, watching to see that the truck came just parallel. His hat was pushed far back on his head and his face and neck were red. He drew alongside and yelled. Mom nodded and turned back to her driving. That was all, but somehow it made me feel good. I pushed the lever that sent the shining wheat emptying into the truck.

We stopped at noon and ate by the combine that gave the only shade in all that blazing sun. Mom had a thermos of cold milk that tasted best of all. And then we were back at it.

The heat deepened. I could feel the platform of the tractor burning through the rubber soles of my old tennis shoes. Everything I touched was hot, even through my heavy work gloves. All the freshness of the morning was gone. The smell of grease and gasoline enclosed me, shutting out the air. The cloud of chaff and dust settled down on us. Particles of the straw stuck to my sweating neck and arms. I kept my eyes on the shrinking size of the standing wheat and the widening desert of stubble, hard and bright and shining like sticks of bamboo. I tried to think of girls working in factories that were close and hot and filled with the stench of grease and steam, of soldiers fighting in tropical countries, but everything was unreal except the strip of wheat and the millions of little grains falling into the truck, falling so fast in the sun they looked like a piece of cloth woven of dark and light gold. Straw crept into my sneakers and gave the heat needles to prick at the soles of my feet. The sun was turning the rimrock pink. It must be after six. My eyes came back to the wheat in front of me just in time. I almost missed a low place. The hail had cut a wide swath in here we hadn't seen. It had been hidden before by the waving wheat. It hurt to see the reels come up without bending wheat between them. Drought years the wheat is like that, scanty and moth-eaten over a whole field.

When I heard the loose sound of broken chain cutting through the noise of the combine, I pulled the cord to tell Mom to stop and signaled to Dad. Dad was with me in a minute. He was clever with machinery. A rancher almost has to be. It was a pity to have something go wrong now when we were trying to finish the field before dark. I hadn't known I was tired, only hot, but now that we were stopped I felt my tiredness. My hands were cramped. I climbed down on the ground and the crunching stubble under my feet was a relief after the steel platform. I wiped my face and went over to tell Mom what was wrong.

The stillness was heavy after the steady noise we had lived with all day. My voice sounded squeaky speaking out in it. Mom looked tired.

"We haven't got much more to do," she said.

"All right, Ellen," Dad called. "I've fastened it with a piece of haywire. I think it'll hold till we finish this."

It was hard to start again. Four times across would do it. I measured with my eyes.

The wheat looked gray by the time we finished. We left the combine and the tractor there in the field and drove back to the house in the truck. Now we'd have to get supper and bring in the cows and milk them and drive a load of wheat over to the elevator.

"That wasn't a bad start," Dad said.

"How long it take you to fix the chain in the morning?" Mom asked.

"Oh, half an hour. If that's all that goes wrong this time I won't do any kicking." Dad was in good spirits.

"You let Yeléna drive the truck to the elevator," Mom suggested.

"We'll see," Dad said. Our house looked little and dark as we drove up to it.

"You go help your father get the cows. I fix supper," Mom said quietly to me. "He's tired."

Walking across to the barn, I looked back at the bare kitchen windows, sprung suddenly to light. Mom was standing in front of the stove. She was tired too, but it was Dad she thought of.

Maybe, all these years she had been trying to make up to him for . . . for tricking him. Always, even when I had worked hard all day, what I had heard that night was there in my mind.

Dad had the three cows we milked already in.

"Want a milkmaid, Dad?" I said.

"Oh, no, you go up and help your mother with supper. She's had a hard day."

I hesitated a minute, then I went back up. We didn't talk much at supper. We were too hungry and too tired. Dad let me take the grain to the elevator. Nobody was ahead of me and I could empty it right away.

"Wheat's running a little light this year," Bailey told me. " 'Tisn't as good as it was last."

On the way back I went around by the Halvorsens' reservoir. It was dark now at eleven o'clock. No danger of anyone seeing me. The water was warm as a bath and so hard I could feel the edge between my fingers, but it felt good on my skin. I lay on my back and floated so I could see the stars. Once a bird flew over me as though it had meant to land on the water and, startled by my white body under the water, darted up again. I could hear the soft flutter of its wings close to me. All the tiredness in my back and legs washed out of me. I didn't feel like Ellen Webb, at all, just light and free. When I put on my clothes again they hardly touched me. I carried my light feeling all the way home.

The house was dark again when I came around the hill, but Mom called out to me. I undressed in the dark and went to bed on the glider. I don't remember when the glider stopped swinging, I went to sleep so fast.

13

THE days went by like wheat sheared off by the sickle, shredded into minutes and quickly lost sight of in the constant stream flowing out of the spout into the grain bin. I lost track of them. One day the johnny bar broke and so we were held up while Dad fixed it. One night it rained and we couldn't start till the middle of the next afternoon. Dad took the big water barrels to fill them with water and Mom did the washing we hadn't done on Monday. I helped Mom fill and empty the tubs, but it was awful to be in the house after being in the fields every day. I felt too closed in, and the house was hot and steamy.

"You don't see young people your own age, Yeléna," Mom said.

"I don't mind."

"You grow old too soon. No use moping no more for that boy."

"I'm not moping. Please let me alone, Mom," I said quickly, and then I was sorry. Mom didn't say another word all morning, but I felt she was still worrying about me as she sat on the tractor seat driving up and back the next afternoon.

That day the sameness of what we did bore into me. I thought of our lives and I wondered what gave them any meaning. When I had Gil to love there was meaning, but now there was none. How did Mom and Dad stand going on and on working to feed themselves and me? What was the use? The question was like a hole in my pocket. Nothing was safe there. But the combine clattered on behind the tractor and the wheat fell beneath the sickle and the grain poured into the truck, on and on, up and down the strip, leaving the sun-bright stubble in a wider and wider swath. My eyes smarted from the heat and my skin crawled with the bits of straw. I couldn't see any beauty today. Last year I had worked like this, but I had been thinking about college. I hadn't wondered about meanings to things. I had to lower the reel again. The wheat wasn't good in here. The flow of grain out of the spout wasn't a full liquid stream, it was scanty and thin.

"If we get seven bushels to the acre out of this we'll do well," Dad said when we stopped for lunch. "It's the poorest crop we've had in five years."

Mom nodded. "It's bad."

"Well, it's better than thirty-three. Remember that year?"

Mom shook her head. Dad turned to me. "That year the drought was so bad, Ellen, that some of the Swedes got a Lutheran minister to come out and hold a service to pray for rain. Everyone around here went except Anna."

Mom made a moue of contempt with her mouth. "We have good wheat as any. Your father can't make up his mind to go or not. He get there for last song." Mom's face was sly and her eyes were bright with making fun.

"Maybe that's what saved us!" Dad retorted, laughing. It was good when they laughed at each other. Dad went over to gas up. Mom and I still sat on the ground against the combine. The grasshoppers kept up an incessant machinelike noise, and yet it seemed quiet.

"Mom, do you ever pray?" I asked. This summer I had grown bold at asking questions.

"Sure, I pray," Mom said. She was tying her handkerchief back on her head.

"But do you believe it helps? I mean, you pray for rain and good crops and it doesn't do any good."

"I don't pray for those. We take what we get. I don't bother God for that. I pray for something hard once and I get it, long time ago in Russia."

"For what, Mom?" I asked softly.

"I pray your father get well. Then I pray to have you. I don't ask things all the time, like in your father's church." Mom stood up as though that was enough of such talk. "You drive the tractor this afternoon. I take combine."

"But, Mom . . ." I wanted her to stay.

"What, Yeléna?" Mom stayed impatiently. I had to ask quickly what was in my head without thinking how to put it.

"You never taught me to pray."

129

Mom's brows lowered over her eyes. "Your father and I, we pray different. We don't teach you. When you feel it, you will pray."

I thought of that Easter Sunday when we almost went to church. I thought of Mom's giving me the icon and how cross it made Dad.

"Do you pray now, Mom?"

Mom looked way off beyond me. She sounded cross. "We won't get done if we don't start. Your father go back with load already."

But all that afternoon I thought of Mom's praying for Dad to get well. She must have loved him then. It was terrible to think of love dying out like wheat pinched off by the drought. I wondered once if it would have done any good if I had prayed to keep Gil. Then I looked up at the endless blue sky reaching way beyond the pale outlines of the mountain, over the stubble and the wheat. It seemed too big to pray to. We three looked too small and unimportant down here on the ground. And there were the Yonkos and the Bardiches and the Hakkulas and the Halvorsens, all out threshing too. If we were all saying prayers, one of us asking for one thing and someone else asking for the very opposite, we would sound like the hungry squealing of the pigs.

Running the tractor was monotonous; it left you too much time to think and we still had another week of threshing ahead of us. Suddenly, I wished we were through.

The night we finished the threshing I didn't get started to the elevator with the load till nearly ten. From the road I could see there were plenty of trucks ahead of me, lined up waiting their turn. It didn't matter. Tomorrow we could sleep late. We could take it easy for a day.

It was a clear moonlight night with the Northern Lights spreading a white tent again over a part of the sky. Threshing was pretty well done around Gotham. As far as you could see there was no wheat, only bare stubble and freshly turned earth where they'd started drilling already for the new winter wheat.

The motion of the truck fanned the hot air into a little breeze. By the store where last June's mud hole was dried into hard ruts the truck bumped so heavily I could feel the load I had on behind. It's a pity that you go through the same motions and work for a poor crop as for a good one.

I stopped at the store and bought a bottle of pop. There were only a couple of people there. Most folks were over at the elevator.

"Well, I s'pose you'll be going back East next week or so," Mrs. Peterson said.

"I may not be going back this year," I said.

"That's too bad. It ain't been a very good year anywhere around here. I heard you folks got hailed out some places."

"We didn't do so badly," I said. I knew it was my father in me. He didn't like to admit bad luck.

Mrs. Peterson's face crinkled up so it looked like a mouse's. "I guess you're thinking of marrying that Eastern fellow that was out here to see you?"

"No," I said. "He's in the Air Force." I went out of the store leaving half my bottle of pop standing there on the counter.

I drove the truck into the line. If Dad had been there, he would have got out to talk, but I stayed in the cab. I was getting so I didn't talk any more than Mom did. The other drivers were in the elevator, watching other ranchers' wheat, or outside where it was cooler, telling jokes, talking politics, smoking. Two men standing near my truck were drinking beer out of bottles. I could smell it on the hot night, along with the dusty grain and the sweaty odor of the men themselves and of my own body and clothes. I was no different from the rest.

Nurmi Maki sneezed so many times it was like a clock striking. Each time he seemed to say "Jerushlem." Somebody laughed. Then Nurmi blew his nose so loud it was worse than the sneezing.

"Dammit, always have hay fever threshing time. Seems like I can't never stand it. Got a boy's the same way," Nurmi spluttered.

"You old pig, Nurmi, I thought you was blowing a trumpet," Minnie Bruhl called out to him. I hadn't seen her before. She talked as loud as a man and swore worse. Klaus Bruhl died the first year I was in high school and she was running the ranch alone. She had three or four children that Bailey said were wild as coyotes. When she stood in front of the headlights I thought I'd never seen an uglier-looking woman. Her gray hair was straight and bobbed unevenly, as though she'd done it herself. Her red face was big-boned and disfigured by two large bristling moles by the corner of her mouth and she had a tooth gone in front. She wore bib overalls that were too tight front and back.

I sat back listening to tag ends of the men's talk. I could see the truck on the elevator tilt and hear the sliding sound of the grain that was like the pound of a heavy rain, then the special creaking sound of the platform legs.

"Good years or bad, I always say wheat in the elevator's same as money in the bank," Norman Olsen declared.

"That's not saying what you'll get for it, though," someone else said.

Chuck Henderson came over to talk to me.

"I been deferred till the wheat's in. I guess I'll have to go now, pretty soon," he told me. I looked at him, wondering what kind of a soldier he'd make. I couldn't think of him as anything but a rancher.

"Are you glad?" I asked, thinking it would be good to have your life taken in charge, to be sent some place and know you couldn't do anything about it.

Chuck looked almost embarrassed. "Oh, I suppose I'll like it all right when I get there. But I'd just as soon stay here, too. How'd your wheat thresh out?" he asked, as though he didn't want to talk any more about the war.

"Fair," I said. "Nothing extra."

"Same here. Gosh, it's been hot threshing."

Minnie Bruhl came back to her truck and stood there, hands on her hips, waiting.

"Say, she can take my place. She's probably in a hurry to get home to her kids," Chuck said, and went over to speak to her.

"Why, damn you, Chuck Henderson, I can wait my turn same as the rest. I ain't askin' nor takin' no favors and I ain't since Klaus died."

Her voice was loud enough to be heard all over the place. Somebody laughed. Chuck walked back to me looking as though he wished himself out of sight. Minnie Bruhl followed over.

"I didn't see you had a girl you wanted to wait with. I mighta known it wasn't my beauty you was after." She laughed as loud as she swore.

"Are you through threshing, Mrs. Bruhl?" I asked, to get her off Chuck.

"Cut the last piece tonight. Tony Bardich came over and threshed for me, him an' Jake. They eat more'n any men I ever fed in my life and Klaus was a good hand to eat, too." She started to laugh and broke off in the middle to turn on the scrawny little girl who climbed out of her truck and came over.

"I told you you'd have to go to sleep and stay if you was going to come with me tonight. That kid tags me every place I go," she complained to us.

The child stood beside her mother as though her words made no impression at all. Chuck handed her a stick of gum.

"Damn you, whaddya say?" Minnie Bruhl asked the child and then without waiting to hear her muttered "Thank you" started talking to Chuck about combines.

"We got the best wheat we've had since Pa died. An' we're goin' to have our own combine one of these days," the little girl piped out suddenly.

"Can't you keep your mouth shut?" Minnie demanded, without seeming angry at all. "If Klaus coulda seen the wheat we had this year he'da pulled through his pneumonia. The year he died the crop failed. He died before we had the damned stuff in." Her voice changed. It was almost tender. "I'd give a lot if he could see it this year."

The man ahead of Chuck's truck was through and Chuck went to drive his up the ramp. Minnie Bruhl went back to her truck.

Driving back home with the empty truck rattling loosely behind me, I tried not to think of Minnie. I couldn't stand any more disappointment and sorrow, even in someone else. A wave of sadness—for the whole world, I guess—came up in me. But I couldn't get out of my head how different Minnie's voice had sounded when she was talking about Klaus. He was a big, hard-working German who never said much. It was strange to feel Minnie's love for him, but I had. There was meaning enough in the threshing for her, I thought a little enviously, but not for Mom and Dad or me.

14

AND so the threshing was done. When I woke the next morning the sun was hot on the porch.

"Mom, what time is it?" I called.

Mom came out with her coffee cup. "After ten. Your father sleep till eight. He is gone down to Bailey's." She sat down on the porch step in the bright sunshine and poured her coffee into her saucer. I had seen her do that so many times before but I liked watching her. It annoyed Dad, so she drank from her coffee cup at the table, but when we were alone she liked it best that way. I used to try it when I was a child but the coffee always ran down my chin.

Mom's hair was still down her back in two thick black braids. She looked younger than she was. I could almost see how she must have been as Anna Petrovna.

"You're pretty, *Mamushka*," I said lazily, calling her by the name she had taught me when I was a child.

Mom made a little face and brushed my compliment away with her hand.

"Don't talk such nonsense, *Yólochka*." I had that queer feeling I have, sometimes, with Mom that we were both talking Russian even though we had said only two Russian words.

"Mr. Henderson was here last night while you are gone. He says do you want Prairie Butte teacherage? The teacher they got is leaving. Too lonesome for her, fifteen miles from Prairie Butte movies. They pay ninety dollar a month and give you wood and school stuff."

"But, Mom!" I was so startled it was like having cold water thrown at me. I sat up straight. "Who told Mr. Henderson I wanted a teacherage?"

Mom's face was, of a sudden, so stolid I felt shut out. We looked at each other across the porch as though we were strangers and spoke a different tongue. She was Russian; I was not.

Mom took her hairpins out of her pocket and began pinning up her braids.

"I guess they need teachers bad now. Mr. Henderson, he knows you have your teaching paper."

"What did Dad say?" I asked coldly. Of course Mom must have asked Mr. Henderson about a job for me.

"I don't talk to him yet. He'll say borrow money and go to school."

I knew how Mom felt about putting a debt on the ranch. Ours was one of the very few around Gotham that was clear. One time when I had complained that even the Bardich girls had a piano in their house Mom had said furiously, "You tell them you have no piano but your ranch is paid for." That was what Mom cared for more than my going back to school. She set her coffee cup and saucer on the porch and I noticed how the saucer was stained from the coffee.

"If I worked . . . I can have my job at the library again. Maybe I can get the cafeteria job back too. It wouldn't cost much except my tuition and my train ticket. They have funds you can pay back after college. I wouldn't have to borrow on the farm." I looked straight at Mom. "The wheat brought something."

"The wheat brought seven hunderd fifty dollar, not counting what seed and gas cost."

"I don't care. You can tell Mr. Henderson I'm going back to school. I'll manage it some way." I threw back the cover and stood up. I wouldn't stay here.

Mom went on sitting on the top step of the porch. I was so angry for an instant I think I hated her. I thought of her scheming to make Dad marry her. Now she was scheming to have me stay here and earn my own living. What could she know about an education?

"It don't hurt you to teach a year," Mom said.

"I'd lose all I learned last year and I'd have to drop out of my class," I burst out at her.

"If you don't know what they teach you last year, no use to learn no more," Mom said.

We didn't talk any more about it. All morning I was really

waiting for Dad to come home. When I saw him drive into the yard I ran out as I used to as a child.

"Hi, Dad!"

"Hello, Ellen." He got out of the truck as though he were lame. "I had to go all the way to town. The man at the store said we were lucky to get through the threshing. He'll have to order a new part."

"Will it cost much?"

"Enough. He's going to come out and see it first time he has business out this way." Dad stopped to wash at the back door.

At the table I'd bring up the subject of school. We'd have it out there. I took the vegetables from the stove and carried them to the table. I felt somehow triumphant over Mom.

"How you feel, Ben?" Mom asked.

"Well, I'm glad we're through the threshing. I'm going to lay up a few days."

"What's the matter, Dad?"

"Oh, I've got a place erupting on my leg again. It hurts so much it must be a big chunk," Dad said. I could see for myself that he was in pain. The steam from the spinach suffocated me. I had a hopeless feeling—Dad was sick again.

"You get into bed and I fix poultice," Mom said. She got up to put the flaxseed on the stove.

I might as well talk about going to school now as wait. Dad would be sick all tomorrow, maybe the next day. Dad pushed back his plate. He would be gone in the other room in a minute.

Mom turned the light on. It was still light, but not over the stove. The bright glare lighted up Dad's face with the lines between his eyes and down from his mouth and the thinness of his cheeks. Mom's face always looked darker in the bright light, darker-browed, darker-eyed than in the daytime. Even the fine black hairs above her mouth showed up. It must show me, too, sitting there stupidly between them. This was the way Gil had seen us, and I felt the color creep up in my face. Dad limped painfully in to the couch in the next room. Mom stood at the stove. I took my dishes and went over to the sink. Why did I see us like this, as though I were standing outside?

I did the dishes while Mom was putting on the poultices. I heard their voices but I didn't listen to their words, and as soon as I was through I went out to the porch to escape from the smell of the flaxseed. I sat there thinking of what I would say. It was the peasant in Mom that made her afraid to borrow. That was foolish. I couldn't stay here all winter.

Mom came out finally. "It's bad this time," she said in a low voice. "It start yesterday but he don't want to say nothing till we was through threshing. Now it look bad."

I braced myself against feeling sorry for Dad. "Mom, you did ask Mr. Henderson about the teacherage, didn't you?"

"That Gil has made you foolish, *Yólochka*. Mrs. Peterson told Mr. Henderson at the store you said maybe you don't go back to school. Henderson came out here while you was still at the elevator. You've had your mad for nothing."

I had to believe her, but I was still angry that she cared so little about my going back to school.

"Will you let me borrow the money to go back?"

Mom didn't answer.

"We borrowed money to buy the combine!"

"But we work for other ranchers till we got it paid back by fall."

"Dad won't want me to stay home and teach. You said so yourself. He always wished he'd gone on and finished."

Mom didn't answer. We were so still we heard Dad walking across the floor in his stocking feet. He had turned the radio on. The static is terrible in summer. He was trying for the war news. The pieces of the news came through the firecracker explosions. The war was miles and miles away. I hardly took in what I heard. I was waiting for the news to be over, then I'd go in and ask Dad.

"I'm going to ask Dad, Mom," I said firmly.

Suddenly, the radio snapped off in the middle of a sentence. We could hear Dad going back to the couch.

"Anna!" he called, and I could feel the tiredness and pain in his voice. "I guess I'll have this poultice changed."

I sat alone on the porch. After a while I went up on the rimrock where I could think about my own plans, but it was no use, my mind was filled with Mom and Dad. When you feel sorry for your father and mother it makes you feel older than they are. Even the line of the rimrock looked stooped and tired, and the house below it seemed lonely. I wasn't free to do what I wanted.

I went over to see Mr. Henderson and told him I'd take the teacherage. They were so thankful to get a teacher at such late notice I didn't even have to meet with the committee or sign a contract. Mr. Henderson said they only wanted me to promise not to leave for some defense job before the school term was over and not to go off and get married.

"I don't suppose we have any right to ask a pretty girl like you to promise a thing like that these days," Mr. Henderson said with a smile.

I said I could promise not to do either. When I came back, I told Dad I'd decided to stay home and teach this next year.

"Well, if you don't like it, remember, you don't have to stay," Dad said easily.

"I promised I'd stay," I said. I hadn't really believed I wouldn't be going back to school until now, but Dad seemed relieved, I thought. It hurt that he didn't insist on my going back to school.

Dad was too sick to drive over to the teacherage with us. The redness had spread all up his leg. I took turns with Mom changing the hot packs. Dad had been feverish some of the time, and irritable. Mom bossed him gruffly and paid no attention to his complaining, but she seemed to grow more stolid and quiet. We took turns seeding the winter wheat, so one of us could be at the house with Dad.

One afternoon I couldn't stand it any longer. Dad lay on the couch with the hot soaks on his leg and his foot in an old bedroom slipper. I was packing my clothes in the bedroom. The house was full of an empty stillness.

"Dad, wouldn't you like me to read to you?" I asked desperately, wanting to fill the room with some thoughts besides our own.

"I wouldn't mind," Dad said, "but I've read all the magazines."

"Maybe I can find some old magazines in the shed you haven't read."

"There's a box of books in that closet in the shed. I guess, though, it would be more trouble to get in to them than it's worth. The box is nailed shut."

I carried the box into the living room and got a screwdriver and a hammer.

"They used to be on the bookshelves in my bedroom in Vermont. When we came out here I never bothered to unpack them."

"But why? I don't see how you could help it, Dad."

"Oh, they're mostly boys' books. I worked so hard that first year I couldn't stay awake long enough to read anything at night, and my hands felt too big and rough to turn a page."

"But later on, in the winter?"

"I know, but I'd turned my face against books," Dad said. "What's in there?"

There was a copy of Emerson's *Self-Reliance* and a *Plutarch's Lives* in the same binding I had seen in the university library and *A Tale of Two Cities* and a ragged copy of *Black Beauty*. I opened the cover and saw Dad's name printed in big awkward letters. I had never seen anything before that had belonged to him when he was a boy. I looked at it a couple of minutes. There was a *Bartlett's Familiar Quotations* that said on the flyleaf "Awarded to Benjamin Oliver Webb for perfect attendance at the First Congregational Sunday School."

I turned over a *Child's History of England* and *The Pathfinder* and a Bible. On the flyleaf of the Bible was written "To my son, Benjamin Oliver Webb, with my love and prayers, from Mother."

"Are there more books of yours back . . . in your old home, Dad?" I asked.

"Oh, yes, at least half of them are mine; half belong to Eunice, of course. Eunice teaches school, you know."

I could count on one hand the number of times I had heard Father mention his sister. I wished he'd go on. "Does she like books, Dad?" I asked.

"I guess so; I don't remember her reading much when we were children. She teaches English, though." Dad gave a little laugh. "She's head of the department in the school where my father was principal."

He didn't say any more. I took out the last book. It was called *Household Gems*.

"Did you like poetry, Dad?" I asked wonderingly.

"I should. I used to have to learn a poem every week to say Friday if I was called on in school. We could pick out our own."

"Why don't you ever recite any of them?"

"Well, I still can. Listen:

"By the rude bridge that arched the flood,
Their flag to April's breeze unfurled,

139

Here once the embattled farmers stood
And fired the shot heard round the world."

We both laughed. "I remember learning 'Invictus,' too. My father thought that was the greatest poem ever written."

I hunted through until I found it. You could almost pick out the poems Dad had learned by the marks on the pages.

"The pack is getting kind of cold, Ellen."

I took off the towels and put them in hot water again. We kept the hot boric solution standing on the stove these days. The redness was going down, but the shrapnel sore was still angry and hard.

"I'd like to take a knife and cut the skin all the way down and get the stuff all out once and for all, and then sew it up and have a clean wound," Dad said. "That's hot enough!"

I lifted the towel to let it cool a little. I think I had done this since I was ten. Dad let out his breath in a long sigh.

"There, read something now."

I had the book open at "Invictus."

"Out of the night that covers me,
    Black as the Pit from pole to pole,
I thank whatever gods may be
    For my unconquerable soul.

"In the fell clutch of circumstance
    I have not winced or cried aloud,
Under the bludgeonings of chance
    My head is bloody, but unbowed.

"Beyond this place of wrath and tears
    Looms but the horror of the shade,
And yet the menace of the years
    Finds, and shall find, me unafraid.

"It matters not how strait the gate,
    How charged with punishments the scroll,
I am the master of my fate:
    I am the captain of my soul."

It made me uncomfortable reading it aloud, it was so desperate and solemn.

"My father used to quote that," Dad said, and went off into his own thoughts.

I wondered if Dad saw how the poem fitted him. His marrying Mother and coming out here in spite of the shrapnel wounds that laid him up all the time—that was pushing against Fate. He was cross and peevish often when he was laid up, but he didn't complain much, and it never occurred to him to give up and sell the ranch and do something easier. I wondered why his soul wasn't unconquerable. It made me feel good to be sitting here in the middle of the afternoon reading poetry aloud to Dad. I felt as though all my life I had been waiting to do just this.

I turned the pages and read a line here and there to myself. I read a long poem by Walt Whitman.

"There was a child went forth every day,
And the first object he look'd upon, that object he became,
And that object became part of him for the day or a certain part
      of the day,
Or for many years . . .

"The early lilacs became part of this child,
And grass and white and red morning-glories, and white and red
      clover, and the song of the phoebe-bird,
And the Third-month lambs and the sow's pink-faint litter, and
      the mar's foal and the cow's calf . . .

"The field-sprouts of Fourth-month and Fifth-month became
      part of him,
Winter-grain sprouts and those of the light-yellow corn . . .

"His own parents, he that had father'd him and she that had con-
      ceiv'd him in her womb and birth'd him,
They gave this child more of themselves than that,
They gave him afterward every day, they became part of him."

These words startled me. They might have been written about Mom and Dad and me. This minute here with Dad's old books and the poems that had thrilled him was part of him that he gave me and was now part of me. First Mom gave to me and then Dad gave to me. Only that night when I had learned about the hate between them had they ever taken away—but then they had taken away so much.

141

I put the books on the table that stood against the wall. Gil might have felt more at home if he had been able to look over and see them.

"Can I take them to the teacherage with me, Dad?"

"Sure. I might just look over the poetry book again."

When we were getting supper that night I told Mom about getting out the box of books.

"Why did you ever leave them out there all these years, Mom?"

Mom was frying potatoes and she had to talk above the sissing sound.

"All his folks was always propped up with books; your father don't need 'em."

"But, Mom . . ." and then I let it go at that.

PART TWO

"The seed haunted by the sun never fails to find its way between the stones in the ground."

—ANTOINE DE SAINT-EXUPÉRY,
Flight to Arras

I

PRAIRIE BUTTE lay eighty-five miles northwest of us. Mom drove me over on Friday. We had the back of the truck full of bedding, towels, clothing, and canned goods. I had to supply my own food. The county furnished wood and furniture and school supplies.

We drove along, silent with our own thinking. I glanced at Mom. She was watching the endless, flat, treeless plains, warm and sunny the first week of September, but so bare. There was no expression on her face. She had always said how like Russia this country is, not up near Seletskoe, but farther south where they grew wheat—only they have more snow in Russia and there are no chinooks to break the cold.

"It's more bare here than down around Gotham," Mom said.

But there were little jack pines growing out of the rocky ground and the sagebrush grew in bigger clumps here. There were no wheat ranches, mostly sheep. The ground was nibbled so close it looked like my old coat with the nap worn off. The last six miles were foothill gravel and full of rocks.

"The mud won't be bad out here in spring," Mom said.

We could see the butte from which the school took its name. It thrust up out of the ground like some earthwork made by children. I would climb up there some day.

"There is your school, Yeléna!" Mom said suddenly.

It was only fifteen miles from Prairie Butte and six miles from the highway. I don't know why I stared at it so hard or why it scared me a little. Teacherages are the same everywhere. I have seen them all my life; this was in better repair than many.

There was the usual long boxlike building painted gray, standing alone in the shadow of the butte, with a line of windows on each side. The last two must be my room where I was to live. Two smokestacks rose up out of the roof: one for the stove in my living quarters, one in front for the schoolroom. In front of the school stood the empty flagpole. In back of the school were the two outhouses.

You look at a place where you're going to live differently from any other place. It is almost as though you look at yourself coming out the door or peering out the window. Your mind goes so far ahead of your eyes.

When I went over to see Mr. Henderson about the teacherage, his wife said:

"It won't be bad, dear, just like the summer pasture farm where the girls in Norway stay alone in the summertime. I liked it. I'd gather wild flowers and do hardanger work and dream. You'll have plenty of time to dream about love up there."

I thought as we walked across to the teacherage that Mrs. Henderson had spent only the summers in her saeter. I was going to spend the winter here, and I felt as chilled as though the wind were already rushing across the plain to flatten itself out against the schoolhouse and the butte.

I turned the key in the door. Flies banged drowsily against the dirty windowpanes. The school board had put the place in order but a good cleaning wouldn't hurt it any.

"The roof don't leak," Mom said. Her voice sounded too loud in the empty room.

A door at one side of the wall back of the teacher's desk opened into a second room where I was to live. It didn't lack for furniture. There was an oil stove as well as a small sheet-iron heating stove, an iron bed, a dresser, a table, one rocker, and one straight chair. A cupboard on the wall with a faded cretonne curtain across it held some dishes. A frying pan and two saucepans hung on the wall under the oil stove. Four pictures of Clark Gable were tacked on the wall by the dresser, one of Walter Pidgeon and Franchot Tone over the bed. On the rack under the table lay a pile of *Photoplay Magazine*. A bright-patterned linoleum rug covered the floor.

I had to do something. I started tearing the pictures of the movie stars off the wall.

"I go see where you get your water," Mom said. "It is better when you get a good cleaning. I can stay overnight and help clean up." I saw her looking at the rain-streaked windows.

"Oh, no. It'll be something for me to do. I can take my time about it; I have until Monday." I wanted her to go before the creeping feeling of depression overwhelmed me.

We went to work to bring in the canned goods and provisions that were to last me most of the winter. I'd get home sometime in October and again at Thanksgiving and Christmas, but I didn't plan to go back and forth often. The jars of fruit and chicken and our own beef and vegetables filled the cupboard. I had to pile the single-portion cans on the floor against the partition.

"I can lie in bed and decide what I'll eat before I get up," I said, trying to make a joke of it.

"You eat right," Mom said sternly. "I make up the bed, anyway." She turned the thin-looking mattress and made it up with the sheets and blankets we had brought. On top she put the quilt Father's mother had made. I was touched at that. Then she brought up from the box of bedding the old icon and the little wooden shelf that belonged in my room at home.

"You have to have something you are used to," Mom said, crossing herself as she turned from hanging the icon.

When I saw Mom driving away after supper with eighty-five miles to go I felt deserted. I sat down on the wooden stoop and looked at the sunset over the butte and the empty twilight. If I had been able to see a thicket of aspen against the soft endless sky it would have helped, but there was nothing but the shabby earth rolling off under the slack wires of the fence that marked the school land from the prairie, and here and there a lonely, twisted jack pine. For the first time in my life I knew what Gil meant by the emptiness. I had taken it in with my mind before, but I had not felt it in my throat and my stomach. The emptiness surrounded me and swept over me until I was nothing.

I put my mind on Mom driving home. Would she be thinking about me, worrying about whether I was lonely? Mom always drove fast when the road lay straight across the prairie, holding the wheel tight as though it were the wheel of the combine. I thought of this summer when she and Dad and I had lived so closely together. I had listened to all they said, trying to find more than the words, scorning and pitying them by turns. At least I was alone now with my own life.

147

I went in through the schoolroom, trailing my hand over the desks as I passed, and lighted the lamp on the table in my room. It made a round yellow light but smelled of kerosene and the singed bodies of dead flies, and left the corners of the room in deeper shadow than before. My throat felt so dry I spoke out loud.

"Well, Ellen Webb, how're you doing?"

The sound of my own voice spilled out into the stillness around me like a drop of kerosene in a pail of water. It refused to dissolve and mingle, but held its own so long I could keep hearing it.

I had never been afraid of being alone or of the wideness of the earth and the sky. I stood there by the lamp, looking fearfully off beyond the circle of the light into the shadowy dark of the schoolroom. Its empty desks were lined up like little ghosts. I hesitated to make any sound. I would turn out the light and get on the bed and cover up. I looked for the little icon, but it was lost in the shadow.

I saw the pail of water Mom had brought and I went over and lighted the kerosene stove. I had to stoop down and tease the flame along the wick. I got out soap and rags and changed into jeans and a shirt. I moved quietly, afraid of making a noise.

When the water was hot I carried it into the schoolroom and went back for the lamp. I began at the front and scrubbed the floor, moving the lamp as I went along the boards. By the time I got to the fourth desk I tried whistling. I whistled the tunes the jukebox in Pop's Place used to play.

"You're doing fine, Ellen Webb," I said out loud when I went to empty my pail, and I threw the dirty water with a flourish on the moth-eaten grass and into the wide, soft darkness. But the splash made so tiny a sound in all that stillness that I knew I lied. I wondered if I could stand it here all fall and all winter and all spring.

2

BY Monday morning I had lived through two whole days alone. The nights had been endless. I kept waking and raising on one elbow to listen, but there was not even the sound of the wind. I think the stillness itself woke me. I slept best after it was light and I didn't get up until ten on Sunday, to cheat the day. That was the longest day I had ever known.

Sunday afternoon, I set out from the teacherage and walked about three miles until I saw a ranch house, but I didn't go up to it. I saw two boys running across to the barn and I knew they must go to my school, but the sight of them made me shy away. I wanted to meet them at school first.

There would be seven children in the Prairie Butte teacherage, Mr. Henderson said. They came from four families. I had only taught a week in the practice school. I hadn't come to know the children at all. When I got back to the schoolhouse, I took out my notebook from the class in teaching methods and reread the notes, but I remembered how often I had thought of Gil in that class. Sometimes, if I walked across the campus to the library after it I caught a glimpse of him. I hadn't thought I would ever use these notes. Along one margin I had figured out the days till Gil would be in Montana. I drew a harsh line through the pathetic figuring.

I was through breakfast by seven this morning and had two sandwiches made for my lunch. When my bread was gone I'd eat crackers, I decided.

"You can make bread and dumplings or muffins. What's the matter with you?" Mom had said. "You got a oven." But I doubted if I'd bother to bake just for myself.

The schoolhouse was clean. The sun and air had taken out any closed-up stale smell or odor of the soap and water, but it was so bare. I wished I had brought over some of Mom's geraniums for the window sills. I did pick a bunch of feathery sage and put it in a pickle jar under Lincoln's picture. I looked at the picture of Lincoln longer than I ever had before. He had known small wooden dwellings and bareness too, I thought. I would like to write that to Gil, but I wasn't writing Gil. Lincoln's eyes seemed to look across the desks through the opposite window. I raised the green shade so he could see the faint rim of mountains beyond the butte.

I had polished the windows. The shades gaped at the sides and had been used so long they looked like relief maps and let in light through all their cracks. Some schoolhouses have curtains at their windows, but I liked seeing out across to Prairie Butte. The sky was so wide it filled the whole upper sash. I would leave the windows bare, like Mom's kitchen windows.

I still had an hour before I could hope to see any of my children. I sat at my desk, facing the wide-open door and the oblong of prairie, and waited. I picked up a pencil to have in my hand so I'd look busy, and I must have pinched it tightly, because my fingers grew stiff. I pulled a piece of paper to me and wrote on it as though I were going on with my biography for Mr. Echols:

"Ellen Webb began teaching September 4, 1941, and taught continuously at the Prairie Butte teacherage for the next thirty-five years." Then I scribbled it out so hard the pencil went through the paper. I'd never do that. Next fall I'd be back at the university. I'd study this year and keep up. I wouldn't be like Dad, leaving my books boxed up in the shed.

I looked up suddenly and saw the boy standing silently on the porch looking at me. He had come up without my hearing him. I wondered uneasily how long he had been there watching me.

"Hello," I said. "You're the first one."

The boy smiled slowly. There was something queer about his smile. He reached up and got his cap off.

"H'lo," he answered, and his voice was too heavy for a child's. It had no tone in it.

"Come in," I said.

He must have been fifteen or sixteen. He looked too big for this school.

"I'm early. Ma said I'd be early. I ain't never been late," he said like a five-year-old. He had a queer disjointed walk, hunching one shoulder ahead of the other. His head looked too big for his body. He was half-witted. I sat still behind my desk as though it were a fortress. Mr. Henderson hadn't told me one of the seven pupils was feeble-minded.

He took the biggest desk at the back of the room by the window. It must have been made especially for him. The seat was knocked together carelessly out of old boards. There was a horrible likeness between the look of the boards that didn't quite join and the look of the boy's shoulders and feet. It was like a cruel joke. He slid into his seat with a loud thud and smiled foolishly at me.

"What's your name?" I asked, speaking loudly, as though he were deaf.

"Robert."

"Robert what?"

"Robert Donaldson." He beamed as though this were something he was sure of.

"My name is Miss Webb." I went over and wrote it on the blackboard and erased it and wrote it again because my writing went downhill. "Can you say Webb?"

He stuttered over the "W" and then brought the name out in a burst.

"Good. Can you tell me what grade you are in, Robert?"

"Four," he said proudly.

"And how old are you?"

He looked down at his hands and frowned. I could hear a truck coming toward the school. Someone shouted. Robert looked up as though to see if I were waiting.

"Five, ten, fifteen," he said. His voice had a flat sound.

He clasped his hands at his desk and smiled vacantly. With a sense of fleeing I went on out to watch the other children come.

"Hi, Mary, there she is!" I heard one shrill voice scream out, but anything was better than that toneless voice and empty smile.

When I faced my schoolroom at quarter of nine I had eight children, representing five families who lived somewhere in the shallow bowl of land between Prairie Butte and the low rimrock. I picked up my record book to write down their names.

"Mr. Henderson told me there would be only seven," I said, feeling more comfortable if I was talking.

"He's new!" a little girl with black braids announced, pointing across the room at a pale-looking boy in the second row. "He's just moved back here," she went on.

"What is your name?" I asked the boy.

"Leslie Harper." He stood up to answer, and his lips pinched together nervously when he finished a sentence. "I moved here from Detroit, Michigan. I was in the third grade last year—you can see my report card." The whole class stared at him.

I started a little speech about the pleasant time I hoped we would have and how much I hoped we were going to learn. I felt like someone other than Ellen Webb.

"We have a chapter of the Bible and the Lord's Prayer and America's Creed first thing in the morning an' we raise the flag and sing 'The Star-spangled Banner,' " the boy named Nels Thorson interrupted. The other boy sitting beside him laughed out loud. Mary Cassidy became convulsed and hid her face in her arms. Suddenly Robert began to laugh as though he had just sensed the joke. The laughter trickled out of his open mouth in a slow thin stream. Then the class began to laugh at him. I quieted them sharply.

"Today we'll skip the usual exercises, because we have so much to do," I began again.

At noon the children ate outside on the gravelly ground in front of the stoop. I made a cup of tea hurriedly on my stove and went out to watch them. I saw how the new boy, Leslie Harper, seemed to sit by himself on the corner of the step, but he was watching the big boys play marbles on the ground. Robert came over and sat beside me. Once I found his vacant eyes on me, his cheeks bulged out with the big bites he was taking. I looked away with relief to the swing, where the wiry little Cassidy girl was swaying, pumping herself up so high the chains screeched.

"Don't you have no radio, Miss Webb?" Nels Thorson asked me. He had won the marble game and rattled the marbles in the pocket of his jeans.

"No, Nels, I'm sorry, I don't."

"You oughta have one. Miss Barnett, our last year's teacher, had one. She used to let us listen to the war news at lunchtime and sometimes if we got through we could hear the three-o'clock quiz program. Gee, she had a swell one, eight tubes. Her boy frien' gave it to her."

"Maybe after Christmas I'll bring one back with me," I said. "Is Miss Barnett teaching this year?"

"Nope, she got married," the dark-haired La Mere boy said. "Her boy frien's a mechanic in the Air Force. He's a sergeant. She showed us his picture."

I looked at my watch. The time was up, but Robert was still chewing slowly.

"Don't mind him. Miss Barnett just let him come in when he got through. His folks ain't going to send him any more after this year."

Robert could hear all Nels said, but he seemed to pay no attention. It made me uncomfortable.

"We can wait a minute or two. Are you almost through, Robert?"

He smiled and began packing what was left in his lunch box.

"Feed it to the birds, Robert," Mike screamed at him. All the children talked louder when they talked to him. "Here, give it to me." Mike snatched the leftover sandwich out of his hands and broke it up on the ground.

"Gee, you wait'll you see the magpies. Sometimes there's ten or twelve," Mike told me.

"If you have any trouble with the pack rats under the floor, Miss Webb, I'll set you a trap and then I can empty it when I come. You won't have to bother with it," Raymond La Mere told me as we went back to the schoolhouse. "I'll help you with the fire, too." I could see that Raymond, as the only sixth-grader, was the head of the school.

A half-hour before school should end, I closed my book. "That's enough for today. I think we'll have a story, an old story many of you have heard, and then tomorrow I'm going to ask you to act it out, so I want you to listen very, very closely." I sounded to myself like the demonstration teacher at the practice class. "Let's see . . ." I looked out the window trying to think of a story simple and dramatic enough to act out. I don't know why, but I thought of Gil on the rimrock at home.

"How many would like to hear the story of Bluebeard?"

"Aw, tell us a war story," Mike Cassidy cried out.

"Yeah, don't you know no spy stories, Miss Webb?" Francis La Mere begged.

"No, not this time. Now listen: Once upon a time, near the city of Baghdad," I began, "there lived a very wealthy man who had the terrible misfortune to have a blue beard." I could see the children settling down. Sigrid Thorson's mouth was wide open. Raymond La Mere's fine dark eyes were intent on my face. Robert was drawing on the piece of paper I had given him. I saw the black-and-white magpies fly past the open door. They were coming for the lunch crumbs, but none of the children noticed them.

"When Bluebeard had to go away on a long journey he gave his wife Fatima the keys to all the chests and rooms of the palace, telling her that everything was hers. But he gave her one key that opened a little closet on the gallery and told her never to use it, and that if she disobeyed him something very terrible would happen to her."

"Our father don't like our mother to use the car keys when he's away, neither," Sigrid Thorson said.

"Shut up!" her brother said sharply.

"But so great was Fatima's curiosity . . ."

"What's curiosity?" Mike asked.

". . . she took the little key and put it in the lock and slowly turned it. When she opened the door it was all dark inside, and then she saw that the floor was covered with blood."

One of the children caught her breath. The only sound in the room was the noise of Robert's crayon on the paper. It was fun seeing these children so spellbound. Even Robert left off crayoning and watched me. I came to the place in the story where Fatima cries out "Sister Anne, Sister Anne, do you see anybody coming?"

"And Sister Anne said, shaking her head, 'I see nothing but dust blowing and the green grass growing.'" I made my voice hopeless and dreary and I looked out the window as I said it. I'm afraid I was thinking again of Gil on the rimrock.

There was a sudden frightened scream. It was the new boy, Leslie Harper. He put his head on his desk and hid his face in his arms. The other children were too startled to make any sound.

"Why, Leslie." I went down to his desk. "Don't be frightened, it's only a story."

"Oh, please, Miss Webb, please let her see something besides . . . besides the grass and the wind. I can't stand it." He hid his face again. I sat down on the desk of the vacant seat behind Leslie. "Listen to the rest of the story."

"Does it turn out all right?" he asked in a smothered voice.

"Yes, it turns out all right," I promised, going on with the story: " 'Sister Anne, Sister Anne, do you see anybody coming?' "

" 'I see,' " replied Sister Anne, " 'a great cloud of dust that comes this way.' "

" 'Are they my brothers?' "

" 'Alas, no, my dear sister, I see a flock of sheep.' " I felt Leslie's hand against my knee and slipped my own down to hold his.

"Then Bluebeard bawled out so loud he made the whole house tremble: 'Naught will avail. You must die!' and he was on the very point of cutting off Fatima's head when two horsemen galloped into the castle, not even dismounting . . ."

"Like the Lone Ranger," one of the children squealed.

"Lone Ranger! Lone Ranger!" shouted Robert, banging on his desk.

"And whipping out their swords they ran them through Bluebeard's body and his poor wife was saved."

"And then what?" Mary Cassidy demanded.

"And then she had all of Bluebeard's money and married the man she loved."

"And lived happily ever after?" Leslie asked.

"Yes, they lived happily ever after," I said. He smiled faintly at me and pulled his hand quietly away.

When the others trooped out Leslie waited behind.

"I'm sorry I cried," he said, "but I couldn't stand it . . . about the dust blowing and the green grass growing, I mean."

"Why, Leslie?"

His small peaked face twisted as though he were going to cry again.

"That's the way it does here, and I hate it."

"Have you never been here before?" I asked.

He shook his head. "I was born here, but my folks moved away right afterward. My father used to live here. My mother's dead."

"Where does your father live?"

"He's in Detroit. He left me with my grandmother and grandfather. We live over that way. There's my grandfather, now."

Leslie ran out of the schoolroom. I followed to see an elderly man driving up in an old Ford truck filled with pine knots.

155

"How d'you do," he called out to me. "After a while this boy'll learn to walk home, but his grandmother's afraid he'll get lost. It's only two miles." Leslie waved to me as they drove off. I watched until they were out of sight, then I stood awhile stupidly staring at nothing but the green grass growing.

3

I WORKED hard at teaching fractions and interest and reading and spelling and yet all the time, underneath, my life seemed to be reaching out like the roots of a cottonwood tree after water. The days fell into a pattern: The Part before School, then School and The Part after School and The Long Evening. I was glad to hear the children arriving in the morning, and every afternoon I had a little dread of the sudden stillness that settled down on the teacherage when they left.

At three-thirty we marched out into the yard and sang "America" while two of the boys lowered the flag. Leslie Harper was chosen first, because he was a new boy. Leslie would hold the folded flag carefully across his flat little chest and march in to put it away.

"The pole looks kind of lonesome when the flag gets down, don't it, Miss Webb?" Leslie said once.

The children were seldom in a hurry to get off. Raymond would bring in wood for me. Francis, not to be outdone by his brother, would bring a fresh pail of water. Some of the children had a swing before they left. I lingered outside with them as long as they stayed. But all of a sudden they were gone. The Part after School had begun.

With a little sinking feeling I realized that today was Friday and I was alone again. I went back into the schoolroom. Somebody always forgot something: a lunch box or a hair ribbon or a cap. Today there was Nels's slingshot over on the window sill and I could see a half-eaten apple in Mike's desk. There was the faint smell of hot dirty hands in the room, and I recognized the scent of the musterole Sigrid's mother had put on her chest. I opened the windows and let it air out. Soon it would be too cold to do that.

Nels Thorson's father had brought a truckload of wood this morning, big chunks of fir and poplar, and dumped it at the corner of the schoolhouse.

"There, Miss Webb, that oughta see you to Christmas. It's January and February that's the worst months," he told me cheerily.

Today I wished it would rain or snow, or the wind would blow hard. Then I would be glad of the snugness of the teacherage and open my books and get to work, but this placid, pitilessly clear fall weather made me feel like a fly held in a drop of honey.

"I must wash my hair," I said aloud, trying to pretend to a great busyness. "I must hurry so I can dry it before the sun goes down. This schoolroom needs a good cleaning," I told myself as I went down the aisle. "I have all those arithmetic and spelling papers to mark. But what are eight papers?" my mind sneered. "The blackboards need washing. I must make a pattern for those paper turkeys. The children can cut them out and paste them on the windows." But I went into my room and sat down on the bed.

Time filled the room and lay across the empty prairie and pushed against the window. There was so much of it that it had pressure and weight. But it was empty. Somewhere there were people who didn't have time enough, who forgot time and themselves.

I wanted to get away from here, to go home and pack my clothes and go back to the city to college. I would work, oh, how I would work, and be busy and hurry! I thought of the hurry down the mall to eight-o'clock classes, and it seemed the thing I wanted most in the world.

When it was five o'clock I started to get my supper. I opened a can of corned beef and cut thin slices, and opened a can of green beans. I heated a potato left from yesterday and made tea in the pot with the broken nose and cut a piece of Mom's fruit cake for dessert. I laid it all out on a napkin on the narrow table by the window. I was hungry.

Then I caught sight of myself in the mirror. Sometimes, last year, I'd catch sight of my own reflection in the shiny surface of the counter as I stood serving, or in a mirror at the Bean Pot, but then it was only for an instant, just time to say hello to myself, not even long enough to think about it. Now there was time for a long stare. I saw how long my neck looked above my shoulders, how my hand around the fork handle looked strong enough to hold a grain shovel. The pink sweater I had bought in Dayton's college shop last year had been washed too many times. I looked dull. "You look so quiet, but so alive," Gil had said once. He wouldn't say that now.

I tried to go on eating, lifting my cup of tea to my lips, but my eyes would find themselves in the mirror. I wasn't hungry. The food was tasteless. My cans stacked along the wall looked like a grocery store. I picked up my plate and went out to scrape it into the garbage can. I put my dishes in the oven and closed the door on them, and went out of the teacherage.

At six-thirty it was dark. The long light nights of summer were over. The top edge of the butte was hidden in darkness, but there would be a moon tonight. The patent-medicine calendar on the wall of the schoolroom said so: three-quarters full. I walked fast at first, away from the butte this time, toward the south. I would stop at whatever house I came to. I had been here five weeks and already I craved people, grown people.

The stars seemed to come out between one step and another. I couldn't see them blink on like street lights, but as suddenly they were there. They seemed to lie just above the rimrock. I climbed toward them, wishing I were climbing the rimrock at home. When I reached the top the moon was up. I could look down on the school sitting there like a doll's house in the center of the flat ground. The flagpole stood out clearly.

I walked along the rimrock a long way, until a ranch house lay below me, and the long squat roof of a sheep shed. There was a light in the house. I ran down from the rimrock almost eagerly. Once I saw two red eyes that I suppose belonged to a jack rabbit.

A dog barked when I came near the gate. The door opened and a woman's voice called out, "Be quiet, Shep!" She lingered there against the oblong of light and I could see that she was small and bent. "Is someone there?" she called.

"Yes," I called back. "How do you do?" I went rapidly up the plank walk to the log house. "I'm the new teacher at the Prairie Butte teacherage."

"Come in. I'm Mrs. Mathew Harper. I was going to send some fresh bread over by Leslie tomorrow. You can take it now for yourself. It didn't turn out as good as it used to."

159

"I wondered if this wasn't where Leslie lived. You're his grandmother?"

"Yes, and mother too, poor boy."

"Leslie told me his mother was dead," I said.

"Dead!" Mrs. Harper gave a kind of snort and went on in a half-resentful tone. "Yes, she is dead and you hadn't ought to talk about the dead, but I think about her and just boil up inside. She went off when Leslie was three, got a 'call' is what she said, to traipse around the country holding religious meetings. It's a queer religion, I say, that calls a woman to leave her own flesh and blood. She'd keep coming back, all dressed-up, and bringing a load of Bibles and books and tracts and then just when Warren'd begin to think she'd settled down, she'd go again. Fin'lly, Warren went and hunted her up in Los Angeles and she was living with the religious preacher that traveled with her. Warren never mentioned her again, and he told Leslie she was dead, as she was a year later. Here, sit down there where you'll be comfortable. Leslie'll be real glad to see you."

The room was like rooms I've always known. Folks on ranches usually buy out of the same mail-order catalogues, but it was different, too. There was a kind of crowded disorder about it. The window sill was piled up with mending. Wood was stacked under the kitchen table and back of the stove. The dishes must have come from dinner and supper both.

"Leslie says you come from Minneapolis?"

"I was there last winter, but I come from Gotham, Montana," I said. "You were just doing the dishes. May I help?"

"Oh, don't bother. I don't make any fuss." As though she was glad to be reminded of what she had been doing, she went back to the sink and picked up her dishcloth. It was too dark over by the sink to see.

"Can I move this lamp over for you?" I asked.

"Father does that for me when he's home. I don't like to move it, I'm so unsteady with my hands."

With the light nearer, I saw how old Mrs. Harper was. Her left hand was knotted up with rheumatism so that she could only use it to hold the dish while she washed it with the other. She was too old to keep things in order. They piled up on her. She was too old to have to raise a grandson.

"How long has Leslie lived with you?" I asked.

"His father brought him here in April. Leslie's a nervous kind of child. His father thought he'd be better off back here."

Maybe it was the light on the shelf above the sink shining down on her face that gave it such a worried look, or maybe I was used to Mom's calm face. She went on talking without my saying anything.

"Warren was a bright boy. I was telling Leslie today I could remember how proud he was when he won the 4H award for raising the best buck, and he did real well at college." Mrs. Harper sloshed the dishcloth over the plates while she talked. She didn't get them clean. I don't think she could see well enough. Her mind was on her son, anyway.

"He got a job the second summer on a boat that went to South America. We didn't want him to go, but, land, he'd have run away if we'd said no, and wool was selling so low and there wasn't anything here on the ranch that summer, so he went. Seems like he never settled down again after that. I knew when he came back from college next year with a picture of a girl that he'd decided to marry her. He did, the end of his junior year. But we didn't say anything. Mathew said there wasn't any use."

I took the teakettle from the stove to rinse the dishes, but it was empty. I didn't want to interrupt to ask where the water was.

"I could tell from the girl's picture she wouldn't do on a ranch. But you wouldn't think to look at her she'd take up with a new religion, either. I forget what they call it. I haven't any use for it, anyway.

"And I never seen such a change in a man as Warren. He stayed in Detroit for six months after he got the wire saying she was dead. I guess he drank some. I'm not excusing him any. He worked hard—Warren always was a good worker—but he looked tired and old enough to be fifty when he drove into the yard last April, and he's only twenty-seven."

"Tell me where these go and I'll put them away," I said.

"Oh, just put them there on the table. I don't fuss."

I was glad to hear Leslie's voice outside.

"Hello, Leslie," I said. "I've been visiting with your grandmother."

The little boy nodded and smiled. He came over toward me. "Grandfather and I went to fill the water barrels."

"Here, I was forgetting about the bread!"

Mrs. Harper brought a loaf from a crock and began wrapping it awkwardly in a towel. Mr. Harper came in with a dog at his heels that seemed too big and wild for him.

"Mathew, this is Miss . . ." Mrs. Harper looked at me blankly.

"Webb, Ellen Webb. We met the first day of school."

Mr. Harper nodded, but I don't think he really remembered me. He was smaller than I, and very frail. I noticed how his eyelids made little peaks above his eyes. His ragged jeans were dirty and he had an old black suit coat that was spotted down the front, but all the same he looked clean. Maybe it was his white hair against his pink skin.

"I'll walk part way home with you, Miss Webb," Leslie said. I looked at Mrs. Harper, but she was too busy trying to tie a string around the bread to hear.

"Not very far. It's getting late," I said.

Mr. Harper sat down in the chair and began taking off his boots.

"That school's got a good roof on it. We put the new shingles right over the old ones," he said, showing me with his heavily veined hands just how it was done.

"I'm glad of that," I said.

When Leslie and I came out of the house it was bright moonlight. I held out my hand to him. "Let's run a ways. I love to run in the moonlight."

Leslie looked at me a minute, then he grinned and took my hand. Running across the hard bare ground, we could see our shadows running with us. The dog's shadow looked like a bear's. I waved my hand in the air and my shadow gestured comically back. Leslie's high, little-boy laughter sounded shrill in that empty place. The dog barked and started echoes way against the reef.

"I think you better go back by the road so you won't get lost after I leave you, Miss Webb," Leslie said soberly. We left off running and went over to the dry, rutted road.

"Do you get scared alone at night?" he asked when we had walked a way.

"No, not scared. I get lonely sometimes."

"I get scared, but not with you and Shep. Would you like to take Shep home with you tonight, Miss Webb?" he asked.

"Oh, no. But if you hear of a puppy, I'm looking for one."

"There're just old dogs around here," he said sadly.

I promised I'd watch him after he left me until he was out of sight. He'd run a little way and then turn to see if I was still there, and wave. In the bright moonlight I could see him a long distance.

I came around the bend in the road and saw the school standing out square and squat on the plain. I ran the rest of the way, partly because of the moonlight, partly to shake off the feeling of the Harpers' house. I would feel old, too, if I stayed there long.

When I lit my lamp and drew the shades my room had a friendly feeling. I liked it for the first time. I moved around feeling natural. I could hum without having the sound stay in the silence. While I undressed I planned out my days: tomorrow I would do some French. Every day I would do some extra work. Sitting on the bed, I looked across at the cans piled against the wall. Why should I wake up every morning staring at beans and soup and canned corn? I went out to the shed and got some cartons to put them in and shoved them under my bed. Then I took red crayon and marked the contents on the box ends.

I put on my coat over my pyjamas and went across to the cistern to get two pails of water. I set them on the stove to heat and dragged out the tin washtub I used for bathing. I had to sit in the tub with my knees almost under my chin, but the hot water was delicious. I made white gloves on my hands and up my arms with the soap, like a child, then I dipped them under the water and watched the soap slide off the smooth skin. My arms, still tanned from summer, looked dark against the white pinkness of my thighs. When I stepped out on the towel I could feel the warmth from the stove and I turned around to feel it on my back and rubbed until I glowed. I unpinned my hair and let it flop softly down on my shoulders. I felt so warm and clothed in my own skin that for a minute I hated to put on my pyjamas. I thought of old Mrs. Harper, and I had a sudden greedy joy in my young, strong body.

It was midnight before I was through with my bath and had the light out. I ran the shades way up and opened the windows. It wasn't really cold, but the air was as clear as ice water. The moonlight was so bright I could see the pattern of the calico on the patchwork squares of my quilt. I didn't mind being alone here any more.

Since I had been in love with Gil I hadn't ever been quite alone. And all summer I had felt so weighed down with Dad and Mom. Now I was free and alone in myself. It was the only way to feel. I wouldn't ever let anybody matter so much to me again. I wouldn't let myself need anybody that way. Dad and Mom had made their own lives and I was separate from them. I was free from Gil now, too—I hardly ever thought of him, I told myself.

It was snowing when I woke in the morning, and I could see my breath in the air. There were two inches of snow on the floor by the window and the top of the stove was covered. The snow came pouring down like wheat emptying out of the truck at the elevator. Prairie Butte was hidden as completely as the faraway Main Range.

4

SUNDAY forenoon Mom and Dad came. I was sitting by the window translating *Cyrano de Bergerac* as hard as though I had a class next hour. My airtight stove was roaring like a furnace and I had the door shut into the schoolroom. Nothing had gone past the window all morning but a sheepherder driving his sheep up over the rimrock. He had his head bent against the wind and his chin down in his coat collar. The sheep kept close together and moved in a gray wall. He went past without seeming to look at the teacherage at all, and yet he must have faced it all the way across from the highway. There was a kind of secretive look about him as though he wanted to be let alone, the look I'd seen on a deer that came down in the wheat field one time. If he had looked up once toward the window I would have called to him. When he had passed, the place seemed more lonely than before.

It was about eleven when I saw the truck coming through the snow. I knew by the blanket tied over the radiator that it was ours. Mom always covered the radiator in cold weather. I ran out to meet them.

"Well, Karmont, I had to come and see where you are," Dad said.

"Yeléna," Mom said very low, and hugged me as though I were a child. How could I ever have thought I could be separate from them?

"They couldn't have found a much more God-forsaken spot to put a teacherage on!" Dad grumbled.

"How are you, Dad? Is your leg all well?" He looked pale to me beside Mom.

"Yes, but he has a cold. I told him I come alone, but he

won't hear. He is stubborn like a pig." Mom scowled when she talked.

"We miss you, Ellen," Dad said, paying no attention to her. We were standing out in front of the school, hardly knowing we were still outside. I can't tell the gladness there was in me.

Mom approved of the schoolroom. Out of the corner of my eye I could see her looking at the floor. I was glad I'd washed it this morning and put the border of turkeys on the blackboard in colored chalks. Mom nodded her head.

Dad didn't think so much of it. "How far would you have to go for help?" he asked, looking out the window.

"About two miles, to Harpers' place," I said.

"Why would she need help?" Mom grumbled.

"Sit down, Mom, and take off your coat." She had been too busy looking. Now she took off the bandanna she wore tied under her chin because of the cold. Then she thought of something.

"Ben, go bring it."

"How did you ever happen to start out a day like this?" I asked.

Mom shrugged. "We plan yesterday, before it get so cold, to come today. The cold don't hurt nothing."

I laughed; it was so good to hear Mom again.

"Mom, I like it here now. I hated it at first, but I don't mind it any more."

Mom's eyes can get brighter while she looks at you. They did now, but she only said:

"You got it good here. Where you put your canned stuff?"

And then Dad came in loaded down. He gave me a box and I knew when I felt the weight of it that it was a radio.

"If you ever needed one you need it here in this place," Dad said. "Let's see if it's any good."

"It came yesterday. Your Dad was crazy to start right out," Mom said.

Dad set it up, but the static was bad. I thought of the first few days when I had been afraid to make any noise. I was glad they hadn't come before, until I was all right alone. Then Dad went back out to the truck for the food they had brought.

"Mom, I can't eat it all!" I shrieked.

"In this cold will keep all right."

"You killed a turkey, Mom!"

"There's one less to run away. She's been out hunting them

166

till the Bardiches complained she keeps them awake." It was Dad's old joke. He always insisted that the Bardiches did nothing but sleep once their crop was in.

Mom was lighting the burner on the oil stove under a kettle she'd brought from home. I knew without asking; it was borsch, Mom's beet soup.

"Oh, Mom!"

"I bet you're sick of them canned soups, eh, *Yólochka?*"

"She won't get the smell out of the school for a week. When your children ask what it is, you tell them they're going to school in Russia now!" Dad teased.

"And cranberry sauce, Mom!" That was one of Dad's favorites.

My room was too small. We spread a napkin over my big desk in the schoolroom and used it for a table. The rows of desks stood around us like astonished children. By now I thought of them almost as being the children who sat in them.

"There's one my size," Dad said. "Who sits there?"

"Oh, that's Robert's. He's not quite bright but he's . . . he's not bad," I said. It seemed a long time since that first day when I had almost fled from him. I told Dad and Mom about one after another. I told them about Leslie crying at the story of Bluebeard.

Dad looked out the window. A fine soft snow was coming down steadily.

"I know how he feels," Dad said. "It's the loneliest damn country in the world."

Silence spread between us; we all three sat staring out the window. I looked at Mom. She was holding a turkey drumstick in her hand. Her face was closed. I think she liked the country because it was like Russia.

"We better start back, soon as we do the dishes," she said. "It's dark quick, now."

"Oh, I'll do the dishes. You go ahead. You ought to stay here all night."

"Because of that little storm!" Dad scoffed.

"We make it all right," Mom said.

When I saw the truck drive off into the snow it was all I could do to keep from running after it. I lighted the lamp and began picking up the dishes. Then I turned my radio on. The static was like the sound of a machine gun, but the dance music filled the emptiness. If the sheepherder passed by now, he'd have to look this way, I thought. It must be funny to have so much music and noise suddenly bursting out in the snow. I ran outdoors to see how it sounded. In the dusk the snow hid the teacherage from sight and the clatter of the radio seemed to come from nowhere.

I liked the snow falling down on the hardpan soil around the teacherage. It was almost a foot deep. I felt the way I do when I see the snow coming down to cover the strips that are planted to winter wheat. I guess you have to live on a dry-land wheat ranch to feel that glad about the first real snow; it seems such an easy way of getting moisture into the soil.

I wondered how it would look here in the spring when fresh grass broke through and it was green for a little while in June. Would there be as many wild flowers as we had on the top of the coulee at home last year when I tried to show them to Gil? I stood out there in the first real snow of winter and I was thinking about spring already! I laughed and ran back into my box of a school. My flesh tingled and my hair was damp from the snow.

It was Sunday night and I hadn't corrected the arithmetic papers or prepared my Monday lessons. The week end I had dreaded was almost over. I sat on the bed with the lamp moved over beside me and the radio playing dance music from the Drake Hotel way off in Chicago, with the cracks and splutters of static in between.

I started marking Francis La Mere's spelling paper. I hadn't been thinking of Gil at all, but I pulled a fresh piece of ruled yellow paper to me and began:

"Dear Gil,

"I couldn't write before because it would have hurt me too much. Don't feel guilty or bothered about me. We were too far apart. Perhaps we could have made a life together, but we would each have had to come a long way and your love was not that strong. Perhaps mine wouldn't have been, either. My parents had too long a way to go.

"We had a poor crop and there was not enough money to send me back to Minneapolis. I am on a teacherage here, a little one-room school set down on the prairie with nothing to see but the snow." Then I scratched that last out and wrote instead: *"with nothing to see but the green grass growing and the dust blowing. The nearest town is six miles away and the nearest ranch is two*

miles away. I have only eight pupils, though one, a boy of fifteen, is feeble-minded. I live here all the time and my time is my own after three-thirty each afternoon.

"At first I was afraid of the loneliness. I know what you felt when you looked at the ranch and the country with such a shudder. You taught me what real loneliness is. But I can stand it here now, Gil. I am no longer afraid of it. And it no longer hurts me to think of you. That is why I can write you now.

"Tonight it is snowing. I went out a few minutes ago and felt the snow on my face and on the hardpan ground. Do you know what I found myself thinking, Gil? I began thinking how green it would be around here in the spring if the snow stayed and there was enough moisture. I wondered if there would be as many flowers as there were last spring on the top of the coulee. I would know better now than to try to show them to you. You have to be more simple and peasantlike like my mother and me to care about our wild flowers.

"But I'm glad we met and that you came out here to see me, even though I lost you that way.

"Ellen Webb"

I read it through. It said exactly what I meant. He would wince at my blunt sentences. It would be kinder not to send it to him. I sat a long time thinking about it. Then I folded it up and put it in an envelope and addressed it. It freed me of him. To make it more final I stamped it and ran out through the snow and put it in the mailbox. I thought of him turning it over in his long straight fingers that I loved even now. He would read the postmark: "Prairie Butte, Montana," and he would take a long time to open it and a longer time to read it. The cover of the mailbox made a loud clang as I banged it closed. The snow came up on my ankles. It was falling so fast the tracks I made on the way out were already filling.

5

THE next morning Mr. Donaldson brought Robert in his big sled. He had stopped by for the Thorsons and the Cassidys. I knew Mr. Donaldson now. He never mentioned Robert's mentality and I had the feeling that he held himself to blame. He was a faded copy of a man who made me think of his jeans, limp and faded against the stout new denim of the patches. Mrs. Donaldson was a big bustling woman who had told me right away how Robert's condition was due to scarlet fever and poor teachers.

The La Mere boys had walked over and were late. The big boys brought in enough chunks of wood to last us for the whole day. We filled the water pail with snow and perched it on the stove to melt.

The deep snow and the lowering sky gave an eerie light to the teacherage. The children's eyes were always out the window while I read the chapter from the Bible.

Mary Cassidy lifted her hand. "Miss Webb, they didn't know what snow was in the Bible times, did they?"

"No, Mary, they lived in a country of deserts and palm trees, you know."

"They had sheep ranches," Nels Thorson put in.

"I keep wishing Jesus knew about Montana, though," Mary said wistfully.

"He musta knowed because His Father made all this and every place else," Nels argued with firm Lutheran assurance.

Leslie Harper raised his hand. I had come to be wary of Leslie's eager interest.

"My father doesn't know God, but my mother did. God holds the whole earth, every place in it, in the hollow of His hand." He spoke with such earnestness that the other children stared.

His gray eyes were like the gray stone that has flecks of shining mica in it. It was like a glimpse of his mother too. I could almost see how she would have enough fire to go out on religious missions even though it meant leaving her child.

"Why didn't your father know God, too?" Francis La Mere asked, his eyes bright and cunning.

Leslie shook his head and his face lost its eagerness and became sullen. "He said he didn't want to know Him."

"Now we'll stand and sing 'The Star-spangled Banner,'" I said quickly.

At noon they opened their lunch boxes and I heated the borsch for them. As Dad said, the fragrance filled the schoolroom. It was a good hearty soup that would warm them up. The cold was beginning to come in around the windows.

"What's this?" Mike asked as he tasted his soup. "I never saw a soup that was red like that."

"Hush up, this is Teacher's soup," Mary scolded.

"It's beet soup they make where it's lots colder than this," I told them. The children had to eat it in every kind of container, because I didn't have enough dishes. Then as a surprise I went into my room and turned on the new radio.

"Miss Webb, you got a radio!" Raymond shouted.

I let them all file into my room to see it. They were crowding through the doorway when the dance music of the Farmers' Noon Hour Program was interrupted by a voice announcing:

"Storm warning: The Highway Department warns motorists to stay off the roads. Snow is drifting and the temperature is dropping. Temperature at two A.M. thirty-two degrees below zero. Below fifty degrees expected by night. Children in rural schools should remain there rather than attempting to go home. Parents are advised not to set out for them until the storm clears."

"We gotta stay here tonight, Teacher!" Mary exclaimed, jumping up and down.

"Where'll we sleep?" little Sigrid Thorson wanted to know. I wondered myself, but I was thankful for the radio; I might have let them start out as usual.

We could feel the wind. It blew the snow like so much sand against the windows and the walls. The big stove roared with the fire in it, but the outside edges of the room were so cold I had the children move up to sit with the others nearer the stove. Robert began to cry. The other children laughed at first. But the sound of Robert sniffling was hard to hear. It mingled with the wind and snow.

"Robert, stop that!" I spoke so sharply I felt the children staring at me. Then I said to Robert in the manner of a teacher at the practice school:

"How would you like to string a macaroni chain for the Christmas tree?" Robert looked interested, so I brought him my pound package of macaroni and a darning needle threaded with string.

I kept the radio on low to hear any other storm warning. I heard the fourth-grade spelling and Raymond's arithmetic, but I was listening to the radio all the time.

The windows were frosted over so we couldn't see out. They made me think of the tall frosted glass windows of the gymnasium at the university. Soon it would be so dark I'd have to light my two lamps.

After the regular schooltime we played games: quiet games, "I See Something" and "I'm Going to New York" and "I'm Going to Take . . ." We played blindman's buff till I was afraid the stovepipe would fall. I lined them up, four on one side and three on the other, for a spelling bee while the room darkened and the snow spattered and drove in under the front door in an icy drift.

When the children had to go outside, I would send two older ones together. I took the younger ones, holding a blanket over our shoulders and keeping our heads down against the wind. It was not safe for anyone alone. When I took six-year-old Sigrid Thorson out she cried and clung to me. "It makes me think of wolves, Miss Webb. Don't it make you scared?"

"No, it doesn't scare me, Sigrid," and I thought how Mom on nights like these, after we had hugged the fire for hours, would say suddenly: "Put your big coat on, Ben, an' we go outside and see the storm. *Yólochka*, come; wrap up your head tight!"

Dad would get up muttering about "that crazy Russian woman I married," and Mom would laugh and bundle herself up until she looked as fat as an Eskimo. Outside, the cold would grab us and hold us so tight we couldn't breathe easily. It would make a pain in my forehead and I could feel it wind around my legs. When it was cold like that it was often clear and Mom would point out the stars.

"Jump, *Yólochka*, up and down, and clap your hands!" She would have us all jump. Dad would seem suddenly young and tall and limber. "Like this!" Mom would say, swinging her arms around herself as she jumped. "Good, Yeléna, but more faster!" I felt as though I were hugging the cold to me.

And once, I remember, when we were out Mom said:

"Hush! I can almost hear the bells on the troikas, Ben."

When we went back in, little Mike Cassidy was crying and the other children were sitting around idle. "I want to go home," Mike sobbed. "I don't want to stay here all night."

I had to think of something, so I said, "But, Mike, we're going to make candy—two kinds, fudge and taffy."

After that they were fine. All these children were used to such storms beating at the walls and windows of small frame houses. Robert dropped his string of macaroni and stepped on it getting out of his seat to pick it up. He looked at me, ready to cry.

"That's all right, Robert," I said quickly. "You can make one of paper rings." Then his face cleared and he laughed instead.

Leslie Harper went over to the window and tried to scratch a place on the glass where he could look out. The sound of his fingernail scratching on the glass window made the flesh at the back of my neck prickle.

"Leslie, keep away from that window, there's too much draft there!"

"I was only trying to get a peek out," Leslie explained sulkily.

It was luck that Mom had brought all that food. I made turkey sandwiches and used up all my butter and then had to make jelly sandwiches without any butter at all. The borsch was gone, but I made a hot soup by pouring three cans of chicken soup with three cans of tomato together. One of the La Mere boys named it "tomatochick." We ate around my big desk and the stove. The two lamps on the desk made a warm yellow light but the back of the schoolroom was left in partial darkness.

"I wonder how Pop likes doing my chores tonight!" Nels Thorson said.

"I got outa washing the milk pails tonight, too," Mary gloated.

"Gram'll worry about my not getting home," Leslie said.

I only half listened to their chatter, but they sounded content. I got out colored papers for Robert and set Francis to cutting them in strips so Robert could paste them. It had come to be almost second nature to keep Robert in busywork.

"Now can we make the candy?" Nels asked.

"Yes, after we do up the dishes. Everyone get in line and bring the dishes out to the work table in my room. There are more cookies if anyone wants some more." They all trooped in with their dishes, but Robert and Francis were the only ones that had room for more cookies.

I had just finished the dishes and come back into the schoolroom when the storm warning was repeated over the radio. "Teachers in rural schools are not to allow children to start home. Parents are advised not to try to go for them." I glanced around the room thinking how comfortable and safe they all were, and suddenly I didn't see Robert.

"Where's Robert?" I asked.

"He was here just a little bit ago, 'cause I seen him come back with his cookies," Nels said.

I grabbed up my sheepskin coat and galoshes and ran outside. I called as I went but the wind took the sound away from me. I ran through the snow to the outhouses by the fence but no one was there. The wind was blowing too hard and there were no footprints but mine.

I ran back into the school, almost sure that I had made a mistake; that Robert must be there. The children were still as I came in. They looked frightened.

"Try to think, children—who saw Robert last?"

"I helped him wipe up some soup off his desk," Francis said. "He kept saying, 'I want to go home' and I told him he couldn't and to go up and get some more cookies."

I remembered giving him the cookies and telling him to bring his paper chain up by the stove. I kept looking into the dark corner of the room at his big empty desk, expecting to see him.

"Raymond, I'll put you in charge. You must all do just what Raymond says till I get back. No running or jumping, and I don't want anyone to move the lamps. The candy will have to wait."

"Miss Webb, where you going?" Mary Cassidy asked.

"I'm going to find Robert," I said, with more assurance than I felt. I went into my room and stuffed my skirt into some old wool pants and tied on a hat with a brim to keep the snow out of my eyes.

"Oh, Miss Webb, you hadn't oughta go, the radio said . . ."

But I didn't wait to hear. I had to cover my face a minute to get my breath. I couldn't see more than six feet ahead of me.

"Robert!" I called into the dark, and then I stood still hoping to hear him, but there was only the sound of the wind. He never walked quite firmly; he must have fallen down; he must be lying now in some snowdrift. I plunged ahead through the snow until I found the mailbox post and leaned against it a minute. Once I thought I saw something dark in the snow. I grabbed for it, expecting to find a mitten, but it was nothing but a frozen tumbleweed. If Robert had come this far he might have worked his way along the fence. I felt for the sagging wire and used it as a guide. In places the snow had piled up higher than my waist. Whenever I came to a rounded humplike drift I thought it might be Robert. I turned around to catch my breath and look at the schoolhouse, but I had drawn the shades to keep out some of the cold. I doubt if I could have seen any light through that snow, anyway.

"Robert!" I screamed into the wind. "Robert!" I never wanted anything so much in all my life as to see that big lummox of a boy with his half-bright smile and his clumsy shambling walk.

"Robert!"

The wind blew so hard I had to stand still a moment. It went through my sheepskin-lined coat as though it were thin cloth. I turned and struggled back through the snow. The wind was at my back. That helped, but the cold numbed me. It seemed to have taken every bit of blood from my brain so that I couldn't think. I had known plenty of blizzards before; I must keep my head now. If I went back to the school and worked out from there in every direction surely I would find him. Maybe he was warmer than I. He was fat; that helped, I told myself. He hadn't shivered the way some of the children had.

I floundered along the wire back up to the school. The vestibule that had seemed like an icebox this morning seemed warm to me now, and a refuge from the wind. I heard Raymond's voice that was changing break as he went through the rigamarole of the game:

"Prince of Paris lost his hat and
Number 4 knows where to find it."

I opened the door of the schoolroom. "Are you all right?" I asked dumbly.

"Yes, Miss Webb," they chorused.

"Did you find Robert?" Leslie asked, his eyes big in his pale face.

"Not yet. I will, though," I said crossly. "Children, nobody remembers seeing Robert after he went up for cookies?"

"I think I remember hearing him close the door. He banged it," Sigrid said.

"Sigrid, think. Did you really?"

Sigrid twisted her head, but said more dubiously, "Well, I think I did." Sigrid had thought she saw a camel one day, too.

But I was wasting time. He would be getting farther away. I cautioned them again about the lamp and saw that the stove was full of wood. I raised the window shades so the light might shine out for Robert to see, and I took time to put on some heavy felt shoes of Mom's, "valenkis," she called them.

The cold seemed more cutting after being inside and it was harder to see, or maybe my fear made it worse. I knew he was lost, and I'd never find him.

I walked into the woodpile without seeing it and fell sprawling. When I stood up my mind seemed to clear. If I could get to the Harpers' ranch perhaps they could help. At least they could get word to the Donaldsons. All these children had stayed alone before. Raymond was fourteen. Nothing would happen to them.

I found the fence post and began the struggle along the wire. After a while there was so little feeling in my hand I hardly knew I had hold of the wire. I slogged through snow above my hips and had to stop to rest.

When the fence came to an end beyond the school land, I had to get down on my hands and knees and feel through the snow for the deep ruts of the road. It was easiest when I came to a stretch where the wind had blown the snow thin. If I stood upright I knew I'd lose the road. I went along almost on all-fours. At times I stood up to look for some marker that I would remember from my one walk back from Harpers', but that had been in the bright moonlight before the snow fell. The snow clung to my eyebrows and eyelashes and my eyelids kept freezing shut, as though they were granulated. It frightened me. I took snow and rubbed at them to get them open. As long as I stuck to the ruts of the road I wouldn't get lost; that kept me going. But the farther I went, the more certain I was that Robert couldn't be alive.

"Oh, God, let him be alive!" I prayed once aloud, and as though in answer the wind flung a sheet of snow from the top of the drift clean in my eyes and my mouth. I couldn't think or pray any more; I could only try to stick to the ruts and keep moving. Then I felt the poles of the cattle-crossing under the snow and I could stand up and follow wire again. I fell after I passed the sheep shed, but when I dug out I could see a light. I heard Shep bark and then was banging on their door.

The door was flung open by a man I didn't know and I stumbled into the kitchen. Leslie's grandmother was there.

For a minute I couldn't talk. Someone pulled a chair out from the table for me.

"Why, Miss Webb," Mrs. Harper said.

"You've frozen your face," the stranger said, and he went for some snow.

"Robert Donaldson's lost," I got out.

"On a night like this!" Mrs. Harper said. She was pulling off my coat. The man came back and rubbed snow on my face. He took off my valenkis. My hands and feet ached. It's queer with Robert on my mind that for a minute I seemed sunk too deep in my own body to do more than sit there, then I came to.

"He went out of the schoolhouse. I tried to find him. I couldn't, so I came here." The pain in my feet and hands and my face was so bad it was hard to talk.

The man brought me a cup. "Here, drink this first," he said.

"Miss Webb, this is my son Warren, Leslie's father. He just got here about three hours ago. He came to surprise Leslie. He wanted to start out for the school, but when he heard the radio he give it up."

"Leslie's all right," I told him. Then I drank the hot coffee he gave me. It was what I needed.

"Do you have a telephone? Can you reach Donaldsons?"

"Mathew, you try. Maybe you can get them," Mrs. Harper said. Old Mr. Harper had been there all the time. I just hadn't noticed him before.

My hands and feet didn't ache so much now, so I could move closer to the heat, but I shielded my face. Mr. Harper turned the

177

handle of the phone and shouted into the mouthpiece. After what seemed ages he turned around to us.

"I got the operator in town. She'll get it through." It was awful to hear him shouting: "He's likely froze to death by now. Ed Donaldson's boy, yep . . ."

"How are your hands now? Do you think more snow would help?" Leslie's father asked, partly, I think, so I wouldn't hear his father.

"Oh, they're all right. I've got to get started back. There'll be enough snow on the way back to put on my hands and face," I said, trying to smile.

"You can't go back tonight," Mrs. Harper said.

"No, you stay here. I'm going," Leslie's father said.

"I can't stay. I've left seven children there alone. I've been away three hours now," I said.

He looked at me a moment. "All right. We'll get started," he said.

I had some more coffee and Mrs. Harper found some dry mittens and a scarf for me. We set out while the old man was still shouting over the phone. I was thankful to have young Mr. Harper with me. He looked very big in his old fur cap and heavy coat.

The trip back was just as bad. It seemed colder. There is no easy way in a blizzard. He had to crawl to follow the ruts as I had before. I was so tired I stumbled and fell and he had to help me up. I could have gone to sleep in a moment and never minded the cold. I must have rested more than a minute one time, because I heard him yelling at me. He helped me on my feet again and stood in front of me so I could get my breath. His body kept off the wind and snow.

"I'm okay," I said after a little.

"Lady, you've got what it takes," he said. He had to shout it to make me hear. His words warmed me, so I crawled along a little faster.

"How are your eyes?" he yelled, but I couldn't answer him in that wind.

It seemed hours before we found the school fence. We leaned against it to rest again.

"We can cut across now," he said, helping me through a drift. The snow was so deep we didn't save any time. Once I thought

I could make out a darker mass that was the teacherage, but a gust of snow blew in front of my face again and I couldn't see a thing. I couldn't make it much farther. I slogged through the snow with my eyes almost frozen shut and almost fell on Mr. Harper. He was bent over shoveling snow with his hands. I knew he had found Robert. I felt it through my body.

It took us a long time to make the little distance to the school-house, although I don't suppose it was a hundred yards. We had to lay the body down on the stoop so Mr. Harper could get the door open. We laid it gently, but I could feel the sound it made, as heavy as stone.

One lamp was out, the other turned down low. The schoolroom might have been a chapel. Three boys were lying on a blanket on the floor by the stove. Someone was wrapped in a coat in my desk chair. One child ground his teeth in his sleep; another turned restlessly. A gentle sound of breathing filled the room. It was warm and they were all safe. Raymond sat up and I spoke to him quietly.

We laid Robert's body on the floor beyond the desks. Mr. Harper struck a match and by that little flame we looked at Robert's cold round face. I touched his hand. It was gripped around a cookie. He had his mackinaw and cap and earbobs on and his galoshes.

Mr. Harper touched me on the shoulder and I realized I was crying silently.

"It's a good out for him, really," he said. "Better than having to drag through life the way he was."

I could only shake my head. Then I said the thing that haunted me: "He was so near. Why couldn't I have found him? Why couldn't I have kept my eyes on him when he was safe here? He sat right over there."

"Don't do that," Mr. Harper said almost sternly. "Have a cigarette?"

I shook my head. I went into my room to get a quilt to cover Robert.

When we had finished, Mr. Harper said:

"Get me some hot water and I'll fix a drink to stop your shivering."

I got the cups and he added some sugar and the whisky he had brought with him.

"Thanks," I said. The hot drink drove the chill from my body, but not from my mind.

I took the lamp and went from child to child. "Here's Leslie," I whispered. He had curled up in my desk chair. Mr. Harper came and stood looking down at him.

"He looks as though he'd had a hard day, doesn't he?"

"I'm glad you came," I said. "Leslie has been a little homesick, I think. He's a serious little boy, isn't he?"

His father's face changed sharply. "Yes, I know he is. He's had a hard God and a hard religion crammed down his throat since he was born. After his mother died I thought on the ranch he'd forget all that and be like other boys out here." The light from the lamp in my hands deepened the lines in his face. "You must be all in. It's only one-thirty and I'll be here to keep the fire going. Why don't you go in and lie down?"

I looked around the dark room. He seemed too big for the desks and seats except for Robert's, but I couldn't quite look at that. The benches against the wall were too narrow.

"Where will you sit?"

"Right here." He picked Leslie up in his arms and sat down in the chair holding him. "He doesn't think too much of me, but I'm glad to see him."

"You can't hold him all night."

"Don't worry about me."

I lighted the other lamp and went on into my room. Mary Cassidy lay in the middle of the bed with fat little Sigrid wedged in between her and the wall and Mike's head on her other shoulder. I put another chunk of wood in my airtight. I was wet through to the skin, so I changed all my clothes and put on the warmest things I had—some old woolen slacks Mom had made for me out of some trousers of Dad's, to do chores in, and a flannel shirt and sweater. I pulled my rocker up to the stove and closed my eyes, but the wind tore suddenly out of the stillness. All the windows rattled and the draft shook my door in its loose catch. I was thankful to be inside; I hadn't been sure I could ever make it to Harpers'.

6

I SAT hunched toward the heat until I must have fallen asleep. When I woke I was stiff. It was still dark, but the blackness had bleached to a kind of greenish-gray. The night was over. The stove was only a little warm and I reached into the woodbox for another chunk and kicked open the draft. The three children on the bed never woke even when I slammed the lid on tight again. All this I did before I remembered. Then the heaviness came back into my mind. I felt Robert out there lying on the cold floor of the schoolroom, dead. At the same moment I heard voices in the other room. I opened the door to the schoolroom without stopping to smooth my hair.

The lamp was set on the floor in the back corner. The light spread out underneath the desks and down the aisles. I could see the dirt on the floor the children had tracked in that day. Someone was kneeling on the floor beside Robert. I could hear Mr. Harper's voice and a woman's. The children were still mercifully sleeping on the blanket by the stove. I was halfway down the aisle when Mr. Harper and Mr. Donaldson stood up. Then I saw Mrs. Donaldson, her broad face red with weeping. Mr. Harper lifted the lamp and Mr. Donaldson's face stood out of the dark, so meek and thin. Their shadows sprang across the ceiling.

"I can't tell you how terribly I feel . . ." I said. My voice stuck in my throat for an instant.

"She don't look to me as though she'd hurt herself any looking for him," Mrs. Donaldson said to Mr. Harper. "I always thought from the first time I seen her she was too young."

"No, no, Minnie, that don't do no good," Mr. Donaldson said.

"I know how you must feel." I tried again. "Robert must have slipped out when the children were bringing their dishes in to me. He had brought me his dishes and I gave him those cookies. That was the last I saw of him. None of the children saw him go and they were all here together. He'd been making a paper chain for our Christmas tree."

I went over to his seat, and more by feeling than sight I found it. He had pasted seven rings together. I gave it to Mr. Donaldson. He held it in his hands as though it were precious to him.

"You know what the night was like, Mr. Donaldson," Mr. Harper said. "She went all the way to our place to get word to you. You saw the road!"

"That was nothing. The terrible thing about it is that all the time Robert was so near," I said.

Mr. Harper covered Robert's body again and he and Mr. Donaldson carried it out. Mrs. Donaldson wept loudly in her handkerchief. I held the door. I could see how Mr. Donaldson's shoulders bent under the load. Perhaps they had always bent a little under that load. It was no longer snowing and the wind was not so strong. Donaldson's sled stood down by the mail post and the deep cuts of the runners looked like trenches. His two big horses were blanketed.

While the two men were gone I wanted to say something to Mrs. Donaldson. She was sitting on the last desk weeping. Two of the boys had wakened and were staring at her.

"Mrs. Donaldson, I do feel I am to blame for Robert's death. I'll resign the teacherage if you think I should."

She looked up from her handkerchief and for a moment her face was exactly like Robert's.

"I don't care what you do, Miss Webb. That's up to the other folks if they want to trust their children to you. I haven't any more children." And she burst out crying loudly.

There wasn't anything more to say, and I had to get some breakfast started for the other children.

Sigrid and Mike woke up while I was stirring the cereal, and roused Mary Cassidy. They looked tousled and rumpled from sleeping with their clothes on, but they were in high spirits because they had slept all night in the school.

"Who's that, Teacher?" Mike asked, pointing at the icon in the corner.

I heard Mary Cassidy trying to shush him. "That's Teacher's

Jesus, Mikey," and she made the sign of the cross quickly. Sigrid stood up on my bed in her stockinged feet to look at it with wide Swedish eyes.

The children were awake in the other room too. One moment it had been quiet with a sleepy half-dark over the room, the next it seemed as though there were at least twenty children. I heard the door slam and saw that Leslie's father had come back in. I went over to the doorway. The children stared. Leslie was the last to waken. He was twisted up in his blanket, so I went over and took it off. He sat up stretching.

"Look, Leslie, look who's there!" I said in a low voice. I expected him to run to his father; instead he stood back against me.

"It's my father," he said wonderingly.

"Yes, he came to see you," I whispered. "Quick, go give him a hug."

Leslie leaned harder against me. "He drinks," he said in a low voice that was strangely unchildlike.

"He came through that terrible blizzard to see you, Leslie. Go on, quick!" I tried to push him forward, but from across the room Mr. Harper had seen it all. It would be hard not to see the quick drawing-back in Leslie's thin little body. "Children, this is Leslie's father." They stared. The older children smiled.

"I'm glad to see you all safe and sound," Mr. Harper said. He came up to Leslie and held out his hand.

Leslie put out his, but he didn't offer to go to him. It was a pitiful thing to see. I stepped a little in front of them. Mrs. Donaldson had begun to cry out loud again. Mr. Donaldson stood beside her, leaning on the window ledge.

"Children, I didn't find Robert when I went out last night. I went all the way to Harpers' for help. Leslie's father was there and he came back with me. Just a little way from the school, under the snow, we found poor Robert. He was frozen to death."

The children were so still that I heard Leslie just behind me catching his breath. Mrs. Donaldson's crying grew louder. It was a terrible sound for children to hear. I hadn't meant to say all this, but I thought the children should know. I found it hard to go on. Raymond was looking down at his feet. Mary had her arm around Mike. The room was only half light; the flame of the lamp was still bright yellow. The snow came above the middle sash of the windows on one side and all of them were frosted so we couldn't see out. Yet in the dim light each child's face seemed dreadfully clear to me. I noticed Nels's square face drawn into a heavy scowl and Raymond La Mere's, blank and stoical.

"I have some breakfast ready for you just as soon as you wash your faces and hands. Raymond, the water is warm in this pail. You help them get washed. Hurry! Mr. Donaldson is going to take you all home." I sounded as matter-of-fact as Mom could have.

Mr. Donaldson and Mrs. Donaldson and the two youngest children sat squeezed together on the front of the sled. Back of the seat on boards lay Robert's body, wrapped in blankets. Mr. Harper and the other children sat on the sides of the sled. No one spoke. Some of them wore things of mine to keep them warm. Mrs. Donaldson had my hot-water bottle at her feet. It wasn't going to be easy to get through those drifts.

"Miss Webb, I don't want you to think we hold anything against you," Mr. Donaldson said to me. "We don't know what Robert was thinking. One time at night he got up and wandered out and I didn't find him till near morning." He stopped and looked off across the snow.

"Thank you, Mr. Donaldson," was all I could say.

"Don't you want to close the school and come over to Mother's for the night, Miss Webb?" Mr. Harper asked.

"No, thank you," I said, but I dreaded staying there. I stood at the window and watched them out of sight. It didn't take long for them to disappear, the drifts were so high.

The schoolroom was a sorry place: dishes were left wherever the children had finished eating. The blankets, dirty from boots and wood ashes, were draped over desks or piled on the floor. In my bedroom the bed was a disordered heap of bedding. The two dishes in which I had cooked all the cereal I had stood on my bureau. There was the soup Robert had spilled on the desk. The lamp was still burning, but the flame was colorless now. I blew it out and sat down on the unmade bed and stared. Maybe I would try to sleep first. I leaned back and switched on the radio. The nine-fifteen broadcast was half over:

". . . one of the worst blizzards in recent years. There were seventeen lives lost in Montana and stock loss was heavy; fifteen hundred head of sheep went over a bank into Deep Creek, five hundred sheep piled up and smothered each other on Willow

Creek. A sheepherder was lost on Black Leaf. From the Prairie Butte teacherage one of eight pupils, Robert Donaldson, wandered off into the snow and was frozen to death. Near Glendive, Montana, two small children were found frozen to death in a fence corner, three hundred yards from their home. . . ."

The radio rattled on. Hearing it like that made last night seem unreal, something you heard about someone else.

I worked hard cleaning the place, and it took me all day. I washed the floor and the blackboards and the dishes. I cut out green paper trees and pasted them on the lower window panes that were still frosted solid. It was hard to make the paste stick. Late in the afternoon, I plowed through the snow to get a little jack pine that grew back of a rocky outcropping. I set it in a pail of water on Robert's desk at the back of the room. I wanted the room to look different when the children came back to it.

It was still snowing the next day. I looked out early in the morning and I knew there wouldn't be any children at school, so I turned over and covered my head with the quilts and tried to go to sleep. But I couldn't. After a while I got up and dressed and made myself some breakfast. I wished now I had left the cleaning until today.

When I went outside, the falling snow shut me into that closed space in front of the schoolhouse. I couldn't see the sky or the rimrock, let alone the mountains. My eyes kept hunting out the exact spot where we had found Robert. There were no tracks in the fresh snow, but still I knew where it must be, because we came up from the fence, a little to the left of the mailbox. I stood there figuring it all out, as though it mattered now. It seemed more horrible than it had yesterday.

To get away from that place in the snow I went back inside. But in the schoolroom my eyes kept wandering over to Robert's desk. I went into my room and closed the door. I looked at the books on my shelves and I didn't care what was in them. I just sat there staring out at the snow.

It gave me a queer feeling to realize how long I had sat there with my hands idle in my lap, like old Mrs. Maki, who sat in a rocker by the stove in her kitchen with no one bothering about her all day. What was happening to me? Mom had a funny saying in Russian that she used to mutter under her breath about anyone she thought wasted time brooding over his troubles. She said it was from the Bible and the priest in her village taught it to her. The English of it is:

"A fool folds his hands together and eats his own flesh."

I broke away from the trancelike feeling and snapped on the radio. The tinkle of a piano fell on the stillness of my room like the tinkle of breaking glass. I lay back on the bed with my hands under my head. The snow fell to the music if I looked long enough.

"Here is your Grain Market Broadcast for today." I looked at my watch, but I had forgotten to wind it. Anyway, I knew by the broadcast that it was near noon.

"Spring and Winter . . . no change. Repeating . . . Spring and Winter, no change. Durum up 2, Flax . . ."

Mom and Dad were probably listening to it, too, and Bailey and the Bardiches and the Petersons, though they had no stored grain to sell this year. I felt closer to Gotham and home hearing it. Then, as though Mom were there to tell me, I started to get my lunch.

7

I WAS filling the lamps that evening when I thought I heard
a car. It was a queer sound after the stillness of that endless day.
I had heard only a dog barking so far away it sounded like a dog
barking in his sleep. I thought someone called. I lighted the
lamps before I went to open the door to make sure I hadn't just
imagined it. Once just before dusk I had thought I heard a child
crying and ran out in the snow. But it was nothing. Then I heard
a good solid knocking on the door.

Leslie Harper's father stood there.

"Come in. How did you get through the drifts?" I asked.

"Oh, the Pony Express. That old truck will go where a snow-
plow won't; and the sled made good ruts," he said. "I tried to
get out to the sheep camp this morning and I got stuck, but the
road's all right."

"How's Leslie?"

"That's one of the reasons I came over here. I wanted to talk
to you about him. The other is that I couldn't think of you here
all alone after such an experience."

"I'm all right," I said.

"Well, I wasn't sure. I thought you might be sick after that
hike through the snow. My mother thought so, too. It's a seven-
day wonder yet that you made it."

"Oh, I'm all right," I repeated dumbly.

"You've got the place cleaned up, I see."

I looked around at it myself. It did look nice.

"How would you like to drive to town and see a movie? The
highway's open and I had no trouble getting over here from our
place. It's only ten below tonight."

I was so surprised I guess I looked blank. "Why, I . . ." I began.

"How many times have you been in to town since you took this job?"

"I haven't been to town yet, but that's not the point."

He laughed. "Well, do we go?"

"That would be heartless two days after Robert died," I said.

"No, it wouldn't be. You can't do him any good by sitting here and thinking about it."

"No, thank you. I really couldn't." I walked up the aisle and sat down in my chair behind the big desk. A schoolroom is an awkward place to have a caller. He seemed like a pupil now.

"I wish you would come. I'll get you back safely; or are you too tired?"

"No, I'm not tired," I said slowly. "I've had all day to rest up." And, suddenly, I wanted to go. I felt I shouldn't; I didn't like the idea of going out with the father of one of my pupils, but . . . "I'll be ready in a minute," I said.

"Fine. It'll do you good. I'll shovel a path for you to the car."

I heard him out there while I dressed in the woolen dress I wore away to college last year. I wore some silk stockings, but I pulled some woolen ones over them. I even carried leather gloves to wear in town. It was wonderful to be dressing to go some place. I set the lamp on the wash table and put on lipstick and brushed my hair till it lay smooth. I couldn't put the lamp any place so I could see myself in the mirror. I had to guess at how I looked.

"You're quick," he said. "We'll stop at our place and take my car. Hang on—this is a through express; no stops till we get there. Once you stop on a road like this, you're done for."

He drove the ruts as well as I could. The old truck bounced and swayed and slid. I had to hang on, all right, but not because I was scared.

"It's a long time since I've driven in snow like this!" he said once. When we got out at the Harpers' ranch he said: "We won't go in, because Leslie'll just be getting to bed and he'll be excited at seeing you. He thinks a lot of you. The only letter he wrote me was half full of you."

Mr. Harper's car was a coupé, this year's model, and had a heater and a radio. I hadn't ridden in anything but a truck since last spring in Minneapolis, with Gil.

"You look as though you like it," he said.

"I do." I laughed. The highway was covered with snow but packed smooth and hard.

"Tell me where you came from, Miss Webb."

"Gotham."

"That doesn't tell me a whole lot. My mother says you went to college last year."

"Yes, just one year. We didn't have much of a wheat crop this year."

"That sounds familiar, only it was always the price of wool with us. When you're away from here you forget how everything really depends on crops and livestock. Going back next year?"

"If I can. You live in Detroit, don't you?"

"If you call it living. I earn my living there."

"What do you do?" I asked.

"I'm in the drafting room of the Seacox Machine Company. It's the kind of a job you think you're pretty good to land when you first get it, but after six years of it you think you were a fool ever to get started in it. I'm taking a little vacation."

He was quiet for a way, with his eyes set on the road ahead. He must have felt me glance over at him, because his eyes came back from the road to me for an instant.

"Let's talk about Leslie," he said. "You said you were glad I came, for Leslie's sake. I'm not sure how much I can help him. You see, he doesn't care very much for me. But I know he likes you and I thought perhaps you could help us." His voice was almost apologetic.

"I'd like to if I can," I said.

He seemed to have trouble going on, then he said:

"I suppose you ought to know something about his unfortunate parents who have made him the way he is. We were married when I was nineteen and Gladys, Leslie's mother, was eighteen. She came from a little town on the main highway, a couple of hundred miles north of here, one of those towns with six beer halls and a couple of stores and two or three gasoline stations. Her father was a barber and her mother's father owned the grocery and the dry-goods store. Her grandfather sent her to college, where we met. She was pretty and liked a good time. I did too. We were married that June and I took her home to the ranch. Mom and Dad went in town, where they ought to be now—you saw how old

189

they are. I was bursting with ideas from school, even thought I'd change from sheep to Herefords. Of course, her home town with the one street looked like Paris next to our ranch. She stuck it all that year, but she hated it. She kept talking about going to the city. She had relatives in Detroit and she thought that was about the swellest place in the world. I didn't take her very seriously. I guess I was busy, and nuts about her, and I didn't really believe she wasn't happy. I have to tell you all this to make you see Gladys's side. My mother thinks she was a regular Jezebel. Well, she wasn't. She was a good kid in her way.

"That spring when Leslie was born she had a nurse who was in some kind of a new religious sect. The nurse stayed six weeks and by the time she left she had Gladys converted. Gladys couldn't eat this and that and she had to read her Bible every day and go to meetings in town. She tried to convert me at first, and then she gave up and I stayed home with the baby while she went to town.

"Finally, she began to have calls to go on 'missions.' She'd leave Leslie with my mother or she'd take him back to her folks. We had some real rows over that, that were finally settled by her agreeing to give them up if I'd give up the ranch and go to Detroit.

"But I don't suppose it was much better for her. We didn't know anybody there but this aunt of hers. Gladys was left alone all day in a little apartment with Leslie. She finally met up with members of the same religious sect and after that she was busy as a bee. She'd take Leslie to the meetings, and from the time he was four he had their brand of religion spooned into him.

"I got discouraged and drank occasionally, and that didn't help. She began to go out on her missions. She'd leave Leslie with her aunt, and then come back and work on him harder than ever, about God hearing everything he said and knowing everything he thought and what a lost soul I was. When Leslie and I were together he'd look at me as though I were an outcast.

"She went away on a mission finally and got pneumonia and died. I guess she didn't have much of a life, and part of it was my fault. But the worst of it is now that Leslie hasn't seen her for two years and he still talks the lingo she taught him and fights shy of me. You saw how he was at school yesterday.

"I sent him home here where I had a great time when I was a boy, and it hasn't helped any. In God's name, what can I do?"

His voice had a hopeless sound to it. "Makes a pretty story, doesn't it? I feel like a fool taking a girl to town and telling her the story of my past for fifty-four miles."

"You didn't begin until we got to Harwood," I said. "That's only thirty-four miles."

"Well, it's bad enough. What do you think?"

I said the thing I knew he wanted to hear, and yet I wondered if it were true. "I think that Leslie will get over it and forget all that, if you're here with him. It's a terrible thing for a child to know there's trouble between his parents." Then I added, almost to myself, "It stays with her."

We were in town. The street lights seemed brilliant, as they always do to me.

Once in the middle of the movie I remembered that two nights ago at this time I had been going up and down in the snow in front of the teacherage, calling Robert. The South American scenery looked as though it were cut out of paper and the actors were dull.

"What's the matter?" Mr. Harper asked.

I was startled. I wondered how he could tell that my interest had wandered from the screen. "I was just thinking about night before last."

"I wouldn't. It won't do any good," he said.

After the movie we had a steak and a green salad and rolls and coffee. I don't know when anything had tasted so good. After those weeks of canned meats and vegetables, the little pieces of young green onions made me think about the garden at home. The tomatoes were hothouse, I suppose, but they were ruby-red. I don't wonder that they call them love apples.

"You were hungry!" Mr. Harper laughed.

"It tasted awfully good."

He dropped a nickel in the slot and the canned jangle of music burst out. It seemed a little like Pop's Place.

"Do you like to dance?"

"I love it," I said.

"How about going some place where we can dance now?"

"Not tonight. I have school tomorrow."

"Sometime before I go?"

"Perhaps." But I was glad he had asked me.

The Harpers' ranch was dark except for a single light in the kitchen.

"I'm sorry to take you out of your way," I said.

"It's kind o' fun. After driving in the city so steadily I'm glad to find I can still drive back country roads in the winter."

We changed to the old truck with the flapping side curtains; it wasn't much better than an open car. The cold came up from the seat through my coat and the wind slid under the curtains. Mr. Harper went back into the barn for an old bearskin rug and covered me up with it, but I believe I was colder than the other night.

We didn't talk much on the way home. On this road again, the night of the blizzard all came back to me so strongly, as though it had been waiting for me. All day I had fought to keep from thinking of it. Now I remembered again the cold of Robert's body and the helpless feeling of the dark and the sting of the snow in my mouth. I lost the feeling of the lights and the music and warmth of the evening as though they were a string of beads I had dropped in the snow.

Mr. Harper went with me to the door of the teacherage. He must have felt my silence because he said:

"Don't be sorry you went. You have your own life, you know. Can I stir up your fire for you?"

I shook my head. "No, thank you." I didn't want to talk any more.

I found something out that night: something that made me feel closer to Mom. A thing doesn't hurt you so much if you take it to you as it does when you keep pushing it away. All day I had tried to keep my mind full of other things, but underneath I knew I could have saved Robert if I had only watched him more closely. Then I'd try to push that thought away. That night, lying wide-awake in bed, I stopped trying.

I remembered Mom telling me about her mother and father's death, when we weeded the beets in the garden. I could see in her face that she remembered it all as though it had just happened and it hurt her all over again, but I felt she wasn't afraid to remember it. I wouldn't be afraid of this; it was a time I had to remember; it was a part of my life.

8

THE next morning I could hardly wait to see the children. I had a panicky feeling that they might not come. Perhaps their families wouldn't want to trust me with them. I hadn't really wanted to teach before; it was just a stopgap. But now I wanted to teach here. The children had driven away with such solemn faces, and I wanted to see them singing or laughing or listening to a story again.

I was ready for school so early I had a long time to wait. I sat at my desk as I had sat the first day of school. The room was just the same as it had been that first day, and yet everything was different. Now I knew the children who belonged in these seats, even the oversize seat at the end of the first row. I knew the color of Raymond's galluses that held up his made-over trousers and how he could snap his fingers, and Mary Cassidy's hair ribbons and Mike's giggle and how painfully Nels Thorson went at arithmetic.

The schoolroom was quiet and orderly and empty, but full at the same time. Lincoln looked out through the windows at the snow-covered butte. The patent-medicine calendar hung on the back wall. I glanced at the calendar and then I wrote on the board, as I always did, "Today is December 4, 1941." A date looks so innocent until you know what can happen on that date.

I picked up the broom and threw a jacket over my shoulders and went out to sweep the front stoop, but really I went to watch for the children. It was starting to snow again—a fine soft snow powdered the air—but there was no wind. The very air seemed gentle. I thought of the snow sifting down on Robert's grave if they buried him today.

The La Mere boys came first, riding double on the old horse

they called Tobacco. I waved to them and they waved back. Leslie Harper's father brought the others in the Pony Express. Sigrid Thorson slid out of the end of the little truck before the others and came running to me with a big box in her arms.

"Mother sent you a cake, Miss Webb," she shouted eagerly. Mary Cassidy brought a jar of baked beans.

"Mamma said she guessed we must have eaten you out of house and home, Miss Webb."

I saw the children glance quickly, almost surreptitiously, at Robert's desk as they came in, and then their eyes came back a second time with eagerness because of the little tree.

"We're going to trim our tree this year in memory of Robert," I said. "Every day that we get through our work in good time we'll make something for it."

We raised the flag this morning in the gently falling snow. The children laughed as the snow tickled their faces and made the Cassidys' and La Meres' black hair gray. We sang Christmas carols at noon and talked about our Christmas entertainment for the parents. And then, because it was bound to, I suppose, the conversation slipped around to Robert.

"They took him on the train back to Illinois," Nels Thorson said. "That's where the Donaldsons come from. I wish I hadn't pinged him with my beebee gun last fall," he said.

"Do you think God'll take him home, Miss Webb?" Leslie asked.

"I'm sure he will," I said.

The mailman came through in the afternoon. He stopped to leave my mail with a great honking and hand-waving. I went out to get the mail because I thought he might have a message for me, but he only wanted to talk.

"Too bad about that boy," he said as he handed me a letter from Mom.

"Yes."

"It's a miracle to me you didn't all freeze; there was a mailman on the Higgins route, Jed Larson, froze to death in a snowbank. I knew him well, often used to see him in town. Mrs. Donaldson was saying in town you should have kept closer watch on Robert. 'Why, say,' I sez to her, 'she oughter get the Carnegie medal for that trip to Harpers'.' I didn't tell her I was glad you saved the bright ones, but I sure was."

Mom wrote: "*Your Father want to see you. He says you are far away as last year in Minnesota. He is still down sick. Can you come home Saturday. I meet you in Clark City. Anna.*" Mom always signed her name that way, even to me.

When the children left that day I got out the letter and read it again and I decided to go home. The bus went past the highway about 10:30. If I started early enough I could walk the six miles to the highway easily.

It was a good feeling to lock the teacherage and know that I'd be away overnight. I was on the road by seven Saturday morning. I wore Mom's valenkis; they didn't make my feet look any smaller, but they kept them warm. I didn't carry anything with me. I had old clothes at home. The sky was still dark and the snow stood out white, as though the two were wrong side around, the sky where the ground should be. The gentleness had given way to cold again.

I reached Harpers' place by eight. Even before I got to their gate I could see a man moving around there. He was too big and straight for old Mr. Harper. I moved over to the outside rut of the road and made up my mind to go by quietly. We had told each other a lot about each other for a first evening's visit. I thought it would make me feel strange and half-embarrassed to talk to him again.

But Warren Harper saw me and came out to the road. The country is bare enough so you can see a person a mile away. He stood at his corral gate as though he were uncertain, then I guess he remembered my black bandanna with the red fringes.

"Hello, Miss Webb," he said as soon as I was near enough.

"Hello," I said. "The snow's packed down good." But I kept right on walking.

"Where are you going?"

"Home for the week end. I can't stop," I said, and then thought that he hadn't asked me to.

He leaned comfortably on the top rail of the fence as though it were summer. "Going to walk all the way to Gotham?"

"Oh, no, I'm catching the bus on the highway."

"Six miles, as cold as it is today! What do you want to do, freeze your face again?"

"It isn't bad when you're walking. Father's sick. I wanted to go home this week end."

"I can see how you might anyway. Come on in a minute and I'll drive you home."

Leslie and Mrs. Harper were not up yet. Only Mr. Harper was in the kitchen.

"Father, I'm going to town to put in a claim for the insurance on those sheep," Warren said. "We lost about five hundred in that blizzard," he told me. I knew what such a loss meant to a sheep rancher.

We talked about Leslie most of the way in.

"He must have been devoted to his mother," I said.

"Yes, he was. She was little and dark and laughed easily, and cried easily, too. He saw her do plenty of both. He heard from her that the ranch was the last place on earth to live and how the wind blew and how cold it got. He's made up his mind not to like it because she didn't."

Then Mr. Harper seemed lost in his own thoughts. I didn't interrupt him. The day was as light then as it was going to be. The sky made me think of a piece of iron covered over with frost.

"I went over to Los Angeles once to see Gladys after she'd been gone over a month on one of her missions," Mr. Harper said abruptly. "I felt so sorry for Leslie I thought I'd see if we couldn't patch things up again. She was living with a man, this preacher fellow. I couldn't tell Leslie a thing like that about his mother even if he'd understood it. So I came back and told him she had died. She did die a year and a half later.

"When I told Leslie that she wouldn't ever come back he didn't cry, just looked at me, and then he said, 'You didn't love her.' That was something for a six-year-old child, wasn't it?"

"That was hard," I murmured. I wanted to say I knew a little how Leslie had felt. I could have told him about Mom and Dad, but that was too deep a part of me.

Warren Harper lit a cigarette and smiled at me. "Did you ever know such a guy? Known you two days and pours out his soul. Well, don't worry, I won't say a word about myself or my child on the way home."

"On the way home?"

"I'd like to come down Sunday afternoon and get you."

"But that's eighty-five miles."

He shrugged. "I've gone a lot farther for less reason."

I made him let me out where our road turns off the highway.

"You can meet Mom and Dad Sunday, if you come. I don't know how Dad is," I told him.

"I'll be here Sunday. You can count on it."

The road wasn't shoveled and there were no ruts through the snow. Dad must have been sick all week. I tried to see the house as I had that day with Gil, unpainted clapboards and all, but I couldn't; it looked good to me. I saw the kitchen window and the gray-white bark of the cottonwood above the coulee and I began to run through the snow.

Mom heard me call and came to look out the window. We could never break Mom of her habit of looking out first when someone knocked. But it was good to see her face break into a smile when she saw me.

"Yeléna!"

"Hello, Mom!"

"We gave you up when we don't get no letter and then we hear the radio."

"Ellen!" Dad called from the other room.

"Oh, Dad, you're still laid up!"

"I'm over this bout. I'm just waiting for the weather to get human and I'll be out." Dad was dressed, but he wore his sweater and bedroom slippers and he looked sick.

I sat down on the couch and Mom brought up a chair. They had set up the heater here in the front room.

"Yeléna, that boy, was he the big one?" Mom asked right away. "Your father was reading the paper and I am setting my bread dough. I wasn't listening much, then I hear 'Prairie Butte teacherage.' I come quick to listen . . ." I'd forgotten how Mom told things. Dad always listened impatiently because she told so many details and then, as usual, he interrupted her.

"I should never have let you go to that place," Dad grumbled. "Do you remember, I asked Sunday when we were there how far you'd have to go for help? Anna asked why you'd need any," Dad finished triumphantly.

Mom made a business of picking up my coat and helped me off with my valenkis. Her face was sulky at being in the wrong. They always argued like this in the winter. Then Dad said:

"It must have been a terrible experience! That was the boy who wasn't quite bright, wasn't it?"

"Yes. It seemed awful that he was so near all the time. I don't see how I missed him, because I hunted back and forth and called and called."

"It was bad storm," Mom said. "I could lose myself going to the barn, almost."

"How did the family take it?" Dad asked.

"His mother blamed me; the father was very kind."

Mom nodded her head. "You can't tell about children. You have to keep your eye on them."

"That boy wasn't bright anyway," Dad said crossly.

My room had been shut off since cold weather. It was cold in there and looked bare without the icon in the corner. The lipstick in my bureau drawer was as stiff and cold as though it had been frozen. I found some green beads I used to wear last year and fastened them around my neck. They were like ice. I opened the drawers and looked in. In the bottom drawer was Gil's picture staring up at me.

"Yeléna, you catch cold in there. Hurry out!" Mom called. I shut the drawer quickly before I had time to look at Gil. But I wished suddenly that I hadn't written that letter. I felt strange here at home with Mom and Dad. I could see so much better now what Gil had felt.

It was better that evening eating supper in the kitchen. Everything seemed so bright in the electric light after my lamps. We had fresh meat and Mom's fresh bread. When we were drinking our coffee, Dad took a letter from his sweater pocket with such deliberateness I knew he meant me to notice. Mom left her coffee and started clearing off the dishes.

"Your Aunt Eunice had occasion to write me last week about some business in connection with our father's house," Dad said. "Several years ago she had to place a mortgage on the house in order to pay a hospital bill. The man who held the mortgage, an old friend of my father's, has died, and his son wants to foreclose. Eunice says he wants the house for himself. She writes to ask if I could help her."

"You have no good from it," Mom put in.

Dad seemed not to notice. "Your aunt wants to keep the house. She has lived there all her life. It has my grandfather's name plate on the door, 'Benjamin Webb, Esquire.' I had to polish it when I was a youngster, with vinegar and salt, I remember." Dad pulled a snapshot out of the envelope and handed it to me. "Your aunt enclosed a picture of it."

I had never seen it and yet when I looked at the picture, the house was so exactly as I knew it must be that it was like recognizing a place I knew well. Only I hadn't known there was an iron grill along the porch or that there was a big bush in the front yard next to the fence.

"What's that bush, Dad?"

"That's a smoke bush, kind of a pink feathery stuff. You could pull it off in your fingers and blow it. My mother was very partial to it," Dad said.

I turned the picture over. On the back was written "I enclose this picture in case you have forgotten what the old place looks like." The writing was so light it was surprising that the words should have such barbs. It wasn't a house anyone would forget. It stood very square with two big windows on either side of the front door, four windows across the second story, and a dormer on the third. The house was built of wider clapboards than I had ever seen, and each window had blinds. I had never seen blinds on a house before.

"Eunice writes that she could perhaps sell the house for a good price. Summer people are glad to pick up a house in Vermont nowadays, but she wants to live in it."

Mom had been picking up the dishes. "If she can't pay, she better sell," she said.

There was a long hard silence in the kitchen, the kind I knew well. I looked at Mom's face set so sullenly and at Dad's, cold and hurt.

"Do you think you'd like to go back there sometime, Ellen?" Dad asked.

"Oh, I'd love to go back and see it."

Mom stood by the table and stirred her cold coffee. "I want no part in it," she said.

"You have no part in this, Anna. This was my life before I ever met you. This is for me to decide." I had never seen him so stern. Mom went back over to the sink. Her face was dark and thick. I knew she minded Dad's talking like that before me. Dad turned to me and went on in a quiet voice:

"After all, Eunice is my only sister. I should hate to see her having to move out of the house. She hasn't had too much out of life. The young fellow she expected to marry was killed in France early in the war. She never went with anyone else as far as I know. I can't forget how she cried the day I went away to the Army. I told her I'd be back, but I suppose to her I never really did come back. She went on taking care of Mother and working hard, and after Mother died she went on alone."

"You help with funeral!" Mom muttered. But Dad seemed to have lost sight of Mom and me and to be back in Vermont. It had never occurred to me before that he might still love this faraway sister. She had never seemed very real to me.

"This is a bad year for ready cash. She needs five hundred dollars by the end of the week. I know she tried to raise it herself first." Dad was really talking to himself. "I suppose she thinks I'm well off. To people back there a rancher in Montana sounds . . . pretty prosperous." I could see that Dad's pride was in this, too.

"How do you think you get five hunderd dollar?" Mom asked from the sink. Her voice was sly, almost sneering.

"I thought I'd go to town Monday and get a loan. I won't have any trouble. Everything I own is paid for."

I went over to get a dishtowel back of the stove. For an instant a kind of anger flashed up in my mind like pan grease that's caught fire. He could talk about a loan for his sister and how easy it would be, but he didn't get a loan to send me back to college. I forgot for the moment that Dad had been sick, and I hadn't really asked him.

"You won't put loan on this ranch," Mom said, looking at Dad across the little kitchen. "She don't mind to borrow money. Let her borrow some more." I held my breath for what Dad would say next.

"That's right, Anna, I put the ranch in your name, didn't I?" His tone was quiet and cold. "I told you you'd earned it, you'd worked so hard."

I glanced at Mom and her eyes seemed to me to gleam under her dark brows.

"Don't worry, I won't put no loan on the ranch," Dad said, mimicking Mom's grammar. "I can raise the five hundred dollars on the combine!"

I think I have never seen Mom move so swiftly. She came over and sat down at the table. "Don't do that, Ben!" Fear made her voice heavier. I knew how she loved the combine.

"I won't see my sister having to sell her house, Anna," Dad said. "That's something I couldn't do."

"What if we get no crop next year?" Mom said.

"Maybe we'll have a bumper crop!" Dad said. "Anyway, Anna, I'm going to raise that money and send it to Eunice."

I was so used to thinking of Dad as sick or tired and Mom as strong, it was strange now to see Mom frightened and angry and feel Dad's strength. Maybe it was because he was sorry for her that he said gently:

"Look, Anna . . ."

"I don't want to hear no more," Mom said like an angry child. "You are big fool, Ben Webb, to make debt on the combine." She slammed the kettles together as she put them away in the cupboard under the sink.

I picked up the snapshot on the table and studied it again, just to be doing something

"Eunice is honest about it. She writes that she could sell the house for a good price." Dad took out a cigarette and went over to the stove for a match. "It must've been hard for her to write and ask me," he said as the match flared out in his hand.

I saw Mom watching Dad as he got out a pad of paper and pen and ink and sat at the kitchen table writing. I finished drying the dishes, and all the time we could hear the pen scratching across the paper. When Dad was through he folded the paper and put it in the envelope and did not seal it. We didn't know what he wrote, but we knew he was going to send the money.

Mom couldn't seem to settle down. She opened the door to my room so the warm air could go in there and brought some flannel pyjamas of mine that were cold from lying in the drawer and hung them behind the stove, then she set the table for breakfast with a noisy clatter of the knives and forks. I wondered why I had come home.

It's a terrible thing the way a child can sit in judgment on her parents without their knowing it.

We had to leave our bedroom doors open that night to keep warm. I lay in bed and heard no least murmur of voices from the other room. They had gone to bed in silence, Mom in anger. I couldn't sleep. About midnight I closed my door and pushed up my window to the cold. I would be glad to be back in the teacher-age.

I was outside all the next morning. It was a bright, clear day. The roof of the house and the long side of the barn laid a bluish shadow on the snow, and the dogwood bush in the coulee was bright-red above the snow, and the willows were as yellow and shining as a new-varnished floor. The strips of fallow ground and the strips of stubble were covered equally by the snow, and the blue sky looked as bright and warm as a blue wool afghan. Way off, the mountains of the Main Range were blue, streaked with white, and looked thin-edged against the sky. It was six below zero on the barn thermometer, but Mom had only a sweater over her shoulders and I had only a leather jacket. The sun made us feel warm, I guess, and the brightness made us a little giddy. This morning I knew why I had come home. I loved this place! The night's trouble was shut in the house.

Mom showed me the turkeys.

"Thirty-eight orders already and the meat man take what I got left. Three cents more a pound I get this year. Pretty good, *Yólochka?*" Mom said, looking at me with a wide smile.

We walked over to the chicken house. I had something I wanted to tell her.

"Mom," I began, "at first I couldn't bear to think about Robert. I kept trying not to remember things . . . you know. Then I thought how you used to tell me about the killing of your mother and father in Russia and I could tell by your eyes how you could see it all over again. So I stopped pushing Robert's death out of my mind. I was to blame, and I just looked right at it. It hurts but not the same way. . . ." I looked at Mom and found her eyes big and dark on my face.

"Sure, is no good to hide your eyes," Mom said.

We were on our way back to the house and I was feeling very close to Mom when I said:

"Don't be that way about Dad's helping his sister. He has to do it."

"We got to think of ourselves and you, Yeléna. We work hard for what we got." She looked out past the barn to the snow-covered wheat fields. "She don't work so hard!" she grumbled.

We might have walked at either end of a strip of wheat—we were no closer together than that, after all.

202

Dad took me out to see the pigs and the two horses we kept in the barn. It was cold enough so their breath was white and thick in the air, pretty plumes that meant life in the coldness.

"Should you be out here in the cold, Dad?" I asked.

"Oh, I don't think it makes much difference. I seem to get these bad colds in the winter whatever I do. Your mother babies me like a child."

It was never so easy to be quiet with Dad as with Mom. I think he was more comfortable talking.

"It's pretty quiet around here without you, Ellen. It seems as though you're farther away over there at Prairie Butte than you were last winter."

I laughed. "Eighty-five miles isn't very far. When the weather's better you can drive over often, or I can catch a ride back."

Dad stopped in the shed where the combine was. Cold bright bars of light came through the loose boards in back of the shed, but even with the front door propped open it was shadowy in there. The combine looked bigger than it was.

"I want to get the model number off this thing," Dad said, bringing out a pencil and an envelope.

I laid my hand on the floor of the combine. It was as icy-cold as it had been blistering-hot last summer. When I was younger I used to pretend it was an airplane standing in our own private hangar.

"I don't know what was the matter with me, Ellen, that I didn't raise some money on this before for you." Dad's voice was muffled, but I could feel the apologetic note in it. "I guess I was so wrapped up in my own misery about that time . . ."

"Oh, Dad, this didn't hurt me any. I can go back next fall." It was easy to be generous now.

"Your mother can't understand how I feel about helping your Aunt Eunice, Ellen." I felt Dad expected me to understand. "I should have managed better back in the beginning with your mother and my family. There should have been some way . . ."

"Do you and Aunt Eunice look alike, Dad?" I asked, partly because I was trying to see her, partly because Dad seemed so sad.

"No, I don't think so. She was dark. I used to think she was the prettiest girl in town. I brought her back a samovar from Russia, but I don't suppose she ever used it."

"Did she . . . was she nice to Mom in the beginning?"

"I think she meant to be. They were so different, of course."

We were so quiet for a minute that I heard Mom calling from the house. I went outside and Mom was standing in the kitchen doorway. Her face was alive and excited.

"Ben, Ellen, come up here, quick!" she called.

She sounded so urgent we ran. Mom had the radio blaring. She always turned it up too high. We couldn't hear it at first for the noise of it.

"It's war!" Mom said as soon as we got to the porch, and the way she said it sent shivers down my back. "The Japs come over Pearl Harbor and bomb it."

Mom stood with her hands on her hips. She looked like one of the figures you see in pictures of the crowds in Russia. She seemed somehow more foreign. I saw her more clearly than I took in the news.

Dad stood by the radio, listening to every word.

"We can't do anything else," he said. His face wasn't sick or pale, now. I could see how he had gone to war before. Neither Dad nor Mom was thinking about themselves or me. "It's time we were in!"

Dad was so excited I felt ashamed that I was so quiet. I had never heard war declared before; I had only read about it. Mom sat down on the couch, listening to every word. Her eyes flashed, but she didn't say anything.

"This'll make the last war look like a neighborhood fight," Dad said.

It was two o'clock before we sat down to dinner. All that time the radio had been blaring. Mom mashed the potatoes and peeled the beets with that listening look on her face. Dad wouldn't stir until the war news was over. He was so excited he wasn't like himself. I had never really known him before, I felt. I could see how he must have been at Gil's age.

Mom laughed suddenly. "Ben, you remember how you was so sick you didn't know there was armistice?"

Dad nodded. "I couldn't believe it. I thought you were all fooling."

"Remember, you said, 'Give me a kiss, then.' An' the Army doctor he laugh and say, 'Go on, kiss him, Anna!'"

"Sure, I remember," Dad said.

"Yeléna, watch out or your Dad go off to war again!" Mom

joked. She gave him a little slap on the shoulder. All their coldness of last night was gone.

I felt a kind of resentment. They were fools. The last war was to blame for Dad's ill-health ever since, it was to blame for his marrying Mom and all their bitterness and hatred and trouble. I couldn't understand them. They didn't even seem to notice that I was quiet.

After a while Dad said, "Well, wheat will go up."

"Just for little," Mom said. "Wars are bad after."

But Dad wasn't listening. He had gone over to sit by the radio again to eat his dessert. I looked at him.

"Dad, I'd think you'd feel all you did in the last war was wasted. I'd think all the men who were crippled and came back sick like you would feel bitter about another war." I had to say it.

"What was that, Ellen?" Dad turned down the radio a little so he could hear me, but they were giving some details of the catastrophe at Pearl Harbor; he turned it up again and bent nearer to hear without waiting for me to repeat what I had said.

Warren Harper came just after dinner. He and Dad started in on the war.

"This makes my mind up for me; I'm going into the Army. I'm twenty-seven and I have only one child. It looks as though they'd need plenty of men."

"Well, you know, I was in the last war," Dad began, "and . . ." I went into the other room as though I had something to pack. I couldn't stand it to hear Dad go over all that again. Mom stood by as though she were interested in every word. I wished I were not going back with Warren Harper. I wished I were driving back alone. I had nothing to take, so I picked up the book of poems. Dad wouldn't do anything but listen to the war news from now on anyway.

"Didn't I tell you I'd come? You didn't believe it, though, did you?" Mr. Harper asked, smiling, as we drove out on the highway.

"I didn't do anything about the bus, though," I said.

"Have a good time?"

"I was glad to see them and the place," I said cautiously.

"They're an interesting pair. Your dad's certainly excited about the war, isn't he?"

"How's Leslie?" I asked, to turn the talk from the war.

"Oh, I don't know. I brought him a knife back from town and he thanked me politely enough, but he didn't holler for joy like any ordinary boy would. I took him out to look at the stars last night when I got home. They were as clear as you'd ever want to see. I thought he'd like to learn the name of the constellations, but he got cold and shivered and said he wanted to go in."

"He probably was cold. Take him out when it's warmer. In the summer I used to like to lie on the hill back of our house and look at the stars."

"I won't be here by then. I'll be in the Army. Let's stop and do the town," he said as we drove down the main street.

"This is something like it," he exclaimed as the waiter set down our drinks. "Last night I had a glass of beer with a hamburger on my way home. Then when I was out looking at the stars with Leslie I picked him up to carry him over a place where the snow was deep. He said, 'Dad, you've been drinking!' as though I'd broken all the Ten Commandments. I didn't tell you that part, but you can see how the star expedition wouldn't be very successful. I'm afraid he'll never do anything but dislike me. It's just as well for him that I'm going into the Army. He's better off without me." Mr. Harper ordered another drink.

"That's not so," I said quietly. "Give him more time. You don't have any idea how the life of his mother and father affects a child."

I had never meant to tell anyone about Ben Webb and Anna Petrovna, but I told Warren Harper, whom I hardly knew. He sat holding his tall glass in his hands, his eyes very bright and sympathetic, his face a little flushed and his hair rumpled from the way he ran his hand over it. I guess I told him because I had just been home and it had all hit me so hard, and because of Leslie. I didn't know whether he took in all I said or not, but he listened. His eyes hardly left my face. I told him about Gil's leaving and how I came home and overheard Mom and Dad. I didn't seem to mind his knowing about Gil.

"That was pretty thick," he said. "I suppose Leslie overheard us plenty. No wonder a kid gets to hate his parents."

"Oh, I don't hate Mom and Dad. If anything, I hate . . . I guess I hate the war. Things wouldn't have happened just this way except for the last war. And now there's another war."

"It's not the war. People do the damnedest things without wars," he said thickly.

I couldn't get him to leave before eight o'clock. We had sat there over three hours. When we left I made him let me drive. He was quiet so long I thought he must have fallen asleep, but he was wide-awake, staring out at the road ahead of us. I liked driving, but it's lonely with someone so sunk in his own thoughts. The world was black and white and cold. There was nothing soft or indistinct or tender about the night.

I drove all the way to the teacherage and turned the car around. He had spoken only once; that was when I got out of the rut and then landed back in it.

"Not bad!" he said.

"I hope you get home all right," I said when I got out of the car. "And I don't know that I blame Leslie," I added brutally, but partly because I was annoyed that I had talked so much.

He didn't say a word. The car stood there for a few minutes, then I heard him driving off. The most he could do was to run in a snowbank and have to walk home.

9

I LIKED waking in my room at the teacherage. Everything was just as I had left it. I looked across at Prairie Butte as though it were an old friend. I hadn't stopped to make a fire in the schoolroom stove last night, so I built one before I was dressed, and opened all the drafts. I went over and wrote on the board "This is December 8, 1941."

The La Mere boys came first, kicking their old horse into a gallop. Francis waited to tie the horse, but Raymond rushed in ahead to say:

"Gee, Miss Webb, I'm fourteen. I might get in the war yet, if it lasts long enough."

I heard Francis and Nels arguing outside before they came in.

"My dad was in the last war, I guess he knows," Nels declared.

"Miss Webb, we're going to beat them Germans and Japs now, ain't we?" Mike Cassidy asked me, his blue eyes shining.

Leslie Harper was late. We were lined up at attention saluting the flag when I saw him running along the road. He slipped into his place while we were singing "Oh, say can you see . . ." Every eye this morning was fixed on the flag floating at the top of the flagpole, very bright against the white of the wide snowy plain. I wondered if the sheepherder saw it there, flying in a kind of no man's land between the butte and the rimrock.

When we broke up to go into school, Leslie came up to me anxiously. His thin face had bluish shadows under his eyes, and he was still out of breath from running.

"Miss Webb, I'm sorry I'm late. I had to walk this morning. My dad wanted to take me but I wouldn't let him."

"I see, Leslie. But if you're late, you'll have to stay after school, you know."

"Oh, yes, I know," he said almost proudly, as though he welcomed the penalty. There was a hardness back of Leslie's delicate little face that wasn't like a child's.

Whatever subject we studied that day came back to the war. At noon we ate our lunch with the war news coming over the radio. Two of the boys amused themselves by drawing Japanese and American airplanes in battle on the blackboard.

I noticed Leslie wasn't eating any lunch.

"Please, Miss Webb, I don't feel good. I'd rather just drink some water," he insisted when I asked him about it.

"How about a cup of hot soup, Leslie?" But he was firm.

The third grade was doing multiplication when I saw Leslie slide off his seat onto the floor.

"Jiminy, Miss Webb, he's fainted!" Mary Cassidy said in a hoarse excited whisper.

I picked him up and carried him into my room and laid him on my bed. When I put cold water on his face, he opened his troubled gray eyes with a little moan. I put the soup on to heat and left him there while I gave the others something to do. But when I took the soup to him he turned away his face.

"Please, no, Miss Webb, I can't. I promised God I wouldn't."

"Leslie, what is this business of not eating and bringing God into it?" I asked a little sternly.

He sat up cross-legged on my bed with very bright eyes. "Promise you won't tell, Miss Webb?" he asked dramatically.

"No. I won't tell," I said. He leaned a little forward and spoke in a whisper.

"Miss Webb, my father went to town yesterday and when he came back he'd been drinking. I promised God I wouldn't eat until he promised to stop." His face shone with an unhealthy glow.

I had to leave Leslie until school was dismissed, then I came back and sat down beside him.

"Leslie, do you really want to help your father?"

He nodded.

"Well, you won't do it this way."

"But his soul is lost, Miss Webb, unless he repents."

I took a long look out the window at the patient face of the butte and the blue sky.

"You don't know about things like that. You're only a little boy. Even your mother didn't know. God wants you to love your father. He doesn't want you to try to teach him." Leslie's solemn eyes hung on my face. I felt uncomfortable. "You sit up now and drink this soup and then go home and don't say anything about this morning to your father."

"But I can't eat. I promised." He buried his head in the pillow.

Even Mom could be no more stubborn than this. I left Leslie there by himself and went outside. I took the shovel and cleared wider paths to the mailbox and the cistern. At four o'clock the western sun was weakening in strength, trading its brave yellow for tinsel pink and lavender that colored the sky but had no warmth. The empty flagpole no longer made a zigzag shadow on the tumbled snow of the playground. The snowman the boys had made and perched on one of the swings had a rakish lurch. Someone had taken a blackboard eraser and inserted it in the wide face for lips. The nose was a stub of wiener from someone's lunch and the eyes were two pieces of charcoal from the stove. I traipsed way across to the only jack pine that grew near the teacherage and broke off a bunch of pine needles to use as mustache and a fringe of hair. I glanced up toward the window of my bedroom and saw a quick movement at the window. Leslie had been watching me.

"Come on and help me build a fort," I called to him. I went ahead without waiting for him, not knowing just what I'd do next. When I heard the door open I didn't look up. "If we get a big enough wall we can have a snowball fight tomorrow noon," I said, pushing up the snow.

He came over slowly and stood a minute watching me. I felt his eyes on me, but I was too busy to look at him. Then he started in. I wondered how he could work so hard when he had had no lunch. We made a wall of snow that stretched about seven feet from the flagpole toward the school. I stood up straight to look at it.

"Gee, lookit how long it is, Miss Webb!" Leslie called. His clear high voice carried way across the empty plain. I threw a snowball at him that broke into fluff on his cap, and ducked down behind the wall. He gave a shrill little laugh that echoed against the side of the schoolhouse.

"Watch out!" he called and threw, but the snowball hit the steps of the porch. I sent one back that struck the snow wall.

"I'm sending that one right back at you, Miss Webb!"

"I've got to get some ammunition ahead," I said, kneeling behind the wall to make a few snowballs. When I stood up I saw Leslie's father leaning on the mailbox post watching us.

"Hello," I called.

"Hello," he answered. Leslie saw him and stopped making snowballs.

"May I play?" Mr. Harper asked.

Leslie didn't look up. His lower lip set against his upper.

"Sure," I said.

"I shan't," Leslie answered. "I'm going home now." He started off down the road, a dogged, stubborn little boy.

"Well, I'll be going on home too." Warren Harper smiled and his whole face gentled. "What would you do?"

It was almost dusk, a cold wintry grayness that made it easy to speak out.

"I'm not sure, but you might try giving up drinking for a while," I suggested. "He's so lonely and really frightened of his hate. It separates him from the rest of the children, too." Then I added, "Hate always isolates you, doesn't it?"

"Well, thanks. I wish I were sure it would help."

The country is so wide here at the teacherage a single human being tramping along the road looks small and insignificant. Warren Harper was a tall man, six feet at least, but his shoulders drooped a little. The growing dark made his hat and clothes one color as he went along the road. I felt a kind of pity for him, going to try to make friends with his own son.

The next morning Leslie came in with the Cassidys. I saw his green tin lunch box with the others on the bench by the door. I knew each one's lunch box now. The blue one with the flowers almost scratched off was Mary's. The black one with the jammed corner used to belong to old Mike Cassidy when he worked in the smelter. Old Mike was lamed in an accident, so he had come out to farm the homestead he'd taken when he first came to Montana. I missed the round red box that used to be Robert Donaldson's.

Leslie looked more rested. He waved his hand frantically in history class. I saw him shoot a paper wad at Sigrid's back and held my tongue.

"When you finish your lunch you can have a snowball fight over my snow wall," I promised them.

"Who built the wall, Miss Webb? It's a good one," Francis asked.

"Leslie helped me after he got through staying after school."

"I bet Mr. Harper helped," Mary piped out. I looked at her quickly.

"No, it was all finished when he came by for Leslie," I said, but I saw Mary roll her eyes at Nels.

Leslie opened his lunch box and ate as eagerly as any of them.

We practiced for the Christmas play in between classes. It was snowing again today, "a flour-sifter kind of snow" Mary Cassidy called it.

"No, that's Aunt Rhody picking her old white geese," Nels said.

After school the children stayed a little later to practice the carols. I sat on one of the desks nearest the stove and the children perched like sparrows near by.

"Isn't it Christmasy, Miss Webb?" Leslie said, hugging his knees, his eyes wide and clear. I nodded and sounded my tuning fork for "O Little Town of Bethlehem." I caught Sigrid's rounded childish tones and Raymond's, newly turned to bass. Mary Cassidy sang with a sweet swinging rhythm that carried all the others.

I looked beyond them out the windows where the sky and the snow were merging into one soft gray light. I almost held my breath. I had the feeling I had had long ago when we had come home from the concert and I had climbed up on the gatepost and heard Mom singing as she covered the tomato plants. It was a feeling of happiness.

I sat there watching them put on their wraps to go: Francis struggling with that rusted zipper on his jacket, Sigrid coming to have her long red scarf wound around her cap and over her mouth, Raymond rushing out as always bareheaded in his thin leather jacket yet never seeming to catch cold. These things had come to be so familiar that they were dear to me.

Leslie came up when he was ready to go. "Miss Webb," he said in a low voice, "Dad said he'd try. He says he don't like making promises but he means just the same thing by it." Leslie's eyes shone with a triumphant gleam that broke the spell for me.

"I'm glad, Leslie," I said. I started to say something more, that if he would just let his father feel that he loved him it would help more, but I didn't. What did I know about love? I was born of unlove. I couldn't hold Gil's love. I didn't watch the children go off as I usually did, but began straightening up the schoolroom. The snow beyond the windows seemed tiresome and endless to me now.

Saturday morning I was mopping the schoolroom floor—I had on jeans and an old shirt and my hair hung down every which way. I was singing the Russian hymn I know, one that Mom used to sing. I don't think it was meant to be sung to work, but it fitted the thrust of my mop. I heard a whistle and my name called out. I stepped over my mop pail and opened the door. Leslie and his father stood there with skis in their arms.

"Hello," Warren said. "We brought a pair for you. Come on and help me teach Leslie."

"I don't know how either."

"Fine! We'll all learn." It was good to see Leslie jumping up and down.

My eyes met Warren Harper's. Leslie ran ahead of us and threw snowballs at his father and chased the dog. His cheeks were red from the cold and he looked almost robust in his heavy jacket and snow pants.

"We have to walk up here about a mile and then there's a good hill to learn on. I was up here last week when I took supplies to the sheep camp," Mr. Harper said.

We walked quite a way before he said, "I went in to see about applying for a commission last week."

"What about your job?" I asked.

"I wrote my boss last week and said I was going in the Army. It makes more sense than anything else for me."

"You're like Dad," I said.

We came to the little slope and put on the skis.

"Those were Mother's," Leslie told me. "She had them when she lived out here."

"Did she like skiing?" I asked.

"Yes," Mr. Harper said shortly.

All the time we were skiing he was shouting directions first at Leslie and then at me. He was having fun now and his face looked younger.

213

"Oh, that was awful. I'm afraid I'm hopeless," I said. The first couple of times I stayed upright but the last time I took a terrible sprawler. "Stop laughing at me!"

He was laughing so hard he could hardly help me up. "If you could have seen your face! You knew you were going to fall and you looked so indignant. Do you think you could call me Warren? It's hard to say 'Miss Webb' every time I pick you out of a snowdrift!"

"I think I could," I said. "Do call me Ellen."

"Look, Miss Webb, see me!" Leslie called.

"You know you've seemed so much older until today," Warren said.

"I've felt old this fall, ten years older than I was last year at school."

"That's not good."

I shrugged the way Mom does. Sometimes I catch myself with some of her mannerisms and some of Dad's big words. "I can't help it."

"I felt a hundred when I came back from Detroit," Warren said, "but then I'm seven years older than you are."

"How did you know how old I am?"

"I guessed," he said, laughing. I don't know why I should have thought of it then, but I remembered how Mary Cassidy had looked over at Nels Thorson and I stopped laughing.

I went back to the Harpers' for dinner. Old Mrs. Harper was rushing around the kitchen, but she let me set the table and help. We ate in the kitchen and it was comfortable and like being home.

"Were you born here?" I asked Warren.

"Right here in this house, in the room off'n the kitchen," Mrs. Harper said. "I remember how the wind blew. I've thought maybe that was why he was so strong-willed and set on having his own way. We'd only been out here 'bout a year. We'd oughta stayed where we was in Wisconsin."

"It's a long sight better climate here," Mr. Harper said. "We set out to raise wheat in the first place, but we had two crop failures an' I said that was enough of that. Wheat's too big a risk."

"How about lambs, Dad?" Warren teased. "Wait'll we get cattle on the place."

"My father raises wheat," I told old Mr. Harper. I had a funny feeling of pride as I said it. "We didn't have much of a crop this last year, but with all this snow the winter wheat ought to do well next year, he thinks."

After dinner, Leslie took me in his room to show me his collection of bird feathers. On the big old-fashioned dresser was a tinted photograph of a young woman in a choir robe.

"That's my mother," Leslie said.

"She's pretty."

"I think she must make a lovely angel, don't you, Miss Webb?"

"Oh, yes, indeed I do," I told him. I went over to look at the feathers carefully laid out on a shelf of an old bookcase.

"Let's see, this is a magpie's and this is a flicker's and this is a chicken hawk's. What's this, Leslie?"

"I don't know. I call it my white bird. Dad says maybe it could be from a sea gull that got too far away from water. He saw one once flying over the reservoir." I ran my finger along the feather. There is a sense of swiftness even in the feeling of a feather, and a little silken sound of wind as you run your finger along its edge.

"I have a blue jay's feather and a red-winged blackbird's at home, Leslie. I'll bring them back to you after Christmas."

His eyes shone and then were grave again. "Miss Webb, can I ask you about something?"

"Of course," I said.

"Miss Webb, Mother told me if I was good and prayed to God, He'd speak to me like He did to Samuel in the night, and I've waited and waited and prayed every day and He doesn't. Why doesn't He?"

Leslie's eyes were on my face, and his whole body seemed to be waiting for my answer. I knew how he felt from asking Mom questions. It is so hard not to be answered.

"I think God speaks in different ways from the way He used to," I began boldly. "I think now He speaks in the things we see in the country and in the snow and the skies and the mountains and the grass. If you don't like this country, God couldn't speak to you through it, and when you were angry with your father God couldn't talk to you if He wanted to." I was glad to get back to the kitchen, where the conversation clung to crops and cookery and neighbors.

Warren took me home in the Pony Express. I told him what

215

Leslie had asked me and of my lame answer. He pushed his hand back over his hair like an embarrassed boy.

"If Gladys had set out to drive me crazy after she died, she couldn't have thought of a better way, could she? I want him to come to like it here, but I wonder if he ever will. I suppose it was this country and the loneliness of it that drove his mother to do what she did, and here I've brought Leslie back here and expect him to like it the way I do."

"Well, he's your son too," I said.

"Yes, that's so, but I wonder if parents and children often see things the same way, let alone understand each other." Warren's voice was sad, and some tone in it matched the late afternoon light and the bare cold look of the country. I wished I could do something to help them.

10

ALL the families came to the Christmas exercises, even to the three-weeks-old baby in the Thorson family. When the Donaldsons came in there was a little stir all over the schoolroom.

I had drawn the shades and lighted two tall red candles on my desk. There was a candle burning in each window.

We began with a Christmas carol. Mary sang the second verse alone and we all hummed the chorus. Then came our pageant of "The News of the Christ Child's Birth" coming to a single shepherd boy off alone with his flock. Francis La Mere was the young shepherd, and the corner of the front of the room with my desk moved out of the way was the hill where he watched his sheep. Warren had brought two sheep over in the Pony Express and Francis kept a firm grip on them. One of the sheep bleated and the audience laughed and clapped.

The young shepherd wanted so to follow the star, but he couldn't leave his sheep because of wolves. Nels made the sound of a wolf from outside the window. So the angels appeared unto the boy and sang carols. Mike kept a flashlight trained on them from behind for a halo. One of the angels guarded the flock while the other took the boy to the stable where Mary and the Baby were. The angel took the sheep out at this point and our audience was hilarious when one sheep balked and had to be pushed down the aisle.

Francis walked after the angel with all the awe and excitement I could ask for. When we were practicing this part Francis said:

"I know, Miss Webb, you mean to walk like I was out hunting and maybe there's an elk over there?"

Mary Cassidy, as Mary, held her own five-months-old sister in her arms and Raymond as Joseph stood by them. The young shepherd had no gift, so he left his crook, which he had made himself out of aspen wood. Then he went happily back to his flock.

Leslie announced the beginning and the end of the pageant. A baby cried and some child coughed croupily so the last words were drowned out, but everyone clapped.

As Raymond raised the shades and blew out the candles at the end, the late winter sun struck in across the room in a blaze of brightness. The parents looked at the papers we had hung along the wall, spelling papers and writing exercises and drawings. I went over to speak to the Donaldsons.

"It was good of you to come," I said.

"I guess it's still our school. We paid our school tax," Mrs. Donaldson sniffed.

"Don't, Minnie," Mr. Donaldson murmured, stooping to put on her galoshes.

"We saw you in town two nights after Robert's death, Miss Webb. We were in the front window of the undertaker's parlor when you went by with Mr. Harper."

I felt my face redden. "I'm sorry I didn't see you," I said stupidly, but my mouth tasted as bitter as though I had been chewing alder bark.

"It looks warmer, don't it?" Mrs. Thorson exclaimed, and I was grateful to her.

"I wouldn't trust it yet," Mr. Thorson said with a big laugh. He was a solid, red-faced man with bright-blue eyes.

"How old are you, Miss Webb? I don't suppose you're at an age yet where you're touchy about it!"

"I'm over twenty," I said in the midst of the laughter, and I could see Warren Harper smiling at me across the room.

"Well, you're all right, young lady. You can have this school another ten years as far as I'm concerned," Mr. Thorson assured me. And Mrs. Cassidy squeezed my arm and told me I was better than last year's teacher. And then they were all leaving at once.

"Merry Christmas, Miss Webb!" the La Mere boys called out.

"Merry Christmas!" I must have called a dozen times. Mr. La Mere had fastened sleighbells on his old jalopy and they made a gay jingle through the late winter afternoon, as gay as the bells on the troikas Mom used to tell about, I thought.

✦

I set the little Christmas tree out in the snow and swept out the litter of popcorn and paper and greens. I would be away ten days. I took a knife and scraped off the candle wax that had dropped on the window sills and tore December off the calendar. My suitcase was already packed. When I heard Warren's car, I locked the door and went out to meet him.

"You did well by Christmas," he said.

"Thank you. The children loved it, didn't they?"

"And the parents."

"I keep forgetting that you went to school here. Did you like it?"

"Oh, yes. That was all I knew. We had the sister of a rancher who lived where Thorsons do now for a teacher. She taught us spelling and reading and arithmetic all right, but I think she was over her depth in geography. The summer before I was married I got a job on a boat going to South America, and I kept thinking of the map in my first geography book here. I thought the world was my apple in those days. I wasn't going to stop till I had been all over the world. I got stymied pretty easy, didn't I? Maybe the war'll give me another chance in geography!"

"Tell me something about South America," I said quickly. I liked to hear him talk when he was interested in a thing. We rode along at seven below zero with the heater on and he told about how awful the heat was when he was unloading fruit in the harbor at Rio. He knew a little Spanish and we tried talking together. All of a sudden, he didn't finish his sentence.

"Ellen Webb, do you know I love you?"

"Oh, please don't," I said. "I'm through thinking about love. It took me all summer and all this fall to stop thinking about Gil. I like feeling alone in myself. I feel free."

"You can't live on that basis all your life."

"I don't know—maybe I can. I know I can live alone. I've tried it this winter."

"What about when you're older?"

"I still think I could manage. I've seen Mom and Dad. I'm sure they don't love each other, but they have to go on as they are."

"That doesn't mean that you and I couldn't be different."

"Don't, Warren, please!" I didn't mean to speak so sharply

but his saying "you and I" made me uncomfortable. I didn't want anyone too close to me again.

There were few cars on the road and the ranches were far apart. Here and there a lonely spot of light gleamed out of the dusk to show where a house stood. I wondered a little hopelessly if there were happiness back of those lights or just lives like Warren's or mine or Mom's or Dad's. I said something like that to Warren; he was easy to tell half-thoughts to.

"Maybe a country settled by homesteads is bound to be made of expectation and disappointment," he said. "So much hope to begin with settling down into so much resignation. Look at that!"

The headlights shone on a solitary deserted building at a crossroad, with broken windows covered with old handbills. "Gold Block" was cut in stone above the entrance, as though it had once been meant for the center of a city.

"Somebody had a big idea once!" Warren said.

I tried to think of threshing time when the country looked so good and everyone felt strong and full of hope, but now the wheat was deep under the snow and nobody knew how it would turn out. The snow in the lights from the car was no longer soft and fresh and white, it was frozen into hard gray banks.

Our yard light was on when we turned off the highway.

"You're all lit up like a church," Warren said.

"Yes, Mom loves a lot of light." I couldn't help thinking what a sturdy light it was in the darkness of the prairie, like Mom. As we drove into the yard I saw Mom looking out the window. Then she opened the door and stood there, thick and plain and so good to see.

"Yeléna!" she called.

"Hi, Mom! Come in, won't you?" I said to Warren.

"I was going to drive over for you tomorrow. Your dad, he is gone back to his home." Mom jerked her head backward.

"To Vermont! When did he go?"

"You don't get his letter? Sure, he go last Monday. You have some coffee, Mr. Harper?"

"Thank you. That would taste good." I could see how he liked Mom.

"Yeléna, you get the cups and some cake in the box. We go in other room." But Mom asked it rather than said it.

"It's fine here," Warren said. So we sat around the table in

220

the kitchen. Mom and Warren talked about the war and the prospects for next year. He told her how good the cake was and Mom cut him another slice.

"It's good with coffee. You like more coffee, too?"

He said he would and Mom got up to pour it and turned her back on us as though she knew we would want to talk by ourselves. There was something in the way she smiled and was so ready to cut more cake that made me uncomfortable, as though I had done well to have somebody to see me home again—like any peasant mother with a daughter on her hands to marry. I wished Dad were home.

"When will Dad be back, Mom?"

Mom shrugged. "He get letter from his sister one day, next day he make up his mind to go." Mom didn't like to talk of family affairs before Warren. And then she added, as though it were forced out of her, "It cost lots of money to go back there." She passed Warren the coffee. "You a rancher, too, Mr. Harper?" Mom looked at him with her bright, inquisitive eyes.

Warren laughed. "At heart. But I've been away a long time."

Mom frowned and waited. I could almost follow her mind with my own. She couldn't understand why anyone would want to leave here, I thought scornfully.

"It seems good to be back here," Warren said.

"Sure," Mom said.

"I was telling Ellen that I admire anyone who raises wheat. That takes lots of . . ."

"Work," Mom said with unusual quickness.

"Yes, and faith, too." Warren could see faith wasn't a word Mom used familiarly, at least not about ranching. I could see him hunting for a better word. "You have to have plenty of patience," he added.

Mom nodded. "We get thirty-six bushel a acre year before last," she boasted.

Warren whistled. "That was all right! Ellen said something about bringing my little boy over here sometime. I hope you'll let him come."

"Your little boy? Sure," Mom said. "I like children. You bring him this spring when we got new baby chicks. Poor boy, his mother dead long time?" Mom asked too curiously, too obviously, I thought.

"Over two years," Warren said. Then he stood up to go.

"He's good-looking young man," was Mom's comment when I came back into the house.

"Not bad," I said. "He's going into the Army."

Mom nodded, her eyes secret with her thoughts. "He like you. He drive way down here just to bring you, eighty-five miles." Mom said it so triumphantly it irritated me.

"He wanted something to do, that's all. Mom, what made Dad decide to go way back to Vermont?"

Mom shrugged and poured a little coffee into her saucer. "He want to see that sister. Once before he went off, but he don't go all the way! He come back when he get to North Dakota." Her face took on that triumphant, almost sly, look that it could get.

"When, Mom? I didn't know. I thought the only time he went back to Vermont was when I was eight and his mother died."

Mom shook her head. "There was other time when we was married, maybe three years. We went for walk one Sunday, way over past Bardiches'. Ben carry you. He was quiet-like—you know? That was queer for him. He kep' walking. I think maybe you get heavy and I say turn back, but he kep' on. I ask him what was wrong.

"After while, he say he going to take trip back home. We had good crop that year an' some money in bank. We plan to buy pair horses and a new harrow with that money, but I say, 'Sure, you go ahead, Ben. Why don't you go tomorrow?'

"So he go. Next night after that I was calcimining the whole house. Everything piled in the kitchen an' me in old dress, bare legs, and my head tied up in flour sack, when I hear someone step on porch. The door open an' in walk Ben.

" 'I caught train back from Fargo, Anna,' he say.

"I say, 'Where you goin' to sleep tonight, Ben? You ain't got any bed.' I show him how I had it piled up with things.

" 'Where you going to sleep?' he say.

" 'Oh, I sleep anywhere when I get done.'

" 'I can sleep where you can,' he say."

Mom laughed telling me. Her eyes were bright and soft with fun.

"But this time I guess he go all the way."

I traced the squares on the oilcloth cover of the table. My

throat ached. I could see how it must have been. Dad must have started out because he was homesick, starved for things and ways he was used to, and then he must have felt he shouldn't do it and turned back home. It made Dad seem younger to think of him wanting something so much. Mom thought Dad had turned around and come back because of her, because he wanted to be with her. She couldn't understand that it must have been his own hard sense of duty, making him feel he shouldn't take the money and go away, that made him turn around. It must have been the same sense of duty that made him marry Mom and take her back to his home and stay with her even after he knew she had fooled him. I knew I shouldn't feel that way about my mother, but I couldn't help it.

"This will be first Christmas without Ben," Mom said, and suddenly I was filled with pity for her. She had tied Dad to her by her rights, by his sense of duty. I thought a little proudly that I hadn't said even one little word to hold Gil.

"I got forty-five turkeys to dress to take into town tomorrow, three more than Thanksgiving. I better get at 'em."

Every year except last year I had helped Mom fix the turkeys for town. Mom's regular customers wrote her every year. Mom raised a special duck-breasted kind that had more white breast meat than others. People had them quick-frozen and shipped them East, they were so good. Mom charged three cents more a pound for dressing them ready to stuff and roast. She always felt she put one over on people charging for that, but she said, "Town women are that lazy an' they faint if they see blood." Mom never counted her own labor as costing anything, so the extra cents were so much pure profit.

I used to catch the turkeys for her, with a long wire bent into a hook at the end. I could hook the wire around the turkey's leg so swiftly he didn't have time to get away, but he made such a squawking you could hear him out to the highway. Mom bled them. I only held them for her, but I helped pick them afterwards out in the shed. Sometimes my fingers would be so cold out there I'd bury them in the soft feathers of the turkey's breast or under the wings where the body heat of the turkey still felt burning-hot. We would fill big cartons with the feathers by the time we were through.

Many a time I have gone to bed with Mom still hard at work fixing turkeys and waked up hours later and found her still working. She wouldn't let Dad help, but he never went to bed until she was through, even if she worked till two or three in the morning. He would sit in the next room and read and call out from time to time that she mustn't do this another year.

"You get yourself something to eat and then you can help," Mom said now.

There were soup and fresh bread Mom had made, and her own butter. After all these years, Mom still made her bread in round loaves. There was nothing so good. I was glad of this vacation, I thought, as I sat there eating. I missed Dad, though. Coming home was cut in half to find him away. I said so to Mom.

"He took idea to go. When he get all that money borrowed it go to his head. Next year when we don't have no crop he'll think a little," Mom said darkly, pulling out a mess of bright-colored entrails from the big carcass in front of her. I watched as though I hadn't seen all this a dozen times before.

"But we will have, Mom. Look at all the snow we've had already this year, and we put in more winter wheat this time!"

Mom shrugged. "We see."

I don't think I realized until that night how fast and deft Mom's fingers were. They seemed to know every hollow of the turkey's carcass. She would hold it up to the light and peer in and nod when she was through. When she laid the finished turkeys in a row on the table, hens in one line, toms in another, they were beautifully clean, the powerful legs crossed and tied, the big wings folded underneath, a string of red uncooked cranberries around each neck. Dad laughed at her for that, but I believe her customers liked it. She had her necklaces all strung and ready in a bag. Mom was systematic without thinking about it. I picked up one cranberry ring, half-expecting Mom to tell me to leave it alone as she always used to, but instead she said:

"Cranberries are awful dear this year!"

It was after two o'clock when we had the tags with the weight marked on them tied to each turkey. We piled the turkeys carefully in two big clothes baskets and a tin tub and set them out in the shed to keep cool. Mom scoured the table and the sink board and I did up the pans we had used. Then we sat down and had some coffee and another slice of bread. When we were through, Mom opened the kitchen door and let the cold air sweep into the hot kitchen till it was freshened of all its odors. She sniffed the air.

"Feel like chinook tomorrow. We better get them turkeys in early."

II

I WONDERED how many trips to town I had made like this, the day before Christmas! It began Christmas for me, and afterward, when all the turkeys were delivered and Mom had the checks and cash in her big black bag, we had lunch and did our Christmas shopping. The one afternoon was always enough for us. We only gave to each other. Dad sent money back home, I knew now. And always every year, a present came for me from Aunt Eunice. Next to the doll, the present I remember best was a pair of white gloves when I was seventeen. I wore them for the first time to Gil's house.

Mom had the list of customers with their addresses in her own handwriting. It dawned on me today as I looked down on the notebook in her hands that Dad must have taught her to write too.

"You better watch the road!" Mom said. I straightened the wheels. I had got over too far looking at Mom's handwriting.

"Did Dad teach you to write English, Mom?" I asked.

"Sure. While he get well, an' on the boat. He don't do so good learning Russian," Mom said, laughing.

"I'll take them in," I said when we got to town. I had been proud the first year Mom let me take the turkeys from the truck to the houses and come back with the money. Mom liked the hard silver dollars best; the paper checks she cashed as soon as we got downtown. I used to wonder why so many of the women looked so hurried and had to hunt to find the money; they knew we would be there that day. One woman borrowed from her maid, and once a woman asked us to stop at her husband's office to get the money from him.

"That's it, the white house. Mrs. Harriman, she get seventeen-pound tom," Mom read.

I thought of Gil as I went around the house to the Harrimans' backdoor. They had a dog that barked, I remembered, but there was no dog there today. Maybe it had grown too old to bark.

Mom had been right about the chinook. The turkeys were soft now as I took them in. Sometimes they were frozen hard from standing overnight in the shed and in the open back of the truck.

"My! Are you Mrs. Webb's daughter?" one woman asked. "I remember when you used to bring our Christmas turkey years ago. You had long blond braids!" I felt ten again.

It took us till nearly one o'clock to get them all delivered. It was good to see the clothes baskets and the tub empty. We had a good many checks, so we went right to the bank and Mom cashed them. I had two monthly checks for teaching uncashed too. I started to deposit them in the savings account I had opened in September, then I decided I'd buy a new coat for myself. I looked at Mom in her old black coat standing at the cashier's window. Mom needed a new coat, too.

I told her at lunch. Mom's eyes sparkled.

"You and Ben, you go crazy when you get money. I don't need no coat. You buy new coat for yourself."

"I am going to, but you need one too. It will be my Christmas present." It was a wonderful feeling to have money of my own to spend.

We went up to the coat department. It was nearly empty. Most people don't leave their Christmas shopping till the day before Christmas. The coat I bought for myself was a polo coat with big pockets and lapels that I could turn up. I put it on and walked up and down over the green carpet past the long mirrors. Mom sat on an imitation white leather chair, and watched me, nodding approval. Mom liked it because the salesgirl showed her the original price slashed down a third because it was so near Christmas.

"Why you do that the day before Christmas?" Mom asked.

"I guess to tempt someone. Most people are home trimming their tree today."

I liked the coat because I thought Vera would approve of it. I wondered where she was this year, and what she would think of me teaching at Prairie Butte. I walked past the mirror again and pretended I was hurrying down the mall to meet . . . well, if not Gil, someone.

And then I got Mom to try on a coat.

227

"No, too tight. I can't move my arms," Mom said, swinging her arms to show the saleswoman. She tried another, a black with a fur collar.

"What kind a animal you call it?" Mom asked, holding up the collar. When she heard it was dyed skunk she wouldn't have it. Each time when she took off a coat she reached for her own old one, till I took it and held it.

Then Mom saw a red one on the rack with a gray squirrel collar. I saw the saleswoman thought it was too young for Mom, but she had already put it on. She walked over in front of the glass and for the first time in my life I saw she must have liked clothes, too. Mom smoothed the soft fur cuffs with her hand.

"You like it, Yeléna?"

"Yes, I believe I do," I said, looking at Mom in a new way. It's hard for a daughter to realize that her mother could be still young. Mom wasn't fat, she was just big, I thought critically.

Mom let me pay for it finally. We argued back and forth while the saleswoman went to have the buttons set over.

"All right, *Yólochka*, you pay," Mom said.

I made Mom wear it out and we took her old coat in the box. We bought a hat, too, but it took time. The hats looked silly above Mom's wide forehead. She sat in front of a glass, her face expressionless. A hat with a veil bothered her and she pushed the veil out of the way. I saw how her eyes kept resting on the red coat.

"It's the color of the cranberries we put on the turkeys, Yeléna," she said.

The hat we bought was dark-red felt. The saleswoman hunted in a big drawer until she found a piece of gray fur to match the collar on the coat.

Mom nodded. "We take that," she said. "You sew the fur on good."

It was becoming. I was ashamed that the red had seemed too young to me too, at first. Mom was seventeen when Dad married her. She was only forty-one now.

"Ben like red," Mom said while the saleswoman was gone. I turned away from the silly smile on her face as she looked in the mirror. "I might go in to town to meet your father's train when he come back." She wanted him to see her in her new coat and hat. I squirmed inwardly, it seemed so pathetic to me. I felt years older.

We went to a man's store and bought a new sweater for Dad and house slippers, the sweater from Mom and the slippers from me.

"Crops must have been good out your way," the salesman said as he wrapped up the gifts.

Mom's face closed up tight. "Crops was bad out our way," she said, and the young man made no more attempts at conversation.

We went to the grocery store and Mom bought all kinds of things she didn't buy ordinarily—powdered sugar and nuts and candied fruits and a tin of caviar and a jar of pickled herring. I sat in the truck outside, but I could see Mom through the big glass window of the store. It didn't seem like Christmas with the chinook melting all the snow and the children going past bareheaded. The road home would be a mess.

We must have been about two miles from home when Mom put a little book in my lap. "There, *Yólochka*, it is yours."

"Why, Mom!" It was a black bankbook like my own.

"I put all the turkey money to you. Two hunderd eighty-four dollar, for school next year."

"But, Mom!" I couldn't say any more.

"Sure, why not?" Mom said. "You buy me this coat, don't you?"

The road was soft where we turned off the highway. I had to tend to my driving. It was dusk when we came to Gotham, a soft warm dusk, almost like spring. We drove with the windows rolled down and I could hear the water running in the culvert when we came to our place. No one had been there to turn on the yard light. I liked the house under the darker ridge of the coulee with the dark fringe of trees above the roof. I shut off the lights and the ignition and we sat there a second in the truck. The wind stirred past us and smelled sweet, of moist dirt and stable smells and some freshness I couldn't name. It was chinook weather for Christmas Eve.

"Ben'll miss being home," Mom said.

"I'll do the milking," I said quickly. "I'll be right ready." I slipped on my jeans and an old shirt and the boy's work shoes I wore around the ranch when it was muddy. After I've been to town these things feel good.

Mom had hung away her new coat and hat, but she was just sitting by the table. Usually, she was so busy the minute we got home from town. She sat idle like that only when she was thinking out some problem.

"Yeléna, it would be good for you to marry. You'd do good on a ranch. How you like this Mr. Harper?"

"Oh, Mom, for heaven's sake, I hardly know him." I let the milk pails clatter together as I went out. I was angry at her for trying to plan things out for me like some old country mother.

It was late to milk the cows, but we had left them in the corral all day with hay to eat. With the chinook melting the snow, the ground of the corral was soft and soppy. I slipped the wooden bar on the gate and talked to the cows as I went in. The yard light reached way over here, so I could see well enough. I led them into the barn one by one. We milk three, and have enough for Bailey and for Peterson at the store.

The light bulb in the barn was mirrored in the cows' big dark eyes. I'm out of practice, but I like milking. May turned her big head and looked at me and I could see myself perfectly reflected in her eyes. She was easy to milk. The milk poured down evenly into the pail. I gave May a pat on the flank and set the pail on the shelf where it was safe and moved to Belle. The cows' names were May and Belle and Dunya. Dad had named the first cow they had on the ranch Dunya after a girl they knew in Russia to tease Mom, and we had had one by that name ever since.

The wide door stood open. I could hear the cows chewing at the hay and the sound of the milk in the pail. I thought how strange a way it was to spend Christmas Eve. Last year I had been with Gil. We had gone downtown and had dinner and danced. Carolers sang carols in the dining room and Gil paid them to sing certain ones for me. They stood by our table and sang "God Rest You Merry, Gentlemen" and "Noel." Gil held my hand under the table. I had thought that I would spend all the Christmas Eves of my life with him. I moved over to Dunya, but in my thoughts I was back with Gil. I remembered Christmas Day and Christmas night last year. I remembered how happy I was.

I turned the cows back out through the corral and heard Dunya's bell as she led the way down to the coulee bed. Their big hoofs made a sucking sound as they picked them up out of the mud.

I stopped to pull down hay for the horses and turn off the barn light. From the wide barn door I could see the yellow lights from the kitchen and the dark top of the tree above the house roof. Patches of snow jumped out of the dark, whiter than they were by daylight. There was a dripping sound of melting icicles. Nothing was like Christmas Eve. I wished I could stay out here and not go back to Mom's questions, but I took the pails of warm fresh milk and went back up to the kitchen.

Mom had changed her dress and had supper set out on the table. She had a fat red candle from some other Christmas in the center. When I came in she looked in the pails to see how much milk I had.

"Good," she nodded. I think she would have said no more about Warren Harper or my marrying, but I didn't wait to see.

"I still love Gil, Mom," I said. I might as well tell her.

Mom made a snorting sound and tipped the pail of warm milk to fill the pitcher for our supper. I took off my sweat shirt and washed my hands at the sink.

Mom muttered crossly, "Why you let him go, then, first time you get mad?"

12

THREE days after Christmas the wind changed again. It blew from the northwest and the temperature dropped so low the bare ground looked cold and naked. It was good to see the snow powdering the frozen earth. The cold made me think of the blizzard and losing Robert. My thoughts always seemed to move close to the weather. We couldn't do much besides feed the stock. I sat by the stove and read. We listened to the radio a lot. Mom was so interested in war news she wouldn't miss one broadcast.

We had a letter from Dad:

"Dear Anna and Ellen,

"I found much that needed attention. Eunice was surprised to see me. She has been quite sick and still looks badly. Worry over money and fear of losing the house have made her worse. She seems lonely here in this big house, but she would rather be here than any place else. I am glad I came.

"I am writing up here in my old room. Nothing has been changed. I find I remember the weeks after I came back from the war and you and I shared this room, Anna, better than the years when I was a boy. Remember how you never could think of the little pegs that held the windows and they would come down with a crash that made you swear in Russian!

"I shall stay a few days after Christmas to see some old friends. You know I miss you both and Christmas at home. I hope the gifts I sent arrive in time.

"Yours affect.

"Ben."

I read the letter aloud to Mom. She sat still to listen. I wondered if Dad were trying to make Mom feel good. He must have remembered so much more than the way Mom let the windows bang! It was odd that he wrote it to both of us and signed it "Ben." But it was true that this winter he had become Ben to me more than Dad, just as Mom had become Anna Petrovna.

His gifts came. Bailey made a special trip to bring them to us. There was a big box of candy and a new leather pocketbook for Mom. He sent me two pairs of nylon stockings. The candy lay on the table in the kitchen where Mom could admire it. Mom loved gifts.

"Ben send it way from there!" Mom said several times. "He spends money!" There was a note of grudging admiration in her voice.

We were sitting by the stove in the front room one late afternoon, five days after Christmas. Mom was knitting. I was reading. Since I had told her about Gil, there had been a little coolness between us—not coolness so much as separation. Talk didn't come so easy.

We both heard the train go through Gotham. I thought how the train would stop only long enough for the mailbags to be thrown off and a few people would look out the windows with bored disinterest. I wished vaguely that I were on it, the way you think about being on a plane when it flies over your head out in the field, or the way you wish it were cool in July when you know it can't be. It wasn't more than a quarter of an hour later that we heard someone call. I went out to the porch and there was Dad walking across the yard, carrying his bag.

"Ben Webb! You come!" I heard Mom say.

"Of course I came." He kissed Mom, then he put his arm around me. "Ellen, I wish I could have taken you with me." I couldn't remember ever having seen him kiss Mom before.

"Why didn't you tell us when you were coming, Dad? We'd have gone into town to meet you."

"Yes, Ben, you should tell us!"

Dad laughed. "I got through before I thought I would, so I just took the first train and came. Where's some coffee? I haven't eaten anything since breakfast."

Mom was busy in a minute making fresh coffee.

"Did you have a good time, Dad?" I asked. I thought how well he looked in his "city clothes." A pleasant air of strangeness seemed to attach to him.

"Well," Dad said slowly, "I don't know, but it was a satisfaction." He looked over at Mom. "Anna, I'm sorry, but I couldn't have done anything else." I knew he couldn't have said that to her before he went away.

Mom was poaching an egg. She kept her eyes on the edges of the white, lifting them gently with her knife.

"I'd say it was worth it even if we didn't have a good crop this year," Dad added.

"If we lose the combine you don't feel so good," Mom muttered, sliding out the egg.

A hopeless feeling rose in me. I felt that Mom must have given me all the turkey money because Dad had given Aunt Eunice money.

"I'll always feel good about it," he said quietly, and I knew he wouldn't mention it ever again. He turned to me. "I hated to miss some of your vacation, Ellen. Your Aunt Eunice was pleased to know you were teaching. I told her how you enjoyed those old books. She's sending you some of my father's. She says she is going to leave the house to you some day, Ellen." Dad didn't look at Mom. He was busy buttering his toast.

"Oh, Dad," I said. I thought how Gil could come and see me there some day.

"Yeléna'll have this ranch some day," Mom said.

When Dad came to his cigarette, I brought him his presents. He put on his sweater and slippers. Mom seemed to forget all her resentment in her pleasure at seeing him.

"That's good sweater, Ben, better than your old one," she said.

"We loved our presents, Dad," I said.

"I wonder you had enough money to get home on, Ben," Mom said, her eyes bright again with fun.

"You should see Mom in her new coat, Dad!" I made Mom go and put it on and the hat and her new pocketbook.

"Well!" Dad said. "Doesn't she look fine, Ellen!" Mom blushed and her face seemed to open and be alive. I looked at her, too. She was . . . why, she was really handsome!

"Stand up there beside her, Dad. You both look so dressed-up!" I said like a doting mother. Dad put his arm around her and they beamed.

"You make yourself foolish, Ben!" Mom said, and moved away.

"Well, I'll go out and see how you two managed the place," Dad said.

"Not in good clothes," Mom warned.

A half-hour later we were all outdoors. Dad, in his old clothes, rode one of the horses up to see about grass on the other side of the coulee. Mom had tied her bandanna over her head and was out looking for the few turkeys she had kept over. I went out, too, in back of the house against the hill.

"You go with your dad, Yeléna," Mom called. "Go ahead!"

I climbed up on the other work horse, just as I was, and rode after Dad. The wind blew my hair and ruffled the horse's shaggy winter coat.

Warren drove into the yard the last day of my vacation. I had dreaded his coming. Mom had kept wondering why he didn't come.

"I thought Mr. Harper was going to bring his little boy some day?" Mom said one night as we were doing the dishes.

"He was probably busy," I said. "I hope he doesn't come."

"Why don't you bring your little boy?" Mom asked him as soon as she saw him. Warren smiled.

"Well, he had a cold. I'd like to do it a little later, if I may." His face was reddened by the wind and he seemed to smile more. He fitted so easily into our kitchen, talking to Dad and Mom. I was glad he had come, after all.

Warren stayed for dinner and he and Dad talked about the war. Their talk shut me out. It was a good thing I wasn't a man, I thought. I didn't see how wars would ever stop so long as they filled people like Mom and Dad with such fervor. Mom listened to every word. When they talked about Russia she interrupted with a boastful laugh.

"Germans don't know Russian winter. They freeze like flies!" I felt that her voice sounded cruel and I hated it. "They can't get Russia *ever*, I don't think!" she added, and the cruelty in her voice had changed to something else, something that vibrated in my own ears and made me proud.

But I didn't mind leaving. I was used now to the coming home and going back to the teacherage. It made a pattern. If you can see the pattern in your days, it's easier, I thought, looking down from a rise in the road on the pattern of fields spread out below

Gotham: strips of stubble against plowed strips, faintly tinged with green and bordered by the faraway mountains striped with snow. The late afternoon sun glinted on the thin covering of snow and polished the shining stalks of stubble. It sparkled on the mountains so we could hardly look straight at them. A warm quietness seemed to hold the whole valley. I thought how Warren was becoming part of that pattern.

We drove through Clark City without stopping and beyond it again to the open country that was clean and bare and wide.

"Oh, I feel good!" I said out of my mind.

"I feel that way when I'm with you," Warren said. "You never seem restless or worried or striving for something."

"Not today anyway," I said. "Tell me about your Christmas. Did you have fun with Leslie?"

"I really did. He went every place with me, up to the sheep camp and into town and over to Lewistown. We stayed overnight in a hotel and Leslie loved that. I went over to see about selling the sheep. They're too much for Dad with me going in the Army. The folks are going to move back into town."

"What have you heard from the Army?"

"The Engineering Corps takes me as a lieutenant. I leave next Saturday."

"That's so soon," I said. I hadn't thought of his going right away.

"It wouldn't have seemed so when I first came out here, but it does now."

"How does Leslie take it?"

"I believe he likes the idea. He acts almost proud of me." Warren smiled as he said it.

"That's fine. I knew he'd change toward you if you were here with him and . . ."

". . . and stopped drinking. Well, I have. But a lot of his attitude is your doing."

"I don't think so."

"You should hear him quote you." Warren laughed. "The other day when we were coming back from the sheep camp, the wind was blowing so hard it took our breath away. He turned his back to it and shouted to me, 'Miss Webb says God speaks to you through the country. Maybe the wind is God's voice.'"

"Oh, that . . ." I said.

"Well, anyway, we stopped on the way back and listened to the wind. The sea has nothing on it for roar. I got the notion while we were listening that the wind in this part of the country, so far inland from water, is kind of a big dry sea, itself. Maybe it has as powerful an effect on the people who live in it as the sea has on people. You know, Conrad stuff."

"Maybe," I said. I hadn't heard him talk in fancies before.

"It has a lot of things the sea has, really, except that it's dry and the sea's wet." He laughed again. "But I didn't bring Leslie along today because I wanted to talk to you, Ellen. What you said the other day about not wanting to love anybody was crazy and childish. You don't mean that."

I looked away from the road over to the east. I saw how the sun had gone from the whole side of the rimrock but for one little spot as big as your hand. It was strange how that spot lingered. If you were up there you could lay your hand against it and feel its warmth. Having someone love you was like that spot. You could lean against it and warm yourself, but when the sun left that place you would be cold again.

"Ellen, I can wait for you to come to love me. I used to be impatient about everything. I've learned a little. You should have seen me last week with Leslie."

He stopped the car along the road and leaned forward a little holding the top of the wheel with both hands. He wasn't looking at me, but down the road at the winter's day that had about run out of light. It's the worst time of day. I hated to have him looking at it without a spot of sun left along the rimrock or on the mountains. The mountains were the worst. They were blue-cold and fading. Maybe he didn't notice them, he went right on talking.

"First, I thought I was too much older. My life has been pretty much messed up, and you should have someone as young as you are. But then I tell myself that we were meant to find each other, because it was all such a chance that I was home when you came to the house in the blizzard.

"I was anxious to meet you before that. Do you know what Leslie wrote me, Ellen?" Warren took a letter out of his pocket. He must have known it pretty well because the penciled writing was hard to read. " 'On the way home Miss Webb took my hand and we ran. She said she loved to run in the moonlight. I'm not

afraid in the dark any more.' Look how he spells moonlight—
'munelite.' " He held it over for me to read.

I tried to remember how I had felt last year with Gil when
he told me he loved me, but it hadn't been like this at all. I hadn't
had to think. I had known long before Gil told me. That time
and Gil and I seemed like something bright and gay and sunny,
like morning. This was like the late winter afternoon, somber,
almost dark, with the light going out of the sky.

"Warren, I'm afraid I still love Gil. I tried not to. I hated
him some of the time last summer, but now I don't."

"Well," Warren said after a long while, "you ought to tell him
then. You ought to let him know."

"I don't think I can do that."

"He's in the Army now, you said?"

"Yes, he was down in Florida the last time I heard."

"If I should ever meet up with him, I'll tell him."

"That wouldn't do any good. He doesn't love me."

"And you're still going to go on loving him?"

"I can't seem to help it. It sounds dumb, doesn't it?"

"Damn dumb to me," he said.

Warren started the car and turned on the radio.

"I wish you would let me take Leslie home the week end you
leave," I said when we reached the teacherage. "It might make it
easier for him to have something special to do."

"Thanks. He'd love that."

It wasn't until the next morning that I noticed there was something in the mailbox. My mail is mostly all educational pamphlets
or advertisements, but I went out to get it before I had breakfast. It was a flat package in brown paper and tied with string.
Then I saw the writing on it. It was from Gil. He had had my
letter, because he had sent this to Prairie Butte. I cut the string
and opened it.

It was a water color on a sheet of drawing paper, fastened to
a piece of cardboard. At first I took in only the colors: the greens
and yellows Gil had wanted to paint that day when we stopped
for lunch by the creek. There was a girl sitting by the bank under
a tree, but her back was turned and her head was bent so you
only saw her hair and the green shade on her skirt.

I set it up on my dresser and went across the room to look at it. It was clearer from a distance, but there were no firm outlines, mostly color. I think it must have been good, because it made me feel like summer. I knew how hot it would be if I went beyond that shaded place. Gil had remembered it just as it was, only he couldn't get the clearness of the stream—maybe no one could. If he had remembered the place and the way the bank turned and that I'd worn a white dress, he must have remembered everything else, what we said and the way we felt. I turned the painting over. He had scribbled a sentence in pencil:

"The mud here is worse than in Montana. Gil."

That was all, but he had sent it in spite of my horrid, smug little letter. I sat reading it over and over the way Robert Donaldson used to read over the sentences in the reader. If Gil could joke about the mud, he wasn't angry about getting stuck in it, any longer.

It was like a Christmas present—maybe he had meant it for that. Last year he had given me a picture of himself for Christmas. This year it was a painting of a creek and trees and a girl in a white dress, hardly even me, and yet this seemed to give me more of him than his photograph. I pinned the painting to the wall where I could see it from my desk.

The Thorsons had come back with colds and Francis La Mere had cotton in his ear because of an earache. He kept saying he couldn't hear and the others burst out laughing every time.

"Miss Webb," Leslie called out to me at recess. "My dad's going to be a lieutenant in the Army!"

"Yes, I know. That's fine, Leslie," I said thoughtlessly.

"How did you know, Miss Webb?" Leslie asked.

"Maybe Mr. Harper told her! They were sitting in the car by the road when we come by from town last night," Mary Cassidy said archly.

But school hardly touched me that day. I wanted it to be over so I could be alone. All through the day I watched the way the sun struck the painting differently at different times.

After school Leslie came back in when he had his cap and scarf and jacket on. I noticed how much healthier he looked than in the fall.

"Miss Webb, Dad told me about your asking me to go home

239

with you this week end when he goes. Gee, thanks!" He leaned back against the desk as though he were going to stay.

"We'll have fun," I said. "You better hurry so you can walk with Mary and Sigrid."

"I don't care. They can go on."

"You better go today, Leslie. I have work to do." I went with him to the door and waved. I had the feeling that he had wanted to stay and talk, but this afternoon I wanted them all to be gone. It seemed strange that I should ever have dreaded The Part after School when the children were gone. The late winter sun lighted up the yellow-green of Gil's painting.

That evening I wrote to Gil. I kept thinking about what Warren had said: "You ought to tell him, Ellen. You ought to let him know."

I held my pen still so long it wouldn't write, and then it blotted when I shook it. I took a pencil instead and wrote him on a ruled school pad held against my knee. Afterward I could copy it.

I told him what I thought of the water color. *"You see you did do it the way you wanted,"* I wrote, because I knew that not being able to do something made Gil cross. He'd never make a rancher! I tried hard to find something about the figure in the painting that made it seem especially me. It might have been any girl under a tree in the sun, but it must have been more to Gil. *"It's all just as it was except the water,"* I wrote. *"And I don't believe anyone could get the way a mountain stream looks into paint."* I closed my eyes and saw the gravel glistening at the shallow bottom and the satin-smooth look of the mud sloping down the low bank, and the clear shine of the water moving swiftly under the alders. It was so real in my mind it seemed strange to open my eyes in the teacherage. I tried to tell Gil how I had felt after he went away last June.

"I saw our ranch and the country as you saw it, Gil. It was bare and flat and the house was a little unpainted shack. I even saw Mom and Dad with your eyes. Mom is a big peasant woman. I may look like her some day. Dad is sick and tiresomely talkative. He doesn't belong out here. You were right in a way. You said you would think they'd come to hate each other. Maybe it was that hate between them that you felt. Maybe that was what made you afraid to love me. I felt that it was in me, someway, like a

240

blight in a sheaf of wheat. After you went away I hated you and Mom and Dad and our ranch and this country. I hated myself even more. Oh, Gil, you don't know what the summer was like or this winter when I first came out to the teacherage!" The words poured onto the paper. It was a relief to write all this to Gil.

"I was never lonely before this fall. That was true when I wrote you that, but when I said 'Thank you for teaching me what loneliness was' it was just boasting. It's not a good feeling. When I wrote you that letter I felt proud of myself because I thought I had been strong enough to put you out of my life. But at Christmas time, Christmas Eve, I knew all over again that I still loved you. And I came back after vacation and found your water color, like an answer."

I had no more to say. That was where I had come to. It had seemed like a miracle to me to know that. Understanding what you really feel and really want is more breath-taking than climbing to the top of the rimrock in the wind. Whether it was good or bad or foolish or wise didn't matter—there it was. I felt light-hearted and sure.

What more was there to say? "How do you like officers' training? What is it like to fly? Can the wind bother more than mud?" Not in this letter. This letter had all that mattered. I wouldn't even copy it over.

I stood on the step a minute before I went in to bed and looked up at the sky. The chinook was over. It was settling down again for a pull of hard winter, dark hard winter, like the name of the winter wheat. I could see the shadow of the flagpole on the moonlit earth and way across the flats, the dark shoulder of Prairie Butte. "It's cold enough to pick your bones," Mom used to say. It was tonight. The cold had picked all that was soft or green or growing and left only the bony skeleton of the earth.

I listened to the radio a long time after I turned the light out. The cold air flowed in under the window that was only opened a few inches. It's a good thing cold can't freeze music! My radio ran on batteries and I should have been saving of it, but I fell asleep with the music still playing.

241

13

THE cold winter days were good days for school. The children settled down to the new term. Leslie seemed more quiet than usual, but I thought he dreaded his father's going on Saturday. He loved stories, and I read aloud longer than usual at the end of school.

On Tuesday the children stayed a half-hour longer while I finished a chapter of *Bambi*. I had a secret feeling of triumph that I wasn't reading about the war to them.

"We're going to move to town next week," Leslie said excitedly as he was getting into his coat. "My grandfather's going to close up the ranch."

"I know that. My dad's goin' to take the hay off'n it," Francis La Mere said.

I thought of the Harper place closed up, no wool caught on the barbed-wire fence from the sheep pushing through, no tracks coming out of the roadway. It must be the rancher in me; I hate to see a ranch house empty and the fields unused.

"We'll only have six in school then," Mary said. "If help don't get easier to get, Pa says maybe we'll move to a big town and he'll go to work for a defense plant." Mary's face looked eager. "It'd be swell to live in a city."

I thought how quickly the war could reach to a place as far away as this.

Nels and Francis stayed to wash the blackboards for me. I sat at my desk marking spelling papers. Raymond brought in wood.

"Look, Miss Webb, a mouse got frozen in the woodpile!" He held up a flat gray body by the tail for me to see.

"Throw it away, Raymond," I said quickly.

"I betcha you can break its tail in two," Nels called out.

Raymond threw it across the room and the other boys dodged with a loud yell.

"That'll do, boys. Finish up now and go. Raymond, take that outside," I said sharply.

"Do you want any mail took to town, Miss Webb? The folks is goin' in tonight." Raymond was trying to make up for the mouse.

I hesitated. I hadn't put the letter in my mailbox. I had kept it on my dresser to think about it.

"Thank you, Raymond. I'll see." I went into my room and took the letter out of its envelope.

"Hey, Raymond, come on!" the boys shouted outside.

"Wait a sec. Teacher's getting a letter."

But I couldn't hurry. I read it again: *"Christmas Eve I knew all over again that I still loved you. And I came back after vacation and found your water color, like an answer."* I sealed it quickly and put two stamps on it and wrote "Air Mail" across the top.

"Here, Raymond. Thank you for waiting."

I watched the three boys straggling down the road until they were out of sight, but I was thinking of Gil getting the letter. It was sent now, anyway, and it was true.

Thursday morning I was wakened suddenly by the sound of a car coming up the road to the teacherage. Then I saw the lights. They shone in the window of my room and laid a strange bright light on the oil stove and the linoleum. I looked at my watch. It was four o'clock in the morning. The car went past the corner of the schoolhouse and left my room in darkness for an instant, then I could see the lights shining up the road. It was snowing again. The flakes danced crazily on the beam of light. The lights went out and the sound of the motor was stilled. I pulled on my warm bathrobe and slippers. Perhaps it was a message from the folks. I lighted my lamp and went through the schoolroom. I opened the door before there was a knock. Warren Harper stood there. He wore his good clothes, but his overcoat hung open and he was bareheaded.

"Warren, why did you come here at this time of night? Is Leslie all right?"

"Sure, Leslie's all right, but he won't be if he sees me! Ed Anderson leaves for the Army tomorrow and I leave Saturday, so we were celebrating tonight. I couldn't go home with liquor on my breath, could I?" His voice had an unpleasant sound.

I set the lamp down on Robert's desk. "But you can't stay here," I said.

He didn't seem to have heard. He sat down in Robert's seat. Then he nodded his head as though agreeing with something I had said.

"Army's a good place for me. Might make a man of me," he said with a mirthless kind of laugh. "Unless it's hopeless." He shrugged his big, loose shoulders.

I stood watching him. I could see why he didn't want to go home. If Leslie saw him like this, all the work of the last few weeks would be undone.

"Go to bed," he said so suddenly that it startled me. "Don't stand there staring at me with sorrowful eyes. Leslie can do that." He clasped his hands in front of him on the desk like a boy in school, but the lamp made his face look older than I had seen it.

"Oh, Warren, why did you do this just before you went away? It meant so much to Leslie." He looked back at me, then his eyes moved around the room.

"I used to sit there by the window, the last seat in the row."

I didn't stay to listen. I took the lamp and went back in my room and lighted the stove. I would heat up the coffee I had made for my dinner. I didn't know much about people who were drunk, but I had an idea that it might help him. I glanced out into the dark schoolroom. He had dropped his head on his arms. I heard his breathing and wondered if he were asleep. When the coffee was hot, I poured a cup and took it out to him. I set the lamp on my desk and then I sat down in the seat in front of him.

"Warren, drink this coffee."

He sat up and pushed his hair back. "Thanks, sister, you're doing the Salvation Army act!" The steam from the coffee went up between us. I saw him jerk his head as he took the first sip and wondered if he had burned his mouth. Then he set the cup down on the desk.

"Came to say good-by," he said. "Got my papers right here." He patted the pocket of his coat. "Report to Texas. Swell! Commission and everything. If I don't get shot it won't be my fault. Maybe they'll hang my picture on the wall here. The children'll be told what a hero I was. If you're here teaching, you remember that!" He shook his finger at me. "Why not? That's the way heroes are made."

"Warren, don't talk like that!" I laid my hand on his arm and he put his hand over mine and held it when I tried to pull it away.

"You're a hero, too, the way you went through that blizzard." I jerked my hand away and picked up his cup.

"Don't go. Sit down. I want to talk. I drove all the way out from town just to talk to you." I stood a minute, hesitating. "You won't have to listen to me much longer. I'll be gone Saturday." I set the cup on the desk across the aisle and sat down again. It was so cold I was shivering.

"It's a great thing to come back where you went to school. You can see yourself as a kid. I was a smart little kid; guess I was the smartest kid in the school. I thought I was going to be a great man. I learned my geography and history lessons well. I can tell you where the Philippine Islands are without looking!" Warren emphasized what he said with one finger that cast a longer finger in shadow on the wall.

"I can tell you the dates of all the wars America ever fought and why we fought 'em and why we're going to fight this one. Isn't this school the cradle of America? Sure! And how the politician loves it!" He swung his arm in a wide gesture and his voice was loud.

"Citizens of the United States, look to the little red schoolhouse if you would safeguard the future of America. Teach 'em the Gettysburg Address and Washington's Farewell Address an' you won't lack for soldiers to fight your battles. If they don't do so well as private citizens, that won't matter now. They'll win the war. America always wins its wars.

"But we've got to learn more than that in the little red schoolhouse; got to learn how to live decently afterward, too." I shivered with the cold, or at some tone in Warren's voice that sounded like Dad's when he gets started on something. It was eerie having him go on and on in the half-dark room. I went over and opened the school stove and put in a fresh stick of wood.

"Warren, please leave now."

"When you're a kid in school here, you want to be great and famous," he went on, but his voice lost its ranting note. "After a while you go away and you forget about that. You want someone to love you the way you love her and you want to make a good living, and live a decent life. When you don't get that, then you're ready to settle for some ideas, but they have to be good ones. That's when a man goes in for religion, I guess, some kind of a faith. But you can't pick up faith at a cut-rate drugstore. A man's lucky if there's a war on that he can go and fight in. If he gets killed in it, his life'll do some good, maybe." He went on and on. Finally I broke in again.

"Listen to me, Warren! You're just talking to hear yourself. You have Leslie. He has to believe in you. He's just beginning to trust you now. His whole life depends on you."

"And then I go and get drunk!" His voice was quiet. He sounded suddenly sober.

"You can't let Leslie know you were drinking."

"I must hide my sins from my son, must I?" Warren said, and that unpleasant sound was in his voice again.

"Yes, if you have to have them. You've got to go away with Leslie proud of you. Can't you see for yourself? I thought you cared about Leslie!" I was so angry I didn't care if he knew it. "I thought you came back here to win his love. Nobody ruined your life for you when you were his age, but you're going to ruin Leslie's."

"You're magnificent when you're angry, Ellen," he said. I saw he was smiling. It made me more angry.

"Get out of here! Go on out to the sheep camp until you're sober!" I think I would have struck him if he had gone on sitting there any longer. He stood up and buttoned his coat. He didn't say anything until he got to the door.

"Thank you for your hospitality, Miss Webb." He looked around the schoolroom. "I always liked this place," he said.

I heard him go down the steps. I went to the door. Outside it was just barely light. I had forgotten that it was snowing hard. And then I saw Mr. Thorson driving into the schoolyard with a truckload of stove wood. He must have seen us in the doorway of the schoolhouse. He got out of his truck and stood waiting for Warren.

"Good morning," Warren called out.

"Well, you're out early, aren't you?" Mr. Thorson said. I stood there wrapped in my bathrobe watching them. They were only a few feet from the steps.

"I just got my orders to leave for the Army. I stopped by to

246

talk to Miss Webb about Leslie," Warren said. I was relieved that he sounded dead-sober.

"You chose a queer time to call," Mr. Thorson said.

"Good morning, Mr. Thorson. Our woodpile was getting low," I said.

Mr. Thorson looked at me, but he didn't speak. Then he looked down at the ground.

"It must have took you some time," he said to Warren. The snow had covered over any tracks going to the schoolhouse.

"Look here, Thorson," Warren said, looking straight at him. He took him by the arm and they walked over to Warren's car so I couldn't hear what they said. I saw Mr. Thorson lay his hand on the hood of Warren's car and I knew it would be cold to the touch. I went back in and dressed hurriedly. It was almost seven-thirty.

I kept going over to the window to watch the two of them by the car. I wondered if I shouldn't call to them. I had a right to know what they were saying. I started out to the door once, but I came back. When I saw them coming back to the schoolhouse, I went into the schoolroom and sat at my desk. Mr. Thorson pushed open the door with a burst. Warren came after him; he looked angry.

"Miss Webb," Mr. Thorson began, "this is a pretty serious proposition for a teacher we send our children to . . ."

"Nels, I just told you that Miss Webb didn't have anything to do with my coming," Warren interrupted. "I sat in that seat over there and talked like a drunken fool for two hours straight. She gave me some coffee and kept trying to send me home."

"Maybe so, maybe so, Warren." Mr. Thorson looked thoughtful. "But she coulda kep' the door locked."

"Mr. Thorson, there was nothing wrong. It is just as Mr. Harper told you," I said.

Mr. Thorson didn't meet my eyes. He studied the crack in the floor. "You see, Miss Webb, I've been defending you for some time back. There's been a party that has seen Warren coming over here and seen you two in town on week ends, and now what I just seen with my own eyes this morning makes it look pretty bad."

"We've told you the truth. You'll have to take our word for it," Warren said.

"Just the same, as head of the school board I'll have to talk with the other members." Mr. Thorson studied the inside of his hat as he talked. "We'll have to hold a meeting and come over here this afternoon to talk to you, Miss Webb. I imagine you won't have any pupils today." He was standing now, but he lingered by the desk, playing with the top of the inkwell in the very same way his son did when he recited.

"Then there's another thing I was going to take up with Mr. Henderson, because he knows your folks. I've heard you mother's a foreigner, Miss Webb, I don't know what. Nels says you have foreign books here that you read out of, German and French and all like that. And the children say you don't seem very keen on the war. Sometimes you make 'em stop talking about it. It don't add up right, Miss Webb.

"Mary Cassidy told how once when the Russians was beaten back you said to think of all those soldiers on both sides that was wounded and crippled for life. That don't sound like a patriotic way to talk to children." He got out his handkerchief and mopped his forehead. I saw the look of disgust on Warren's face. I didn't quite believe what I had heard.

"Mr. Thorson, my father fought in Russia in the last war. He was wounded and has never been really well since. Naturally, war means wrecked lives to me. That doesn't keep soldiers from going to fight, or us from sending them." Suddenly, I said boldly: "The man I love, Mr. Thorson, is in the service right now. He's learning to be a pilot." It did me good to say "The man I love."

Mr. Thorson looked startled. "You oughtn't to be going out with Warren, then."

"I . . ." But Mr. Thorson tramped out of the room without another word. Warren was still standing there, but I didn't look at him.

"I've made a pretty good mess of everything, haven't I? I suppose they're all as evil-minded as Nels, or worse. It makes me gag to think I talked about coming back here to live!"

"Well, there's nothing we can do about it, and I wouldn't want to stay on if they won't believe us," I said. "But, Warren, what about Leslie? He mustn't hear any of this. It would spoil everything."

Warren's anger had disappeared, but his face looked so hopeless it hurt me to see him.

"I guess he just has the wrong father and the sooner he gives him up for a bad job, the better for him."

"Don't talk like that!" I said.

"I'm going to see Cassidy first. He's pretty human," he said. I followed him out to the porch and watched him going through the snow that had plenty of tracks now.

14

I MADE my bed and straightened my room and still it was only seven-thirty. Mr. Thorson had said I wouldn't have any pupils today, but perhaps some would come after all. This morning seemed like the morning after Robert's death when I waited for the children. Only then I had felt guilty; today I didn't.

I went out to the schoolroom and arranged my books in order for the day's lessons. I went through the back spelling words and made a list for a test. The parents must know every single thing that happened in school. I was glad that I hadn't known it before. It gave me a spied-on feeling. I thought of Mr. Thorson saying "I've heard your mother's a foreigner."

I heard the sound of the doorknob that was loose and always rattled a little.

"Good morning, Miss Webb." I knew before I looked up that it was Leslie. He slid into his seat and bent his head to look inside his desk. It was eight o'clock. None of the other children were coming. There was no sign of anyone else on the road. I wondered what I should tell him.

Leslie sat up straight and clasped his hands, as the children were asked to do as soon as they came into the schoolroom. I couldn't help thinking how his father had sat there earlier this morning, talking in such a tormented way.

"Well, it looks as though you were going to be the only pupil this morning," I said, smiling at him.

"Miss Webb, want to see what I found on the way over?" He came up to the desk, smiling mysteriously. When he stood beside me, he reached under his sweater and brought out a long gray and white feather. He had been so excited about his find he hadn't heard me.

"Oh, Leslie, what a big one! What kind of a bird do you think it belonged to?"

Leslie looked at me with shining eyes. "I think it belonged to a eagle, Miss Webb, 'cause it's such a strong feather—the eagle that lives on top of Prairie Butte!"

"Maybe you're right," I agreed.

"I know I am, Miss Webb. D'you want to feel it?"

I riffled the feather against my finger. "You don't think it could come from a chicken hawk?" I suggested.

"No." Leslie scowled and shook his head. "Why, Miss Webb, it'd be darker. This one's almost white, and it's so long and strong."

"That's right," I said. I was wondering what I should do with him. Mr. Thorson and the school board might come any time.

"Where're the other kids?" he asked. He hadn't thought about them before.

"I guess they're not coming. Most of the parents are coming for a meeting, so the children are lucky and have a vacation today. Maybe your father forgot to tell you."

"I didn't see Dad this morning. He's getting ready to go away."

"Well, you had a walk for nothing, but you won't mind that since you found the eagle's feather."

Leslie looked out the window at the snow. "I brought my lunch. I'd just as soon stay awhile. Can't I wash the blackboards?"

"Yes," I said impatiently. After all, it was only eight-thirty.

Leslie had to stand on a bench to reach the top of the blackboards. The wet slate had a sour, claylike smell that set my teeth on edge.

"Besides, you want the school board to think you keep the blackboards clean," Leslie said. He went outside and I heard him clapping the erasers together. While he was out there, Nels Thorson and Francis La Mere went by. Francis had his rifle. They called out and Leslie called back. They walked backward a way to see him, but they didn't stop. They would go home and tell their families that Leslie was here.

"Leslie, how would you like to take a book home with you to read?"

"Okay, Miss Webb." He went over to the bookshelf and took a book. "You want me to go now, don't you?"

"Well, I hate to have you waste the day here when the other children are out shooting and playing."

"I'm going now," he said. When he had his galoshes and cap and jacket on he came back to the desk. "Would you like my feather to keep, Miss Webb?"

"Oh, thank you, Leslie." And then I had a better idea. "Why don't you give it to your father to take with him to the Army?"

"That's a swell idea, Miss Webb."

I watched him go. He stuck his feather in his cap and before he was past the fence post he was eating a sandwich from his lunch.

I waited so hard the back of my neck ached. I was tight all over, the way I've been after a whole day on the combine when something goes wrong with the machinery. I couldn't keep my mind on anything to read. I couldn't go for a walk, because they might come and think I had been afraid of them. I tried to think what I would say to them, but I couldn't. I would just have to wait till they came. I thought of Gil, but that didn't help. Gil would hate anything like this; this had mud in it, and hate.

I watched them getting out of Mr. Thorson's car; he had brought Mr. La Mere and Mrs. Cassidy and Mrs. Donaldson. Mrs. Donaldson kept nodding her head and talking fast. Mr. La Mere looked down at the snow while Mrs. Donaldson was talking. I went to the door and said how do you do, as though they were coming to the Christmas exercises.

They had to sit on a bench and the front seats around my desk. Mrs. Donaldson wouldn't look at me. Mrs. Cassidy smiled and then covered it by blowing her nose. Mr. Thorson rose to talk. He put his hands in his pockets and looked out the window. There was a long minute of embarrassed silence.

"Miss Webb," Mr. Thorson began, "we're sorry we have to come here on such an errand. We've seldom had a teacher as promising, I might say, in the Prairie Butte school . . ."

"Nels Thorson, quit beatin' around the bush. She's not fit to teach young ones and she oughta go tomorrow," Mrs. Donaldson interrupted.

"Now, Minnie . . ." Mrs. Cassidy said, but I didn't wait.

"I'll be glad to go, Mr. Thorson. If you don't care to take my word and accept the explanation I gave you, I wouldn't care to stay."

Mrs. Donaldson sniffed. Suddenly, what I wanted to say was clear to me.

"There's just one thing I want to insist on, Mr. Thorson. I want to be sure that none of the children get any idea of the bad things you are thinking about me and Leslie Harper's father."

"Some of them have seen things for themselves," Mrs. Donaldson put in.

I could feel my face getting hot and my pulse throbbing in my neck.

"It doesn't make any difference to me or to Mr. Harper what you think," I said, "but I don't want to see a little boy's faith in his father destroyed by lies. Mr. Harper goes to the Army Saturday. He may not come back!"

"It'd be a shame to turn the boy against his father," Mr. La Mere said. "We kin say it was sickness that took you home, Miss Webb. We kin put a piece in the paper that reads that way."

"Teachers are hard to get in the middle of the term, Nels. My Mary's very fond of Miss Webb," Mrs. Cassidy said almost guiltily.

But Mr. Thorson shook his head. "Warren Harper threatened to sue me if Miss Webb lost her job . . ."

"I'd like to see him try! You saw him sneaking out of the teacherage this morning with your own eyes!" Mrs. Donaldson bristled. "His boy ought to know the truth."

I lost control then and I'm not sure of all I said. I remember that I looked at Mrs. Donaldson and Mr. Thorson when I said:

"This war we're fighting now is against people who have forced others, especially little children, to live in a world without hope or faith. Most of you feel there is no truth in what you are saying about me, but you want to believe there is, just for the excitement. You don't care if a little boy's faith in his father is destroyed by your gossip. I'm leaving! I wouldn't stay now if you begged me to, but I want a promise from each of you that the children won't hear a story that will break Leslie's heart."

Mr. Thorson was studying his hat. Mrs. Donaldson was red in the face. Mr. La Mere looked at me, but his face concealed whatever he thought.

I was trembling so that I gripped the edge of the desk while I waited for them to say something.

Slowly Mr. Thorson got to his feet. "Well, I don't see as any harm'll be done if we agree to that."

"Suits me fine," Mr. La Mere said, almost with relief, I thought.

"For the Lord's sake, yes!" Mrs. Cassidy sounded as though she might cry.

"I don't like it this way, but as long as she can't hurt my Robert no more, why, I suppose she can let on she's going home 'count of sickness. But I won't have her here!" Mrs. Donaldson declared.

I hardly listened to Mr. Thorson's remarks. He said there was no hurry. I could wait till the county supervisor notified me. I heard myself repeating that I wouldn't think of staying any longer than I had to.

But after they had gone I came back in and sat down at my desk. I put my head down on my arm like one of the children. I guess I was tired out. I didn't want to leave. This place was mine, as the rimrock back of the house is mine. Mom and Dad would believe me, but it would hurt them to have anyone saying these things.

It seemed as though everything I touched turned out wrong. I couldn't hold Gil's love, not at first, anyway, and now I couldn't hold my job. I remembered how Dad had said that other time: "If that boy's made Ellen unhappy, we've got paid back for our sins." He might even wonder if maybe I had been . . . like Mom.

I hated the way their lives and mine seemed so mixed up together. I almost wished I didn't have to go home, that I could be free of Mom and Dad and their hate and even their love for me. But I knew I couldn't. If I went away and got a job somewhere, in the city, I would feel I had run away.

Warren came back in the early evening.

"I couldn't do a damn thing to help you out of this mess," he said. He sat there, staring down at his hands. I felt sorry for him, more sorry than I had for myself when Gil went away.

"Don't worry any more about it. I don't care," I told him.

"I'll drive you home and tell your mother and father how it was," he said.

"No, you don't need to do that. I can tell them. They'll believe me. You only have two more days with Leslie."

"Please let me. I only have that long to see you, Ellen." He looked up at me so quickly I couldn't look away. I had never seen a man's face so plain before. Nothing was covered up in it. I didn't doubt that he loved me, it was there so clearly, but it didn't seem to touch me.

"I won't ask you again to marry me. Even if you didn't love your Gil you'd be a fool to take a chance with me, but a thing like last night won't ever happen again." When he smiled that way he looked like Leslie. "I don't know why you should believe me."

"But I do, Warren," I said. The funny thing about it was that I did.

"I wish I could have found you, Ellen, before you met Gil. He must be blind."

"No," I said. "He's just the way he has to be. I suppose we all are."

"Well, when I come back, I'm coming to see you."

"Of course! I'll be glad to see you." I laughed a little to make things easier between us.

"If there was just something I could do to make it up to you."

"You don't need to make anything up." Then I thought of Leslie. "Except I'd like to see you make it up to Leslie."

His face changed and seemed to brighten under the weariness. "Do you know when I got in the car to go to see Henderson, Leslie came running out and wanted to go along. He's never done that before without my asking him. It was a poor business to take a child on, but he sat out in the car. He gave me this to take with me to the Army." Warren took the feather out of his pocket. "He says he's sure it's a feather from the eagle that lives on Prairie Butte." Warren smiled as he told me about it. "Leslie slept all the way home. I carried him into the house and put him on his bed before I came over here."

"It didn't really take long to win him over, Warren, did it?"

"Now he'll hear about last night!"

"No, he won't. Saturday when you leave you're going to bring him out to our place as we planned. Then the next week your mother and father will be in town, anyway."

"How about your mother and father? Do you think they'll want him after all this?"

"Of course, Warren, they're not like that." He looked so relieved I saw he had been worrying about them. "Go on home now and get some sleep. I'll be ready to go in the morning when you come for me. You'll have to bring the Pony Express, I've got so much stuff."

He was so tired he didn't say any more. He just went.

I worked until late that night putting the teacherage in order. I washed the floor again, but I couldn't see to wash the windows. It was hard to remember how I had felt those first days here, but that was way back in the fall. Now I felt at home. I had come back here from the ranch last time with relief. I didn't want to go away so soon. The reason for going didn't seem to touch me—it was just the going.

I had grown used to living alone by myself. Now I didn't want to go back to our house, where my room was so close to the folks. I had come to like the stillness that had seemed so empty and ghostly at first. Gil would say our ranch house was far enough away to suit anybody, but it was full of Mom's and Dad's living. The fields pushed up so close to the house with their crops and the need to worry about them. Here there was nothing. Even the sheepherder drove his herd across this bare place to better grazing ground. But it didn't seem like nothing to me. It seemed wide and sunny and wind-swept, and I loved it, most of all, perhaps, because I had come out here feeling I had lost Gil and I had found him again while I was here.

I would never be able to make Gil understand how I felt about this place. I would know better than to bring him to see it. It would look only crude and desolate to him. His not understanding seemed for a minute like one of those sharp cuts that the spring rains make in the gumbo. The cut goes deep sometimes.

I remembered how Warren had stood against the door the other night, just last night, really. He had looked around the room and said:

"I always liked this place."

I went into my room and started to pack my things. I took down the icon and Gil's water color first.

PART THREE

"Sow the seed in the wide black earth and already the seed is victorious, though time must contribute to the triumph of the wheat."

—ANTOINE DE SAINT-EXUPÉRY,
Flight to Arras

I

WE turned off the highway at our place near noon. All the way I had pictured Mom and Dad. They would both be home, waiting to hear the noon broadcast of the grain market. When Mom heard the truck she would come to the window and look out above the geraniums.

"Let me explain to them. I'm responsible for the whole thing," Warren said, almost like a young boy bringing a girl home late.

"Oh, no, I'll tell them. I'll wait till you are gone."

But Mom came across the yard as we drove in. Her head was tied up in a white dishtowel. She had on an old coat of mine that didn't quite come together in front and some canvas gloves.

"Yeléna, what is wrong?" she asked when she saw us.

"I had trouble with the school board, Mom. I'm not going to teach the second term. Warren brought my things home for me."

"It wasn't her fault at all, Mrs. Webb," Warren said.

Mom's face was heavy with thinking. "You bring everything home?"

"Yes, everything."

"Just put them things all on the porch. Yeléna, you can get them from there." Mom went ahead to take off the old blankets that covered the glider in winter. "Your father's down to Bailey's," Mom threw back over her shoulder. She didn't ask anything more. The things piled in the truck looked dreary as we started to unpack them. I took up a box of things: the icon, my water color, Dad's books. Because there was so much to say that we didn't say we worked twice as fast at unloading the truck.

"Mom, Warren's leaving for the service Saturday. I invited Leslie to stay with us this week end before I knew that. I thought he could come anyway. Warren can bring him in when he goes and then we can take him back."

"Sure," Mom said. "Mr. Harper, you bring him." I was grateful to her for the warm tone in her voice.

"Warren's family are moving into town. He'll be going there to school," I added, because there didn't seem much to talk about.

"Don't the little boy want to stay here right along? Town is no place for boys," Mom said. "We need a boy 'round here." Mom looked from me to Warren. I could almost follow her thought in her face. Her eyes narrowed a little and were bright and almost shrewd.

"Well," Warren said, "that's awfully good of you, I . . ." He was embarrassed. I felt him looking at me.

"I'm afraid he might be lonesome if he stayed here," I said.

"Not out here," Mom said so positively that Warren laughed and I had to smile. "Pretty soon now we get those baby chicks. He can go to school in Gotham. That's where Yeléna go when she was little."

"But, Mom, Warren's family want Leslie, and anyway he likes living in town." I heard my own voice sounding irritable, and I said more gently, "But you would like having a boy here, wouldn't you?"

Mom paid no attention to me. "What do you say, Mr. Harper?"

"Ellen?" he asked. "You don't want Leslie here underfoot."

For a minute I didn't, and then I thought of Leslie offering me his eagle feather.

"Of course I would. Would your family let him come?"

"I think they would like to have him here. Mother is so old, and they'll only have a little place in town. I would want to pay his board of course, and . . ."

"Oh, he can help so much as his living cost," Mom interrupted. I busied myself picking up the odds and ends that were put in the truck loose. "We see," Mom was saying when I came back to them. "I talk to Ben. When you come we settle that."

Warren wouldn't stay for dinner. I didn't urge him.

"You're sure this is all right with you, Ellen? You must be fed up with the Harpers, father and son." His face had a comical expression, as though he weren't quite sure that he wouldn't be scolded.

260

"Don't be silly. It will be fun to have him here if he really wants to come. Tell him he can bring his feather collection."

His face lighted. "Thank you, Ellen."

Now that I was home, I wondered if I had been too hasty in leaving my job without a fight. I felt a little self-conscious walking back to the porch with Mom standing there.

"You better open up your room and let it warm up first," was all Mom said. "You can take these things in the front room."

I picked up my suitcase and my old jacket from the glider and took them in. The kitchen seemed hot and steamy. The front room hadn't been put in order yet this morning and a last night's newspaper lay in a heap by Dad's couch. The radio was on too loud. I turned it off before I heard whether the wheat was up or down. I didn't care. I had never noticed until now how low the ceiling was above my head. I opened the flimsy door into my room and the cold air of the closed room was like a wall against me. How could you be homesick coming home? And yet I was. For a minute it didn't seem to me that I could ever fit into living here again. It felt too small.

"Here, you have something to eat first," Mom said. She poured a cup of coffee and brought out some bread and cold pork.

I sat down at the table in the kitchen, but I wasn't hungry.

"What happen?" Mom asked.

It seemed so hard to go back over all that. I began at the beginning. Mom nodded from time to time. I told her about Warren's coming in the middle of the night.

"He had been drinking and he didn't want to go home. You see, on account of Leslie . . ." It was hard to explain why a grown man should be afraid of a little boy. I wasn't sure she understood what I was trying to say about Leslie, but Mom said suddenly:

"I know. Your aunt was like that. Wine was something of the Devil, so was anything Catholic. Your dad was brought up like that."

It was easier than I had thought it would be. "So I left. I couldn't go on teaching there after they had thought the worst things about me."

"No," Mom said. "You do right. We need you here in spring. If we have early spring we can get started pretty soon now."

I had most of my things put back in the drawers they had come from. The icon was back in the corner and a few of the books on my dresser. It didn't take long. I went back out to the kitchen. Mom was chopping cabbage on the table.

"Yeléna, did Mr. Harper ask you to marry him?"

I was so surprised at her asking like that that I had no other answer ready. "Why, yes, he asked me," I said. "I told him I couldn't."

Mom nodded. She went on cutting cabbage with hard chops against the wooden bowl. "I guess he like his little boy come here." Mom left out more of her little words than usual.

"If Leslie likes it. His grandparents are quite old," I said, thinking about them. "He's a strange little boy, very religious."

Mom stopped her chopping again to say: "I see Bardiches' tiger cat over here looking for mice around the barn. I think she maybe have kittens. You tell Tony we like one." Mom smiled as though to herself. I marveled at how simple she was. She thought she could make any child happy with a new kitten, and she thought she could make me want to marry Warren by having Warren's boy here till I grew so fond of him I didn't want to let him go.

"I guess I'll go down and meet Dad," I said.

I put on the old sheepskin hanging by the door and set out in the wind. I was almost glad of the wind. I didn't feel still or calm, myself. I walked in front of Peterson's store. Let them wonder why I was back home; I didn't care. Then I cut across the road to the elevator.

When I ran up the ramp to the elevator I could hear the radio going in Bailey's office. The door was closed to shut out the cold. I stood still a minute to hear the light spattering sound of grain sifting out over the top of the full bins. The wooden joists high up creaked as though the elevator were alive and had a voice. Someone had figured a sum in pencil on the cardboard sign tacked by the door. "One Dk. Hard Winter," I read, but it didn't give me any feeling of courage.

I knocked on the door of the office, and when no one answered I turned the knob. Bailey and Dad must have gone somewhere together. The cribbage board was out on the counter by the window, and a deck of cards. The radio was going full-blast. A voice sang "I'll be down to get you in a taxi, honey, Better be ready at half-past eight . . ." I turned it down until the voice

262

was only a whine, no louder than the sound of the wind. The room was like an oven. It was a snug little place in winter. The wind blowing against the tall frame walls made it seem even more of a refuge. I sat on the counter where I used to climb up as a child. I used to think it was like a watchtower in here, the windows gave on such a wide sweep of country.

The ground was half covered with snow, half bare, but the mountains showed way at the edge, beyond our place and Bardiches' and Halvorsens'. I was tired of winter and bareness. I wished it were spring. I tried for a minute to think how all this would look when it was warm again, but I couldn't. It scared me a little. What if when you were old you couldn't remember what it had been like to be young? You could tell yourself what it had been like. . . .

"My hair used to be yellow. I had the fairest skin, I was slender then, as slender as an aspen tree. . . ." That was the way women loved to talk about themselves when they were old. But maybe it would be like talking of spring. I could tell myself how it was then: "The wheat is green in spring, every other strip, and the sky above it is a bright blue. The low hills are green, too, for a month or so, and the prairie flats are blue and yellow and pink with shooting stars and crocuses and lupin. New sage grows in the palest green clumps and the road is still muddy."

But I couldn't see it. I could only see the bare late-winter look of the country.

I was disappointed not to find Dad. I wanted to see him first alone. I wanted to tell him, without Mom there, how I had come to leave Prairie Butte. But when I came home Dad was there in the kitchen, reading.

"Well, Ellen, it's good to have you home. I didn't like having you off out there in that God-forsaken spot."

I went over to him, but I felt Mom holding her spoon in the air above the saucepan to watch me, and I felt big and awkward standing by Dad. I couldn't say anything. Mom had told him anyway. Dad put his arm around me and drew me closer to his chair. I stood there just long enough so I wouldn't hurt his feelings, then I drew away.

"Come back like a bad penny, Dad," I said. "I guess I better change my shoes, they're wet."

"Like a lucky piece, you mean," Dad retorted. "Your mother's got some baked beans for supper. You came the right night, Ellen."

They tried so hard to make me feel welcome; it made me feel more strange.

2

THERE'S something that hurts about a thing broken off before it's finished, whether it's a job or a branch of a tree or a row of wheat. It bothered me to be home this way. I thought of the teacherage there waiting for me. I wondered if it would stand idle and empty so long that the pack rat that lived under the floor would bore a hole through.

Mom had agreed that I couldn't have stayed after they had talked that way about me, but Dad fretted about it to himself, I think, because he would say something now and then.

"When I think about the way they treated you, I'd like to go to Prairie Butte myself," he said one day.

"Oh, I think Mr. La Mere and Mrs. Cassidy and maybe Mr. Thorson were sorry at the end."

"I guess Mr. Henderson told them plenty!" Mom punched her bread dough as though it were one of the school board.

I had known that Mom and Dad would stand back of me, but I was grateful that they didn't blame me or doubt me.

Saturday morning I said: "I'll give Leslie my room. He'll go to bed earlier than we do, so he'll need a room to himself." Mom nodded as though that went without saying. "I can sleep on the couch," I said. "Are you sure you want to take Leslie to board, Mom?"

"Sure. We can use the little money he want to pay. It please Mr. Harper to have him here." Mom had made up her mind.

I was helping with dinner when Leslie and his father drove into the yard. I stopped to wash my hands while Mom went right out. I knew Dad was in the barn and would see them too. I don't know why I hung back so.

Leslie climbed out first. I saw how the wind seemed to blow

against him. His thinness showed up as he stood there. His hair needed cutting. He took off his cap and then it was so cold he pulled it on again. I saw Dad shake hands with them both. Warren was smiling, but I had the picture of him in the schoolroom still in my mind. It didn't seem to fit.

I couldn't delay any longer. Mom and Leslie were walking back to the house. When I stepped outside Leslie ran to me and put his arms around me.

"Miss Webb, I brought my feathers and everything!" he said. I hadn't expected him to be so glad to see me. I felt better about his coming. I went over to speak to Warren.

"Hello, Warren."

"Hello, Ellen. You don't know how happy Leslie is to come." I felt Leslie's hand squeezing mine. "I'm glad your mother and father were willing to let him come," I said.

I took Leslie into my room and helped him arrange his feathers on the table by the window. It was strange to have him here. We opened his suitcase and took out his things: overalls and socks and shirts and underwear, little-boy things. He had the drawings he had made at school and a rock and a bag of marbles and his mother's big indexed Bible and some pamphlets and the picture of his mother wrapped up in a pyjama top.

We set dinner in the front room. It was dark enough at four o'clock so we had to turn on the light. The bulb in its green paper shade shone down on chicken pie and candied sweet potatoes and Mom's rolls. When Mom wants a meal to be especially nice, she cooks the kind of thing Dad likes best. The light shone, too, on the sterling silver spoons and all the knives and forks that were plated silver from the dime store. Gil had made me aware of these things now for the rest of time. I wondered how soon I would hear from him. Surely he would write. I had expected a letter by now. I had thought he would rush to write me as I had hurried to write him.

Mom enjoyed seeing Leslie eat. Dad and Warren talked the war together.

"The Thorsons are moving into town too, Miss Webb," Leslie looked up to say. "I guess they aren't going to get a new teacher for the rest of the year. There's only the La Meres left, and the school board'll pay their fare into Harwood. Dad says it's because they couldn't find anybody good enough to take your place,

Miss Webb. Miss Webb, couldn't I please call you Ellen the way Dad does?"

"Surely you can if you want to, Leslie," I said. I felt Mom looking at me and my face blushing.

"Ellen, can I please go outside? That's all I can eat, honest." Leslie asked me questions as though he were still at school.

"Of course, but stay around. Your father will be leaving in a little bit," I said.

I think we lingered at the table because Warren had to go right afterward. Dad was doing most of the talking, as he had when Gil was here. I had minded it then. Now I didn't care. I got up to take off the dishes and empty their ash trays and then I came back to sit with them, only half-listening to what they said.

"Yeléna, you get some wine before Mr. Harper goes," Mom said. "Get the dandelion wine."

Mom made two kinds of wine, dandelion and raisin. The dandelion was a beautiful color. It was too bad Mom put it in a brown bottle and the only wineglasses we had were bright-green. I took it in to the table to pour it.

"Well, Warren, here's good luck to you! I wish I were going with you," Dad said.

"*Na zdorozye!*" Mom said, which is Russian for "Your health."

As we lifted our glasses I met Warren's eyes. He was pleased by the little ceremony. Then for an instant I held my breath. I saw Leslie's horror-struck little face looking in at us through the window. He must have come to see how soon Warren was leaving, and he had seen us with our glasses raised.

"Warren, Leslie was there at the window!"

"Tell him to come back in. Here, I get him," Mom said, but I was already on my way to the porch. As I opened the door Leslie ran past.

"Leslie!" I called. "Come here—we're just wishing your father good luck." But he kept on running without turning his head. "Leslie, your father's going now. Come and say good-by," I called again. He could hear me easily, but he didn't turn his head. He disappeared inside the barn.

"What on earth struck him?" Warren asked beside me.

"The wine, I guess. He saw us drinking."

Warren's face showed his exasperation. "There's no use chasing him then."

"He'll come when he hears you start the car," I said. We went back in, but the moment was spoiled. Dad and Mom drank their little glasses of wine standing. Warren held his by the stem. "I know how good it is, but I guess I won't drink it. You tell Leslie, sometime." He looked embarrassed. I carried out the glass and emptied mine into the sink with it. Mom and Dad couldn't understand what it was all about, I could see. I heard Warren talking to Mom about Leslie's board and his pen scratching as he wrote a check.

"He'll be fine, don't worry none," Mom was saying as they came out to the kitchen.

Dad had gone out to the barn to find Leslie but I saw him coming back alone. Warren went out to speak to Dad. Mom and I stood at the window watching them.

"He's going now, Ellen. You better go say good-by," Mom said.

I picked up my jacket and went out. I walked up to them slowly so they would be through talking.

"Not many people would treat me like this after I was the cause of Ellen's losing her job. I can't tell you . . ." I heard Warren say.

"Well, it can't be helped. Folks in little towns are a suspicious lot," Dad said. His voice that sometimes seemed slow to me sounded kind.

"I had been celebrating or I wouldn't have been so thoughtless."

"Forget it now," Dad said. Then he saw me. "There's Ellen. I'll take another look for the boy."

"I'm so sorry that happened, Warren. I'm sure I can explain it to Leslie."

"It won't be easy. I told your mother if he's sullen or unmanageable just to take him in to my parents. It does kind of wipe out what progress I made with him, doesn't it? Anyway, it's a wonderful thing for him to be here."

"The folks are going to be glad to have him. I may go in town and get a job, and he will keep them from getting lonesome."

"You'd rather be teaching. You don't like it back home here, I could see at dinner."

"It's all right. I'll like it when there's work to do. Just now, while it's so cold, it's dull."

268

We stood there awkwardly. The wind blew so that I pulled my coat around me tightly.

"Here, put your arms into it," Warren said, and I minded him.

"I hope you do like it in the Army," I said finally. "I guess you will. Dad sure did."

"I'll like it all right."

"Leslie is proud of your going."

Warren's mouth twisted a moment. "I don't know. He seemed different the last few days, stuck to me tighter than a bur, but he hasn't said anything about hating to see me go."

"But he does," I insisted. I couldn't stand to have Warren go feeling like this about Leslie. I looked over at the barn and even up on the rimrock, hoping to catch a glimpse of him.

"Ellen, I know I talked the worst rot the other night. I don't know just what I said. I drank too much in town and instead of feeling hilarious I kept getting lower all the way back home. I got to thinking about what I'd meant to be when I was a kid and where I was . . ."

"Don't do that," I said, as sharply as though I were speaking to the school children. "I've forgotten it by now."

"You're better to me than I deserve. Well, I've got to go. Ellen, would you write me once in a while?"

I didn't like seeing him so humble. "Of course," I said. "You'll want to hear about Leslie. He'll be writing you, too."

Warren hesitated with his hand on the car door. I think he wanted to say something more. "Wait, I'll call Leslie again." I ran way to the barn and called: "Leslie, please come. Your father wants to say good-by." But there was no sign of him. I looked back at Warren standing by the car waiting.

"Never mind. Maybe it's better not to say good-by. You tell him I'll be writing," Warren said. He didn't shake hands or even say good-by. He just waved as he drove away.

I felt I really knew Warren better than I did Gil. Hearing him that night in the schoolroom when he was only half talking to me was like being inside his mind, feeling things the way he did.

As I watched him drive away I seemed to know how he felt, both glad and sorry, glad of a new life for a while and a chance to do something that seemed bigger and more urgent than just earning a living, but without much that was happy to look back

269

on. And now he wouldn't be able to forget how Leslie had run off just as he was leaving.

"Good luck, Warren!" I called, but Warren couldn't hear me. I walked back to the barn to look for Leslie, but I went on thinking about Warren. I wondered what his life would be like after the war. Finally I gave up hunting for Leslie and went back into the house.

It was dark by five o'clock. I was just going out to milk when I heard Dad calling. He was coming up from the big shed where the combine stood, carrying Leslie. I held the kitchen door open for him and he carried him in and put him on my bed. I covered him up without waking him and we closed the bedroom door.

"You mean that little kid was so mad about the wine he ran off like that?" Dad said in the kitchen.

"Sure, you ought to know. Like your folks he is!" Mom slapped the dishcloth against the sink as she polished it.

We moved around the house quietly. We didn't talk about him, but I guess we were all thinking about him or his father. Mom set out bowls of soup in the kitchen for supper about seven, and the house was quiet except for the clink of our spoons.

But we were all waiting for Leslie to wake up. It was close to eight when we heard the bedroom door open, and Leslie's feet on the linoleum-covered floor. He stood in the doorway, his hair tousled, his face pale and white-looking in the bright light. He had rings under his eyes and there were dirt streaks on his face.

"You must be hungry. I get you some good soup," Mom said.

"Sit right down here," Dad said.

Leslie ate everything Mom gave him. When he was through Mom brought him some old funny papers. She always saved the old papers in the shed. Leslie smiled and said thank you and spread them out on the table. No one said anything about his father. We went back to what we had been doing.

At nine o'clock I said it was bedtime.

"Oh, Ellen! I have to read my chapter first." Leslie hurried into his room and came back with his mother's big Bible that was marked with different colored crayons and had many strips of paper sticking out between the pages.

"I'm on my way through it. I've got to Numbers, the thirty-third chapter." He laid the big Bible on the table and opened it at the marker. We were so still we could hear the fire in the stove. Leslie moved his finger under the line he was reading. "Ellen, it's all names. Could you help me?"

I came and looked down at what he was reading. His finger pointed out the line. " 'And the children of Israel removed from Rameses and pitched in Succoth,' " I read for him. He looked up beaming.

"I could say 'and the child of the Harpers removed from Prairie Butte and pitched in Gotham,' couldn't I?" We were all smiling with relief.

I looked down the long list of Biblical names. "I think you could skip this part," I said.

"Oh, no, Mother wanted me to read every word."

"Here, Leslie, bring the Bible over here," Dad said. "I used to read in the Old Testament when I was a boy." Leslie climbed up on Dad's knees and leaned back against his shoulder. Dad read aloud; whether he knew how to pronounce the names or not, he never hesitated, but brought them out with a brave ringing sound of authority: " 'And they removed from Dibongad and encamped in Almon-diblathaim. And they removed from Almon-diblathaim and pitched in the mountains of Abarim, before Nebo . . .' " Once he looked above Leslie's head at us and smiled. Leslie's face had the intent listening look it used to have in the teacherage.

"Thank you, Mr. Webb," he said gravely and carried the Bible back into his room. We could hear him undressing—his boots on the floor and then the sound of his belt buckle against the back of the chair. Suddenly we heard from the other room:

"Dear God in Heaven, bless the Webbs, and Grandmother and Grandfather, because they're old. And give my love to Mother . . ." There was a long pause. I saw Mom lean forward. ". . . And bless the Army and Navy. . . . And may my dad feel the burden of his sins and fight temptation and the Devil. A-men."

Mom crossed herself. Dad shook his head. I went in to open the window and tuck in the blankets.

3

IN a couple of weeks' time it seemed natural to have four at the table, to hear Leslie call Mom and Dad Aunt Anna and Uncle Ben, and to hear him ask grace before meals. Every noon Mom would stand outside the kitchen door or watch out the window to see Leslie come running up the road from school. More often now we heard his high, shrill little laugh. He always thought the pigs were funny and the gobbling of the turkeys, and he never could get Dad to tell him enough stories about when he was a boy. Whenever we couldn't find him we knew where to look—in the combine. There was a big tarpaulin over part of it that he called his tent, and that was his retreat.

When a letter came from his father he brought it to me to read. Warren told Leslie all about the camp and what he did all day. At the end he said, "I miss you very much and I miss Miss Webb. I hope you'll both write me soon. Love, Dad." When I gave Leslie back his letter, he ran to put it in his bureau drawer. I wondered what he was thinking.

But I was waiting for another letter, a letter from Gil. If Dad was away when the train came in, I pretended an errand at the store so I could go for the mail.

Tony Bardich was in the store when I went in one day.

"Hi," he said, "I see in the paper where you left your teacher-age because of sickness at home. I didn't know any of your folks was sick!"

"Dad hasn't been well," I said. "I thought you'd be in the Army by this time," I flung back at him. I didn't wait to see what he would say. At least, the school board had kept their promise. I took my package and went on down to the elevator to get the mail.

272

I walked on the rails a way, the ground was so wet with melted snow. It was February now and as warm some days as April. The sun on the ramp was so bright I had to blink a minute when I went into the darkness of the elevator.

"Well, I expected Ben over this afternoon. I guess you just come when you know you're going to get a letter, is that it?" Bailey said with a grin.

"Sure," I said. I walked up to the little counter and looked at the pigeonhole above our name. There was a letter in it, a thick-looking letter. Bailey seemed so slow, stopping to fasten the half-door of the counter behind him, before he reached out for the envelope.

"Looks like you're hearing from some soldier!"

"Thanks, Bailey," I said, and slipped it in my pocket as though I got a letter every day. I went back out of the elevator, down the ramp, and across the tracks. I was out of sight of the cross-roads before I took it out of my pocket. I saw the postmark and the word "Free" written at the stamp corner. "Wm. Richards, Lt. A.A.F." was written in the other corner. The handwriting was strange.

I tore the envelope across one end and a little newspaper clipping fell out on the ground. I picked it up and read that first.

"5 Army Fliers Killed

"Jan. 10th. Three officers and two enlisted men were killed and six others were injured today when a large Army bomber from the air base on a routine flight crashed and burned in a farm field near here. Names of the casualties were not released pending notification to first of kin."

There was another loose sheet in the envelope. It was just a sheet torn out of a tablet, with a sketch, really a sort of cartoon on it—a drawing of a man sprawling in the mud with a silly little flower near his head. The man was smelling the flower and there was a broad smile on his face. Underneath was printed "It takes a fall in the mud to make you see a wild flower. G.H.B."

Then I read the letter:

"*Dear Miss Webb,*

"*I am writing you because Gil seemed to think a great deal of you. He used to talk a lot about you and I found an envelope*

*with your address on it in his things. I know your last letter was
in his pocket. The enclosed clipping tells all there is to know. His
personal belongings were sent back to his family. Gil was my best
friend. He was a quiet sort, and I think the Army was hard on
him at first, but he was one of our best pilots. I know he would
have done great things if he had ever gotten over.*

*"I am enclosing this cartoon because he said one day that he was
going to send it to you.*

> *"Sincerely yours,*
>
> *"William Richards, Lt. A.A.F."*

I folded the letter and the drawing and put them back in my
pocket. January 10. I had written Gil the week after I got back
from Christmas vacation. That was the first week of January,
January 5 or 6. The letter had just reached there. He had never
had time to write me. I would never know how he felt.

I took the letter out and read it again: "Gil seemed to think a
great deal of you. He used to talk a lot about you. . . . I know
your last letter was in his pocket."

I went on home because there was nothing else to do. I felt the
way I did when Gil went away and I was sure he wasn't coming
back. I had put him out of my life then; but that was last year
when I didn't know how deep my love went and that I couldn't
stop loving him. After he sent me the little water color I had
known that he couldn't stop loving me, either. Of course I knew
how he felt. I clumped through the middle of the road, not bothering to keep on the hard edge.

"You got the mail, Yeléna! Your Dad and Leslie go over, too.
Bailey say there was only mail for you," Mom said as I came into
the kitchen.

"Yes," I said. I took the letter out of my pocket. I felt Mom
waiting. "Gil's a flyer now," I said dumbly.

"Well! I wonder can he run a plane better than the truck!"
Mom stood there in the kitchen with her arms on her hips,
laughing.

I went on into my room and closed the door. I looked at the
yellow-green water color tacked up by my mirror and I told myself that Gil would never see the sun like that again, but I didn't
really believe it. I looked at the cartoon again. He must have
drawn that after my smug little letter from the teacherage.

I took out the photograph of him, but he was looking past me in it. The thread of his cigarette smoke went up heartlessly. He hadn't loved me then, or been in the Army or learned to fly. All that must have changed him. I had only heard from him twice, and I hadn't kept those letters. I had torn them to bits in a rage. Why hadn't I written him sooner? Why had I been so slow to know I loved him? That was the trouble with this country out here; it is so far away, so slow, there is as much time as there is sky.

I heard Leslie's voice and Dad's. I pushed Gil's picture into the drawer, and the cartoon, but I carried the letter and the clipping in the pocket of my shirt like a secret. I wished I had been married to Gil, so I could go out and tell Mom and Dad and they would let me have my grief. Now if I told them they would be glad that was over with. But it wasn't, and they wouldn't understand. They didn't know what love was, I thought with scorn and pity.

In the kitchen Mom was dishing up the meat and dumplings. There was a warm good smell of food. Leslie was drying his hands and talking excitedly to Dad about the water standing on the field across the road.

"It was really melted today and there was real live ducks on it, Uncle Ben. You know, with black heads and white on them!"

"Look at you, Yeléna. Are you going to eat in those clothes?" Mom asked me.

I had forgotten about the way I looked. Only in harvesttime did we eat in our work clothes. Even Mom always changed into a clean housedress. Dad said he couldn't eat if he smelled dust in his clothes and I think Mom was proud of it in him. I looked down at my heavy work shoes that were gray with dried mud, and the ragged hems of my jeans.

"That's right," I said. "You sit down and I'll be back in a minute."

"I guess the mail make you lightheaded," Mom said.

In my room I stripped off my clothes and sponged with cold water from the pitcher, then I dressed for Gil. Gil used to like my light-green sweater and the gray skirt. I used to wear it last year in the library. I brushed my hair and fastened it with a black velvet bow and did my lips. I hadn't bothered since I came home.

"Just last year at this time, Gil," I whispered. I looked in the mirror and I looked pretty even to myself, pretty for Gil. I had a foolish notion—I pretended I was already married to Gil.

Then I went back out to the table.

"That's better!" Mom said.

"Oh, Ellen, you look nice," Leslie said with his mouth full.

Dad looked at me and I could see that he liked having me dressed up, but they didn't know why I looked so different.

I talked all through dinner. I told them I'd seen Tony Bardich and what he said about reading in the paper that I was back home because of sickness in the family. "I told him you hadn't been well, Dad." I saw Leslie's eyes on me, but that wouldn't tell him anything.

Mom made a sound of contempt in her throat. "That Tony should keep his nose in his own cabbage field!" she said, and Leslie burst out into a giggle.

"Does he have a big nose, Aunt Anna?"

It was a funny thing, I wasn't sad. I felt elated, as though nothing really could touch me because of my secret. In a strange way I felt I was close to Gil.

After the dishes Mom said: "You and Leslie better write his dad tonight. He'll be worrying, off in Army like that."

"All right," I said, and I got out a pad of paper and a pencil for Leslie. "Come on, Leslie, you sit here." I drew up a chair for him at the kitchen table.

Leslie came, but he sat back against the chair. "Couldn't you write him, Ellen?"

"Oh, I'll add a note, but he wants to hear from you. You've only written him one little short letter."

Leslie picked up the pencil, but his lips were set in a sulky line. "DEAR DAD," he printed. "I AM FINE. I SAW WILD DUCKS TODAY DOWN ON THE FIELD WHERE THERE IS LOTS OF WATER."

"That's all I can think of," he said.

"You can write more than that. Tell him about playing in the combine and how you miss him, and ask him about the Army," I prompted. It was easy to do tonight. I wanted Warren to have a letter from Leslie that would make him feel good. A letter was so important.

Leslie shook his head, then he picked up his pencil and began printing, "DID YOU BRAKE YOUR PROMISE AGEN? YOUR SON, LESLIE

HARPER." "There!" He handed it to me as though he knew I wouldn't like it.

"Oh, Leslie, what a thing to say! You know that night when we drank to your father's health? He didn't drink any. He left his glass there, not because he thought it was wrong but because he didn't want to make you feel bad."

Leslie's eyes seemed to study me and his mouth was as stern as any adult's. I saw Mom looking at him.

"You mean you think my good wine I make from them yellow dandelions is bad?" Mom asked him.

Leslie nodded his head. He took his jacket silently and went outdoors. Mom made as if to call him, but I said: "He'll be all right. Dad is out there." I erased Leslie's last sentence. "Send me a picture in your uniform," I printed, making it look as much like Leslie's as I could and I put in the word "love."

Then I wrote a note to Lieutenant Richards thanking him for writing me. There was so much I wanted to ask him. Most of all, I wanted to write: "Do you think he loved me very much? What did he say about me? Did he seem happy the day he got my last letter?" But I couldn't do that.

Mom thought I was writing to Gil. She didn't like it, and clattered the cover of the soup kettle as she pushed it back on the stove.

After a while Dad came in with Leslie. Already Leslie stamped his feet on the step the way Dad did and wore his cap as steadily as Dad did his hat.

I was glad when the house was dark and I lay on the couch in the front room. I could give my whole mind to Gil. I went back to that first day in the library and all the other days. I saw Gil as plain as if he were there again and I remembered all kinds of silly little things: the way Gil dropped his whole hand in the pocket of his coat when he was talking and the slender look of his ankle above his long shoe and his hands. Always I could see his hands that were so warm and quick when he held mine and so perfectly shaped.

When we sat in front of the fire at his house Christmas night he had held my head against his shoulder, and I could remember how his fingers felt against my face. I let all the things we said run through my mind.

I have seen them lift the gate in an irrigation ditch and watched the clear silver water flow in. It was just like that with my thinking of Gil.

I thought how he used to say, "You're like silver," and the day by the creek, the green-and-yellow day: "I used to think I'd never really fall in love, and then I saw you that day in the library. I had to know you. I watched you all those days almost afraid to talk to you for fear you'd spoil yourself, someway . . . every day you were just the same. On a bright day all the sun would seem to center on your head and on a dull day your hair would give it brightness and you'd look cool and gentle and quiet and yet so alive, Ellen." I thought of the time, too, in Pop's Place when Gil said he'd never change about loving me.

I know how the dry gumbo feels when the water soaks into it. It can come alive and can breathe and it's easy for it to push up the wheat. I felt that way with Gil's words running through my mind.

And then I knew I had to go back over Gil's visit here. I had to think of the day Gil went away. First I lay there not thinking about it and then I lifted the gate and let those thoughts flow through after the others.

The water wasn't clear and silvery; it was dark and brackish, but it flowed as fast as the other. I thought of the way Gil had seemed to change out here. He was uncomfortable and quiet, and he kept asking how Dad had stood it here. I thought how he had said: "How do people stay in love with each other after years alone in these places?" Gil was so sensitive he could tell about Mom and Dad. He could feel their bitterness and hate.

He was right about that, but he was wrong in thinking it had anything to do with us, or that we would be that way. He knew that now; that was what the cartoon meant. He still loved me. He had my letter with him in his pocket. He knew I loved him. I couldn't have stood his not knowing. If he was frightened, if he had time to think when he crashed, he knew.

I turned over in the pillow and cried. I had to hold the pillow tight so the folks wouldn't hear me.

"Oh, Gil," I kept whispering over and over, and each time it hurt me more. I put my arms around my own shoulders and tried to comfort myself.

4

I NEVER woke up till I heard Mom making breakfast in the kitchen and Leslie came and tickled my nose with the end of a feather. I bounced up with a little scream and he jumped back, laughing.

"Never wake me with anything but an eagle's feather, Leslie," I said as I picked up my blankets and went into my own room to dress. But all the feeling of yesterday had gone out of me. The weather had changed, too. It was cold and the wind was blowing again. It was almost too dark to see Gil's water color. The gray-dark light swallowed up the yellow.

"Below zero again," Dad said at breakfast. We sat down to eat with the naked electric light glaring down on us. Dad looked tired and unshaven. He had walked with a limp when he came to the table and I knew his leg was bothering him again. He turned the radio on to catch the early morning news broadcast. Leslie asked grace under cover of the news.

"You get same thing you get last night, Ben," Mom said doggedly, as she had said so many times before.

"Why, no, you don't. They get news all night long," Dad answered. "You see in London now . . ." Dad took out his watch to figure the time exactly, "it's seven hours later . . . that would be about three P.M. there. . . ."

"I bet bombs are falling on them, aren't they, Uncle Ben?" Leslie asked.

I drank my coffee and hoped they wouldn't notice that I had nothing to say.

"Yeléna, you an' me clean chicken house this morning. Your dad don't feel so good," Mom said.

"Are you going to get the baby chicks? Can I go with you?" Leslie asked between bites of toast.

"Be still, Leslie. We gotta get place ready first. March we get the chicks," Mom told him. "You put your scarf over your ears today an' wear your mittens, like I tell you."

After Leslie had gone and breakfast was over, it seemed to me that the house settled down into dreariness. Dad took yesterday's paper that he had already read in on the couch. The radio still jangled and would go on all day while Dad was sick. Mom moved around the kitchen, stolid and busy as though there were no difference between the days. I poured hot water to rinse the dishes I had washed and began to wipe them. My life seemed as coarse and ugly and dull as the cracked white plates I wiped, as far away from the kind of life I had meant to have as the fine china Gil's mother had.

Keeping Gil's death secret had helped to make it not seem true, but this morning it did no good. I emptied my dishwater out beside the back door and I looked on the bare, empty ground that lay flat and dead under the sky.

"Close that door, Ellen," Dad called from the front room. "The cold goes right through me. See what the temperature is now."

I looked at the thermometer nailed to the house. It read three below.

"I wish there were more snow. Cold on the bare ground doesn't do the wheat any good. After it's been so warm, it's likely to winter-kill," Dad fussed.

"Don't worry so much, Ben. Cold won't hurt the wheat none," Mom said, almost crossly. She was always like this when Dad was sick. "You better let me start them packs right now. I felt it an' it's going to fester way up."

"You fix the mash and I can do the rest, Anna," Dad muttered. He hated to be waited on and it made him grouchy. Twenty-four years, almost a quarter of a century, they had done this. The deadly dreariness of their lives lay on my own. I was glad to get out of the house. I wished I had gone right into town and tried for a job. I knew now that I had been waiting to hear from Gil. Well, now there was no more use. But there was no use getting a job in town now, either. With Dad sick, Mom would have to have me here.

I milked the cows, but it wasn't like that other time. The electric light in the barn gave off a hard, thin light. There is no comfort in a light turned on in the daytime, even though it's still dark. The milk pail was so cold my hand stuck to the handle. The milk sent up a little cloud of steam in my face, and I could see my own breath.

But I didn't mind the cold. It was better to be off by myself. I sat on the stool by Dunya, sheltered between the side of the stall and the cow's body. I leaned back against the wall, and for a minute I wished I could stop thinking and remembering and feeling. I wished I could just stay here or hide out in the combine the way Leslie did. I sat there till the cold cut in on my thoughts and drove me inside.

As soon as I opened the door, I smelled the flaxseed mash on the stove. Mom was in the other room with Dad. It was a day when the house was too small. It's all right when everyone's well and we all have work to do outside, but in winter there is no place to be by yourself. Dad must have felt that all these years. And there's nothing important to do except the chores. Winter is a waiting—only for me there was nothing to wait for now.

"It's going to warm up. Maybe you can start whitewashing the chicken house, Yeléna," Mom said. "You think it's too cold?"

"No, I'll do it," I said. "I'll put on a sweater underneath and my valenkis." I tied my head up in a woolen scarf. I looked like a peasant, all right, but Gil couldn't see me.

There was a kerosene stove in the chicken house that we kept going in cold weather. Mom thought it made the chickens lay better. It was so cold some of the turkeys had got in there. They looked shabby inside. Turkeys need sun and space to strut in. Cold doesn't hurt them, Mom always says, so I chased them out. I was taking wide strokes with the sloppy brush by the time Mom came down.

"Well, you got good start," Mom said. "Is not so cold in here. Did you look for eggs? I never see such a girl—come in the chicken house an' don't look for eggs!" Mom went around picking them out of the nests.

"How's Dad?"

"His leg hurt bad. Always he think he don't need no poultice this time, an' he always must have them. I tell him, but 'No, we see,' he says."

I went on painting. Mom poured some of the whitewash into another pail and began on the opposite wall. The chickens pretended to be scared and set up a noise whenever we made a sudden movement. Mom talked to them, half in English, half in Russian.

After a while, Mom said, "What did he say, *Yólochka?*"

"Who, Mom?" I asked, though I knew perfectly well.

"That Gilbert."

I shrugged. "Nothing much."

We painted on without talking till Mom said: "He'll never marry you. You waste your time. He ain't nothing you want, anyway."

Anger burned in me so I could hardly see where my brush went. Then I said, squatting down to get the bottom board, and my words came out as hard as hailstones:

"I'm not like you, Mom, so I'd do anything to get a man to marry me!"

Mom held her brush still. She looked at me so blankly it made me all the angrier. I couldn't stop then.

"Don't look as though you didn't know what I was talking about. I know how you tricked Dad. I overheard you the night after Gil left. I know he married you and took you back to America because you told him you were pregnant. Then you made him bring you out here on this ranch where he never wanted to come. And when he knew you weren't going to have a child it was too late. He was married to you, and he was too honorable to go away and leave you."

I couldn't seem to stop. I watched my words fall like blows on Mom's face. I don't think she took in all I said; I talked too fast. Mom couldn't understand if a person didn't speak slowly.

"And you've gone on all these years hating each other. Gil felt that hate. He could tell just being here. That's one of the things that drove him away from here, from me." I almost choked on my own words. I guess I was crying. I sat down on an old box and covered my face.

Mom was still so long I looked up at her. All the color had gone out of her face, except in her eyes. She shook her head.

"You don't know anything, Yeléna. You are child like that Leslie. In our church if baby is not christened we say she go blind in next world. I think you go blind in this world—blind dumb!" She stopped and then went on slowly. "No, Yeléna, I never hate

Ben an' Ben don't hate me. *Gospode Boge!* I love him here so all these years!" Mom touched her breast and her face broke into life. Her eyes were softer. "Me hate Ben!" She laughed. I sat there dumbly watching her. Her laughter seemed far away, like the children's laughter I'd heard through the closed windows of the teacherage.

"But, Mom, I heard Dad say you had tricked him. It was true, wasn't it?"

Mom nodded. She was a long time answering. "Yes, that is true. I was seventeen year old. I never love anyone before. If war don't come I would be married before that to some man from our village. But my people was killed an' I went to nursing. Ben was brought in almost dead. I take care of him. I never seen no one like him. He was always good and full of fun. Even when he hurt bad he make joke.

"When he get better we go out for walk around. I teach him Russian words, just for fun. But when he teach me English, I learn, not just for fun. I say them over and over till I know them good. I want to speak his way. I never have such good time. He was only twenty-one. He make love to me an' kiss me. Once . . . You are grown, *Yólochka*, you know how those things can be. . . ."

"No," I said. My face felt cold and hard. But Mom didn't hear me, she was living so in what she told.

"When it get spring an' ice melt in harbor an' he talk about going home I can't stand to think. He feel bad, too. 'I'm going to miss you, Anna,' he say, 'but I come back.' I talk about going with him now an' he try to tell me it can't be. He try to tell me about his mother an' sister an' father. He say he have to go back an' tell them about me, let them get used to me. I can't think what they are like then, but they don't worry me.

"They get orders for sail an' Ben come to say good-by. I see how he love me. I can't let him go without me. I love him so. I can't help it, Yeléna, I tell him I'm going to have a child. Lots of soldiers, in Russia, they don't care; they just go away, but not Ben. Ben is a good man. He feel awful bad, but he don't get mad. Then he say 'We get married.'

"We was married an' we was happy. Ben was happy. Even after we are in his home, when he come upstairs to me and shut the door we are happy an' laugh together all the time. Ben was different when he was young; he make more fun.

"I hope an' I pray I get that way with baby before he know, but I don't. I think I play sick an' lose the baby. . . . I can never lie to Ben no more. When we are in Montana here, Ben know. He is very angry. Three days he says not a word an' he sleep in other room. Then he sleep with me but not like he love me. But I love him. I try to make up to him with my body for all things. . . ."

"He must have hated you," I said. I wished Mom wouldn't tell me these things. I stirred the whitewash with a stick.

"I don't blame him none. I feel bad. If he had beat me, I wouldn't blame him. I love him so much. One night I go to put down his plate for supper an' he reach up an' pull my face down an' kiss me. You see, *Yólochka?*" Mom asked, as though that answered everything.

I couldn't look at her, but I had to say what was in my mind. "But all these years, even when I was a child, I've felt that you hated each other. When I heard you that night you both sounded cold and hard."

Mom made a sound of disgust in her throat. "That don't mean nothing. We get mad, sure! Like ice an' snow an' thunder an' lightning storm, but they don't hurt the wheat down in the ground any." Mom picked up her whitewash brush and slapped it against the rough boards. "*Yólochka*, you don't know how love is yet."

I went on painting, too. I only had a little more to do. I was wondering how two people could love each other after all that and if Dad had ever really forgiven her.

The sun was up at last. It came through the dirty window-panes on the fresh whitewash and made it glisten. I glanced at Mom. In the bright sunlight her face showed more lines, but it had that closed look. I wondered what she was thinking. She finished her wall and poured the whitewash that was left back in the bigger pail.

"You can write that young Gil of yours that he don't know what he think he does. Sure, we fight sometime, but we got no hate here." Her eyes flashed.

I don't know why I told her then, but I said:

"Gil is dead, Mom. That letter was from his friend. He was in a bomber that crashed."

I heard Mom draw in her breath. "He was young," she said, so gently my eyes filled.

"I'll take these to the barn," I managed to say. When I opened the door the cold wind stung my eyes.

5

LIKE that other time I found myself watching Mom and Dad.
They were so middle-aged, they said so little that mattered:
whether to lease the quarter-section from Bailey again, how much
to plant to spring wheat, whether the house roof could go another year without shingles. . . .

Of course, I could see how dependent they were on each other.
"How you feel, Ben?" Mom was always asking. And she knew
how to make Dad comfortable. Dad explained things to her.
"Read what it say, Ben," Mom would say, giving him the paper.
Then she would sit down beside him, her face withdrawn and
empty, listening. But love . . . love was more than that. They
had just made the best of a sordid, wretched mistake. Maybe
Dad's hate had cooled in all these years, but hate, cooling, was
no better than love cooling, it was like mud drying to dust.

Dad was sick a long time. "It's good you be sick now in winter," Mom said, trying to cheer him up.

"I don't like you doing all the barn work," Dad said.

"With Yeléna here I got it easy. That way I keep her from
going off to town for job." Mom laughed.

We did the chores easily. Dad stayed inside reading or listening
to the radio or working on his accounts. When his leg got too
painful he just lay on the couch without talking. Then Mom was
more silent, too. I was glad Leslie was there. Leslie seemed untouched by the housebound feeling of sickness. Perhaps I had
been at that age, or perhaps he had always lived in an atmosphere
of tension. He liked school in Gotham. There were two rooms
and more children than at Prairie Butte. I was grateful for his
chattering through a meal and when he perched on the end of the

couch Dad made an effort to talk to him. One day Leslie found that Dad had been in the last war.

"Were you really, Uncle Ben? Did you get to see any fighting?" he asked, climbing up beside him.

"Sure I did. That's how I got this," Dad said, touching his leg.

"Gee, I didn't know that! I thought you just got sick." His voice was awed and when Mom changed the poultices Leslie would sidle up as close as he could to watch. He kept a tiny piece of shrapnel that came away once, on the table with his feather collection.

The cold relaxed a little in the middle of each day. There were chickadees chirping from the bushes along the coulee and under the warm sun the snow melted to water on the low fields, but by late afternoon it was cold again. The water froze to ice and the country looked dead. I thought I had been lonely at the teacherage and I had looked forward to the week ends at home, but I was more lonely here.

One day I took down Gil's water color. It hurt me too much to see it. I stood there holding the picture and the cartoon and Gil's picture, trying to put them away, when Mom opened the door.

"Yeléna," she began, then she saw what I had in my hands.

"I was just packing them away," I said. I put them in the bottom drawer and banged it closed.

"There's no hurry," Mom said. "He was good-looking young man." It was the first nice thing she had ever said about him.

"You didn't think so till he was dead," I said. I didn't feel mean like that, but it seemed to say itself. Mom's silence made it sound childish and crude.

"Don't take it that way," she said. "Before this war gets done lots of girls got to lose their sweethearts. You aren't only one. You got no need to act like it."

I was grateful for her calling him my sweetheart and I scarcely listened to the rest.

"Maybe if he hadn't die an' come back after war, maybe you don't love him no more. He was lots different from you, Yeléna."

"You and Dad are certainly different," I said.

Mom leaned against the dresser. "Yes, Ben an' me are different, but we are different from you an' Gil. Ben don't go away like Gil, an' I don't let him go."

"But . . ." I began angrily.

"Look, *Yólochka*," Mom said in a soft calm voice. "Soon we be outdoors working. You feel good again when you get out more." Mom moved her shoulders as though they were muscle-bound now. "Sun an' wind make you feel different. Same way with me, same way with Ben, too. After that time I tell you about, when Ben is angry that I trick him into taking me, even after he forgive me, we are quiet. That spring we work all day out in the fields; sometime we hardly talk a word. It was good we was both so tired. I never work so hard. I want to show him what I do for him. We plow under our bad feelings. Same with you, maybe, you put your feeling bad down in ground."

"I don't know," I said.

"You wait an' see!" Mom said. "Them baby chicks is in Clark City. You drive in town an' get them. Take Leslie to see his folks an' take your time. Winter will be gone before you wear your new coat."

"Don't bother about me, Mom, I'm all right," I said. I felt like a big, overgrown child she had tried to comfort.

By the time it was warm enough to work in the machine shed, Dad was up again, looking thinner and paler than ever, but he was bound to get out there.

"I'll just putter around and see what there is to do," he promised Mom. But when he had been out there almost an hour Mom said,

"Go out, Yeléna, and see if you can help him."

I pushed open the shed door and the early spring sunlight split on the black metal disks he was taking off the harrow.

"Put something against the door, the sun feels good," Dad said. "You're just in time to give me a hand here."

"Mom doesn't want you to work too long down here, Dad," I said.

"I'm all right. I've laid up long enough."

"Leslie will love watching you get the combine ready."

Dad nodded. "He thinks the combine is the best thing on the place. He's all right. You tell Warren when you write how much I like him. Here, if you want something to do, you can take off all these bolts for me." Dad stopped to light his cigarette. "Ellen, don't grieve so hard over Gil. It makes us feel bad to see you."

I couldn't say anything. Dad loosened the last bolt and took off the steel blade.

"But it's pretty tough to see a young fellow like that 'go West.' It makes it worse, in a way, that he was still in training."

I didn't want him to go on. His expression from the last war made me squirm a little, it seemed worse than saying "die." "I suppose that's what you have to expect in wartime," I said lamely, like Mrs. Peterson or Bailey. In Gotham folks jump from one safe and tried remark to another as though they were stepping-stones, not wanting to get their feet wet in their own feelings and thoughts.

"Hand me that grease can over there, Ellen."

I watched Dad work. The sun was bright but I could see that his hands were cold by the bluish look of the skin.

"Well, next year you'll be back in school," Dad said. "You're only twenty. By the time you're through you'll have forgotten you ever stayed out a year." He was putting the blade back now. I held it in place while he tightened the bolts.

"If we have a crop, I'll go back next year," I said.

"There's no if about it this year," Dad said firmly, the way he likes to talk. Then he said, "I thought you were through with Gil last summer, Ellen."

"I thought I was, Dad. But you were right that time you said he couldn't get me out of his mind. I couldn't stop loving him either." It was hard to talk and yet it was a relief, too.

"Look here, Ellen, you don't want to be like your Aunt Eunice. She loved Jim Robinson; his father was president of the bank back home. They weren't engaged, just had an understanding, I guess, and he was killed in Belleau Wood. Eunice never got over it, never looked at anyone else after that. When I was back there last winter, Ellen, I thought she was just like the parlor at home. It's closed up tight. No life gets to it. Don't be like that." Dad straightened up and looked out across the yard.

He stood idle so long I looked to see what he was watching. Mom was there waiting at the top of the road for Leslie. When he came up to her he showed her his school paper and we could see by the way she raised her hand that she was admiring his work. Then she laughed at something. Leslie laughed, too. She took his hand and they ran back to the house.

289

Dad turned back to the blade he was tightening. He had a kind of smile on his face as though something had pleased him.

"I used to watch Anna come into the hospital when I was sick. It wasn't a hospital, really, just a sort of cellar hole. She was slender then and younger than you are, but she was strong and full of life. I was pretty weak and it did me good just to watch her moving around."

It hurt me to think of Dad watching Mom and feeling her strength and health when he was sick. That was why she had attracted him, I thought. I stirred the thick grease that stood in a can, just to be doing something.

"Ellen, bring that light over here and hold it so I can see what I'm doing," he said. I unhooked the powerful bulb in its wire cage and took it over where Dad was working. The light was on the machinery and his grease-covered hands but it shone up on his face and spread a glint on his hair below his cap. It was yellow, like mine. His work shirt showed a little white place at the base of his throat that didn't seem to match the leathery skin above his collar. He looked younger and healthier than he had when he was cooped up in the house. When Dad was sick I guess I never quite looked at him because I knew how he hated it. When I was a child he had seemed so different from the rest of the people around Gotham I had thought he was wonderful. Since last June I hadn't seen him without thinking how he had seemed to Gil. I kept looking at him now, the way you do with a stranger, sometimes, to see how much you can tell about him.

"Hold that light down a little, there. Don't shine it in my eyes, Ellen, or I'll have to get a new helper!" Dad grumbled jokingly.

I lowered the bulb. Why couldn't things have been different for him, I wondered angrily. The feeling of injustice boiled up in me so that I spoke without thinking.

"Don't you feel bitter, Dad, about the way things have turned out for you?" I asked. Then I was ashamed of my question. I knew he did. Why did I make it worse by asking him? I couldn't stand the silence so I went on talking.

"That's why I've hated this war so, even before Gil was killed. I've thought how the last war took your health and twisted your life around."

"I don't feel that way," Dad said mildly, not looking up from the screw he was tightening. "I guess the war gives as much as it takes away from you. It has for me, anyway."

"I mean," I squirmed, "you could have done something with your head, something easier than ranching."

"Ranching takes plenty of head. Of course, I might have done something I had more of a knack for, but Anna wouldn't have been happy back East."

"That's what I mean, Dad! If you hadn't married Mom. She's so . . . well, she wouldn't want to live any place but a ranch. I love her, but I mean . . ." My voice trailed lamely off into silence. I couldn't look at Dad. He can't face the truth, I thought, and I didn't blame him. I was trying to think how to put the words to tell him I knew what Mom had done. I wanted to say that I didn't blame him if he couldn't forgive her for deceiving him and spoiling his whole life. He stopped turning the wrench in his hand. It was as though we were frozen there. Dad was the one who liked to talk usually, Mom was more silent, but it was harder now to talk to Dad. I wondered if he wished I would go.

Then Dad said, going on with his work, "Sometimes it's hard to understand your mother, Ellen. She wasn't born in America, you know; that makes a difference. She had a harder life as a young girl than you can imagine. The first year out here was hard on her, too. Sometimes I think she's forgotten all about those bad times, but once in a while I can see she hasn't. When she first saw this place she took to it. She could hardly wait to get the house built so we could start plowing. I remember how we stood out here one day, deciding where to put the house. It looked pretty bare to me and all of a sudden Anna said, 'It's good to see so much sky.'

"I told her she'd be sick of seeing just sky before we got through out here, but I don't know that she has. She's liked it here." Dad said it as though it gave him a good feeling.

He dropped a bolt and I got down to hunt for it.

"I've laid up so long doing nothing I'm getting to be a regular butter-fingers," Dad muttered when I found it for him. Then he was quiet so long I was afraid he had forgotten what we were talking about.

Finally he said, "I don't suppose you can get any idea of how this country seemed to me when I came out here, Ellen." I was disappointed, he wasn't going to say anything more about Mom and I had heard him tell before how the country looked to him.

"It looked like the end of nowhere except for the glimpses of the mountains. I couldn't get used to it at first. I'd known little villages back home, I didn't come from a very big place, but villages back there have a church with a tall white spire sticking up on them instead of a grain elevator, and houses with lawns and streets with trees. I got pretty homesick for them that first year. Everything was different out here, even the dirt. Why, we wouldn't have thought gumbo was any kind of soil worth bothering about back home. I don't understand it yet. Sometimes when I'm plowing I look at it and wonder about it, how it holds enough moisture to grow wheat! But I guess it doesn't make any difference whether I see how it does it or not!"

Dad stopped to light a cigarette and I hung the bulb back where it belonged. My arm ached from holding it for him so long. He was off on the country. I wasn't listening very well.

". . . crazy darned country, lonely as Time and as violent as the everlasting wind out here. Maybe you never quite understand why, but it gets to be a part of you when you live with it. It was a funny thing, but last winter when I was home I was actually homesick for this place. I couldn't get a good look at the sky back there and I knew what Anna meant." Dad gave a little laugh. "I packed up and came home before I'd planned to."

Perhaps Dad would have said more, but we heard the house door bang and Leslie came running across the yard.

"Uncle Ben, Ellen! Dinner's ready. You better hustle right in here 'cause Aunt Anna's got that red Russian soup all dished up. What are you doing?"

"I've been getting things ready so you can help me, Leslie," Dad said. He laid down his wrench and cleaned off his hands with an old rag. "Come on, Karmont." Then he kicked away the prop that held the shed door open and we started back to the house.

6

WE went across the yard that was full of puddles from the melting snow. Leslie ran ahead and jumped them all. Mom stood in
the doorway waiting for us.

"What you think, Ben? Will it rain?" she asked.

Dad turned his face up to the sky. "I wouldn't wonder; it's a
whole lot warmer."

Inside, the kitchen was steamy from the hot soup. Leslie giggled
aloud. "Aunt Anna never dished up! I just said that to hurry
you!" He shrieked with delight at his fooling us.

We took turns washing while Mom filled the soup bowls and
cut the bread that was so fresh it was hard to slice. Leslie was
asking Dad questions about the machinery.

"You're coming on, Leslie. Couple of months ago you'd have
thought a belt was just something you wore on your pants," Dad
teased him.

"Is much got to be done, Ben?" Mom asked.

"Oh, there's some work on it. It makes me anxious to get out
and get started."

Mom nodded her head and gave a little laugh. "You start plowing in the snow maybe, too!" Mom reached over and gave him
a little nudge and I saw how her dark eyes gleamed with fun.

I sat at the table taking spoonfuls of the hot soup.

"It tastes good, Mom," I said.

"Sure." Mom nodded. "Borsch is good. Even Ben'll stand the
cabbage smell for it."

"You notice I went down to the shed, though," Dad retorted.
This was the way they talked, laughing at their old jokes.

Maybe it was from eating alone at the teacherage or maybe that
I so often found myself thinking of Gil when we sat here at the

table that I didn't have anything to say. If Mom noticed that I was quiet she never said anything about it.

In the middle of the meal she remembered she had seen the name of a Russian town she knew in the paper and she brought it for Dad to read to her. While he read out loud she sat listening, stirring her coffee round and round without knowing that she was doing it. When Dad mentioned a Russian name she said it after him, differently, but he paid no attention and went right on. It was funny to hear them.

From where I sat I could look out the window by the sink and see the sky above the roof of the barn. I thought back over the things Dad had said. Even when I had made it easy for him he wouldn't say anything against Mom. He had acted almost as though he had not liked my criticizing her. And he had gone on to try to make me understand her as he did. . . . My own thought startled me . . . I had to stop and look at it.

AS HE DID!

I had been so sure that there was no real understanding between Mom and Dad. He had said himself: "Sometimes it's hard to understand your mother, Ellen," and then in the next breath, as though he were embarrassed, he had gone on about this country and how different it was from the East. "Maybe you never quite understand why, but this country gets to be a part of you when you live with it." Could he have meant that he felt that way about Mom, too? It struck me all of a sudden, as though I had been trying to read something in the half-dark and now I had come outside where there was light.

"You have more soup, Yeléna? Look, I got plenty meat left in the bottom." Mom stood at the stove lifting the big soup ladle to show me.

"No, thanks, Mom," I said, looking at her as though I had never really seen her before. I looked at Dad. He was listening to Leslie tell about school. Their faces told me nothing. They were just the same.

I thought of Dad saying, "Sometimes I think she's forgotten all about those bad times, but once in a while I can see she hasn't." I began to see how it must really be between them. He could look at Mom without saying anything and know how she felt, even when they were talking like this about nothing that mattered, or when they were working all day in the fields. That was what I had wanted Gil to do, to understand sometimes the way I felt without my telling him.

I kept looking at them in wonder as the sense of their strange understanding and love grew on me. I thought of a hundred little things whose meaning was changed now: how Mom had said, "This will be first Christmas without Ben." And how she had looked in the mirror in the store and wondered if Dad would like her in her new red coat. I had thought she was pathetic then. I thought of her fixing a poultice in the middle of the night and of the days when Dad lay on the couch watching Mom through the doorway. I had thought of him as being trapped and frustrated by illness and our ranch. Maybe he had watched Mom as he used to do in the cellar hole in Russia.

"It did me good just to watch her moving around . . . she was strong and full of life," Dad had said.

I even looked at that night again; the night Gil went away, when I had lain against the side of the hill and looked in through the window at them. I thought of Mom's bitter, angry words and of how Dad had gone into the front room to sleep. But now I remembered how I had heard Mom go in to him, saying without any anger at all in her voice that he would be lame in the morning if he lay there all night. And Dad had gone back with her.

And Mom had said, "Sure we get mad, but that don't hurt nothing. Thunder an' lightning an' cold an' snow don't hurt the wheat down in the ground." "Why you let him go, then, first time you get mad?" she had asked when I told her I loved Gil. I couldn't swallow the bread in my mouth for a minute; something choked me. I felt like the night out in the barn when I was milking the cows and I had suddenly known that I still loved Gil, that kind of a feeling that changes the whole world and you with it.

"*Solnieshko,* did somebody give you a present? What struck you? You sit there looking like it was your name day!" Mom said.

My thoughts must have shown through in my face. Mom and Dad and Leslie were all smiling at me.

"No," I laughed. "I just feel good, I guess."

Mom gave a little grunt. "That don't hurt you none."

There we sat in the kitchen with the cooking dishes piled in

295

the sink, at the table where I had so often shrunk from the picture we made, with the silverware from the dime store and the china that didn't match, and I didn't mind at all. I did feel good. I felt as light as though a weight had been taken from me.

"Leslie, how would you like to ride down with me to get the mail? I've got to go down to the store anyway," I said.

Leslie loved to ride in the truck. He held on tight to the side and I hit the bump where our road went into the highway so that he bounced. We swooped up to the tracks and down the steep pitch on the other side and came to a stop just by the ramp with Leslie shrieking with excitement. I let him run in. I hadn't been for the mail since the day I got the letter about Gil. I wished I could write him about Mom and Dad—how wrong we were about them.

Leslie came running back with the paper and a letter from his father. "It's raining, Ellen, big drops. Whyn't you turn the windshield wiper on?" I had sat there and not seen the rain.

"Shall I read your letter to you?"

"If you want to," Leslie said.

Warren's letter told him about the company's mascot and the soldier who asked about his eagle feather, and how hot it was there.

"There's a letter for you, too. He always writes you, doesn't he, Ellen?"

"Yes," I said. "It's nice of him." I tucked it away in my pocket. It was usually about Leslie.

"Ellen," Leslie said slowly, "Dad didn't say whether he kept his promise. Do you think he hasn't and he's ashamed?"

"Oh, Leslie! That's not the important thing. Stop worrying about what your father does, and love him."

"I should think you would think it was important! Nels told me. I know all about how Dad came to the teacherage when he'd been drinking and he stayed all night and then the school board fired you. Miss Webb, I mean Ellen, I hate him for that. I wish he wasn't my father!" Suddenly he was crying with his fists dug into his eyes. I put my hand on his knee, but I didn't dare to put my arm around him. His shoulders looked too independent.

"He hurt my mother, too, and broke her heart," he sobbed.

"Leslie, look here!" Suddenly, I understood. He was as mixed up as I had been. "I'm just like you. I used to think my mother had spoiled my father's life and it made me angry and unhappy."

"About Aunt Anna and Uncle Ben?" he asked unbelievingly.

"Yes, but I didn't know how things really were. That's the way with you. You weren't very old when your mother died. You can't remember how things were. Maybe I can explain some things to you." It seemed easy to talk with the sound of the rain and the comfortable rub of the windshield wiper against the glass.

"Your father loved your mother and wanted her to be happy," I went on. "She was like you. She didn't like it out at Prairie Butte. She wanted to get away from there. Going out preaching and to meetings was a chance to get away. Your father moved to Detroit so she would be happier, but by that time she liked the meetings and traveling, so she kept on, even though she had to leave you a lot of the time. Your father took care of you. I have an idea he was often lonely and unhappy because you weren't old enough to be company for him like you are now."

"He drank and he didn't go to church or read the Bible," Leslie said, watching the windshield wiper. "Mother said he was lost."

"Leslie, the thing that matters is that he loved your mother and he loves you. You can't be lost when you love someone!" I opened the window a little. The rain felt warm and fresh.

"I gave him the eagle feather you told me to," Leslie said almost defensively.

"I know you did. He showed it to me and said it was the nicest thing that had happened to him. You wouldn't have given it to him if you hadn't loved him."

Leslie shook his head. "I gave it to him because he looked so sad that day driving in to town. He didn't hardly talk all the way. I meant to tell him I knew he'd broke his promise and gotten you into trouble. He did that, Ellen. You know he did. You can't forgive him that!"

"Yes, but, Leslie, that doesn't hurt your loving him." From where we sat I could see the wheat shining green under the rain. It made me think of what Mom had said to me. "Look at that wheat, Leslie. It's been there all winter and it's had cold and snow on it and it hasn't been hurt any. See how green it is? How it's coming in spite of everything? That's the way love is." You can say things to a child sometimes that you couldn't say even to yourself.

Leslie didn't say anything. I didn't look at him.

"Wheat can stand a lot," I went on. "The hard wheat doesn't grow in warm countries, you know. And wheat grown on irrigated land lacks the strength of dry-land wheat. I guess it takes cold and snow and dryness and heat to make the best wheat."

Leslie laughed and gave a little bounce on the seat. "You're funny, Ellen. First you talk about love and then you talk about wheat."

"I get them mixed up, don't I?" I said.

Mom was outdoors when I drove into the yard.

"Like spring!" she said, holding up her hands to the rain.

"Wet, though," I laughed.

"That don't hurt nothing. Look at it take the dirty snow. That's all that's left of winter."

We went up on the porch, just out of the rain, and watched it.

"Smell!" Mom said. Leslie stood on the top step with his palms out to feel the rain.

"You should see the wheat from the hill, shouldn't she, Ellen? Gee, it looks green."

"Yes, but it looks spotty down by the road," Mom said.

That evening, after supper, Leslie got out his tablet and pencil. "I thought I might tell Dad about the rain and how far the wheat's up," he said, looking at me.

"Tell him we're going to start plowing tomorrow," Dad said.

Then I remembered Warren's note to me. I took it out of my pocket and read:

"*Dear Ellen,*

"*Thank you for telling me about Leslie. He sounds very happy. I am grateful to have him there. Whenever you are tired of him you must say so.*

"*I am sorry to hear about Gil. You cared so much about him, you will miss him badly. I think of you a great deal and hope the spring doesn't hurt too much with Gil gone.*

"*We are almost into summer here, but I missed the spring back home. This is a curious life. I like it, but I shall like it better when the training period is over, and we move on to our real work.*

"*Warren.*"

298

I looked over at Leslie writing at the kitchen table. I saw he had covered a page with large printed letters. He gave a big sigh.

"There! I guess that's enough. Can I print my name in ink, Ellen?"

I brought the ink bottle and Mom's straight pen and I saw him print LESLIE under the penciled word "love."

"I think Dad'll make a good officer, don't you, Ellen?" he asked. His eyes were only a little anxious.

"I'm sure he will," I said.

Dad heard him. "Your dad, Leslie? Why, he's the kind it takes. If I was picking an officer to be under, I'd choose him, I'll tell you."

"Would you, Uncle Ben?" Leslie's smile spread over his face. He hitched one knee over the other in a way he had when he was excited. "I'll tell him that. I can put it in a P.S., can't I?"

7

SOME folks begin their spring plowing when the county agent tells them to, some folks watch their neighbors, but we always wait till there's life in the ground. There was life in the ground by the last week in March that year. Some years it didn't come till later, as late as May, one year. After the hard dead look of frozen gumbo the earth changes, shows cracks around the roots of the windbreak, looks darker. Ground sparrows dart up from the stubble, ants crawl across the bare ground, and green shows bright in the winter wheat and up the side of the coulee. It's a thing you can feel. Then you know it's time to plow.

It was good to be out working in the fields again with nothing between me and the sky. It was still cold early and late, but the sun was warm on my head and the back of my neck by mid-morning. I was glad I wasn't in the library at the university or in the teacherage at Prairie Butte. I was glad I was back here riding the tractor across the fields.

There's one thing about plowing: trying to keep a straight line with the tractor, you forget other things. A ground sparrow will fly up from the furrow ahead of you or a Chinese cock pheasant will flaunt his colors against the plain dirt and take your mind off what you were thinking.

But I thought often of Anna Petrovna and Ben Webb plowing this same dirt their first spring in Montana. I thought of them hardly speaking all day. I knew so well how Anna Petrovna's face could look when it closed all her feelings inside, and I knew how Ben Webb could look when he was discouraged and tired and sick. I thought of them going up to that unpainted house under the coulee and eating in silence and lying down beside each other at night. That they could plow under their hate and bitterness and grow any love for each other seemed a greater miracle than the spring. Sometimes it was hard to believe, I had believed in their hate so long, but I could look over and see the green of the winter wheat. Because of what Mom had said, I took it as a kind of proof.

One day, the first week of April, we had a turn of cold. The wind blew so hard it lifted the fresh dirt I had plowed. By afternoon, a thin snow came down and covered the fields an inch deep, but the wheat stuck up through it as green as life. It gave me a good feeling all day.

I thought often of Gil as I went back and forth over the field, and I tried to plan out my life and think what I would do after the harvest. I turned the tractor at the corner and felt the extra pull of the moist spring earth, then I faced across the field to the east again.

Some days I forgot everything but the good feeling of the spring day and the soft cool air and the wideness of the field. When I stepped down off the tractor I liked even the stiff, sticky sqush of the gumbo furrows under my feet. I was glad it was an early spring; the winter had been long enough.

The sun stayed longer each week. We could work later in the fields. Mom seemed to know I wanted to be outdoors. She was the one who always went up ahead to tend to meals and she and Dad did the chores while I was still riding the tractor. They left me a lot to myself. I felt a sense of understanding between Mom and me, without any words. It seemed to grow with the green that spread up the coulee.

I remembered how impatient I used to be with Mom because she never seemed to be excited or to look ahead; she just worked through the day as it came. But I knew now that there were times when you couldn't look ahead. It hurt too much if you tried to think what came after spring and what after summer. It was easier to go along and work so hard in the day that you were tired at night. It came to me one morning, going back and forth over the field, that maybe so much had happened to Mom back in Russia that work out here had seemed peaceful. Maybe it had seemed good to Dad, after being sick so long, just to be out here in the sun. I began to understand how they had stood that first year here. Maybe it hadn't seemed like being exiled to Dad, after all.

It was after eight o'clock when I stopped some nights. Leslie often came down to wait for me by the fence and I would let him drive the tractor a few rods across the field. The wild flowers were out, but I didn't have time to climb the rimrock these days—maybe I didn't want to. But Leslie would try to bring me something new he had found: the first pale lavender crocus, some little bright pink flower, no bigger than an ice crystal on a frozen windowpane, or a bluebonnet as bright a shade as the Thorson children's eyes. And in my mind I would show each one to Gil.

Once Leslie took a flower home to press and send to Warren in a letter.

"Maybe, by now, he's lost the feather I gave him," he told me.

Leslie and I walked back up to the house together, leaving the tractor in the field for the next day. Oh, yes, Warren, the spring hurt. Sometimes it hurt most on these walks back up to the house at the end of the day. I thought of writing that to Warren in one of Leslie's letters, because Warren must know for himself how spring could hurt. But I didn't write.

"Bailey says up on the high line they've lost half their winter wheat crop; they're going to have to reseed to spring," Dad said one night at supper.

"How, Uncle Ben?" Leslie asked.

"Winter-killed," Dad said. "So many hard freezes after warm spells this last winter. A freeze on the bare ground does it."

"You know how that water stood in places, Ben, an' then froze solid!" Mom's face was as solemn as wood.

"That's what does it," Dad said.

"The ground heave up," Mom added, showing Leslie with her rough red hands.

"You see, it tears the wheat loose from the roots, Leslie," Dad explained. He could make sentences out of Mom's phrases when I couldn't get the meaning at all.

"You mean that could happen to our wheat?" Leslie asked, his eyes bigger with sudden alarm.

"Sure," Mom said darkly.

"But it's green now. Ellen said it could stand cold and snow!" His voice was like a cry of protest. I knew what he felt. It was more than wheat to him. It was more to me, too. I got up to fill Leslie's glass with milk.

"I was looking at the wheat today," Dad said. "I pulled up

302

some stalks here and there that weren't really rooted. But you can't tell how much of it's that way."

"You mean, we might have to plow it up and reseed the whole thing?" I asked.

"Sure! All that seed an' gas an' time gone for nothing!" Mom said. "You won't get that money paid back on your combine this year, Ben Webb. An' I don't see you've heard anything from your sister yet about what you send her!"

I held my hands tight together under the table. There was that sharp, almost taunting note in Mom's voice that went through me. "Don't do that! How can you?" My mind cried out as it used to when I was a child. I couldn't look at Dad. I wished Leslie didn't have to hear them.

"Well, maybe I won't, but we won't lose the combine, either," Dad said, setting himself against her taunt so firmly I was suddenly all on his side. "We'll pay off half anyway." Dad had a different kind of strength from Mom. I could feel it.

"No, we just go on dragging a mortgage after us. Work so many years to be free an' then go out and ask for more!" Mom was so angry her face blotched with red, her eyes flashed, and her voice was heavier.

"The combine isn't the biggest thing in the world to me, Anna." The coldness of Dad's voice separated the two of them as far as Russia was from Vermont, I thought.

I started to clear the dishes. Here I was again, as I had always been, pulled this way and that by their attitudes. I was glad when Dad went into the front room with his magazine and Mom went out to the chicken house. Leslie came to stand by the sink to dry the dishes. I didn't quite meet his eyes.

"But, Ellen, I thought you said for sure that the wheat could stand the cold?" he insisted.

"It does mostly," I told him. "It isn't the cold that hurts it. It's these warm spells that melt all the snow and leave the wheat exposed, and then the cold strikes." But my voice trailed off. I felt there was nothing you could say "for sure." I dumped my dishwater outside and hung the pan against the house. I stood there by myself in the dark. The house was too full of feeling and tension.

"Oh, God!" I said, as I had that night in the blizzard, and only the snow had blown in my face.

"When you feel it, you will pray," Mom had said.

"Oh, God, don't let the wheat all die," I prayed with my whole heart.

That night I made up my bed again on the glider on the porch. It was still cold at night, but I couldn't have stood it in the house.

I woke next morning to an all-day rain. I helped Dad in the shed all morning, but in the afternoon there was nothing more to do.

"It won't hurt you to take time to fix yourself up," Mom said. "Put on that white dress, for once."

But when I dressed up in the white piqué dress I could only think how I had worn it to town last spring with Gil. I looked at my hands and they were red and rough against my skirt, like Mom's. When I combed my hair it caught on the rough places on my fingers. My nails were dry and worked down close to my fingertips. Gil would wince to see them now. I felt such a longing to see Gil's hands again, to feel them against my face, that it was like a pain. "I know he was coming back to me," I said out loud in my room to the icon and the peach walls and the mirror that Gil had looked on. That was what the little water color meant. That was why he sent it.

All that next week we watched the wheat without saying much about it. I saw Leslie on his way to school stop by one of the long strips of wheat. He pulled up a single stalk. I couldn't see from where I was how it looked, but it seemed to come out easy. Then he walked slowly a way before he began to run.

The second week of April came off warm. The grass around the house was green, the aspens in the coulee shivered in their pale green leaves. The box elders that sprang up wild against the bank held out tight-furled green torches at the tips of their bare branches.

"Well, let's go down and look at the wheat again," Dad said one morning, as though we hadn't been watching it every day.

"How you think it look, Ben?" Mom asked.

"I don't think it did any harm to wait," Dad said. "Some folks have plowed up and reseeded already, but there's too much good wheat left there."

Once again, the three of us sat on the seat of the truck while we went to see the wheat. I was driving and I went the long way around.

"The road's muddy the other way," I said. I came around the first strip of stubble and parked. We made a procession across from the road. The stubble creaked like an old basket as we walked over it.

"There's some brown, all right," Mom said, pointing.

We each studied every strip with our own eyes. Through the green wheat that stood already four inches high there were spots where the blades had turned brown and lay along the ground or drooped with a sick whitish-green, and here and there were bare moth-eaten places. I walked up a row and pulled up one of the brown withered stalks and felt it come away in my hand. I looked out over this strip and the one beyond. The brown stalks were only scattered. There were places where the wheat was deep green and thick. I pulled at a green stalk beside my foot, but it clung to the earth as though its root reached two feet deep.

I looked at Dad. His face was thin and already burned by the wind. He had a stick or a match in his mouth and his lips gathered up around it as he considered. I could feel his impatience, that was still part of him even after all these years out here, in the way he took off his hat and put it on again and then felt for his package of cigarettes and lighted one with so much attention he hardly seemed interested in the wheat. When he got it lighted he turned back to the field. Mom had tramped ahead of us to look for herself.

"How about it, Dad?" I couldn't wait any longer.

"Well," he said slowly, "it's spotty. There's places where it winter-killed, but some of those spots were just wind-blown. It came through better than I thought it could. There's enough good wheat there for you to ride to school next fall on a first-class ticket, girl! All that through there has been slowed down a little because of the rain and cold these last weeks, but it'll blaze now. Anna!" he shouted.

"Ben!" Mom's voice across the strip had a warm excited sound to it. "Look over here! It's good here. She done better than she look last week!" Mom came back to stand by Dad.

"I thought you said I'd lose the combine!" Dad had a laugh in his voice.

"Well, you might yet with hail or grasshoppers. Watch out!"

Mom looked up at him with her eyes sparkling the way they did over a joke.

I went back over to the truck. This afternoon I would bring Leslie down here to see the wheat that didn't winter-kill.

"See," I would say, "it didn't die out. Oh, in a few places, but look here—try to pull it up. See how strong and green it is?" Leslie would know what I meant. His eyes would shine.

I slid in on the seat of the truck to wait for Mom and Dad. They had walked a little way along the strip. Now they were standing together. They looked smaller under the too-wide sky, Mom so thick and peasant-looking with her bandanna tied around her head, Dad spare and angular and a little round-shouldered.

Why had I worried about them? I had been as blind in this world as Mom had said. They had love that was deep-rooted and stronger than love that grows easily. It gave me faith for my own life.

"You can't pick up faith at the cut-rate drugstore," Warren had said. I must tell him sometime that faith had to grow like wheat, winter wheat. Love was like that, too.

I thought how I had sat in Dunya's cold stall and wished I could stop feeling and thinking and remembering after I knew Gil was dead. How had I ever felt that way? I didn't feel that way any more. Now I wanted to live my life with the strength of the winter wheat, through drought and rain and snow and sun.

I honked the horn. It grated noisily on the bright spring day.
"Come on!" I yelled. "It won't grow while you watch it!"
Mom waved.
"Hold your horses!" Dad yelled back. They came up the field together.

I had not always been glad that I was their child, but today I had a kind of pride in being born to them.